About the author

Samantha Booth has always loved writing. As a child writing stories about her naughty baby brother, as a journalist and working for a national charity. This is her first published novel, but she hopes it will be the first of many. She lives in a village near Glasgow, Scotland and when she is not writing, she loves yoga, being with her partner, Martin, family and walking Border collies, Freddie and Cassie.

Author photo credit: Laura Coventry

THE MANY DEATHS OF AURORA FLOWERS

SAMANTHA BOOTH

THE MANY DEATHS OF AURORA FLOWERS

Vanguard Press

Dedication

To Dad, wish you were here.

Acknowledgements

Martin, Mum, Steven, Simon, Joyce, Gill, Samantha, Jan, Stewart, James, and of course, Freddie, Cassie and Cooper x

And a special thank you to Evax.

Prologue

The ground trembled beneath their feet, lifting and lurching as the world roared to its own destruction.

Cas and Max grasped each other's hands tightly as they stared at the high priestess, dignified despite her struggle to stay upright. The enormous crystal skull standing on its rose quartz plinth behind her glowed with a relentless light even as it groaned and creaked in response to Armageddon.

"Please hurry! Cas, with her long dark hair still twisted beautifully around her skull and her youthful skin still glowing with vitality, destined to be obliterated shortly, urged the priestess. "I am not afraid to die, but I want to die with Max as my husband."

Max, his sun-kissed brown hair brushed back from his face and his smooth, toned chest gleaming in the deathly light from the crystal skull, nodded his calm agreement. His eyes were filled with nothing but unconditional love for Cas, his best friend since that day they were both born, seventeen years before, and the love of his life since *that* day in a shimmering wheat field when they looked at each other and realised what they felt for each other was more than simply friendship.

"This is irregular in the extreme." The high priestess, in her shimmering, translucent rosy, pink robe, looked from one to the other perplexed.

"The world is ending, Magenta, Atlantis is falling, and nothing is regular any more. I know we have not been through the usual preparations, but it is now or never."

"Make your last act in this world one of love, Magenta, please." Max's voice was as soft and calm as ever, just like his deep blue eyes as they held the gaze of the priestess. Steady and unfaltering, as if the floor wasn't starting to split and contort around them, revealing terrifying glimpses of the molten fate awaiting them.

Taking a deep breath, the older woman righted herself and straightened her robes, thinking how incongruous that, in just moments, these two young, glowing, vital people would be no more. Her own demise was of no consequence, she knew it was not the end, but for these young lovers to be robbed of the chance to enjoy all that was sweet in the world seemed such a shame. Her heart swelled with familiar feelings of love as she raised her arms and began to intone the sacred words of marriage.

Cas and Max turned to face each other; his strong arms wrapped around her slim waist barely concealed beneath her diaphanous violet gown. Fire now erupted from the chasms in the broken floor but neither noticed, lost as they were in each other's eyes. Magenta announced them as husband and wife and, as Max bent to kiss Cas's lips, an eerie piercing scream came from the crystal skull - its swansong before it exploded into a million pieces. Beneath them, the floor finally became an open maw and all three fell into the fire.

Chapter 1

Aurora Flowers, as she was known today, gasped out loud as she woke up from her dream, her forehead beaded with sweat. It was the flames again. Those terrible flames. And yet what was harder for Aurora to bear was the way Max held her tight, still trying to protect her even as his beautiful face contorted with agony. Max. She sighed as she pulled back the bedcovers. Where was he? Knowing that there would be no more sleep for her that night, Aurora pulled on her dressing gown and headed to her kitchen.

Flicking the switch on the kettle on the way past, she glanced at her mobile phone where she had left it on the counter — 2.10 a.m. It was always 2.10 a.m. Was that significant? Was that when they died together, newly married, all those thousands of years ago?

Making herself a cup of chamomile tea, she sat at her kitchen table. Taking her first sip, she remembered the tea they had drunk in Atlantis. The taste so pure and fresh, stronger and more flavoursome than any she could find today. But then that's how everything had seemed in Atlantis — bright, bolder, lighter, more colourful. Until the end, of course. Or perhaps, Aurora wondered, that was the curse of having a memory like her own. Not only could she remember every lifetime she had ever lived, but she also looked back on Atlantis as halcyon days never to be relived or revived. But perhaps that was simply a trick. Perhaps it had not been like that at all. The lifetimes which followed certainly hadn't always been like that. Some had been brutal in the extreme; so brutal she was glad when the moment of death came. Others had been pleasant and even joyous, but none had ever come close to the lost world of Atlantis.

And then there was this lifetime. What was this lifetime, she often found herself pondering? The world felt strange to her now. She was a successful life coach and she enjoyed helping people to find their way through life finding that, with her unique perspective, she had an uncanny knack for it. Sometimes her clients were people she had met before in previous lives and with that extra knowledge, she was able to help them make seemingly miraculous changes. After all, she knew better than anyone, how everything was connected and dying from starvation in one life could lead to gluttony in the next.

She was content, she thought, and had lots of friends, but she struggled with twenty-first century living. The noise, the fast pace, the endless stimulation. Everyone seemed to race around from pillar to post, missing out on life's precious moments. They were too busy posting selfies to relish the experience, so lost in the latest fad game they forgot to look up and see the glorious sunset and so self-absorbed in their own dramas they often failed to notice the man dying in the street. And yet, it would be those self-same people who would take to social media to express their moral outrage that a man could die in the street, jump on the latest cyber bandwagon. Or become yet another social media crusader determined to have their say and join whichever digital gang seemed most right-on in that moment before going back to quietly allowing their lives to slip past half asleep. She despaired at the endless obsession with so-called celebrities and the need to have the latest fashions. She couldn't comprehend hours spent in front of a television, much less the TV shows themselves. She was a woman out of time. Without her friends, who were all gently rebelling against twenty-first century living in their own ways, even without the extraordinary ability to remember all their previous incarnations, she would go mad.

But, of course, Aurora knew that the main reason she couldn't settle in this world she had inhabited for nearly forty years this time round was that she hadn't yet found Max. Always before, often before she had even really had time to miss him, he would appear in her life in some shape or form. This time, though, he simply hadn't appeared and without him she felt bereft.

The Child

The child's mother held the baby close, unable to understand why the baby cried so much when she tried to lie her down close to the fire. The snow was deep outside and she was terrified the baby would freeze unless she stayed close to the fire pit. Besides, she had chores to do; she couldn't keep the child close to her breast all the time now she was nearly six moons old, but even resting her on a skin a man's length away from the flames was enough to set off the most piercing screams. Screams that then set the hounds off, and in the close confines of the roundhouse in the depth of winter, it was becoming too much to bear. The woman had seen the look in her husband's eye. She knew that the child's own father posed more of a threat to her than the flames, but she was at her wits end to know what to do to stop the child crying. A combination of a wife who didn't do her chores and an endlessly crying child who set off the dogs would soon be enough to drive her husband to leave the child in the snow for the wild beasts.

Glancing in the direction of the man, to where he himself hunched next to the fire pit, a great fur over his shoulders, she noticed again that he was once more idly whittling a piece of bone. She had thought he might be making a toy for the child, something to keep her entertained, but she saw now he was making a knife handle. Grasping her child tighter to her breast, she moved to the far end of the roundhouse, as far away from the fire as she could go in the hopes of keeping the child quiet, even though she knew they would both be cold.

The next night there was a commotion beyond the door skin. All eyes turned to look, ears straining to hear what was happening beyond that vulnerable flap of animal skin. Moments later, the fabric that had once been a deer burst open and a figure so bundled in furs encrusted with snow it was hard to tell if it was a man or a woman, fell into the roundhouse. The woman's husband was on his feet in an instant, knife at the ready as he grabbed the figure by the scruff of the neck, or at least by the furs there, and hauled him to his feet to reveal the face of a young man, a boy rather, perhaps no more than twelve years. His knees clearly buckling with exhaustion, his arms lolling at his side.

"Help." The word was no more than a whispered croak. The woman looked on – the baby held close to her, her tiny face just visible above bundled fur blankets, bright innocent eyes blinking – wondering what her husband would do now. Time passed. "Help." The croak came again.

"Why?" Her husband's voice was questioning but not brutal, as he could sometimes be, or even unkind. She remembered he had only survived his childhood through the kindness of others and she wondered if those memories would guide him now. Though, she also knew, he was just as likely to slit his throat, steal his furs and leave his body out for the crows.

She felt her heart beat loudly in her own chest while the child grew more and more animated in her arms. Looking into her baby's grey-blue eyes, which seemed overspilling with the need to communicate, something inside her shifted. In the days that came afterwards, she would never understand why she did what she did next. Her husband was the leader of this small band and he never took kindly to his authority being questioned but she simply knew that this boy was important and his life must be saved.

"Husband." Her voice quavered but she didn't stop. "He is young. Let him warm himself by the fire and put some stew in his belly, then he can talk."

The man looked at his wife steadily, appraisingly. She waited for a blow, but after several long moments of consideration, he let the boy fall to the floor and turned away. The baby wrestled in her arms, limbs flailing with unfettered excitement as she moved in to help the boy sit up next to the fire. She pulled another blanket over his shoulders and then hastily handed him a clay beaker of meat stew with a bone spoon. His eyes spoke his thanks even though the words never quite reached his mouth.

It was only then she realised that, despite being crouched next to the fire, and the child being half out her blankets she had wriggled so much, the baby wasn't screaming. In fact, she was ignoring the flames altogether as she stared at the face of the man-child who had just fallen into their lives.

The sun rose and set many times and the boy was still with them. The woman looked on in wonder as he happily played and cared for the normally restless child, relishing the baby's presence as much as she clearly adored his. To begin with, he sought her permission with his eyes to touch or pick up the child, but the longer he remained in their shelter the more he naturally began keeping her with him as a mother bear with a cub. He would jump to help with any chore that might earn him a share of the night's meal, but always with the child crooked under his arm or slung over his shoulder. In the dark, as they sat round the fire, he would dangle a bone for her to play with or pull faces to make her giggle, never paying the slightest attention to the closeness of the flames. Even the woman's husband seemed to look on with tolerant bemusement at this nanny goat that had unwittingly landed in their midst.

But the woman knew there was danger in this. She knew her man would not let peace reign for long. He was spiteful and malicious and while he was content for the moment, no longer bothered by the child's cries and spared as he was by a dozen manual chores, thanks to the boy's presence, she knew it was only a matter of time. As soon as the thaw began, she reckoned, a shadow would hang over the boy's future. And she worried about what would happen to her child when the man killed the boy as he undoubtedly would.

In the end, the thaw never came. About one cycle of the moon after the boy arrived, the man drank too deeply from his antler horn one night. The boy, languidly lying back on some furs, the baby on his lap, let out an uproarious laugh as the child repeatedly caught his finger and tried to put it in her mouth. The woman stared aghast at his reckless joy. How could he be so foolhardy in front of the man? She knew he knew he was dangerous; she had seen how he shielded the child from him and watched him to see what his mood might be in the exact same way as she did herself. All those thoughts flitted through the woman's head in a heartbeat. A heartbeat later, the man was on top of the boy, his hands were around his throat, the child's muffled screams crushed beneath the monstrous weight of her own father. Grabbing a heavy antler spade, the woman hit her husband again and again, but he never stopped or even flinched as he squeezed the life from the boy and flattened his tiny daughter. It was only when they were both silent and still that he stood up, grabbed the spade and backhanded the tool across her cheek.

By the time the woman was able to open her eyes the bodies were gone. Meat for the wolves.

Chapter 2

Aurora was meeting a new client. She quickly plumped the cushions in her small living room that doubled as a consultation room and glanced around to see everything was in order.

It was painted fresh white to contrast with her bright turquoise rug and large cushions in pinks, blues and greens. Two low armchairs sat on either side of an arched brick fireplace housing a log-burning stove in which flames cheerily gyrated safely behind a glass and iron door. A large amethyst crystal sat on one side of the stove. A piece of polished reclaimed wood formed the mantelpiece which was adorned with a row of broad white pillar candles.

On the other side of the room a large, colourful painting of a magical woodland alive with hidden creatures and watching eyes dominated the wall while French windows, framed with light, billowing white curtains, opened on to a small balcony opposite the door. The whole room, consciously or unconsciously, paid homage to those vast palaces of light and calm that she remembered from Atlantis. Places where a person could be healed simply by sitting in the presence of giant crystals, breathing and believing.

The doorbell rang. Shaking off her nostalgia, Aurora headed for the door. Pulling it open, she found a nervous young man, hands deep in the pockets of his anorak, nose moist from the cold, waiting for her, invoking a familiar but always unsettling sensation which came with meeting someone she had known before. This man was not Max, though. In another life, he wasn't even a man.

Calanthe
Dawn

It was Beltane again. Calanthe was awake before dawn to prepare for the day ahead. She might not yet be twenty summers, but she was High Priestess and her people looked to her for guidance. Or rather, she reminded herself, to her and Adair, Chief Druid and the reincarnation of Max. Not that he remembered the way Calanthe did, but he was wise and learned and understood how to look within to find that which is hidden from view. He had caught glimpses and what she had told him resonated in a way that he knew could not be denied. In the same way, even the elders of their community had listened when she spoke about the mysteries of life even when just a young girl. They knew how to follow that deep resonance inside themselves even if the words made little sense.

That was how she had become priestess at such a young age and it was a role Calanthe enjoyed. In fact, this life, living from the land in accordance with nature in the shadow of the magical Tor where Calanthe could sense deep power akin to that of Atlantis, was possibly as close to Atlantis as she could get without being able to travel back in time.

It could be harsh, especially in wintertime when the young and the old seemed to die with such heart-wrenching regularity, but the summers were long and bountiful and their people, in the main, lived, in peace. Calanthe was glad to be able to ease this suffering as much as she could and to guide the people with an unwavering gentle wisdom that generally brought contentment.

Calanthe could consider herself happy except for one person — Seana. Calanthe was pretty, and she knew how to draw on her power to make her eyes flash with whatever she wanted them to — mainly power or passion — but she also knew how unimportant looks were. She understood that every living creature was a spark of the divine, whether they were the greatest warrior with muscles honed as if made of marble or the lowliest beggar with a face ravaged by disease. But Calanthe struggled to keep her lower thoughts in check when it came to Seana.

Seana was beautiful. Beautiful in a way that made men stop and stare, to watch hungrily as her willowy frame move seductively, hips swaying slowly, in a way that suggested sensual confidence, just below the wispy ends of her lustrous raven-black hair. She caused the peaceful tribe more problems than any of their fractious neighbours and she hated Calanthe with a passion. Not just because Calanthe held power, but because she wanted Adair. Adair struggled not to respond to Seana's overt sexuality, and in return, Calanthe struggled not to respond to Seana with all her lower aspects — malice, spite, jealousy and anger. It took Calanthe all the composure of her rank, and wisdom from her time in Atlantis, not to grab the woman by her dark tresses and rub her face in the dung pile.

And, today, Calanthe knew Seana would be dogging her steps at every turn. She would want to humiliate Calanthe if she could, jeopardise the sacred ritual, the coming together of chief druid and high priestess as the God and the Goddess, to ensure the success of the year's harvest regardless of what that might mean for the entire tribe. All so she could jump over the Beltane fires with Adair and lure him into the woodlands.

Calanthe was determined she wouldn't allow this to happen. If Adair really wanted to sleep with the woman, then he could do so at any other time if he wanted. Calanthe might even encourage a brief union to help Adair to get it out of his system. She couldn't bear the thought, but she knew brief physical relationships, born from lust, rarely lasted. She also knew that, if sated, it would soon pass. She wouldn't allow it to happen at Beltane, though, not on such an important festival when the threads of the universe would be strummed by human fingers and shift in accordance with their touch. And yet, the scrunching sensation in the pit of her stomach told her that's exactly why Seana would try to do something today if she possibly could.

In an attempt to shake off her thoughts about Seana, Calanthe wrapped herself in her cloak and took a clay beaker of tea out of the roundhouse. After a few minutes' walk, she came to her favourite spot, a rock nestled on the side of a small hill offering her views of the Tor and the flat lands laid out at her feet. The air was still fresh but promised a warm spring day, as did the wide-open sky above as the deep blue of night gave way to lighter shades, casting a strange ethereal glow on the land below.

Calanthe sat and remembered Atlantis. The nights always seemed short there, and even then, there was a divine quality to them, one that she struggled to see in the night skies now, even when the stars shone in all their magnificence. In Atlantis, she felt she could read the history of the entire universe in the night sky and it wasn't uncommon for people to spend whole nights staring up at them, lost in contemplation. The days in Atlantis were different too - always long and full of sunshine. There were seasons, they were just gentler than what she experienced now, and she remembered a festival very like Beltane.

Bonfires were lit, there was feasting, dancing and lots of laughter, Calanthe remembered, but at the heart of that celebration, like every other in Atlantis, lay the ceremonies in the crystal temples. So very unlike anything Calanthe experienced in this life. Incarnated as she was now, Calanthe could feel Gaia's pulse beneath her feet, sense her own life force in her veins and feel the powerful energy of life on Earth. In Atlantis, though, in the presence of the glowing crystals, Calanthe could remember what it felt like to experience transcendental love, a feeling so blissful you simply lost yourself in it and never wanted to leave.

The sun was now fully risen. The bustle from the village was growing by the minute as more people emerged from their beds and went about the day's tasks. Calanthe could sense the added anticipation of the night to come. This was, after all, one of the year's eight major festivals, and they meant a lot to people who worked hard, day in and day out, not just as a break from their normal duties but as a way of connecting to the world around them and finding meaning. Calanthe slowly rose and stretched, arms raised in salute to the sun, head tilted back to drink in its warm energy. She had plenty to do herself.

Dusk

The energy always shifted with the darkening of the sky, even when it was barely more than a gentle deepening of the day's azure glory. Calanthe could sense it, even from deep within her own dark chambers, and knew it was time for her to become the Goddess. She had spent the last two hours having her flesh massaged with rich rose oil before bathing in a large, luxuriant copper bath. Her ladies had drawn her hair back in braids at either side of her head so it hung down her back beneath an elaborate headdress of twisted wires of precious metals, decorated with flowers and jewels. Her gown of heavy silk the colour of early spring leaves hung loosely over her oiled body, the blue dragon tattoos on her arms flickering beneath the rustling folds as she moved. Pausing for a moment, she closed her eyes and breathed deeply, tuning into the power coursing round her veins.

Drums began to beat somewhere nearby. She could sense the excitement building, but it didn't matter because she was ready. Ready to be Goddess for her people. Ready to greet the God. Ready to re-enact the sacred union that would harness the energy for the coming year and ensure all their survival. The drums grew louder and she didn't need to be able to see the sky to know it was deepening still.

In her mind's eye, she could imagine the people gathered around the processional way. They would have come from far and wide during the day to see Calathne and Adair, known, even if not understood, to have power beyond most of their ken. They would be pressed close to each other, the faring and feasting of the afternoon forgotten as they gathered to be in the presence of the Goddess.   Of course, their minds would also already be turning to who they might jump the Beltane fires with before spending the night beneath the stars, joining in a sacred union of their own.

Calanthe breathed deeply once more. Not quite yet. She stood swaying slightly in her robe, hidden from site behind the door of her round house, confident that she would know when the time was right The drums grew in strength. Their beat now at home inside Calanthe. With her eyes still closed, she followed their rhythm as she prodded the world around her with her mind and heart. One more deep breath. One more round of drumming. The darkening of the sky. And then, stillness. Her eyes opened. "It is time."

Calanthe felt both more in her physical body than she had even been before, and simultaneously, as if she was floating beside herself. Thinking had stopped. She was now the Goddess. She could feel the divine power pulsating around and through her, setting alight her eyes as she gazed majestically around the gathered people, taking in their awed wonder as she stepped slowly, languidly and yet oh so powerfully along the processional way to the beat of the drum, her green robes trailing behind her like ribbons on a stall or pennants on a boat.

Each step she took was eternity itself, as if there was nothing more important in the history of the universe than that moment. Every eye she caught, she let that person know, that in that moment, they were all that existed. Flames and faces swirled before her as she walked slowly up the Tor, many more falling in step behind her, until, eventually, they reached the top where Adair was waiting with a torch clutched in his hand, resplendent in a robe of green to match her own and a headdress of stag antlers.

From now, he was all that existed for Calanthe, both as the human and the Goddess. Stepping forward, she took the proffered torch, and with great ceremony, lit the waiting bonfire on her left. Handing it back to Adair, he did the same to its twin on the other side of the Tor's summit, never taking his eyes from Calanthe. Sparks and hissing quickly transformed into leaping, towering flames and Calanthe was taken back to that last day in Atlantis, and for a moment, thought they were going to experience the same fate again.

Remembering that today she was the Goddess, she cast her fear aside and stepped toward Adair, casting her robe to the ground as she did so. He responded in kind, wrapping his arms around her waist and hers rose to encircle his neck. Huge cheers went up as they fell to the cold surface of Mother Earth, conjoined in the sacred union.

Calanthe lost herself to the sensations of both woman and Goddess, enjoying the feel of Adair's strong body against her own, knowing that he, like her, was drunk with lust and love. So drunk that neither of them noticed Seana appear from the shadows, wearing a robe and headdress no more than a mockery of Calanthe's own. Her knife drove into Calanthe's neck just as the last whispers of pleasure escaped her lips. The sacred union had been despoiled at its most sacred point. Silence fell, the heavens opened and within moments the fires were extinguished. Calanthe was dead, her last image, caught over Adair's strong, glistening shoulder, was of Seana standing triumphantly, eyes glittering dangerously, her own blood dripping from the ceremonial knife that had brought her death. With her, the hopes and future of the tribes died too

Aurora remembered all this as the young man slumped into one of the armchairs next to her fireplace, breathing deeply to quell the anger she still felt at the memories.

"Give me a moment please and I will make us some tea." Aurora needed the time to compose herself. To centre and let go of residual feelings of anger and hurt. She knew she was just as responsible for what happened as Seana was, their own energies had drawn the event into their lives and they both bore their own karma. She also knew she needed to find compassion for Seana as she was now, a forlorn looking young man, desperately in need of help. Karma, she realized, had not been easy on Seana.

Taking her tea tray back to the fireplace, she focused on her heart centre and allowed the peace there to bubble up to her lips so she could greet the boy man with a smile.

"So, it's Sean, is that right?" The man boy nodded meekly. "And you are twenty-two, right?" Aurora smiled encouragingly, but he only nodded again. "Well, thanks for coming, Sean, would you like to tell me why it is you have sought my help?"

Sean took a teacup, his hands shaking as he busied himself taking a sip of the still-too-hot drink. Aurora sat back in silence, allowing him a little time to muster his courage. Finally, he spoke. "I have these terrible dreams," he said. "Where I murder someone."

Aurora sat up. Now she was interested. "I'm sorry, they sound terrible. Can you tell me more about them?"

"There are more than one. I mean it's like I am always killing someone, but in different places. Sometimes I am a man and sometimes a woman."

"OK, can you give me any more detail?"

"I'm always filled with anger and jealousy when I kill. It's like I can't control it."

"And how are you with anger and jealousy, Sean?"

He looked abashed. "I never mean to get so possessive of girlfriends, it's just... I care so much that it's like I can't think properly. I have only had three girlfriends, but the relationships have all ended terribly because of me."

"That's OK, you have made a big step admitting it. Have you ever had hypnosis before?"

Sean shook his head, looking so frightened and miserable, Aurora felt a stab of compassion.

24

"It's really just a way of making you so relaxed I can talk to your subconscious, are you happy with that?"

He nodded.

"OK, then, please come and lie down on this rug, take your shoes off and I will get you a blanket and pillows."

Half an hour later, Sean lay deep in a hypnotic trance.

"Sean, I would like you to go back even further now to before you were born in this life, can you go back beyond that darkness for me? What do you see?"

Sean murmured and stirred. "It's muddy. I'm covered in mud. And cold."

"OK, Sean. What are you wearing, can you see?"

"Like brown... Or maybe green... It's a uniform, I think."

"Can you hear anything?"

"Yes, there are loud bangs and smoke. I can't see very far. There's a knife in my hand."

"So, you are a soldier. What's your name?"

"Private Stewart Ratcliff."

"OK, Private Ratcliff, what are you doing?"

"I'm trying to find him."

"Who are you trying to find, Private Ratcliff?"

"The major."

"Why, Private Ratcliff, why are you trying to find the major?"

"He stole my girl, Lisbette. Oh, she was so sweet. Works on one of the farms nearby. I knew she liked me, but the major stole her, took her away to a hotel."

"What are you going to do when you find the major, Private Ratcliff?"

Sean's face contorted as he lay, lost in another time, wearing an expression Aurora recognized. "I will kill him. I will slit his throat and watch the blood run down my hands. That will teach him."

"OK, enough. Sean, go back further, leave Private Ratcliff, go back into the darkness. Breath. Relax. Breath. Relax. Where are you now?"

Sean's head rolled from side to side. "I'm moving. Everything's moving. I feel sick."

"OK, Sean, stay calm, what can you see?"

"Wood. Darkness. I can't move. There's something round my ankle. Something heavy. It's sore."

"What's your name in this time and place?"

There was a long pause. "My name is Abayomi. My mother named me that because I brought her joy. Now I must bring her pain as I am never to go home and sure to die."

"Hello, Abayomi, are you on a ship?"

"Yes. I have been taken."

"Do you know where you are going?"

"It does not matter because I will never see that place. I have a blade hidden and I will kill the man who took me away and stole my family. I will gut him like a boar. I will taste his blood on my skin before I die... I will..."

Sean's eyelids flicker as he stops talking, distracted by what he sees in his past.

"Abayomi? Can you hear me Abayomi?"

"He is coming, I can smell him, now is the time. Now I will make him pay!"

"OK, Sean, let's leave Abayomi, keep moving, back into the darkness, breath and relax, where are you now?"

For a few moments all Aurora could hear was Sean's deep breathing.

"It's dark. I am outside. The stars are so bright."

"OK, can you see anything else?"

"My feet are bare on grass. I am wearing a long dress. I sense... Excitement... Anticipation. Something is happening."

"That's good. Tell me, what is your name in this life?"

"I am called Seana."

As Sean said the word his voice changed and Aurora was once more face-to-face with the woman who killed her so long ago. Her blood chilled.

"Hello, Seana. It is me, Calanthe." The temperature in the room plummeted. Aurora could sense the hate pulsating from Sean's inert body. Calling in light to protect herself, she ploughed on. "Why did you want to kill me, Seana?"

"You have him. You always had him. I wanted Adair. I wanted Adair to look at me the way he looks at you with your power and haughtiness and… And that way you have of… Knowing… I hate you. I want to be revered and adored by everyone, but it is always you… I am so much more beautiful than you and yet people never pay any attention to me. Not really. Oh yes, they look and I see the lust in their eyes, but it is there one minute and gone the next… You, though… They always want to be with you… To listen to you… I am just a beautiful bit of meat." Sean was writhing now where he lay, trying to contain the hate and jealousy passed down through the ages. "I just thought, without you, Adair would turn to me… See me for what I really am and everything would be different… But it wasn't… It wasn't at all."

Aurora felt her heart race as conflicting emotions tumbled through her — anger, hurt, sadness, sorrow, compassion, guilt. With a voice sounding calmer than she felt she asked, "What happened, Seana, what happened after you killed me?"

"I loved it. I loved taking you by surprise. I loved watching the look on your face as your blood ran into the ground. Oh, it was so sweet… What a glorious moment… I was waiting for Adair to see me… To see the power I had, and what I could achieve… But when he turned to see me, he looked so… Outraged and in pain — as if it was him I had stabbed! He came after me, put his hands around my throat. He was so strong… I can still feel them pressed there… I thought he would kill me there and then, but the elders pulled him away. They said I had to stand trial. They said they had to give you a proper burial and then they would deal with me… Even in death, it was you first."

Aurora was transfixed, the scene as clear in her own mind as if it was one of her own memories. "What happened then?"

"They kept me locked in an outhouse. Bound so I couldn't move. I don't know how long for, days. I remember they brought me food maybe seven or eight times. Then I was brought out to face the elders. Adair was with them. He looked older… Like he hadn't slept. I tried to smile at him, but he just stared."

Aurora swallowed hard, feeling pain even now at the thought of Max's suffering. "Then what?" she asked, more curtly than she intended.

"There was a lot of talking… I didn't listen I just looked at Adair… Then I suddenly caught a word… I heard 'fire' and I realized they were talking about burning me… They said there needed to be a sacrifice to make up for the despoiling of the sacred union…" Seana now sounded scared.

Aurora had tears in her eyes, despite herself. "Did they burn you, Seana?"

"Yes… It was awful… The smell… The pain… Just when I thought I couldn't stand the flames… They were just beginning to burn my feet… Adair stepped in and cut my throat. He looked in my eyes as he did it and I knew he forgave me… But… But I don't think I have ever forgiven myself." Sean convulsed with emotion; tears ran down the young man's cheeks.

"I forgive you too, Seana. It is over now. It is past. Let's help Sean to have a life."

Sean's sobbing eased slightly.

"Sean… Sean… This is Aurora… We are going to come back to the room now… Let's leave the past behind… I'm going to count you back… ten, nine, eight… Breath and relax… You are wakening now… seven, six, five… Come back to the room… four, three, two, one, and you are awake."

A while later, Sean sipped at a fresh cup of tea, still looking like a deer trapped in the headlights.

"So, I murdered you in a previous life?"

"Yes, I am afraid so. I know it is a lot to take in."

"And I was put to death for it. And that's what started a pattern through all my lifetimes?"

"Yes… A combination of karma and your own beliefs about yourself — that you were no good, that you deserved to be punished — meant you kept repeating the same mistakes. You have broken it now, though, by coming here today. This is the end of that cycle."

"So, I won't get those awful dreams any more?"

"I don't think so… But I think we still have some work to do on the beliefs you have about yourself in this life. You need to learn to love yourself and be centred, when you do there's no room for anger or jealousy and then you stop drawing those type of situations into your life… It is all connected… The world is a mirror of what's happening inside ourselves. Does that make sense?"

"Wow… I think so."

"As I say, it is a lot to take in, I would advise you go home and sleep and come back next week and we can work on what you need to do in this life now we have dealt with the issues from the past."

Sean might have been dazed as he left, but Aurora could sense the change in his energy. He was already far more at peace. She, too, felt a peacefulness. She was glad to have put something else from her past to bed, but there was one thing she couldn't put aside so easily — Max's pain. Oh, how she craved him, missed him, needed him; where was he?

Chapter 3

Aurora was on the tube. There was something she liked about the subterranean trains. It was stolen time. She could lose herself in her own thoughts or sometimes simply allow herself to sense the energies of those around her. She liked to send love to those who seemed sad, peace to those who seemed angry and light to those who had a darkness around them. She knew that on some level, even if just in a very small way, her efforts would make a difference to them.

Today was a day where her mind was blissfully quiet. The work repairing the ancient history with Seana had left her with a deep sense of peace. Max was never far from her thoughts, but the deep yearning was only a muted whisper today. Some days were like that, and on those days, Aurora was able to remember that life was about joy and love. She was able to look at the trees, and despite being able to remember having looked upon them for thousands of years, see their incredible beauty. Hear bird song and feel uplifted and smile at the sight of dancing heads of daffodils. There were still days when the beauty of the world could stop her in her tracks as if she was seeing it all for the first time, and on those days, she felt nothing but deep joy at being alive and even grateful that she could remember. Smiling to herself Aurora knew that today could be one of those days.

Idly, she watched as the train pulled into the station, her eyes pausing for a moment on a man on the platform in a blue jumper — unshaven, but not quite bearded, in his forties with a lived-in face, but not unhandsome — and something clicked inside her. She knew him, remembered him. With her heart in her mouth, she watched him board, moving with the same capable ease he had done all those years before. He had always been completely at home in his physicality. He had grace, ease and gave the impression that he was able to do anything. Capable in the extreme. She remembered watching him train for battle, lithe and toned rather than muscular, he had wit, more than brawn, quick reflexes rather than brute force and the easy sweeping movements of a dancer. He had been formidable.

Aurora caught her breath as he took the seat directly opposite her then audibly gasped as their eyes met. They were exactly as they had been before — tawny brown, soulful and knowing, with only rare glimpses of humour. He held Aurora's gaze just as he had done all those hundreds of years before and Aurora was sure that, on some level, he remembered too. After what seemed like an age, he pulled his gaze away and looked down at his hands. Aurora could tell, though, he was struggling with the same emotional jolt she was feeling — instant attraction, recognition and a deep sexual desire. She knew he would be wondering how he could feel such deep, intense desire for a stranger on a train. She knew it was because they had been passionate lovers in a lifetime long ago.

Ailidh

Ailidh was in the woods collecting herbs and flowers. She was glad to be away from the villa on her own to have some time to think. Having just turned sixteen years old in this life as a slave, she had been informed by her master that, as a young woman of remarkable beauty, she was to be gifted to one of his most important commanders for him to do with as he liked. Ailidh knew that could mean just about anything. She could be raped and murdered, or she could be treated with kindness and even earn the respect of a wife. If the commander — yet to be selected — felt so taken, he could even make her a wife. Ailidh found it hard to feel anything other than despair at the thought. Her life at the villa was fairly pleasant. They lived deep in the country surrounded by beautiful woodlands that seemed to call to her, her chores were never too onerous and her master was kind as masters go — he had only ever hit Ailidh once.

The only thing missing for Ailidh was Max, but she was young enough to be filled with hope that he would appear in time. It would be hard for Ailidh to leave, but her real despair came because she could remember the freedom of other lives. Running free in Atlantis and the power of being high priestess. In the here and now she had absolutely no control over her destiny and she was, for want of a better word, sulking over it. Yet Ailidh also knew, with the wisdom of ages at her disposal, that if she just stopped wallowing for a moment, she would hear the quiet voice inside her telling her that she always had a choice. If nothing else she could focus her thoughts on what she wanted to happen and trust the universe would take care of the rest.

Dropping down beside an ancient oak tree she closed her eyes and rested her back against the rough trunk, enjoying nothing but the sensation of dappled sunlight playing on her face. Breathing deeply, she began to imagine, imagine what she would ideally like to happen. She saw herself with a strong handsome man, Max, of course, who loved her and cherished her and gave her freedom. She saw them having lots of children, living in the country and having long happy days in the sunshine. "Oh, Gods and Goddess, let that or something better be mine." The spoken words hung in the woodland air, heard only by the birds, rabbits and the small deer watching her with quiet interest as it chewed on grass at the other side of the clearing.

Ailidh trusted completely her prayers would be heard and that her vision would come true, but a few weeks later, she was given to a cantankerous ageing commander, who wanted her to be available for groping and waiting on in equal measure. And he was quick with his fists if she dared to complain or pull away. They lived in a dark villa deep inside Londinium and so rare was it that Ailidh was allowed out that she feared she would never see a tree again.

And it was in this dark life that she lived for five years, always wondering where Max was and if she had been forgotten completely by the Gods, Goddess, the Divine Mother, the Universe or whatever you might want to call those supernatural forces people called upon in times of need. Yet, in bed at night, she still escaped to her vision of her handsome prince, her Max, who would somehow help her change her life.

Then, one day, Ailidh heard an unusual commotion. Running out to the courtyard, she saw the commander wrest his old limbs into the saddle of a horse. Then, shouting to his men, they all galloped from the villa into the streets without a backward look, gates hanging open behind them. Ailidh stood stunned in the silence, which hung at their backs. There didn't seem to be another living soul left in the villa, only Juno the dog, who was staring up at Ailidh as if looking for her to tell him what to do. Wrapping him in her arms Ailidh dropped a kiss on his scruffy brown head. "It looks like it is just us, Juno," she whispered in his ears.

Ailidh spent three days wondering what to do. This was her chance to escape, but where would she go? What if they returned and caught her running away? At best, she would be whipped, at worst, killed. But what if they never returned? What if she was now free? At first, she kept up with her chores, but the more she swept and cleaned the now undeniably empty villa — the other servants had vanished too — the less likely it seemed that anyone would return. Peeking round the gates, she could tell that the streets outside were deserted too and she decided that the safest option would be to lock herself in.

As the hours became days, though, she liked less the idea of being abandoned in the dismal villa, even with Juno for company. Wandering from room to room, she began putting herself together a pack of essentials, wondering as she did if it constituted theft. On her third night alone, she decided she would leave at first light, just her and Juno on foot with her pack on her bag. The idea made her feel quite queasy, but it was a sense of excitement that filled her as she fell asleep on her last day in the dark place she had never called home.

At first light they set out, Juno's jaunty gait matching Ailidh's own liberated steps, though she continuously looked over her shoulder half expecting the old commander to come chasing up behind her, demanding she be hanged, or, worse, return to her life as his slave.

As the sun rose in the sky, though, the more her sense of freedom grew. It was so exhilarating to be outside and master of her own destiny that it overrode her disquiet. She saw very few people and those she did, scuttled away as if scared of her or at least scared to be seen. People had obviously fled, she could see the signs of that quite clearly in the broken urns and discarded belongings littering the streets, but what they had fled from was something Ailidh chose not to think about.

By midday she had reached the edges of the city and could see countryside. An hour or so later, she stopped by the banks of a stream to dip in her dusty feet and eat some bread and cheese. She laughed as she hadn't done in years as Juno frolicked in the water like a newborn lamb.

The old dog was as rejuvenated by their freedom as she was. That night, they slept curled up beneath a huge sycamore tree, listening to the hoot of owls and Ailidh felt safer than she had in a long time.

It was mid-afternoon on the next day that she met him. Having stopped at another stream to wash and eat, she was just pulling her hair back into a braid when he stepped out from behind a tree on silent feet. A cry failing on her lips, Ailidh found herself unable to move, held still by his eyes. Tawny and deep, she knew instantly this was not a man to be messed with, but it was something else which held her, something similar to what she remembered with Max, yet different. Her body could barely contain the convulsion of attraction she felt and knew he felt it too.

Neither of them spoke, Ailidh tried to find a smile but there was no response to the tiny twitch of her lips. His eyes simply continued to hold hers with undiminished intensity. With the ease of a wolf, he took another step forward and raised his hand gently to her cheek.

"Who are you?" he asked in a throaty whisper.

"Ailidh," was her only answer and then finally there was a twitch in his own lips.

"Of course, you are, I should have known." His calloused fingers gently, almost unwittingly, caressed her cheek with tiny, feather-light touches. "Where are you from, Ailidh?"

"Londinium."

"You don't look Roman, are you a slave?"

Ailidh felt a trickle of fear run down her back but found herself unable to speak anything other than the truth to this man. "I was," she replied, struggling to think beyond the pulses rampaging through her body.

"Was?"

"They fled and left me."

He raised his eyebrows. "Leave you? How could they." His lips touched hers, infinitely gentle and Ailidh felt her body rise in response, her breath deepening.

He pressed her against the trunk of a tree and her body turned to liquid. Nothing in the world existed except him and his touch.

Later, as they lay together naked except for his cloak over them, she turned to him. "What is your name?"

34

"Sloan, it means warrior."

"I know what it means. What will you do with me now then, warrior?"

"Do with you? Nothing unless you want me to. I hope you will come with me of your own free will. Will you?"

Ailidh was caught in those tawny eyes once more, there could only be one answer.

Sloan was the leader of a band of warriors made up of disparate British tribes, intent on reclaiming land from the Romans. It had been this band who had chased the beleaguered garrison from Londinium, although the Romans reclaimed it soon enough.

They spent their life on horseback and sleeping in woods and caves. Ailidh didn't mind any of it, though; she felt as if she was born to it, and besides, she would have lived in whatever way it was needed for her to be near to Sloan. She craved his touch constantly and he, hers. They took the chance of every moment alone to satisfy their desire, but it wasn't only a physical attraction between them, there was a deep, easy understanding which became love. Ailidh did still wonder about Max, but the desire for him was dimmed by Sloan's presence.

When they made love, they lost themselves completely in each other, and even as months turned to years, the passion between them never dimmed. As long as Sloan was present, Ailidh only had eyes for him and Sloan still found himself staring, mesmerized by Ailidh long after initial passion should have waned. He had to school himself not to simply give into his desires at any given moment, understanding as he did the need his men had for a leader. Someone who could keep his wits about him and stay one step ahead of the Romans.

He was pleased to see how Ailidh fitted in with the small troop of soldiers. Nobody else would dare touch the leader's woman, but Ailidh made it clear she only had eyes for Sloan in a way they respected. She earned their respect even more when she showed she could ride all day without complaining and yet was still happy to fetch wood or water with the rest of them. Her medicinal skills and plant knowledge, which grew year on year, also proved vital. In time, none of the troop could imagine life without Ailidh and many even began to look upon her as their lucky totem as, while Ailidh was there, they never really suffered any devastating injuries or loses.

Perhaps, Ailidh mused often, it was just as well she never fell pregnant as all that they had would have to change. She couldn't take a baby on the road, could she? Sometimes she would dream about having Sloan's child and riding with the child strapped to her chest. It would be a boy, destined to follow in his father's footsteps from an early age.

Years passed but Ailidh was later to remember the old saying that you had to be careful what you wished for, take care where you placed your focus and intention, as, twelve years after she first met Sloan, she did eventually fall pregnant. It was a secret that Ailidh had been nursing until she was sure, but now she wanted to tell Sloan and she hoped he would be as happy as she was, even though she knew it would bring them a new set of worries. That night, limbs woven together beneath their furs as they lay next to their fire, having once more lost themselves in each other's bodies, Ailidh rose on her elbows so she could look directly into those undimmed tawny eyes. They had many more creases around them now, but their intensity remained.

"My warrior," she began, using her name for him. "I have something to tell you." As usual, he gave nothing away, just calmly held her gaze with all his focus. "I believe I am with child."

Moments passed under his direct scrutiny before, finally, his hand in her hair, he pulled her towards him and kissed her. "It is right a passion like ours should produce a child, my love."

"You are right, but won't it make things difficult?"

"Children have been born throughout time to people without a proper home or roof. We will manage, I am sure."

And to begin with, they did. Ailidh's pregnancy didn't change things beyond the occasional stop for her to be sick in the bushes and the men didn't seem too perturbed by the turn in events, after all, many of them had wives and children in homes in the country that they would visit when they could. Why shouldn't Sloan have a child too? As the months passed and Ailidh's stomach grew, though, a sense of unease grew among the band. Things were beginning to go awry and it felt like, with Ailidh's pregnancy, their luck had run out. She was close to term, though, when everything came to a disastrous head.

Ailidh woke up feeling terrible. She felt huge, ungainly and as if she had heavy weights round her legs. She caught Sloan watching her as she

36

struggled to her mount, but for once there was deep concern, rather than desire, etched in his brown eyes. Every moment of the morning passed like an eternity for Ailidh as her body rebelled with every step the horse took. Finally, she slumped forward over her distended belly, knowing she could go no further that day. As quick and agile as ever, Sloan swept her from the horse, and with almost imperceptible gestures to his men, he had them come off the trail and organise a makeshift camp. It was not a place he would have chosen to stop, but there was nothing he could do about it and he showed no thought for that as he bent over Ailidh, mopping her brow and massaging her stomach.

"Is the child coming?" he asked urgently.

"No. No, I don't think so," a fevered Ailidh managed in response. "I am just unwell."

Sloan sat by her for hours, building a large fire to keep away the chill, until she finally fell into a deep, exhausted sleep.

She woke in deep darkness to the sound of steel on steel and the calls of men deep in fight. The fire had been doused, though, and she could see very little. Hardened by years as part of a warrior troop, she knew better than to call for help, instead very slowly she eased herself to her knees and then, with the support of a tree, to her feet. Gingerly, she placed one foot in front of another. Careful to make as little noise as possible, she made her way towards the sound of battle. A body fell at her feet, one of their own band, with a Roman spear through his chest. Ailidh wanted to cry out — he had been a good man — but her thoughts were taken up with the need to find Sloan.

Moving forward, burdened as she was, she found a position behind a tree where she could see men fighting in a clearing, picking out Sloan from amongst them with incredible ease. In his mid-forties now, he had lost none of his easy grace and agility. He danced through the melee with his sword swinging high and low, catching Roman soldiers at every turn. Ailidh was entranced by his poise and the way he made something as ugly as fighting quite beautiful. Her heart swelled with the knowledge that he was hers as she was his, just as she knew in that moment that he would never see another sunrise. It was only moments later that he fell, taken down by the last Roman soldier as they retreated. He was cowering behind a bush waiting to strike like a snake in the grass rather than a true

37

warrior. Ailidh forgot her sickness, and her huge belly, and burst from her hiding place and ran screaming to where he had fallen.

He was still living when she got to him, if only just. For one last time he raised his hand to her cheek and held her eyes with his still, steady gaze. "If he is a boy, name him for me but let him be a poet not a warrior, if he so chooses." He paused to catch breath, one of his last. "I never expected to love the way I have loved you, Ailidh. Remember that." The man who was always so strong and capable then took one last strained, rasping breath, his hand squeezed tight for a moment around Ailidh's, and was gone.

Ailidh sobbed over his body until the men that were left pulled her away. She went into labour shortly afterwards, and not without kindness, the men left her with a secret order of druid priestesses, living deep in the marshes, to have her baby. And despite her sadness and the deep raw wound that the loss of Sloan had left, the moment her baby boy was placed in her hands, her heart leapt with a new joy. Max. Her child was Max. Her and Sloan's child was Max. To keep her word to his father, she had him named Sloan, but to Ailidh, there was only ever one Sloan and one Max so between themselves in private that's all she ever called him. He grew up as Ailidh grew old and content amongst the druid priestesses, learning their almost forgotten lore as they hid amongst the marshes.

One day, Ailidh looked up from where she sat in the sun contentedly weaving and gasped as she thought it was Sloan walking toward her, but no, it was their son grown to a man and looking as much as his father as could be, and yet still undeniably Max too. He had his father's strength and flexibility, intensity and wit, yet he had never wanted to be a warrior. Perhaps his father knew something as he had lay dying, as his son had become a revered bard. A new Taliesin, passing down their druidic history and traditions in verse so they would never be forgotten, and Ailidh knew, Sloan would have been a proud father. In fact, she decided that would be the first thing she would tell him when she saw him in the afterlife as she fell asleep that night never to wake again. In that life anyway.

On the tube, Aurora couldn't stop herself from looking at Sloan, incarnated as he was now, on the seat across from her. Their eyes had met several times and held far longer than strangers, even those attracted to each other, ever would.

Aurora wanted to speak, to say so many things, but couldn't quite find her voice. Now, the train was rolling into her stop, and she would have to walk away from him, perhaps never to see him again. Standing up, she felt an overwhelming sense of loss, but what could she say? "Hi, remember when we were lovers in ancient Britain?"

She turned away to step on to the platform, tears prickling her eyes, when she felt a hand on her arm. It was him, looking at her just as he had all those hundreds of years ago. "Hi, sorry, I didn't mean to startle you, I couldn't just let you go. Do I know you from somewhere?"

Aurora smiled. "Maybe somewhere, a long time ago."

His eyes were still on hers. "I'm Jack," he said, his face perilously close to hers, their breathing ragged. "Can I take you for a drink?"

Aurora grinned now. "There's nothing I would like better."

Chapter 4

It was three weeks since Aurora had set eyes on Jack. Three weeks in which she had allowed herself to be completely distracted by lust, to the point she almost forgot she had been watching the moments of this life tick by simply waiting for Max to appear.

They had gone straight from the tube station to the nearest bar, so conscious of each other they were unaware of everything else. Aurora, thinking back later, thought it was one of those chain places. She had a glass of wine and he ordered a lager, but the drinks had barely been touched by the time Aurora suggested they go to her flat. A bemused but clearly delighted Jack took a large mouthful, as if for Dutch courage, then took her by the hand and purposefully pulled her out onto the street. A moment later he turned back to her, more than a little bashful.

"I don't know where you live," he said simply. "Strange, it almost felt like I did… As if I should, for some reason. Like we have done all this before."

"I know," was all Aurora could think to say. After all, telling him that they had in fact been passionate lovers one thousand five hundred years ago may well have put him off.

Once they were undressing in her candlelit bedroom, though, it was as if all one thousand five hundred years fell away. His hands felt like Sloan's on her skin, his muscled torso held the same contours, and more than anything, his eyes held the same intensity. They simply lost themselves to the same fierce physicality they had always enjoyed all that time ago. Afterwards, they lay in heavy limbed satisfaction, studying each other's faces.

Aurora wanted to say, *it's lovely to see you again. I have missed you.* But she contented herself with, "I can't believe I met you on a train. We just locked eyes and now you are here."

Jack stroked her face, his hands just as rough and gentle as Sloan's had always been. "I couldn't take my eyes off you; I never felt such instant attraction before. And with a total stranger!"

Not quite a stranger, Aurora thought, but she simply smiled back and leant forward to kiss his lips once more.

Jack dragged himself away to work — he was a photographer — the next morning. Aurora said goodbye with a sense of sadness as she told herself it had to be a one-off.

She had, gradually, over the last few lifetimes, stopped having romantic relationships unless it was with Max and only then if he incarnated in an appropriate form. Rarely these days could she find herself drawn enough to anyone to distract her herself from her thoughts of Max, and besides, she knew it wasn't fair on the other person. They all deserved to be loved wholly and completely by someone, not to be given half her attention. When Jack texted the next day, though, she found herself smiling, and then responding. That night they went for dinner and Jack, once again, came back with Aurora to her flat.

"I can't stop thinking about you," he said to her as they lay in each other's arms. "It's strange, though, it's like you have come back to me and I don't know why."

While with Jack, and especially while they made love, Aurora forgot everything else, just as she had all those years ago when she was Ailidh and he was Sloan. When in Jack's arms, feeling his touch, losing herself in his smell, she found herself in the moment, joyfully alive and in her body, which, for someone who could remember all her incarnations as Aurora could, was sheer bliss.

When her thoughts drifted to him, as they did almost as often as she thought of Max, she always found herself smiling. She even experienced the odd twinge of guilt. How could she lay aside her desperate need to find Max in this life so easily?

She even spent one fun-filled evening in Jack's studio posing for the camera. One of the benefits of remembering so many lives was a sense of being completely comfortable in your own skin: little fazed Aurora as she often felt like she had done it all before. She couldn't remember posing for a photo shoot before, but she had posed for paintings, and after all, played the role of Goddess in many ceremonies.

Afterwards, Jack presented her with a stunning black and white portrait — he had caught her half unawares as she pulled back the voile curtain in his studio to look out to see the sunshine come out after a storm.

"You are beautiful," he said simply. "Timeless. I don't think I could guess what age you are from that photo." He looked at her with an amused look. "You know you have never actually said what age you are."

Aurora smiled. "Let's just leave it with timeless."

And so, it went. They met most nights for three weeks. Mainly eating and going to bed, but occasionally they walked, hand in hand, through London's parks, talking idly about not much in particular. Aurora enjoyed the light relief from questions posed by her clients and by her own unique view of life.

Freed as she was from the fear of death, it was normal for her to nonetheless be beset with ponderings over the reasons why she incarnated when and where she did, how and where she had accrued karma and how and why Max finally appeared. That's if he did appear this time. He always had before, but what if this time was different? It was that question more than any other which kept Aurora awake in the middle of the night, but more recently, while she still did awake in a cold sweat at the thought that Max might not appear, she found all she had to do was think of Jack to soothe herself.

The problem was that now, after just three weeks, he was beginning to make murmurings about a future. Nothing quite as serious as living together or children, but his brother was getting married and he hoped she would be his partner for the day and he had mentioned being together for Christmas, which was still a good couple of months away. Situations which spoke of a fully-fledged relationship, the kind Aurora had avoided for decades if not centuries And yet, Jack had soothed her soul in a way she couldn't remember happening for quite a few lifetimes and lifted her from sinking into a complete depression. With Jack around, she felt less brittle, less like the hustle and bustle of modern life was closing in around her and threatening to drive her insane with its endless assault of the senses. Jack had made her feel real again, and fully present in her twenty-first century body. Is that something she was ready to give up? Aurora decided to go away for a night. Whenever she needed some time to think and meditate, she headed out of the city, and as usual, there was only one place she really wanted to go — Glastonbury.

Aurora could feel the power of Planet Earth, the life force of the universe, God, Goddess or whatever else you wanted to call it when she was in Glastonbury. It was a pulsing beneath her bare feet as she walked on the grass around the Tor and in the hit of pure light she felt as she drank from the Chalice Well. Here, more than anywhere else she had ever been in the world, she felt closest to Atlantis. Here she could remember more easily than at any other time what it was like to live in a time when people lived without rancour or judgement. To accept the beating heart of nature as the twin of your own pulse. Which is why it was to Glastonbury she had fled for many hundreds of years whenever she needed to think. Ever since her life as Calanthe. Or since she was left amongst the community of holy women there after Sloan's death.

Those women who lived their lives hand in hand with Mother Nature and who, by staring into the flames of a fire or the depths of a still moonlit pool, could travel the threads of the universe and see beyond the limitations of time and death. Wise women who had lived on what is now the flat land at the foot of Glastonbury Tor, then a marsh where mists would descend quickly. She could still remember the words the sisters used to draw in the power needed to control those mists, parting them to let through visitors and drawing them down when danger threatened. Ever since her time there, a time which offered her peace and contentment after losing Sloan, she had thought of it as her own personal sanctuary, somewhere she could be and reconnect to the universe. Somewhere she could always find answers.

Now, as she slowly walked the path to the Tor, the sun low but bright and the crisp autumn air tingling pleasantly on her skin, she let herself calm her mind to see if the magical place could help her find some answers to help her with her feelings for Jack and her search for Max.

Uther

"Uther, I don't want to hear you calling your brother Max again do you hear? His name is Wolfstan and well you know it."

Uther hung his head at his mother's reproach. He did indeed know that he was called Wolfstan in this life, but in his heart, his name would always be Max. Young as he was, he also knew, though, he would have to try and watch his tongue as his family didn't understand about his memories and he had already been beaten once by his father for repeatedly calling Wolfstan 'Max'.

It pained Uther, though, that Max didn't remember. The minute he had seen his baby brother, wrapped tight in swaddling clothes, he knew he was Max and his heart had filled with delight. How funny that they would be brothers, he had thought to himself. It was a thought Uther revelled in, as, in the life he had been born into just a few years before, brothers were everything to each other — family, friends, comrades and more.

Uther knew they would spend lots of time together learning to be warriors and then actually as warriors, even if the idea of battle or killing someone horrified Uther. His memories of Atlantis were too fresh to not be dismayed by how little life was revered here in his new body. Death was a daily occurrence and for men in particular, it was better to die well in battle than to live into old age. At night, when they gathered round the fire in the great hall to listen to the bards, their tales always told of battles and death, and perhaps unsurprisingly pondered the transience of life. Uther had once spoken out at the end of one of these tales.

"No wonder life seems so short," he had said to the gathering of his people, "when all you want to do is fight and go to battle."

His father had beaten him for that too and banished him to kitchen duty for a few weeks. "If you want to think like a woman then you will live like a woman," he had said.

Uther realized voicing his thoughts was pointless, but when Wolfstan was born, he thought that perhaps he could try and enjoy this

44

life as a warrior if it meant being able to spend every waking moment with Max. And so far, he had. Seven years his junior, he had taken his baby brother under his wing, and to his father's satisfaction, it was Uther who gave the toddler his first sword, a small wooden one he had carved himself. They played together, ate together, trained together, were given lessons together and even slept together in the same hay filled pallet beneath the same soft furs.

Uther's only disappointment came when he took Wolfstan aside when he was about three years old and said to the wide-eyed toddler, "You remember, don't you? You remember your real name is Max, don't you?"

For a moment, the child just stared back at him, his pale blue eyes thoughtful, but then a deep fear seemed to take over and the little boy shook his head angrily. "No! I'm Wolfstan. Don't call me that again."

Uther, now twelve, still accidently called Wolfstan 'Max' despite his best efforts and the threat of his father's heavy hand. It was hard as, while Wolfstan didn't really look like Max, his smile was very like the Max Uther had known in Atlantis and the way he laughed, with such gleeful abandonment, was all Max.

"Now," said his mother, still looking at him, her eyes carrying a strangeness he did not recognise, "your father wants to speak to you. Stand straight and don't, whatever you do, call your brother Max, do you hear?"

"Yes, mother."

"Good, now off you go."

Despite all his training as a young warrior, his experiences through many lifetimes and his memories of a different way of being, Uther still trembled at the thought of going before his father. Aelfric was every inch the Saxon warrior. He was large in every sense of the word, almost as broad as he was tall, his presence seemed to fill whatever hall he sat in and dominated whatever hearth he sat at. Uther had seen him in battle too and seen how his mighty persona almost cowed his enemies before his sword or axe cleaved their skulls..

Now, as Uther entered the great hall, dim and dusty in comparison to the bright sunshine outside, to see his father sitting in his carved oak seat on the dais, his enormous fingers adorned with large ornate gold rings pulling pensively at the matted strands of his dirty blond beard, he felt his insides turn to liquid.

"Father, Mother said you wanted to see me." Uther stood as straight as he could, though his head bowed a little naturally out of deference.

The warrior looked down at his son for a long moment, his dark blue eyes thoughtful as his top lip almost curled in distaste. Who was this child of his? So dark and lithe, more like a Pict than a Saxon, and with his queer notions. Aelfric sometimes thought he should be a shaman rather than a warrior He certainly knew how to make the hair on the back of his neck stand up with his strange looks and otherworldly statements. But as Aelfric's eldest son, he could be nothing other than a warrior so it was up to the warrior king to try and make him the best he could be, a credit to his name – named as he was for the great British king as a respectful nod to the land where they lived -and dynasty. At least, he thought, he possessed skills with the sword and he had an agility not often seen amongst bulky Saxon warriors.

Beneath his father's stern, calculating gaze, the seconds seemed like minutes for Uther. Terrified as he was, he didn't want to shame himself by being seen to shake or worse.

"As my eldest son you are destined to be a great warrior."

"If only I could follow your greatness, my lord." Uther knew what he was meant to say well enough.

"I believe your training is going well and that you move well, with a lightness and quickness."

"Thank you, sir." Uther's mind reeled, wondering where this could be going.

"I have decided, though, that to make you a true Saxon warrior you must be fostered."

Aelfric watched closely for his son's reaction. Uther swallowed hard, his heart sinking, his mind racing in panic at the thought of being away from Max, but all he said was, "Whatever you think is right, my father, I am honoured."

"You are. I am sending you to an island off the coast of Alba where women have been teaching war craft for generations. They are Celts, but we have a truce and I think their skills would suit you."

"Thank you, sir." Uther felt like crying, but the knowledge of the outrage it would cause in his father stemmed the tears.

"Do not forget your roots though, son, you are Saxon and must return to us a Saxon still, do you understand?" His father's voice became almost sinister.

"Yes, sir."

"Good. You leave tomorrow. Tonight, we shall give you a farewell feast."

Everyone came together in the great hall for the feast. There was singing and dancing and a pig, roasted on a spit, slaughtered in his honour. Every single person toasted Uther on his journey, his success in training and his ultimate return as a true Saxon warrior. Even his mother hailed his journey, though Uther could tell by the tightness around her eyes that she was worried, but what could she say? The king's mind was made up. And for Uther, it was the thought of leaving Max that pained him most. He kept his little brother by his side all night and he could tell that Wolfstan was upset about his departure, but in the way of five-year-olds. One minute, holding on to his arm saying, "Don't go Uther!" and the next giggling happily as he ate a piece of juicy pork crackling. Uther found it all hard to bear, but nobody seemed to really notice that he wasn't smiling and before the sun had risen, he found himself on the back of a horse with his belongings packed in a saddle bag and flanked on either side by his escort. Six warriors to take him to his new home. Uther wondered if his father feared he might try and run away. Little did he know that he wouldn't, purely because it would mean he would likely never see Max again in this life.

He had hugged his mother and then bent to Max, held him by the shoulders and looked into his innocent eyes. "Don't forget me, brother, I will come back and then we will never be parted again, do you understand?"

The little boy simply nodded, tears threatening.

There was nothing more to say or do except hold his hand high in farewell as they rode away across the fertile farmlands of his father's kingdom.

It was more than ten years before Uther returned. And when he did, it was no hero's homecoming. He had, once he had become accustomed to the wildness of his new home, a place where the wind seemed to bite deep even when the sun shone bright on the summer solstice, thrived. Unlike some of the other Saxon youths sent there to be trained, he had had no problem being taught by a woman — he could, after all, remember being a woman, and in Atlantis, men and women were equal, just as it was understood that the divine feminine and masculine had to be balanced in all things. There was a beauty and grace about the way they fought, too, which appealed to Uther. It was more of a dance then a battle and more about defence than aggression. He even enjoyed the extremes of weather, feeling an exaltation in his veins when the rains lashed the rocks. He took to riding his horse hard along the beaches when the storms were at their worst, earning himself the nickname of Stormchaser amongst the hardened warrior women.

Over the many years there his muscles stretched and hardened, the skin darkening and tightening around them. He grew tall, but never bulky and he began wearing his soft black hair in braids down either side of his face like the Pictish warriors he met. And despite knowing the outrage it would provoke in his father, he allowed himself to be tattooed with dark swirling patterns in the manner of the men of the north. Out there on the island, his father's anger seemed impotent. The only remnant of his childhood, which still burned bright in his mind, were thoughts of his little brother. Every day, Uther spent time looking out to sea wondering what he was doing, how he had grown and if he thought of his missing brother at all. He tried to send him thoughts, wondering if perhaps Wolfstan would hear him calling over the empty miles. Remembering the holy woman of another life, he even tried scrying to capture images of him, but the fleeting glimpses he managed told him little, even less than the messages from home. But even thoughts of his little brother, the soul he had loved through the ages, were eclipsed for a while when Uther met Luguswelwa.

Coming from Gaul, she was as dark as Uther. She was small and light too but there was a fierceness about her that she carried in the jut of her chin and the fire in her eyes. Most kept their distance when she first arrived, but not Uther. He was captivated instantly. He wondered at the strength of his feelings, wondered if he was seeing Max in Luguswelwa as Wolfstan was hundreds of miles away, but he quickly put those thoughts aside as he realised it was Luguswelwa herself he was captivated by. Not that she seemed interested in him,. Whenever he tried to extend a hand of friendship he was rewarded with an icy stare or even a snarl. Yet Uther couldn't help but continue to try, showing her where to forage for food to supplement their rations, helping her weatherproof her leather armour and even offering her his pallet, when he realised she had none.

For months, this was the way of things although, as time passed, Uther began to notice that while Luguswelwa still snarled at him, she sometimes accepted his help and didn't get up and move away when he sat beside her, happy to be companionably at her side if nothing else. Uther hoped the softening might continue, so a little warmth might thaw the tautness that vibrated through her every sinew. He fantasised about a melting in her eyes and yielding in her lips that turned a snarl into the beginnings of a smile, nothing more. He wouldn't allow himself to believe he could hope for anything more. One day, though, everything changed and it wasn't in a way Uther wanted. Watching her as he always did, he unthinkingly rushed to her side as she stumbled backwards under a parry during training, catching her by the elbow as he might his mother.

Luguswelwa was barely steadied when she swept her sword arm backwards across Uther's face, slashing his cheek from eye to chin. Blood dripped to the ground as they stood staring at each other, each with eyes as bright with dangerous swirls of anger, humiliation and frustration as the other. Later, nobody would be able to tell who moved first, all they could say for certain was that they both uttered screams of such guttural ferocity that all the other warriors stopped what they were doing to look towards the clashing swords. They were like two tigers fighting. It was bloodthirsty, barbaric and savage. Matched as they were, neither could find dominance and as sweat joined the increasing swill of blood at their feet, they both forgot their swords and fell to a murderous form of wrestling where eyes were gouged, arms twisted cruelly and nails clawed at flesh. Uther finally had his hands round Luguswelwa's throat and he found himself squeezing with all his strength as the swell of months of frustrated passion, and years of feeling not good enough, found a release in violent hatred. He might even have killed her if Alata, one of the

49

trainers, hadn't thumped him expertly on the back of the head with the hilt of her sword and knocked him out.

It was that lump that finally roused Uther from the depths of unconsciousness. The swelling pressing torturously against the rock on which he lay was too much for the blackness to contend with. His mind foggy, for the first few moments he was lost in the mists of half memories and confusion even as his bitten tongue pressed at his raw and ravaged cheeks and lips. Had he been in battle, he wondered. He could remember holding his sword. Feeling the fire of battle lust in his veins. Yet, he knew that wasn't quite right. Tentatively he opened his eyes, or eye, as one was swollen shut, eyelashes crusted with blood. He had certainly received some serious blows. A flash of memory came — a sword flashing across his face, but who was its owner? Time to move his legs. Slowly he bent the knee of one and then the other, flexing each ankle and foot as he did so. They were whole and unbroken, but by Lugh did they hurt. Now for the arms. He fought the urge to tilt his head up to look as he knew at best it would make him queasy at worst, send him back into the blackness. His left arm moved a little, but as he tried to splay his fingers he cried out in pain. They were broken, he knew. Now for his right arm. There was something wrong there too, it felt trapped, as if he was tethered. Had he lost it? Gingerly he began to raise his head, the world tilting as sweat broke out on his forehead, to look down at his wrist. At first, he could make no sense of what he saw, why he was in this situation, but then it all came flooding back to him and he lay back down with a wrenching thud, aghast by the fact his arm was actually tethered. It might have been better if it had been hacked off.

"Luguswelwa." His dry lips barely managed the name.

"Yes." It was the first words he had ever heard her speak in his own language. "You were going to kill me, remember?" The question was a challenge but not really an accusation.

"Yes, I remember." Uther felt weary beyond words and wished the blackness would return.

"Alta stopped you." Uther didn't respond. "They were going to whip us both, but Cruachan said this would be a better lesson." She pulled her wrist up fiercely, dragging Uther's painfully with it. "We are to stay like this until we learn to be comrades if not friends."

Uther could manage no more than a wry smile, the irony not lost on him.

In the end, he never knew how long they stayed tethered together, their wrists bound tightly by multiple leather cords tied in intricate knots, but those first few days felt like years. Both wounded and bloodied, neither could move from where they had been left on a rocky outcrop until they had helped each other heal. Long before Uther had awoken, Luguswelwa had managed to reach and retrieve the bundle left for them, containing salves, food, water, blankets and clean clothes.

He noted that, while she had somehow managed to dress her own wounds, change clothes and wrap herself in a blanket, she hadn't bothered to lay one over his unconscious form. With more than a little effort, as Luguswelwa watched with belligerent amusement, he managed to prop himself on to one side long enough to grab a corner of another and awkwardly pull it over his broken body. Moments later he was asleep again. When he awoke again, he realized with some despair that he desperately needed to relieve himself.

Raising his head a little, he found Luguswelwa curled with her back to him, one arm stretched back to where his right hand lay next to his side. With a sigh he lay back to consider his options — wake Luguswelwa or go where he lay. He didn't fancy either choice, but with the pressure in his stomach mounting to unbearable proportions, he had to make a decision quickly.

"Lug." His voice was sharp, authoritative in a way he had never heard himself sound before. "Wake up, I need to piss."

He moved before she had time to react, ungainly hauling himself to his feet before she had really stirred. Hobbling to a rock, a goodly number of strides away from where they slept, as best he could before she really got to her feet.

"Hey!" she called as she stumbled behind him.

Uther felt ridiculously satisfied at having been able to disconcert her for once, but by the time he was ready to undo his flies and pass water she was back to her truculent best.

"Don't expect me to help," she said matter-of-factly as she watched him struggle, then simply looked on with indifference as his broken fingers finally undid his trousers and urine spurted forth.

51

By the time they made it back to the blankets, though, they were both exhausted, too exhausted to quarrel. When Uther suggested they make a fire before sleeping again Luguswelwa did nothing but nod, and for the first time Uther could remember, they worked together in companionable silence, intuitively using their tethered hands in the best way possible.

With a fire roaring, they made tea and ate some hardened bread. Uther changed clothes and even managed to rub some salve on the worst of his cuts and bruises. By the time they lay down again, sleep stole upon them in moments.

The next time they woke, the wind was blowing fiercely and the fire had died.

"We need to find better shelter," Uther said as they stood looking at the purple hues forming in the sky. "We are in for a storm." Luguswelwa nodded. "Are you ok to walk?" Uther asked her, aware that his own injuries would make it painful for him.

The look she gave him was murderous. "Worry about your own endurance, warrior," she almost spat at him.

There was no time to argue, though, and between them they packed up the few possessions they had, and unhappily handfast, made their way across the isolated rocky outcrop where they had been left to the protection of the trees on the horizon.

By the time the thunder finally roared, they were deep in the trees, sheltered by a man-made canopy contrived in silent necessity and sitting on a bed of gathered leaves and ferns. They had built a small fire in a protective stone circle at their feet.

"Well, this is like being in my father's great hall compared to the last couple of nights," Uther tried to joke, but Luguswelwa remained silent and Uther fell to sipping tea from a clay beaker held awkwardly in his damaged left hand and listening to the storm.

Sometime later, as they lay back beneath their furs, walking distant paths as they listened to the rain in the trees above them and hissing in the heat of the flames, Luguswelwa finally spoke. "Has it occurred to you, warrior, that we could free ourselves?"

Uther was taken by surprise as in all honesty it hadn't. "No, it hasn't. Could we? Would we? Should we?" He raised himself so he could look

52

down at her, reminding himself, as he looked down at her sharp cheekbones and flashing eyes, her beauty not in the least diminished by the bruises on her face, swollen lips and ragged cut across her left eyebrow, that they were not lovers. Yet she stared back at him in a way that almost made Uther lean forward and kiss her.

"We could."

"Do you have a knife?" Uther asked softly as a shiver ran up his spine, whether from attraction or the prospect she may have a secret knife that was likely to end up between his ribs.

Luguswelwa looked disgusted. "Why would we need a knife? There are stones. We could find something sharp."

Uther considered it for a moment. He had a feeling there was more to those knots than just twine — he had seen first-hand what could be done with magic in this life and others — and had a feeling attempting to cut through them would have serious consequences. Or would they? Perhaps they were just ordinary knots and the thoughts they were having were all part of a test? Would they be punished further for attempting to escape their bondage? Uther wasn't sure, he was also well acquainted with the contrary notions of the warrior tribe who lived on these islands, perhaps they would fail by not attempting to escape? Not showing the courage and gumption needed to seek their freedom could be seen as a terrible failure by them. And finally, Uther thought, did he want to lose the tether to Luguswelwa? He finally had her undivided attention. He smiled ruefully as he suddenly realised how they were now connected in a strange, twisted version of the ceremonial hand-fasting used to symbolise men and women's commitment to each other.

It dawned on him that he had been silent quite some time and Luguswelwa's eyes were on his face. He felt himself flush slightly, unnoticeable, he hoped, in their gloomy makeshift bedchamber.

"You are thinking many things, warrior. Tell me?"

Uther smiled down at her. "I am just wondering about the true nature of this punishment. I can't decide if we will be punished further by escaping or failing to try."

Luguswelwa looked back steadily without a trace of a smile. "Was that all?"

"Yes," Uther lied.

Luguswelwa looked at him a moment longer. "You might be right. We do nothing for the moment."

In fact, they did nothing for many more days and the more time they passed tethered, the more Uther sensed the tiniest of thawing in Luguswelwa. Nothing he could put his finger on, just that she was a little less aggressive and more at ease in his company. They waited out the storm in the woods, nursing their wounds and regaining their strength. By the time the rain stopped, the supplies left for them had run out.

"So, warrior, what do we do now?" Luguswelwa asked him. Uther was astounded she was looking for him to take the lead.

"We make a spear and hunt deer. We make a line and catch fish. We forage. We make a better camp. When we have built up our strength and supplies, we try to find our way back."

There was that long stare once more. "Yes, I agree." She now sounded as if she had been a teacher setting him a problem.

A few days later, a small deer cooked on a makeshift spit over the fire in their new camp — a low cave deep in the woods — Uther noticed Luguswelwa rubbing at the twines that tethered them.

She caught him looking. "They are beginning to chafe. The looser they get the more they rub."

Uther turned the spit with his healing left hand. "Is now the time to try?"

"Try what?" Luguswelwa asked irritably, distracted by her bonds.

"Cutting them." Uther looked down at her, his eyes gentle, and for a moment he saw a softening inside her, just before a huge raven burst from the trees, screeching like a banshee, and tore at their dinner.

Now well used to moving as one, they leapt to their feet and chased the bird.

"I think that's a no," was all Luguswelwa said, but as she looked at Uther there was the tiniest of smiles on her lips.

That night they lay beneath the furs facing each other for the first time, holding the tethered arms above their heads so their bodies lay close. There was silence for the longest time as a storm gathered in the space between, those few inches separating their flesh. Finally, Uther raised his good hand to Lug's face, the back of his fingers gentle on her cheek and then they kissed. Her response was greater than Uther could ever have

54

hoped for and for a few hours that night they were the only people in the whole world.

After that, everything changed. Luguswelwa was still surly and brittle at times, but she began to laugh and even sing. Uther too found himself grinning in a way he could never remember doing so before in this life.

Days merged into weeks as the lost themselves in each other and their forest world. They would hunt for food, turning a chore into a beautiful expression of the unity they had found. Moving as if they had one body and mind, they would move silently through the forest, a lithe, four-legged creature able to move in ways beyond any other creature's ken. In between times though they frolicked. Uther could hardly believe Luguswelwa was capable, but frolic was the only word he could think of to describe what they did. They swam and splashed about in rivers and streams, they chased each other through the trees squealing with delight at the futility of such a game given they were attached at the wrist. They tickled and teased each other. And ultimately, they made love wherever and whenever they pleased. They both glowed and they both seemed to completely forget that they were tethered or that they were meant to be setting out to find their way back to the village.

Eventually, after several years, the world found them. It was springtime and the forest floor around their cave was carpeted in fresh, springy grass dotted with daisies. Uther and Luguswelwa lay naked, except for the cords at their wrists, languid after love making and relishing the cool press of grass beneath their limbs. They were relaxed and carefree, yet their warrior instincts remained and they both sprung to their feet at the sound of a twig breaking beneath the unmistakable tread of a human foot.

Grabbing a spear each, they stood unashamed in their naked state, and stared to where the noise came from.

"Who's there?" Uther called.

No answer bar further rustling and then, from between the leaves and branches, stepped Uther's father. The old warrior took in the scene before him in one world-weary glance.

"I must be getting old if I allowed you to hear me approach," he said, watching his son with an unreadable expression.

Uther glanced anxiously between his father and Luguswelwa, caught between a need to stand proud before his father and the desire to cover his and Lug's nakedness.

Enjoying his son's discomfort, his father did nothing to help, simply stood surveying the rustic camp.

It was Lug who came to the rescue. With an unhurried calm, she bowed slightly to the old king as if she stood before him in his great hall in her best gown. "My lord, it is an honour to meet you at last." She smiled slightly but Uther knew his father would not miss the proud, determined jut of her jaw. "If you could give us a moment to dress then we could receive you properly?"

Lug gave him a moment and then no more before dropping her spear and reclaiming her now worn trews. Uther followed suit, suddenly aware of his tether to Lug in a way that he hadn't been for a long time.

When they were dressed, Uther stoked the fire as Lug placed a pot over it for tea.

"Please, my lord, sit and we will take some tea."

Uther's father sat on the proffered flat stone as if he were in his great hall. "Hrumph, no ale?"

"We have none, Father." Uther's voice was steady and he looked directly into his father's eyes for perhaps the first time in his life.

"I don't imagine you would, living out here like animals. No more, though, I have come to fetch you home." His father watched his son's face, hand resting on the hilt of his sword as if expecting to fight.

Uther and Lug looked at each other, communicating without words as they so often did.

"We don't want to leave, Father."

The old man was on his feet in an instant, causing Uther and Lug to once more dive for their spears, but the hardened king was too fast for them and had brought down his sword before either of them could turn and defend themselves. It wasn't flesh and bone the sword cut through, though, it was the worn, weathered twines of leather which had bound their wrists together for so long that Uther's father cut. The young couple fell apart as if they had been felled by the blow, too stunned by the sudden and brutal loss of the connection to be able to react.

Uther felt as if he had been stabbed, or worse. His stomach convulsed in grief at the realisation he and Lug were no longer linked. They had been tied together so long it was as if she were a part of him and he, her. They couldn't remember life when they were not linked. Uther looked at Lug as she cradled her wrist to her chest, tears streaming down her face.

"My love, it changes nothing." She nodded in response, but Uther knew that in that instant everything had changed and life would never be the same again.

His father sheathed his sword and sat back down again, satisfied. "Good. We leave at dawn."

The closer they came to the warrior's village, the more Uther felt as if he were in a dream. As they passed farmsteads and crofts, people came out to look at them, taking in their wild appearance. Uther looked back as if it were they who were the wild creatures, beasts he had maybe once seen pictures of but had never seen in life, familiar and yet foreign. The further away from their forest haven, the more withdrawn Lug became. Eventually, after days of walking, they came to the top of the hill and saw the buildings of the warriors' village below them sitting where they had done for many years on the top of a cliff.

"What will happen to us now?" Lug asked, having not uttered a word since the morning they had left.

Uther's father looked at her. "What will happen to you, I have no idea, but my son and I leave for our own lands as soon as the ship is ready."

"No!" Uther's voice was horrified. "I am not leaving without Lug."

"Does she want to come?" His father, as always, was unperturbed.

"Lug?" Uther turned to her, desperate.

"I don't know, Uther. I don't know anything." And with that, Lug walked away towards the village leaving Uther baffled and distraught.

"Leave her, son. You've had your fun. I will find you a nice Saxon wife at home."

Uther was too bewildered to reply.

Three days later, they sailed for the mainland without Lug. Uther couldn't understand why she wouldn't leave with him as she had clung to him and begged him to stay with her there, but Uther's father made it clear that if he didn't leave with his father, he would kill them both. So, he had stood leaning against the railing watching her slight form, still standing, hair whipping in the wind, where he had finally left her, vanish from sight.

He spent the voyage in stony silence and it wasn't until they were on the horses his father had left for them on the mainland that his thoughts turned to home. And more particularly, Wolfstan. His brother that he had thought of less and less in the last years, even though he still remembered the lives, and love, they had shared before.

He had talked often about them to Lug, who listened with rapt attention, as he told her how he could remember living in other bodies and how he had known his brother before and that once, a long time ago, in a place called Atlantis, they had been young lovers who were married just as the world swallowed them and the world as they knew it. She never doubted him and always wanted to know more of what he could remember. One day, though, she had asked, "Do you love him more than me?"

Taken aback by the question, Uther had to think before he answered. "No. It's just different. I love you here and now in this life, and who knows, I might love you again, but my love for Max is eternal and boundless, it will just always be."

Uther had worried his answer might upset her, but she accepted it with a quiet nod. Maybe, Uther wondered as he rode behind his father but in front of his men at arms, that was why she had refused to come. Maybe she thought he wouldn't love her when he was back with Wolfstan? Wolfstan, Max. Uther felt a sweep of emotions when he thought about his baby brother. How many years had it been? He wasn't sure. How old would he be now? Sixteen? Maybe seventeen? He would be a man, a young warrior and he may not even remember Uther. All at once, Uther wanted the miles to vanish so he could be home while also feeling desperate to turn on his tail and flee back to the island and Lug's embrace.

As it turned out, when they arrived at his father's homestead, Wolfstan wasn't there.

"He's out riding the borders with his men," the guard told them when they enquired.

"As always," his father replied in a way that left Uther wondering.

"What do you mean, Father?" he asked, no longer afraid to ask his father anything.

His father looked at him appraisingly before answering. "Your beloved little brother has ideas above his station. He has a band of young warriors who hang on his every word and they are always itching for a fight. I had him whipped in public just a month ago but it seems to have made him worse rather than cow his bloodlust." Uther noticed for the first time how strained his father looked. "I need my sons to be warriors not battle hungry fools and that's what your brother has become. It was one of the reasons I came to find you. He used to listen to you and I need an ally. You are many things, Uther, but never a battle hungry fool."

Uther nodded, accepting his father's compliment of sorts as he took in this new information. "Where's my mother?"

"That was the other reason I came to find you." He sounded weary. "She died. I am sorry."

Uther spent the rest of the day in a daze. Familiar faces floated before him, clapping his shoulder in sorrow and welcome but he barely registered them. His father held a feast in his honour, welcoming the prodigal son home, yet making no mention of his mother or the fact that he had been living in a cave tethered at the wrist to Lug for the last few years. He barely touched the ale pressed into his hand, finding the bitter taste unpalatable after so long of drinking nothing but fresh spring water and teas made from foraged herbs and leaves. Besides, the noise, the heat and smells of a great hall filled with unwashed people devouring food from mountainous platters, laughing, singing and falling into each other made him feel nauseated enough.

As soon as he reckoned everyone was too drunk to notice otherwise, he slunk away to find somewhere quiet to be by himself, deeply missing Lug and deeply aware that he was yet to see his brother. He climbed to the top of the nearby hill, enjoying the fresh air in his nostrils and the star filled space above him. Finding the spot, somewhere he had often hidden out as a youngster, he lay down in the long grass and stared up at the sky. His hand automatically straying to run where, until very recently, he had been linked to Lug for every moment of every day. Lug. How he missed her. He couldn't help but wonder what she was doing and wishing she had come with them. Lug's dark features shifted in his mind, though, and it was his mother's he now saw. It had been so long since he had seen her face, yet in his mind, he could remember how she had smiled at him as if he had just left her at the feast. Tears welled in his eyes, how could she be gone? He didn't even know what had happened to her, nobody had told him and he hadn't been capable of asking.

And then his mother's face became that of Wolfstan and the image of that little boy Uther remembered looking so sorrowful at his brother's departure almost instantly transformed into Max. Slim, toned Max with his easy charm and quick smile. Strong yet gentle. Joyous, yet calm. How Uther wished more than anyone else that Max was with him there and then, his presence itself would be reassuring and Uther knew he could tell him all that he was thinking. But he wasn't, and by all accounts, the man that was now Max was far removed from that young Atlantean man he once was. As hard as it was for Uther to believe, Wolfstan seemed to have become violent and vicious. With his long memory, Uther understood that such emotions ultimately arose form unhappiness and Wolfstan would have felt Uther's departure and then his mother's death keenly, but still, the thought of his younger brother rampaging around the country killing filled him with horror and dread.

Uther had been back at home for close to a week and still there had been no sign of Wolfstan. In those days, though, Uther had slowly begun to readjust to living once more in his childhood home, although thoughts of Lug were never far from his mind. He spent time speaking to those he remembered from his childhood and his father's men to find out what had been happening while he was away and the state of play with neighbouring tribes, although whenever his mother came up in conversation, Uther was greeted with brisk changes in subject, awkward shuffling and darting gazes. Eventually he strode into the great hall to confront his father.

"Father," he called loudly to get his father's attention. He was sitting on his throne staring into the middle distance, something Uther noticed he did a lot now. It seemed almost a struggle for him to draw his gaze away to look at Uther.

'Son?" he asked wearily.

Uther felt sorry for him for the first time in his life, but he needed an answer. "What happened to my mother?" he asked, perhaps more gruffly than he intended. His father's face darkened and Uther braced himself for his anger. Instead, the older man simply buried his face in his hands. Uther stood staring. His father's shoulders shuddered as he gave in to sobbing. "Father?" Uther asked more gently, placing a hand on the older man's heaving shoulders.

Without looking up at his son, Aelfric almost whimpered, "Wolfstan killed her. Your own brother killed your own mother, we are cursed, Uther. I don't know why but we are cursed."

There was no time for Uther to take in this news as, just a moment later, the alarm horns were blown. It could only mean one thing — armed men were approaching. Pulling his sword from the scabbard, Uther ran to the gate, demanding to know from the guards what they had seen, only dimly aware that, without realising what he was doing, he had stepped into his father's shoes.

"There's someone out there, my lord."

"What do you mean 'someone out there'?" Uther demanded. "Soldiers? Wolfstan?"

"No, at least we don't think so. It's just one figure, but he is flitting from cover to cover as if planning to attack."

"A single warrior?" Uther asked wonderingly. "Open the gates I will go and find them."

"Uther." His father's voice rang out behind him. As he turned to face him, Uther half expected to be upbraided but instead his father just put a hand on his shoulder. "Be careful."

Years spent living in nature had honed Uther's senses in a way warrior training never could. His sword was held lightly in his hand, but once he heard the gate close behind him, he knew his greatest boon was to stand still and silent for a moment and allow his senses to find what they would, hunting with his ears, nose and another sense altogether, like a wolf.

The rippling breeze tickled his nose, and behind the scent of grass and damp earth, Uther could smell the musk of an animal, deer, he thought, and another smell too, something faint yet familiar, sweet and yet sour. He could hear nothing more than the birds and the scuffling of a small animal nearby, and scanning the rolling hills stretching out before him, he saw nothing unusual. Closing his eyes, he tuned into that other sense, the one that alerted him to things that all his other senses missed. In Atlantis, he remembered, people used that extra sense as naturally and as frequently as people now used their voices. And there it was, telling him there was someone out there and exactly which way to go to find them. Moving catlike on silent feet, he stalked through the undergrowth. He paused to allow his breath, ragged in his own ears, to regulate. Nothing would give him away more than his own breath. Then, taking another few steps, he spun around behind a boulder and pulled the figure crouched there to the ground, a bundle of arms and legs beneath an oversized cloak.

He didn't need to see to know it was Lug.

"Woden's teeth," he swore, feeling his heart leap with delight. "Lug, it's you." Finding her face, dirtied and bruised as it was, amongst the cloth he caressed her cheek. "What are you doing here?"

She smiled back at him, her eyes filled with love and relief. "I missed you," she said simply.

Bundling her to his chest he held her tight and felt some tension ease from her muscles. Then, pulling her back, he crushed her lips with his. "Oh, I've missed you too, why didn't you just come with me?"

He saw her swallow hard. "I didn't want to come between you and Wolfstan. I know the love you have for your brother, but I felt like I didn't want to live without you, so I had to come."

Uther smiled. "I am so glad you did." He kissed her again. "I have so much to tell you, but let's get you inside first. It's not safe out here and I think you could use a good meal."

Lug nodded wearily. "You are not wrong. I haven't eaten for two days."

Uther hauled her to her feet and put his arm round her waist to help her along, while he held his sword in the other.

"Surely this close to your home you don't need your sword?" she asked.

Uther made a noise in the back of his throat. "You would think, but things have changed. My brother…"

Uther never got to finish the sentence. An arrow whizzed in front of his face and embedded itself deep in Lug's throat. He saw her eyes stretch once in knowing horror before the beautiful light went out in them, her body now heavy in his arms. The cry he let out was beyond guttural. It was wild and animalistic. He laid her gently on the ground, closed her eyes and then spun to face the attackers he knew were closing in on him, enraged and engorged, made mindless by grief. He screamed out all his pain as the warriors emerged from the undergrowth only to be cut down as easily as if they were grass by Uther's unstoppable blade. And then there was only one man standing before him. He may not have seen him for many years, and in that time, he had grown from a little boy into a young man, but Uther knew in a heartbeat it was Wolfstan. And it was only a heartbeat before the two were locked in deadly combat, unaware of the anguished wail that came from an old man who had once been a strong and indomitable king.

The bloodlust only lessened when Uther pulled the sword from his brother's heart and collapsed at his side, crumbling beneath the weight of what had just happened. Lug lay dead just feet away and now, his beloved baby brother, Wolfstan, who was Max, was choking on his own blood as it pumped from his mouth. Dead at his own brother's hand just as their own mother had been killed by her son. The brothers grasped hands, tears in both their eyes.

"Max, I am sorry," Uther sobbed.

"I am too, brother. For everything." Wolfstan took one final rattling breath and was gone, his hand limp in Uther's.

Uther folded his brother's hands peacefully on his chest and closed his eyes before standing, staggering as he did so, sword dangling from his right hand. In the stunned silence, he shuffled to where Lug lay and kissed her cold brow. Then, looking up at the ramparts where his father stood, he held his sword high in acknowledgment.

"Father... I am sorry," was all he said, then, turning his back on his father and his home, he looked out over the rolling hills, stained pink in the setting sun, and thinking of Atlantis, he thrust his sword deep into his own chest. His last breath forming a name, the name that followed him from life to life — Max.

Aurora jolted awake, the setting sun painting the sky before her pink and orange, just like Uther's last view of the world. She had fallen asleep where she had sat on Glastonbury Tor, her back resting against the ancient brick of St Michael's church. Groggily, she stumbled to her feet,

63

aware her steps also echoed Uther's final ones. Why, she wondered, had she dreamt of that lifetime? She had been looking for an answer about her relationship with Jack and dreamt of a brutal lifetime where she had killed Max. Out of grief and heartbreak, granted, but still, as Uther she had murdered Max in that life and she knew there would have been karma to pay. Had she paid it? And what did it mean that she dreamt of it now?

Aurora, feeling stiff, cold, tired and greatly unsettled by her memories, started to make her way down from the Tor, the stirring leaves promising a storm to come. It wasn't Max or Jack she was thinking of as she walked down the ancient processional way, in the footsteps of her own self when she had walked Earth as Calanthe. She wasn't even thinking about Calanthe. It was Lug. Uther had loved Lug, not in the transcendental way that Aurora loved — loves — Max, or really in the earthy passionate way Ailidh had loved Sloan, but in a devoted, gentle way which came with its own sweet physicality, but like Sloan, until she had met Jack anyway, she didn't remember ever encountering Lug again in any lifetime. It was strange, she thought, that while there were people she was friends with, or related to, that she met again and again in lifetime after lifetime, aside, of course, from Max, there were others she never saw again. . Or at least, not that she remembered. But, as far as she knew, the part of her that was Uther had loved Lug deeply and yet Lug had never reappeared and until now, Sloan, who she had also loved with a passion, had never reappeared. Was that something important? Is that why she was remembering Lug now? Aurora felt like she couldn't think any longer. All she wanted was to get back to her B&B, have a bath and sleep.

The next morning, she felt refreshed and decided to spend some time pottering round the esoteric offerings of Glastonbury high street, wandering aimlessly among the eclectic bookshops and stores filled with intriguing bits and bobs. It was something she always found relaxing, perhaps, she had wondered, it was because so much of the merchandise seemed familiar from other times, other lives she had led. Maybe, she thought, it was because some of the people who ran the shops and the customers, had also been alive at those times too, but unlike Aurora, they simply didn't remember. Or didn't remember with the utter clarity she did. It was also a good way of distracting herself for a while from her musings over Jack and her longing for Max. Jack had messaged her that morning. She felt both pleased and unsettled, so a few hours of retail distraction followed by good coffee and a slice of homemade cake was exactly what she felt like.

An hour and a half and three new books, plus a crystal ring, later and she was taking her seat for a mid-morning coffee feeling a little more at ease. She was idly flicking through one of her new books when the waitress came to take her order. Flashing her a bright smile, Aurora, distracted by her book, didn't really take her in as she asked for coffee and a slice of Victoria Sponge cake. It was moments later that it registered in her subconscious that she knew the girl. It was Lug. Aurora could almost see the universe moving the pieces on the chess board. This was all happening for a reason, these things always did, but the reason was, for the moment, beyond Aurora.

She tried to watch the girl subtly, feeling the strange bubbling of emotions that always came with meeting someone in a different life who had meant a lot to her in a previous one. Excitement, love, happiness and familiarity mixed with something akin to anxiety and even nervousness. The girl had the same cheekbones and eyes, but her hair was more brown than black and she was taller and curvier, but Aurora knew with that deep knowing that had been her companion for more years than she cared to count, that it was Lug. What should she do? Smile. That was always a good start, especially as she was coming back towards her with her coffee and cake

The girl who had been Lug smiled back, open and friendly but showing no sign of recognition.

"Thank you," Aurora managed, suppressing an urge to reach out, take the girl's hand and tell her how nice it was to see her again. The girl smiled and nodded and made her way back to the bar without another word.

By the time it came for her to leave, Aurora tried to make a more meaningful connection, but the girl who had been Lug simply gave her a distracted smile and moved on to another table. What did it all mean, wondered Aurora?

Chapter 5

By the time Aurora arrived back in London, she had decided to keep seeing Jack. She wasn't quite ready to admit it, but her feelings for Jack were beginning to feel a lot like love. Max was still there, somewhere in her head and heart, but it was Jack who was taking up pole position right at the moment. That and her growing preoccupation with the memories that were arising unbidden as she encountered people from her many pasts again. Not that it was unusual, she had always recognized people. The lady who owned the local newsagents was once Aurora's boy servant, a taxi driver Aurora had recently recognized as a butcher she knew a few hundred years ago. These encounters were so common they barely registered with Aurora any more. What was happening now, though, seemed loaded with significance. Each memory seemed to follow naturally from the next, as if she was being prompted by some greater force to examine each of her lives – and the people in them - in turn. But why? What did it all mean? Where did Jack fit into it all? Why had he, of all people from her many lives, returned to her with such force? Ultimately, though, it did all come back to one question for Aurora; where was Max?

On the train home from Glastonbury, Aurora had allowed herself to sink into a daydream of remembrance, back to when she was Cas and she and Max literally glowed with love, pure unconditional love, for each other. She remembered the verdant meadows alive with the buzz of bees as they dipped and soared above the jewel-like wildflowers. She remembered how animals roamed contentedly, safe in the knowledge that their human companions felt nothing but love and gratitude for them.

Back then, Aurora, as Cas, had known that their corner of Atlantis was the last place on Earth to still be such an idyll. She knew that in other places, not that far away, people were living very different lives, lives filled with fear and violence. Lives focused solely on survival. She remembered wishing they could all feel the blissful love she felt for every person in her life and especially Max, her twin flame, her soulmate, her other half. She remembered idyllic hours spent together playing beneath crystal clear waterfalls, lying, hands entwined, in the long grasses, simply being and breathing. It felt like it could not possibly end, such a wondrous existence amongst nature's bounty, but in the end, the darkness forming on the rest of the Planet encroached on their little paradise Their blissful existence was swallowed up by flames and Atlantis was sent to the bottom of the ocean to become a myth.

With their greater awareness and expanded consciousness, Cas and her family, her people, understood the need for this to happen at a higher level and felt no bitterness. They happily offered their lives up in service of the greater good, but as a human, Aurora was doomed to remember what once was while pining for the other half of her soul and the love they had known throughout incarnation after incarnation. Yet she knew it was also an extraordinary opportunity, a gift she had been given. Perhaps her work helping people was the full potential of that gift, but she sensed the universe had still a greater plan for her – was now the time it came to fruition?

She sent Jack a text asking if he would like to meet that night. They must talk. How much, though, could Aurora tell him?

They went for dinner then walked hand in hand along the Thames. Jack was delighted to see her and seemed to accept her invitation as an acknowledgment that she felt their relationship could go further. They went back to his studio apartment and made love with a deep intensity, hands and eyes locked. It was afterwards, as they sprawled languidly in bed, that Aurora broached the subject that had been whispering in her ear all night.

"Jack?" she asked, as her fingers gently swept his hair back from his brow.

"Mmm," came his sleepy response.

"Do you believe in life after death?" Silence. He roused himself, raising onto one elbow to look at her with lazy quizzical eyes.

"Eh?" was his ineloquent response.

"I know, it is a random question, but I just wondered what you believe. Do you think we have been here before?" She held his eyes intently and saw what she was hoping for, the tiniest spark of awareness, recognition of a truth that Jack himself might not even be consciously aware of. For Aurora, though, it was enough.

"Is this because of what you do?" Jack had a little understanding of her job, but she hadn't delved into all the details with him.

"Yes, perhaps. Sometimes I hypnotise people to remember past lives — they speak in languages they have never even heard, in this lifetime, give details they could not possibly have known from history books and even sometimes reveal something which is completely contrary to what has been written."

"Must be fascinating. And you believe them? You believe this knowledge comes from past lives rather than some subconscious computer we all have holding knowledge we simply aren't aware of?"

"Yes, I do. Do you?"

"I've never really thought about it, to be honest." He paused, brow furrowed. "Is this because of us?" he asked.

"Why would you say that?" Aurora asked, her heart racing, as she realised she was getting to the moment of truth.

"Because, from the moment I laid eyes on you, I felt like I knew you and I know you felt the same." He watched her; his masculine features gentle in the half light.

"Yes, I knew it," she replied, lifting her hand to stroke his cheek. "The thing is, Jack, I also remember how and where."

"A life we had together before?" His voice was incredulous, but she knew there was something he was remembering, subtly perhaps but it was there, enough to stop him from declaring her mad there and then.

"Yes, do you want me to tell you about it?"

Jack's eyes were awake now and intent, full of curious, if slightly disbelieving, interest. "Yes."

Aurora lay back on the pillows and pulled Jack's head on to her chest so her arms could wrap around him, then, almost like a mother telling a story to a child, she told him all about their life together from beginning to end, giving every detail she could remember. The only detail she left out was the fact that their son was Max. The sun was beginning to rise by the time she had finished, her voice thick with talking.

Jack lay still for many moments. She allowed him his time, lost as he was in his own thoughts. Finally, he spoke. "When I was a child, I always wanted a sword and a horse. I wanted to ride on horseback through woods. I called myself Sloan the Barbarian."

Aurora smiled, a sense of relief washing through her. "Do you believe me then?"

Jack drew himself round, pushing her hair from her face so he could look her in the eyes. His own tawny ones filled with their customary gentle seriousness. "I do. I always knew you were different."

Aurora looked back, her face serious too. "I am, Jack. I can't help it. Do you mind?"

Jack shook his head. "No." And then lent forward to kiss her yet again.

Jack seemed less perturbed than fascinated. Over the next few days, he bombarded Aurora with questions, mainly about their life together but also about what else she could remember. Aurora was as honest as she could be with him. It was refreshing for her to be able to talk about it, to share the burden, but for reasons she couldn't quite explain, though, she never mentioned Max.

"So how does karma work then?" Jack asked her one evening as they picked at a bowl of olives in a bar dressed for Halloween.

"How do you mean 'work'?" Aurora asked as she chewed, shivering slightly despite wearing a thick navy jumper.

"Well, you must have seen it in action, haven't you?"

Aurora chewed slowly, thinking about Jack's question, feeling a little disconnected from the world around her.

"I have," she started hesitantly, "I have seen karma play out time and time again. It is not a punishment, you know, though, it is just a balancing, a learning. At a higher level, our souls agree and understand."

"Do you have karma to play out in this life then? I mean, I guess we all do. I must have karma from all those people I killed as Sloan, mustn't I?"

Aurora frowned. "I think the answer to all three is yes. You may have already worked off the karma from Sloan's lifetime, though, maybe you had a lifetime where you lost a lot of people you loved. I remember experiencing karma in action, but then it is happening all the time. You keep the change when someone gives you too much in the shop in the morning and in the afternoon, you drop a tenner. That kind of thing."

Aurora was aware of her words slurring as her shivering of a few moments ago turned to heat.

"Aurora? Honey? Are you OK?"

"Actually, I don't feel very well, do you mind if I go home?"

Caedmon

Bells were ringing, echoing the panic in the air around them. Brother Caedmon held his habit high above his knees so he could move with greater ease, his worn leather sandals slapping at the flagstones beneath his feet. Fear pulsed through his veins. The ship had been sighted off the coast only half an hour before, but it was close to landing already, the Viking warriors on board straining at the prow like hungry wolfhounds on a leash. Thankfully, Caedmon thought to himself as he raced through the cloisters, most of the monks, including the old abbot, had fled on his command. He had a presence and wisdom that fostered respect amongst the community and he had used to his full advantage in the hours leading to this point.

He intended to be the only person on the mainland when the Vikings arrived, but he wanted to be found serene and praying, not hightailing it around like a child at play as he tried to hide as many of the monastery's manuscripts as he could. He knew the Vikings wouldn't value them, it was gold and blood they were after, so he had to at least try and save them from the bonfire.

Panting, he finally found himself kneeling on the cold stone before the cross. In the distance, he could hear the bloodthirsty howls of the invaders, but it was not fear he felt. Even before he had heard the teachings of Jesus, which so appealed to him as Caedmon, he knew there was no death.

As a child he had awoken with nightmares of falling on his own sword, the bodies of a woman and a man at his feet. His mother had brought in a priest when he told her of falling into the flames of Atlantis and even of the time he was a lady and worshipped the Goddess. Thankfully, for Caedmon, the priest was kindly and wise and never admonished Caedmon. Instead, he liked to ask the young boy about his memories, listening to his answers with great gravity and pondering, almost to himself, how this knowledge fitted in to Christ's teachings. It was inevitable, really, that Caedmon would become a monk himself. As a young man, when the old priest asked if he was sure he wanted to take the tonsure, Caedmon had replied that he had to be a monk because it was his destiny in this lifetime to die as a monk, he had known it from the moment he was born. The old priest simply nodded sagely, acknowledging what the boy said as simple truth.

What the boy never revealed was that he was to die at the hands of the physical manifestation of the other half of his own soul, Max. Did he not tell him because he felt the old man wouldn't believe or understand the love that stretched back over eons? No, not that, it was just, because for Caedmon, it simply felt too personal. The death of Max, or Wolfstan, at his own hands haunted Caedmon's soul and he knew he would not feel at ease until the balance was redressed.

And he knew that was exactly what was about to happen and karma's hand, bedecked in furs and wearing a long beard,, was charging up the pretty white sand of their beach as he knelt praying. Prayers he believed in; the Christ may be a recent addition to the minds of humanity, but Caedmon recognised his light of old and he felt more than comfortable in its presence. He prayed that his death wouldn't be too painful and that the balance would then be redressed, and that if and when he incarnated again, it would be like a fresh start. He also prayed for Max, whose soul would be accumulating karma by balancing his own, and he prayed that in their next life together they might once more know each other in love.

The man snarled as he burst open the door to the chapel. Caedmon could smell him, the sweat and filth overlaid by something else. Bloodlust, possibly. He waited to see if he was about to be struck prone where he knelt, but when it never happened, he rose slowly and calmly to his feet before turning to face Max as he was in this lifetime. He smiled. "Max, it is me, Cas," he said, almost happily.

The Viking, tall and muscular and every inch a warrior, strutted back and forth across the breadth of the small chapel, weighing the sword in his hand in anticipation of the move to kill the monk he saw before him, smiling incongruously. The Viking looked afresh at the monk. He should have killed him before he had risen but something had held his hand. Sometimes these Christians seemed to welcome death, he mused. Not always, some screamed like piglets, trying to squirm away even as the blow caught them. Here was one, though, who was ready and prepared, not like a warrior, but in a peaceful way. It was baffling to the Viking. To embrace death was one thing but do so with a sword in hand and your chin held high and defiantly. Not like this monk who looked like he would happily hold his habit out the way to make it easier for the sword to cut him down. And he was speaking. The Viking didn't understand the language, but there was something in those words that struck him, as if he had heard them before somewhere. Max. Cas. He took a step closer to the man, towering above him as he did so, yet the monk did not baulk. Instead, he smiled calmly up at him.

"I welcome you, Max. I know you must redress the balance and I welcome that too. I pray for your soul."

There's that word again — Max. The Viking stared back at the smiling monk. Was it the eyes? Were they familiar? Did they remind him of someone? He couldn't place it, but what did it matter, the monk was going back to meet his maker and the sooner he did so the better. It was over in an instant. Caedmon's head lay next to his crumpled body on the flagstones before his smile had time to fall from his face.

The Viking staggered backwards, suddenly and unexpectedly overwhelmed with a despair deeper than anything he had ever felt before. When his comrades found him, he was kneeling beside the body of the monk, cradling the severed head. The best option, they decided, was to send him to join him.

Aurora felt groggy when she woke. The metallic taste of blood still in her mouth. For a moment, she didn't know where she was, but as her eyes slowly opened and adjusted, she realised she was lying on Jack's couch, in the dark with a blanket over her.

"Jack?" There was no sound. Hesitantly she pulled herself up to a seated position and felt better for grounding her feet on the floor. "Jack?" She was surprised to hear the quaver in her voice, the need for his solid presence. A door opened and there he was, smelling of darkroom chemicals. He still liked to develop some photos the old-fashioned way.

"Hey, you are awake." He was crouching beside her in moments, his gentle hands pushing her hair from her face. "How are you feeling?"

"Better, thanks. I think. What happened?"

"You had a funny turn. I brought you here as it was closest and the moment you lay down on the couch you fell asleep."

"How long have I been asleep for?"

Jack glanced at his watch. "Close to three hours."

Aurora stretched, testing her body to see how it felt. "I do feel better, thank you for looking after me."

Jack put his arm around her shoulder and dropped a kiss on the top of her head. "It was strange, we were talking about karma and you just started talking oddly then said you felt unwell."

Aurora frowned. "That's what I dreamt about. Karma."

Jack looked at her quizzically. "How so?"

"I was remembering a life where I knew I had to die, gruesomely, to balance the scales for a life I had taken before."

Jack held her close. "It must be so strange for you, to remember all that."

Aurora yawned, stretched again then leant into Jack's embrace. "I don't know any different."

"Want to forget about past lives for a while and go to bed? Create some new karma?"

Aurora laughed. "How would we create karma? We are two consenting adults, there is no one else involved."

Jack grinned a rare grin. "Yeah, but what I am thinking about doing to you might not actually be legal."

The next day, Aurora went to her friend Felicity's house for dinner after she had finished with her last client. She was unsurprised that Felicity asked her to dish the dirt on Jack even before she had put the wine glasses on the table. Aurora smiled knowingly.

"Oh, I see, that good!" Felicity raised her dark eyebrows until they were obscured by her floppy dark curls. "So, is he a keeper?"

Aurora sighed. How could she possibly explain? Felicity believed in past lives. Aurora had helped her to regress to understand patterns she was repeating in this life, but how could Aurora tell her that she remembered Felicity well, in France, during the French Revolution? Felicity, a spoilt young darling of the French aristocracy, living a pampered life while surrounded by suffering.

Aurora could remember keenly the biting cold in a way it can only be felt when you are nothing but skin and bones and you have long since stopped having any feeling in your feet. She remembered the sickening gnawing in her stomach, the desperation in the eyes of those around her and the strange mixed emotion that came with the silencing of a child's cries. Sadness at the death, gladness that they were no longer cold and hungry. But she also remembered the kindness of Felicity. The food she secretly stole from the kitchen to give to the people living in the streets, the clothes she took from her own wardrobe to give out to the poorest and even just the time she took to stop and smile, understand.

None of it had stopped her from being dragged to the guillotine when mob rule became frenzied. Aurora remembered watching with abject horror as a terrified and tear-stained Felicity, with a look of baffled confusion on her face, was forced to lay her head in the deathly contraption. Aurora knew, without a shadow of a doubt, that that experience was what made it difficult for Felicity to trust in this life. She always feared she would be treated unfairly. She had taken her back there in regression but had never as yet admitted to her own memories.

"I think he might be," was the best answer she could give.

Felicity looked at her, her large dark eyes thoughtful. "Good. It's about time. You have waited long enough, time to start living."

"Waited?" Aurora glanced up sharply. What did Felicity mean? Did she somehow know about Max?

"Yes, waited. It's always like you are waiting for someone else, as if you are less living than sitting in a doctor's waiting room, whiling away your time reading out of date magazines."

Felicity's words stuck with Aurora. Her friend had struck upon a truth, she was sure, one that, because she had been so caught up in her memories, her centuries-old yearning for Max,— she had somehow missed. Perhaps Max wouldn't make an appearance this time round? Perhaps her lesson this time was to let go of her attachment to him? Give herself wholly to someone else? Jack? Aurora felt the sands move beneath her feet in a way she had rarely felt before in her many lives. Remembering all your incarnations gave one a sense of permanence and stability that other humans lost with their memories, but now Aurora suddenly felt as if the rules had been changed and she was yet to see the new rule book. The one constant in her life now seemed to be Jack. Surprisingly, the thought brought her a lot of comfort.

Chapter 6

Christmas was fast approaching. Aurora's favourite time of the year. It seemed to bring together all that was pure and lovely about being a human that she remembered from all her lifetimes. She knew there was a special energy around at this time of year and she just wished other people could feel the magic. Miracles could happen at Christmas, she was sure, they just didn't come in an Argos catalogue

And yet, here she was, tired but happy after an afternoon lost on Oxford Street. A present for Jack still alluded her, but she had still enjoyed the hustle and bustle, the festive music, and above all, the lights. In small doses, she found it all wondrous. Now, though, laden down with bags which made finding her keys tricky, she was thinking of nothing more than putting on her pyjamas, thermal socks and an old cardigan and snuggling up in front of the fire with a book and a glass of wine.

With Jack away seeing his parents for a few days she knew she could slob in peace, even while the thought of him not being with her caused an aching pain in her heart. She really did miss him. She found herself considering the fact as if it were a truly miraculous revelation. Where did this leave her feelings for Max? It was a bit as if her previous life, when Jack was Sloan, was repeating itself. Why, though, she asked herself? And did it mean that Max might again appear, as her and Jack's child? If so, did it mean that history would also repeat itself in that it would also mean the death of Jack? Aurora frowned. She couldn't allow that to happen. If patterns were repeating themselves to draw her attention to something, then she had to learn the lessons sent to her in order to let Jack live. Or would that matter? If Jack was destined to die at a certain time and place then surely, he would, regardless?

Aurora shook her head as she finally got the door open. For tonight, all she wanted to do was curl up and daydream of Christmas with Jack. As the door closed behind her, she never noticed the figure lurking in the doorway across the street.

Edyth

"Christmas is fast approaching, come now there's work to be done!" Edyth dared not linger when she heard that tone in her mistress' voice.

She had been up since long before daybreak as it was and her limbs, young and fit as she was, already ached with fetching and carrying. It was only a week before the Twelve Days of Feasting, heralded by Christmas morning, got under way, but the guests would all be arriving in the next day or two and Lord and Lady Athelstan were desperate to impress their new Norman king who had given them the dubious honour of hosting his first Christmas on English soil. Why, was anyone's guess, although Edyth did wonder if it was simply because none of the dozens of castles he had ordered built since the Hastings battle were ready for people to live in yet, so he headed to the best of the closest burghs, more of a town behind palisades with a great hall at its centre than the kind of castles the Norman seemed to prefer.

Lord Athelstan had fought alongside Harold at Hastings and lost one of his sons to a Norman arrow, and the attention of the new king was giving him sleepless nights while adding an extra frisson to the normal festive preparations.

Edyth went about her chores with only half a mind. As usual, her thoughts were in part taken up with Max and where he might appear this time round, and much to her chagrin, why she had incarnated into a life as a servant. With very human fits of pique, she was known, in private, to stamp her feet and wonder why, if she could remember her lives, couldn't she pick better situations for herself? And yet, the nineteen-year-old maiden in her couldn't help but also wonder at the dashing young knights from Normandy who would be housed with them for the next few weeks. Maybe, she dreamed as she folded yet more linen, one of them would fall in love with her and sweep her away. Maybe one of them would be Max. Afterall, she knew she was beautiful with her long golden hair, shapely figure and cornflower blue eyes. She saw how the men watched her and the women looked at her with envy. Stranger things happened — she, more than anyone, was well aware of what life could throw up. Although one glimpse at her red raw hands set her heart sinking again. What knight would want a maiden whose hands were as rough as a stable boy's?

Arwen, the chatelaine, arrived at that point and ensured Edyth didn't have any more time for thinking that day. The next morning, though, she made sure she was by the burgh's main gate when the first of the guests arrived in their flurry of clanking bridles, flapping pennants and the confident cheerfulness of conquerors. This wasn't the king arriving, just his advance guard to ensure everything was ready for their monarch, but to the serving girls of Lord Athelstan's household, the sight was as grand as anything from the tales told by the bards in the great hall on feast nights. They squashed together and squeezed each other's arms with excitement as they watched the dozen or so men noisily dismount, their cloaks swinging dramatically behind them. The girls took in the strong leather-clad legs, the tanned, muscular and scarred forearms exposed above the gloves and below the elbow despite the weather and their careless grace. They had only just arrived, Edyth thought, yet they walked within the palisades, talking and laughing with easy confidence, as if they had just come home. She could see the men, many of whom had fought and been defeated at Hastings, eyeing them warily, but if the new arrivals noticed, they pretended not to.

Edyth knew within moments that Max was not amongst them: she would have known the second they rode in, she told herself, but once her initial disappointment subsided, she found her eyes trailing time and time again to one warrior with sallow skin and large almost silver-blue eyes. Unlike his comrades, his hair was cropped short to match a dark beard, with barely more than a day or two's growth. He wasn't as loud and boisterous as the others, although she saw his lips twitch in amusement as he listened to their nonchalant banter. Yet she could tell just by the way he carried himself, and by the way the others deferred to him in small ways such as when he stepped up to the water barrel to pour freezing water over his bare head despite the biting cold, that it was likely that he was the most proficient warrior amongst the group. He also, she noticed, took in everything around with those pale eyes of his. Which is how he came to stand before Edyth, his eyes appraising as he removed his soft leather gloves.

"Have we captured your interest, maiden?" he asked in accented English, his eyes alight with calculating amusement.

Edyth felt herself blush even as she smiled suggestively at the handsome knight before her. She had learned early in this life to use her beauty. "Not sure why you say 'we', my lord. You have." She was being bold. It was risky, but the man before her simply threw back his head and laughed with gusto.

"You are a brazen one! Serving maidens in Normandy would not be so forward." He smiled, his cool eyes alive. "What's your name, girl?"

"Edyth, a good Anglo-Saxon name." His eyebrows shot upwards; she knew she was pushing her luck but for some reason she couldn't quite stop herself.

"Well, Edyth, perhaps you could show me where I can find the lord of this burgh?"

Edyth considered asking his name first but decided she had taken enough risks in their small discourse and instead led the way, lips twitching with a barely suppressed delight and hips gently swaying with just enough suggestion to keep his attention, unaware of the group of servants that were now arriving on foot and by wagon. Amongst them, a young fletcher by the name of Piteur, who couldn't take his eyes off Edyth. He felt as if he knew her from somewhere. Little did he know that if Edyth had only been paying attention, she would have realised that, here on the cold, wet cobbles, with dark hair falling in his rich amber eyes, shivering beneath his leather vest and thick wool cloak, was her Max.

Edyth though was too distracted by her infatuation with the lord with the icy silver eyes, whose name she discovered was Lord Jonas, a cousin of the conquering king, to give Max much thought over the next few days. She found a reason to be close to him every second she could and when she wasn't, she was daydreaming of him sweeping her away to be his lady in a Norman castle. Her wisdom of previous lives was swept aside in very Earthly desires for jewels, beautiful gowns, and above all, to be loved, cherished, worshipped even, by a man like Lord Jonas. She found herself standing, staring after him, the way he moved with his warrior limbs sending quivers through her body. Arwen lost patience with her time and time again, even slapping the young girl's face in an attempt to draw her attention back to matters at hand, but Edyth barely noticed. Her every moment was filled with yearning and daydreams hung on the remembrance of those moments where he seemed to notice her - an occasional small nod but sometimes a quick conspiratorial smile - which were enough to send Edyth's heart spinning.

Piteur watched, as the entire burgh did with varying degrees of tolerance and exasperation, as Edyth giggled and flirted her way through the days. If Edyth thought she was being discreet, she was greatly mistaken.

Christmas Eve was a magical night for Edyth. The snow finally stopped falling and settled into a sparkling blanket over the land, washed an unearthly blue by a low-lying, almost full moon. The preparations were almost complete, the main hall was bedecked in huge boughs of ivy and holly, whole pigs and sides of venison were roasting over spits in the kitchen, and most importantly, the king had arrived that morning. Edyth had barely registered him and had needed an elbow in her ribs to remind her to curtsey deeply, as distracted as she was trying to catch yet another glimpse of Lord Jonas.

The entire burgh, from the lowliest servant to the king himself, were ready for the night's festivities and a frisson of anticipation hung in the air. Edyth knew she looked her best, having changed into her one good gown of deep crimson, the perfect tone to draw colour from her cheeks and set alight her fair hair. She had enjoyed the sweet wine they were allowed to drink and had danced the evening away, ensuring she was always in the view of Lord Jonas.

She knew he watched her. She loved to know his eyes were drawn to her even as she pretended not to notice, to flirt with the young lads of the household and laugh in a way that she knew would leave him filled with desire. Excitement coursed through her veins. Something told her that this was her night, this was the night that would change her life forever and she believed that meant riding off into the sunset with Lord Jonas.

The festivities were slowly beginning to wind down when he finally came to her outside. She knew he would. He appeared behind her on silent feet and dropped his cloak, heavy and oh so soft, around her shoulders.

"You look like the winter queen tonight," he said, his accent heavier with wine, as he moved round to stand before her. He raised a hand and ran a finger across her lower lip. "Your lips are like the holly berries." His drew the back of his fingers gently down her cheek. "Those cheeks are almost as... What is the word? Vibrant? Succulent?"

Edyth smiled coyly, eyes flashing. "Succulent is for pigs. Ladies are... Delectable or, perhaps, ravishing."

He smiled seductively. "Ah, but the question is, Edyth, are you a lady? Delectable, yes, ravishing, yes, but a lady?"

Edyth felt the first murmurings of discomfort but fuelled by wine and the headiness of the night, she shrugged it aside. "Mais oui, bien sûr, my liege." She spoke slowly, temptingly lingering on each word, as she swept into a graceful curtsey before him, her head bowing just before his groin.

His lips found hers even as he drew her back to standing. Edyth felt herself respond with equal vigour. He swept her easily into his arms and into the warmth of the stables, deserted by all except the horses.

"No, wait!" Edyth put her hand on his chest.

He looked down at her, his cool eyes filled with lust and impatience. "You having second thoughts, my little chicken?"

"No, I just thought we might go somewhere a little... More comfortable?"

He laughed. "So, were you expecting the king's chamber, my little serving girl?" Edyth could feel herself blush at being called that.

"Of course not! But perhaps your quarters?" She placed all her wiles into that smile. She could not let him take her on the stable floor.

"Why not?" Jonas chuckled, more drunk perhaps that Edyth first realised. "I did say you were a winter queen after all!" Standing her on her feet, he took her by the hand. "Follow me, my lady."

It was the bells which woke Edyth the next morning. At first, she couldn't remember where she was, the feel of the rich cotton felt strange on her cheek and the air, heavy with the scent of the warm male body lying next to her, foreign to her nostrils. And then it all came back to her. The giggling as they stumbled into his chambers in the dark, the hasty undressing by moonlight, the impassioned love they had made again and again, broken only by mouthfuls of wine until they had fallen into a sated, drunken sleep. Edyth lay very still for a moment, allowing herself to remember every detail, relishing the trace of his touch on her skin and already hungry to feel the press of his lips once more. She let out a contented sigh and rolled over to where Lord Jonas lay inert, allowing one hand to dance languidly across his chest. He stirred, reaching up to take her hand.

"Stop." His voice was thick and heavy with drink and sleep

"Morning, my lord, am I distracting you from your rest? Not that I remember you complaining last night."

His hand tightened round her wrist. "You go too far, wench. They will be missing you, I am sure. Leave."

Edyth, the bedclothes now clutched to her chest, stared with confusion and dawning horror. "But, my lord, I thought—"

He cut her off, his voice dripping with disdain. "What did you think? That I would fall in love with you? That you were more than a bit of fun when in our cups? That I would marry you? You are a serving wench, no more. Fit to empty my piss pot. If you are lucky, I will allow you to polish my boots. Now be gone."

Ashen-faced, Edyth stumbled from the chamber, pausing in a dark corner only to hastily pull on her robe. One thing Lord Jonas was right about was that they would be looking for her, and if she didn't show her face at some point, she would pay the price. But with bile rising in the back of her throat as she stumbled through the dark corridors, silent except for the odd groan and snore from beyond chamber doors, all Edyth could think about was getting into the fresh air.

She emptied her stomach into a corner of the inner courtyard, realising by the smell that greeted her downturned face that she wasn't the first person to do so that morning. It was only when she righted herself did the tears come, streaming down cheeks, prickling in the bitter cold. Snowflakes, which seemed so full of magic the night before, only served to taunt her. *You thought we were filled with promises*, they seemed to say, *but with just the lightest of touches we vanish to nothing, leaving nothing but a cold puddle behind.*

"Are you OK?" Another heavily accented voice broke through her misery.

"Do I look OK?" Edyth rounded on the owner of the voice. "Do people who are fine stand in the freezing cold, crying and throwing the contents of last night's festivities up on the straw? No, I am far from OK, but what would you know?"

Piteur, for it was Piteur, hesitated, shuffling his booted feet on the slippery cobbles. "I know not, you are right. I… I wanted to see if I could help. I don't like… To see a lady in distress. Especially not you."

Edyth's sharp eyes focused properly on the young man for the first time. "What do you mean? Especially not me?"

Piteur paused, searching for the right words. "I… Noticed you… It was like I had been waiting to see you all my life. I know that doesn't make sense."

Edyth stared at the man. "Max?" The word was barely audible.

Piteur continued on, a look of earnest consternation on his face. "I didn't like when I saw you go with my liege. He takes a different girl in every town…"

"Oh, that makes me feel much better!" Edyth railed. "Not only am I a maid silly enough to think he might have wanted me for more than a roll in the hay, I hear I am one of dozens, if not hundreds!"

"You really think that?" Piteur asked, eyebrows raised with incredulity. "You must see men like my liege here all the time…you must know what they are like."

Edyth swallowed hard. She did, there was no doubt. And if she was honest with herself, she knew she was dreaming. She knew that if she had been born into the life she had now, with no memory of all that had gone before, she would not have strained at the shackles quite so much, but to know what more life could be, to have freedom and control of your own destiny made it all the harder to simply stay put and obey another's rules, dependent on the whims of others for her security, safety and even happiness.

She looked at Piteur, finding comfort in finally seeing Max there. "I do. I was a fool. It's just… I don't want to live like this, beholden to others and never to know happiness beyond being given an extra portion of sweet wine on high days and holidays."

Piteur uttered a very Norman sound in the back of his throat. "C'est la vie, mon amie."

Edyth smiled wanly. "Maybe so, but it doesn't have to be." With that, Edyth pushed herself away from the wall and headed to the kitchen where, if she was lucky, she would get away with just a severe ticking off.

Edyth kept a very low profile in the days to come. The household may have been celebrating the twelve days of Christmas, but Edyth simply wished she could disappear. Knowing eyes seemed to follow her everywhere, some filled with sympathy but others with judgement. In a show of penitence, she didn't really feel, she took to wearing her hair beneath a more modest cap than was the fashion and spending hours on her knees in the chapel. She didn't really feel penitent. She felt frustrated and foolish, but she couldn't believe she had done anything wrong — after all, what was wrong with hoping for more from life? At least she found some peace in church. And in that peace, she had time to think and wonder.

Her other solace was Max — or, rather, Piteur — who always seemed to be nearby with a consoling smile or a few words of friendship. When their duties allowed, they would sit together in the stables enjoying the warmth of the great war horses, or perhaps Edyth would sit watching his clever hands work the feathers of the arrows, talking amiably.

By late February, Edyth knew idle chat of dreams and futures could no longer be enough as not only was the day drawing near when Piteur would leave, she was now certain she was carrying Lord Jonas' child. Necessity, rather than desire, prompted her to be bold this time. She hung around the courtyard in the early morning cold, waiting for her chance to speak. Not to Lord Jonas, but to Piteur.

He smiled when he saw her and she saw his eyes crease with concern when all she could muster was a thin grimace in return.

"Piteur." She uttered with enough urgency to make him stop in his tracks. "I need to speak to you, please."

"You carry his child?" he asked, with gentleness that carried an unfathomable edge.

"Yes," Edyth whispered in return. "How did you know?"

Piteur blushed. "I have noticed you looking… Fuller. I wondered."

Edyth said nothing, the words she needed to say failing on her lips.

"You want me to help?" Piteur asked.

Edyth nodded. "Together we could have a better life."

Piteur looked at her for a long moment. "It won't be easy," was all he said.

He was right. The pair of them found themselves prostrate before the lord, and under the sneeringly amused gaze of Lord Jonas, for more hours than they could count that evening as they explained that they would like to be married and allowed to leave to start a life of their own. Eventually an agreement was reached, but the couple had to promise that their first son would go into Lord Jonas' service when he came of age, and their first daughter would be a replacement for Edyth when the time was right.

Edyth almost choked on the promises — how could she buy her own freedom with the service of her as yet unborn children? But Piteur squeezed her hand, stopping her from speaking further. "Perhaps by then they will all be dead," he whispered.

And so, that autumn, as their little cottage, built with their own hands amidst lots of laughter, basked in the golden haze of evening, their first son, for Piteur always considered him so, was born. They called him Max and never did he end up in the service of Lord Jonas. Nor did their daughter, Cassie, born two years later. For many years, the little family lived happily on the edge of the wood, with hens scratching in the grass, growing vegetables, voluptuously leafed every summer, on either side of the little path and a pig, cow and pony all happily sharing a small meadow beyond.

Piteur earned a decent living from fletching and Edyth surprised herself by finding peace and happiness looking after family and home, never happier than when watching her husband work and children playing in the sunshine. Her and Max, the man she had loved through the mists of time, and their children.

Their idyll came to a cruel end one winter's evening when a band of brigands descended upon the cottage and murdered the whole family as they slept. Edyth was the last to be put to the sword, being kept alive for sport before a sword was thrust deep in her belly, leaving her to endure a slow, agonising death staring into the cold glassy eyes of Piteur, but before she could look to death, she was forced to look into the eyes of the man who had driven the murdering spree which had wrecked her happiness. Cold blue eyes. The eyes of Lord Jonas. He grinned viciously when he recognised her before leaving in a flurry of footsteps and snowflakes.

With every weakening breath, though, Edyth felt no fear or anger, only peace. Into the cold darkness her lips moved one final time. "I am coming, Max," is what might have been heard if there had been anyone to hear.

Aurora's breath hissed in her throat as she awoke. She hadn't thought about that life for a long time. Why now? The frustration of living a life of servitude when you knew what else life could be, the shame and foolishness of thinking Lord Jonas wanted her for anything more than her body, and perhaps most painful of all, the sweetness of living in domestic bliss with Max. With children. Two beautiful, bright children who had never lived to see double figures.

What was she meant to be learning from reliving it all again in this lifetime? A thought dawned on her then that she had never had before. Had she ever had a child that had survived her? Other than Max, as Sloan's child, she couldn't think of one, not one from all her many lives. A sense of sadness overwhelmed her and tiredness rushed in at its back. How she wished Jack were there. Without him, she poured herself a strong measure of brandy and turned on the TV.

Outside, a man stared up at her window in the dark, wintry night. A man with cold, blue eyes.

Chapter 7

When Jack arrived home a few days later, Aurora was overjoyed to see him. Suddenly, despite being used to her own company for centuries, she felt lonely and found herself craving his presence.

"I take it you missed me then?" he asked as she snuggled into him on the couch.

"I did, I really did." She looked up at him thoughtfully.

"Good," he answered, dropping a kiss on her forehead. "You've that pensive expression again, what is it?"

Aurora paused. "Well...you know how I can remember my past lives."

"Yeah?"

"I have been kind of having really vivid dreams, as if I am there, in the different times, again."

"While you are sleeping?"

"Sometimes, but it can also be like a trance. I had another really strong memory while you were away." There was a flicker across Jack's face — a flash of interest followed in hot pursuit by wariness.

"Oh yeah?" His nonchalance was loaded as he tentatively processed something unknown to him. "Was I in it?"

"No, not this time," Aurora admitted. "As I said as far as I can remember, we have only had one life together before now."

"So, what was it?"

"It was bittersweet. Happiness followed by the brutal slaughter of my family."

Jack's arm tightened round her as he looked down at her in concern. "Oh, Aurora, that's horrible. I'm sorry, I wish I had been here."

"I wish you had been here too but there's nothing you could have done to help."

"I could have held you. Told you that you were safe." Aurora, at that moment, felt safe, and loved.

"I did wish you had been there."

Neither said anything for a moment or two. Then Jack broke the silence. "Aurora?" He said it like a question.

"Mmm," came her slightly distracted response.

"Do you think it is wise to keep remembering things like this?"

"How do you mean? I have always."

"You've always had memories, but you've not always fallen into dreams where you almost relive things, have you?"

Aurora thought for a moment. "No and I have been wondering why now. I think it has something to do with you. I am not sure I could stop them, though."

"No, I guess not."

Jack kissed her again. "Just promise me, next time, whatever happens, will you tell me please?"

Aurora snuggled into him once more. "I promise."

It was only a few days before Christmas and Aurora had decided to clear her diary so she could spend time with Jack and enjoy the festivities. The two of them spent a pleasurable afternoon wandering around the Christmas markets, drinking hot cider and warming cold hands on hot syrupy waffles.

Aurora allowed herself to get lost in the festivities, enjoying the feeling of being with an attractive man she was beginning to wonder if she loved. Old instincts die hard, though, and even as she wandered, hand in hand with Jack, hats pulled down low over their foreheads as the winter chill really took hold, a familiar face would catch her eye every now and then and a flash of reminiscence would cross her mind. A woman she once laughed with many generations ago, or a man she knew as a child a long time ago in the past. A face that might have been Max, but which Aurora knew with long honed telling, within a spilt second, that it was not her twin soul who had been with her through lifetime after lifetime until now.

Though, for the first time in all the thousands of years of human life that she could remember, she no longer felt utterly desolate by Max's absence. Her eyes still sought him in the crowds, her mind still roved on its endless search, but her heart, though always Max's on some level, was now more focused on Jack. And it was Jack, not Aurora, who first noticed the man with the cold, hard eyes.

They were sitting by a roaring fire pit in the beer garden of a riverside pub, enjoying a warmed cider after a day spent ice-skating in the park. They had been idly chatting about the holidays, Jack gently trying to persuade Aurora to go with him to his family, given she didn't seem close to what family she had, when he stopped to stare over Aurora's shoulder with a crease between his eyes and a serious set to his mouth.

"Jack?" Aurora nudged his arm playfully. "Jack? What is it?"

He looked back at her, shaking his head. "Probably nothing. It's just this guy. I seem to have seen him about half a dozen times in the last few days. How weird is that?"

"Which guy?" Aurora felt a rippling of concern as she involuntarily scanned the faces of those sat around her.

"He's gone. He's dressed all in black, but it's his eyes I keep noticing. They're really icy, blue, like a wolf's."

Icy, blue eyes, just days after she had remembered her experience with Lord Jonas, could not be a coincidence, Aurora thought to herself.

"Strange," she said to Jack. "Why don't we head home anyway. My place or yours?" It took all of her willpower not to look over her shoulder every two minutes as they headed back to Jack's studio flat.

Aurora was once more walking around her small flat on Christmas Eve morning, tidying away letters that didn't need tidying, checking the Christmas tree lights were off even though she could clearly see they were and glancing out of the window every three seconds to see if Jack had arrived. She had finally agreed to go with Jack to his parents for Christmas, and for Aurora, it felt like a monumental decision. There was no doubt that she felt it was almost a betrayal of Max, and yet she could not deny that she felt a girlish excitement at the idea of spending a traditional family Christmas with a man she was becoming increasingly happy to admit she was almost besotted with.

She was also nervous. She would be meeting his parents — what did that mean for her future? Would they like her? Questions that hadn't truly bothered Aurora for centuries. Her unusual view of life left her feeling more and more removed from the minutiae which dominated the thinking of people unable to remember all their incarnations and see the patterns and threads which wove through them. Now, she felt like a teenager who couldn't remember having any experience of what lay ahead. It was quite nice, refreshing even, to be doing something for what felt like the first time.

Bang on time, she saw Jack pull up in his Land Rover. Jumping out, his face broke into a huge, sexy grin as he saw her at her window. Her own reaction mirrored his and her heart leapt, and flipped, at the sight of him, slightly unshaven and bundled up against the cold in a stylish navy jacket and colourful cashmere scarf. A few minutes and a bruising kiss later and they were heading off, just as the first few flakes of snow started to land on the windscreen.

"What about *Classic Christmas*?" She asked with barely suppressed excitement as she flicked through the music on Jack's phone. "No? OK then, *Jazz Christmas*? *Swing does Christmas*? *Country Christmas*?"

Jack simply glanced round at her, daring only to take his eyes off the increasingly blurry windscreen for a second or two.

"What?"

"I don't think I've ever seen you like this."

"Like what?" Her tone was light, playful.

"Girlish." Jack threw her an equally boyish smile. "You know, red cheeked, bright eyed, squirmy... Except, of course, when... You know." Aurora threw a glove at him.

"I feel girlish. I feel like I haven't felt in a long time... As if I am actually doing something new! Any idea how hard it is to do something new when you can remember all the lives you have ever lived?"

"I would say I can imagine but the truth is I can't! You mean you've never done Christmas?"

"Of course, I have done Christmas! I have always loved Christmas, even when life wasn't exactly being kind to me, but I don't remember a Christmas like this."

"What's different?" Jack asked, keeping his eyes firmly on the now heavily falling snow.

Aurora paused, watching the whiteout beyond the windows. "You are," she said finally.

"Me?" Jack sounded genuinely surprised.

"Yes. I mean I have spent Christmases with people I care about before, but never really like this. Never in a normal two-people-who-like-each-other-introducing-each-other-to-their-families kind of way."

"So, you are getting a kick out of being Mr and Mrs Normal."

"Yes, but only because it is you I am playing with." Aurora looked across at him, his handsome face, thoughtful as he slowed behind a bus. He took the chance to look at her, his face serious.

"I'm happy to be playing with you too, Aurora Flowers."

They fell into a companionable silence for a while, carols playing gently in the background as the snow muffled the world around.

"There's one thing missing with your game, you know," Jack finally said.

"How do you mean?" Aurora answered, her voice almost sleepily content.

"Your family." Jack glanced at her, catching the slight frown between her eyes. "You have never really mentioned anyone."

Aurora stared out the windscreen into the blizzard wondering how she could explain. "I know. It's complicated."

"Because of your magic memory, you mean?"

"Yes, because of that."

"Well, you must have a mother and father?" he asked. "Or is it 'had'?" he asked gently.

Aurora sighed. "Yes, I have parents, it's just…"

"I'm sorry, you don't need to talk about it if you don't want to."

"No, it's OK, if we are being normal then it is only normal that I tell you about my parents." Aurora kept her eyes on the snow. "I believe we live lots of lives so we have a chance to rectify mistakes, do better next time, and in essence, learn and grow. You get that, right?"

"Yes. Like karma."

"Right. Except, while most people could potentially glimpse past lives through regression or maybe visiting an important place or even dreams, I remember all my lives in the same way you remember your childhood or what happened a few years back."

"OK. Got that."

"Well, I remember who my parents in this life were in previous lives."

"That's not surprising, you seem to meet the same people again and again… Me included."

"Yes… Try as I have, though, I can't get beyond what they did to me before."

"What happened?"

"Well…"

Hilda

Hilda ran to the door of the cottage to stare out into the glade beyond. She was sure she heard hooves. Arthur hadn't returned from market and she was alone. She had never been a nervous girl before, and she was someone who liked her solitude, but now Hilda found the thought of approaching horsemen was enough to make her blood run cold.

The glade was beautiful in the summer sun, dappled as it was by the dancing shadows of leaves. Birds trilled joyously above and Hilda could hear the stream gushing delightedly after the heavy rainfall a few days before. Sounds that once would have made Hilda laugh and dance in glee.

That was before, though. Before she had been accused of using witchcraft on a woman in their nearest town. Arthur had thought if she stayed at the cottage in the glade, so many miles from anywhere, as it was, they would, in time, forget all about her, but they both now tensed at every snapping twig and the sound of approaching horsemen brought nothing but a sense of dread rather than excitement.

Hilda strained her ears, listening for anything that might warn of danger. The birds had gone quiet. There was someone out there, someone or something. On silent feet she fled to the barn.

"I must hide, Barney," she said to the old donkey. "Please don't let anyone near me until Arthur comes back."

Oh, Arthur! she thought. Or Max, as she had known him so many times before. So devoted to her, so caring and so gentle, if he were here, she knew she wouldn't feel as scared. If he were close, she could face anything, safe in the knowledge that he would do all he could to protect her or that they would die together. Hilda, with her unusual memories, knew that this life was not the be all and end all, she knew there would be another one to follow or eternity elsewhere, but this life with Max was

91

sweet and easy. Together they were young lovers with nothing to worry about other than tending their small land and making love in the hay.

Or, at least it had been, until Matilda Redgrave had named her as the cause of her pox. Certainly Hilda, with her lifetimes' worth of plant lore, had suggested she try clay mixed with cider vinegar on a rash, but both she and Matilda knew that was not the cause of her pox. Matilda's vindictiveness had named Hilda, jealous as she had been of Hilda since she was a young girl. Jealous of Arthur, with his thick blonde hair and kind blue eyes, and how his eyes never strayed from Hilda.

Hilda buried herself deep in the sweet-smelling hay of Barney's stall as the animal took up stance as sentry with no more than a snort and without even pausing mid-chew. Laying as still as she could, she prayed as hard as she could that Arthur would be there soon while trusting that Barney's keen ears would alert her if anyone came near.

It was Barney's unsettled whickering that woke her. Someone was close and by Barney's reaction, it wasn't Arthur. Hilda's heart thumped in her ears, making it impossible to hear what else might be happening beyond the barn's wooden walls. Was that a footstep? Did she hear a creak? Barney stamped the ground nervously. There was someone outside.

"Come out, lass. We know you are here. You may as well come out and face the music." The voice was gruff and sounded almost amused.

"Watch what you are saying, Neville. She might turn herself into an owl and be off."

"Oh, I forgot she is a right little witch, isn't she?"

The door to the barn swung open, flooding Barney's stall with bright evening light. Barney guffawed defiantly and stepped toward the man now looming large in the doorway, pike in hand.

"Well now, this makes a pretty hiding place," the man muttered, almost to himself. Using his weapon's butt, he pushed a stubborn Barney out of the way before delving the sharp end into the hay. "This will soon rouse you if you are there, lass." One. Two. Three. Nothing. Four. Five. It just missed her. Six. Surely, he must give up soon. Seven. Barney butted the man's rear. A sharp swipe back and the animal backed off with a loud complaint before the man plunged the pike in once more. Hilda couldn't hold onto the scream as the sharp blade sliced through her arm.

92

"A needle in a haystack, eh, lass?" the man spoke, unperturbed as he pulled Hilda, bleeding, from the hay. "Come with me now. Got her, Neville."

The man dragged Hilda out to meet a gathering of people waiting in the glade. Hilda, her mind fuzzy with pain, struggled to understand what was happening. Then she saw Matilda and her brother, Bishop Steven. And then she saw Arthur, bound, gagged and on his knees with blood soaking his clothes and streaking his beautiful hair, hair normally the colour of wheat fields.

Hilda almost didn't realise when they began wrapping a rope around her, lost as she was in Arthur's eyes, speaking to her of sorrow and pain and fear. "Arthur... What happened?" she managed as they pulled her towards a tree.

Weakened as he was, he could do no more than shake his head then whimper in protest as they dragged Hilda to the tree and bound her to the trunk.

"Arthur... Arthur..." Hilda's voice was panicked now. As much as she had faced death many times before, she didn't relish a painful end, especially as she had been there before and knew how painful it could be. "What are you doing?" she screamed at the faces around her, at Matilda's smirking pox-marked face and her brother's stern hate-filled expression.

"Hilda Green, you have been charged with witchcraft." Bishop Steven's spittle landed on her face as he spoke, so charged with self-righteous hatred as he was. "We cannot stomach witchcraft, it is an abomination to God and—"

"I am no witch!" Hilda screamed. "Matilda caught the pox dallying with Harold Black and well she knows it!" Hilda felt a moment's satisfaction as she caught the look of horror cross Matilda's face, but the darkening on her brother's told her the revelation had sealed her fate. There was no way she would be allowed to live now.

"A witch's tongue to boot, I see. Well, we have a test for the likes of you," the bishop sneered, then, with a nonchalant hand, motioned for his soldiers to bring Arthur forward to kneel between them.

"No... No..." Hilda was weeping openly. "Please don't hurt him, please, he is innocent."

"Innocent? How can he be innocent when he married a witch?" The bishop was pleased with his own cleverness.

"What chance do I have?" Hilda called back at him. "You have already decided I am a witch; all tests are futile as the outcome will all be the same. Just kill me and be done! Just leave Arthur be."

The man laughed, his grey eyes glistening with malice. "Perhaps, but we must follow the correct procedure, don't you think?"

The slightest of nods was all he gave and the soldier who had found her before thrust his spike through her stomach until it was buried deep into the wood behind her. Hilda slumped in her bindings, pain swamping her every sense and mirrored acutely in Arthur's mute expression.

"As long as the spike stays there you will actually take quite a long time to die." The bishop's voice was matter of fact, as if discussing the building of a wall. "Plenty of time to watch us cut Arthur to bits here, piece by piece." He smiled at her. "Of course, you could always prove your witchery by using your dark arts and save him, couldn't you?"

Hilda shook her head hopelessly, pain rendering her speechless as her tears fell to the earth at her feet.

"Well, let's see, shall we?" Another delicate nod and the soldier sliced Arthur's ear from his head. Holding it for a moment, they watched the bishop for their next orders. On seeing nothing from Hilda, he nodded again and Arthur's other ear ended up in the dirt, his cries muffled by the filthy rags crammed in his throat. And so, it went on, until the sun had fallen well beneath the horizon. Until, finally, just as the first hint of dawn teased the skyline, and with Arthur in bits and long dead at her feet, Hilda found the sweet release of her last breath.

Aurora took a deep breath. "And I imagine you have guessed, the bishop is my father in this life, and Matilda my mother." Aurora had told him everything except who Arthur was -her gloomy tale making the cheery carols still playing in the car now sound incongruous. Jack could do nothing but gape in horror.

"Oh, Aurora," he finally managed.

She smiled sadly in response. "It is awful, isn't it? But they have never understood why their daughter is so cold towards them and I have never been able to explain, they would think I had gone mad if I mentioned past lives."

Jack was silent. "But Aurora… And you know better than me… But isn't reincarnation about trying to resolve these things?"

"Yes. Absolutely. And that's what I am always telling my clients, but in this instance, I find it really hard to put into practice."

"I can understand that," Jack answered. "But maybe, that's part of everything that's happening? Maybe you need to try again?"
Aurora looked at him gravely, her emotions clearly torn between agreeing with him and the need to hold on to her old hurt.
"Maybe." She admitted.

"OK… Let's leave that for another day. Tell me, what do you hope Santa's brought you?"

Aurora grinned, glad of the subject change. "Santa? Or do you mean Jack?"

Christmas turned out to be lovely. Jack's parents were perfect as far as Aurora was concerned. Warm and welcoming without being nosy or intrusive. Their home, an old farmhouse, now part of a quaint village, was exactly how Aurora imagined a home at Christmas should be — bedecked with holly, candles in every nook and cranny and with a huge real tree sparkling in the light of a roaring fire, by which they ate sandwiches and drank wine after their arrival on Christmas Eve. Presents were opened in their pyjamas on Christmas morning as the snow continued to fall outside — Jack had bought Aurora a beautiful silver locket on a long chain, while she had given him an elegant leather portfolio book, and a painting she had done of him as Sloan. Afterwards, they had a proper sit-down Christmas feast, followed by a long, lazy walk in the snow with Frodo, Jack's parents' Border collie, who had taken a real shine to Aurora. At Jack's gentle suggestion Aurora even phoned her own parents to wish them a Merry Christmas. The call was short and stilted, but Aurora felt something shift when she hung up.

The evening was spent playing games by the fire while sipping at brandy. When it came time to leave on Boxing Day, Aurora felt almost desolate despite promises to return soon and it was only when she left her flat the day after that she remembered the man with the ice blue eyes who Jack had noticed. And she only thought of him then as she was sure he was standing watching her from the other side of the road. And in a heartbeat, she knew it was Lord Jonas.

Chapter 8

Aurora stood rooted to the spot, torn between the desire to run back upstairs to her flat and barricade the door behind her or stomp across the street and look defiantly into the eyes of the man who had broken her girlish heart so many lifetimes ago. But with a composure born of many centuries of existence, Aurora drew air deeply into her lungs and walked slowly up the street to the coffee shop, giving herself time to find the inner calm that she knew lived inside her beyond the fear and anxiety, the hurt and the anger. She knew he was following her, but for the moment, that was OK.

As she ordered her drink — to sit in now when she had been planning to take it with her before she had spotted Lord Jonas— she let her thoughts wander back to that life. To the dangerously dark and handsome Lord Jonas and her youthful belief he would sweep her away from her life of drudgery. She remembered her anguish and his disdain, but more than anything, she shuddered at the thought of how he coldly killed her children and Max before her eyes.

Even though she knew death was not the end and even though she knew she would know them all again in different times, different places, the human agony of the moment still had to be endured. And yet, she mused as she sipped her coffee, only half aware of the man with the icy blue eyes sliding into a seat on the other side of the café, that was only half a story.

It was because of Lord Jonas' actions she had enjoyed a long spell of idyllic happiness with Max, and those souls who had been their children. And she knew that while the manner of their deaths was the kind of horror that reverberated through time, she knew it could never have happened if it did not serve them all, at a soul level, in some way. What, though?

It was another flag to Aurora that something was nearing completion, that there was a reason so many coincidences and reliving's were happening now, so many people coming back to her, when she had lived the longest she had ever lived, without any trace of Max in her life. There was no sign of her twin soul reappearing as he always had, but meanwhile she was falling in love in a way that was almost new to her and did the man with the icy eyes have any memory of their shared connection? Or was he following a much more worldly intent by following her and Jack?

Finishing her coffee, she decided there was only one way to find out. Rising with natural grace, she moved between the tables and slipped into the seat across from the man with the icy cold eyes in one fluid movement.

"Hello," she said calmly, her voice neutral. The eyes stared back, the hatred harboured there as plain to Aurora as if she were looking at the back of her own hands. No answer. "You have been following me," she tried again, voice still devoid of emotion. "I would like to know why."

The icy eyes sharpened and Aurora felt herself flinch involuntarily, remembering Lord Jonas taking the life of her children with that exact same look.

Nothing.

Aurora held his stare, allowing the hate to wash over her, telling herself inwardly that hatred only ever comes from fear and this young man must be very frightened.

"What are you scared of?" she asked now, her tone now enquiring. Then, with a hard swallow, she found herself saying, "I can help, you know. That's what I do, help people understand where their fears come from, help them become free of them."

Silence. Then, jerking his seat back with a clatter, he drew a finger swiftly across his neck and vanished out the door.

Corba

The year was 1209 and while the sun was bright, the earliest of autumn air had watered down its strength a little. Every now and then, when the gentle breeze stirred in the right direction, Corba could smell a hint of that uniquely earthy scent that defined autumn in her mind, and as always, it gave her a thrill. There was something about this time of year that she loved. Summer was wonderful, especially where she lived, as a respected figure in a small religious community in the verdant hills near

Carcassonne, but there was a sense of warm anticipation in the smokiness of autumn that thrilled.

With a small jolt of excitement, she turned away from her contemplation and made her way down from the gated wall of their home, offering as it did fabulous views down the valley to the far more splendid walls of Carcassonne, and headed back towards the main building lying at the heart of their small complex of rose gardens and vegetable patches, all golden in the evening sun.

Corba wished for a moment, as she rarely did, that she could speak to Max. Share with him the simple joy she felt in the turning of the seasons, nature's wondrous cycle which always reminded her of home, their home, she meant - Atlantis. Instead, she had to settle for a smile as he walked out to meet her, tall and grand in this life as a wise Cathar bon homme called Raymonde, although between them it was, as always, the kind of smile that plucked universal threads. In this life she had never shared a normal conversation with Max, taking a vow of silence as she had at the age of just fifteen after seeing a vision of Mary Magdalene. Max had arrived in her life just two years later, only ten years older than Corba but exuding the calm power of a wise master.

Corba had never been able to ask if he knew who she was or remembered their lives together. If he did, he never mentioned it to her and he spent many hours conversing with Corba as if she could speak with her tongue. He seemed to be able to understand what she would have said if she could have spoken anyway so it rarely mattered and Corba was mainly content simply to be in his presence, to work together with him as they oversaw the running of their small community and ministered to those who needed them.

The Cathars lived in love and tolerance, meaning that, by and large, they all lived happy and contented lives reminiscent of the way things had been before the fall. Corba's silence meant she could connect deeply with the world around her and follow the wisdom provided in its depths. Which was why it was so very strange that she never knew what was coming. That she had no sense of the disaster that was about to befall her people. In fact, the first she knew of it was when it arrived at the door of their community that autumn, just weeks after Corba had sensed the changing season in the air.

"Lady Corba." The young girl's voice carried a sense of urgency, panic even, rarely heard in their small community, causing Corba to look up from her quiet contemplation of the flames in her fireplace with some alarm. "You must come." The girl rushed on at the sight of Corba's mute question.

By the time she reached the door, Raymonde was already there, ushering drenched people into the main hall and ordering hot food to be brought up from the kitchen. One woman, blood pouring from her head and side, was being all but carried by another, who also bore marks of violence. Corba ran to Raymonde's side and grabbed his arm to draw his attention.

"Their farm has been attacked," he said shortly. "The king's men."

Corba felt her blood run cold. Why? Why would the king's men attack honest farmers? Especially here, in Cathar land, where peace, prosperity and hospitality ruled. Corba felt a sense of trepidation the like of which she had rarely before experienced, yet under the rule of her vow she was unable to express. Raymonde, understanding her silent communication as easily as ever, squeezed her arm. "Corba, I fear they have been attacked because they are Cathar," he whispered. Then, more loudly, to the household, he called, "Come, bar the doors and shut out this miserable autumn night, we have guests to care for and listen to."

A while later, Corba sat on a trestle table watching the scene before her as if it were a tableau. Their visitors, about ten in total, men, women and children, hunkered before the large fire with blankets and robes having replaced their sodden clothes. The injured women lay on the fireside rugs, pillows propping their bandaged heads and limbs. All still silent and shaking with shock.

"My children." Raymonde stood before them, his voice gentle. "I can clearly see something terrible has befallen you. Be assured you are safe here and will be well cared for, but I must ask you to tell us your story if you can." His eyes ranged across the anguished faces, all reluctant to speak. Finally, it was a young man, no more than seventeen years who spoke.

"We had just sat down to eat." His voice was flat. "They just burst in and started killing. My da's blood went all over the table. There was

100

nothing we could do. There was no time to even find a weapon — all we could do was run."

"I'm sorry, son. How many others were killed, other than your father?" Raymonde's voice was resonant with sympathy.

"Three, maybe."

The boy looked at his companions for verification and an older woman spoke. "They killed Arnauld, this boy's father, as well as my husband and poor Isabella's two daughters. Only little, they were, too. Lovely girls, blonde and as bright as sunshine." The woman's voice trailed away, her pain evident.

"I am sorry for you all and your losses, we shall pray for them all." Raymonde paused a moment. "Do you know who the men were who attacked you?"

"Aye," called the boy, his grief replaced briefly by chagrin, "it was the king's men. They carried the king's crest on their halberds."

One of the women began to sob softly. "Why would they do this to us, holy one? Why?"

Raymonde placed a comforting hand on her shoulder. "I do not know, my dear, I do not know but I will pray for answers."

As autumn turned into winter, barely a week went by without the community hearing of similar atrocities across the Cathar lands while the numbers of their small community doubled as people fled from attack.

"Carcassonne is become overwhelmed," Raymonde said to Corba one night as they sat late, pondering, once again, why their people had come the victims of such indiscriminate violence. "The streets are filled with people. They are all, of course, being taken in and cared for, but one can't help wondering how long for." He paused and looked at Corba's tense face. "We are OK, for the moment," he said, again reading her thoughts. "We have enough to last years, even if our numbers double again. We have been blessed with bountiful harvests in recent years and it is our duty to care for those of us who have lost everything."

Corba bowed her head slightly in a silent prayer and acknowledgment of the truth of Raymonde's words.

"Perhaps it was God's way of preparing us for what is to come." Corba didn't need to ask what he meant.

Since their first visitors had arrived, they had both been plagued by dreams. Disturbing violent dreams that ended in fire. At first, Corba wondered if she was once again dreaming that old dream that followed her through her lives, of the end of Atlantis when she and Max fell to their fiery deaths as newlyweds, but this was different.

Years passed and Corba's small rural community became a refuge for many more. They became a secret safe house for refugees fleeing the crusade instigated by the pope and heartily carried out by the French king. They also became a hub of resistance activity as Cathar soldiers appeared at all hours of the day and night, some simply looking for a bed and decent meal while many others needed medical attention. Only the worst injured would stay any length of time though, anxious as they were to be back protecting their people and worried about bringing the crusaders to the community's door.

No longer did the community spend its days tending the land with grateful hearts, enjoying the simple pleasure of sunshine on their skin or in commune with God and Christ. Instead, they tore old blankets into bandages, made giant vats of stew and soup, eking out their dwindling reserves as far as they possibly could and reinforcing their walls and gates so, if the crusaders did come, they stood a chance of protecting themselves. The dozens of children were corralled every day in makeshifts schools or set to simple tasks such as peeling potatoes while long, thoughtful theological lessons and discussions were replaced by dispatches from Carcassonne and eyewitness accounts of happenings across the Cathar region.

Predictably, the crusades did finally come to the community. They had held out well, offered five years of refuge and help to those who needed it, but by the time the crusaders arrived, they were almost on their knees, weak with hunger and overcrowding. Yet Corba wasn't simply going to open the doors and allow them in. She may have hair streaked with grey and a tongue she hadn't used for speech in many years, but her heart was filled with defiance.

Early morning mist hung spectre-like in the air as Corba, an eternal peace already settling in her heart, pulled opened the huge wooden door to her beloved community for the last time, the neglected hinges moaning loudly in the pre-dawn quiet. She waited as she heard the massive iron bars slide in place at her back, just as she had ordered Roger, a young man she trusted and who was the only person to know her plans, to do, in writing.

Her resolve still intact, a sense of peace light in her heart, she drew in a deep breath, relishing the myriad scents of home she found there. The grass, the dew, the special earthiness of the land. The cool morning air fresh on her cheeks, reminding her, as always, of her childhood in the magical mountains. Corba waited a few more moments as the light crept in from the east and the earliest risers among the birds began their daily song. The sound of the first stirrings of the crusade camp soon joined the birds in a discordant harmony, signalling to Corba it was time to start her walk across the rough meadow that lay between them.

The guard blanched a little to see the ethereal figure emerge from the mist, but as a hardened warrior, he soon swallowed his supernatural fears and lowered his spear almost nonchalantly in Corba's direction.

"Who goes there?" he asked, as if he didn't know. Corba held her silent tongue and looked back at the scarred face with compassion. "Well? Not saying anything, *bonne femme*?" Silence. "Cat got your tongue, eh? Well, maybe a spear in your side will help, what do you think?" Corba continued to look back, unperturbed and meeting threat with love. The man shuffled awkwardly, not sure how to handle the calm and dignified old lady who showed no fear, even when she was only inches and possibly moments away from certain death. Finally, filled with uncertainty, he grunted disgustedly to himself and beckoned to Corba to follow him as he led her to his commander, gesturing to a younger man lounging nearby to take his place on sentry duty.

Curious eyes followed the white-robed woman as she made her way serenely through the makeshift camp, unsure why the sight so unsettled them. Even as she was made to stand for what seemed like an absurd amount of time outside the tent of Lord Guiscard, one of the French noblemen currently rampaging around Cathar lands, wilfully killing on the orders of the French king and the pope, Corba kept her calm. The soldiers' eyes were unwillingly drawn back time and time again to the woman who almost seemed to be surrounded by a strange light.

At last, she was allowed to duck her head beneath the doorway to stand before the man who would undoubtedly be the cause of her death, in this lifetime. She let dignity ripple through her body as she lifted her chin with a gentle defiance to meet his gaze, only to almost quail as she met the ice-cold eyes of Lord Jonas. A deep breath of air drew her back to her senses as she sternly told herself that this was not Jonas, but Lord Guiscard.

"Madam, you look like you have seen a ghost," the man sprawled in a leather camp chair said, having clearly hurriedly dressed just moments before, said as he took a long draft of watered wine. "It seems to be a ghostly morning," he continued, rubbing at his dark stubble. "My men thought it was you who was the spectre."

Corba held on to her silence a moment longer, suddenly filled with grief at the thought of breaking her vow. But eventually she spoke. "Perhaps, Lord, they are right, as I doubt I will live to see sundown. I am breaking a vow of silence to do as I do today and that's not something I take lightly, so listen well." The words felt strange in her mouth, but she could see she had the man's attention. "Take me as your sacrifice. Let the woman and children leave our community and take me as payment for their lives. Before them all I will willingly submit to any death you so desire and say whatever words you wish me to utter." Lord Guiscard considered her with a look of mixed respect and contempt.

"We are here to kill heretics." He paused, his eyes as cold and malicious as ever. "Like you." He took another drink. "Your death is inevitable. It is God's will. It is God's will, though, that you should all die, why should your words stop me from carrying out God's will?"

Corba knew he was right. Her move was always going to be a gamble. She hadn't wanted to say more, but she knew she needed to. "Because you will score many more points by killing me publicly and painfully than by killing them all. Rather than fight and risk your men's lives, kill me and let them carry the word through the country of your strength and your wisdom, how you should not be defied. Let them do your work for you." A heavy silence hung between them. Corba instinctively knew it wasn't enough, so she added the words she had hoped to avoid completely. "I can add the life of our bon homme, Raymonde, to my own." They were met with a nasty smile that told her she had won, at quite a cost, but she knew she had won.

She was in prayer when Raymonde arrived, having received her message, and instantly knew she could not hold to her desire to speak no further until she had passed over to the next world and eventually, as Corba knew all too well, her next life.

"Raymonde." She rose from her knees to reach out to her old friend in this life, her twin soul through eternity. His face, serene except for a small wry smile, told her she didn't need words, he understood as always and yet Corba felt compelled to explain. "I am so sorry to have brought you here. I had hoped to spare sacrificing you. It is one thing to sacrifice your own life, but I am presumptuous in sacrificing you too." Corba felt her voice crack, emotions breaking through the peace of certainty for the first time.

Raymonde took her in his arms. "Ah, Corba, it is almost worth it just to hear your voice this once." He kissed the top of her head and pulled back so he could look in her eye. "I have known for a long time that this was the sort of end that awaited me and if it is in your service, the service of God, while also helping to spare our people, then I am glad. Don't be sad, Corba." His voice was cajoling, as though chivvying a child out of a tantrum. "Besides, is the cornerstone of our belief not that we will now be with God?" His eyes were gentle, yet Corba could also see the sadness. "We will meet again, won't we Corba? We are in this together, as they say, are we not?"

Corba nodded and moved away, walking the small floor space in the tent where they were being held. "We are, Raymonde, perhaps more than you realise. I have always wanted to tell you this, but it would be very hard to explain without speech."

"Oh, yes?"

"I remember." Corba looked at Raymonde, standing as patient as ever, waiting for her to explain. "I remember our other lives together. We are always together, you and I, in different ways each time, but we are always together."

"Corba, that's quite a privilege... A God-given gift." Raymonde's eyes were alive with interest.

"Sometimes it feels that way, at other times, less so."

"Can you tell me?"

So, for the hours they had left in that life, Corba and Raymonde sat on the rough flooring of the tent, his arms comfortably around her as Corba spoke more than she had the rest of her life, telling Raymonde all her memories of all their lives together. By the time the soldiers came for them, their imminent deaths seemed almost insignificant, although it was hard not to quiver still when they realised the manner of their passing.

Corba didn't see the pyre at first, instead she breathed a sigh of relief as she saw the trail of people, carts and animals slowly moving down the hill, the head of which already far ahead. A group of men Corba recognized were being held by soldiers, being kept back, Corba realized, to hear their declaration and witness their deaths before, hopefully, they too would be allowed to leave.

"They wanted to stay and be with us right until the end," Raymonde said, conversationally from her side. "I ordered them to go."

Corba nodded, her breathing now shallow. Lord Guiscard appeared before them, looking far more commandeering than he had early that morning, and Corba noted, looking like he was about to greatly enjoy the evening's sport.

"So," he spoke in a loud, cheerful voice designed to travel, "you were right, Lady Corba. You would not live to see sundown." He smiled cruelly. "How does that feel then?

"I will see many more sunsets in another life."

"Ah, reincarnation!" the French lord almost gloated. "Do you hear that?" he called to the gathered soldiers. "Another one of their heretical beliefs. They don't just go to heaven like proper Christians, they are reincarnated and return to earth time and time again." There was jeering from the soldiers. "I think," the lord continued, performing as if part of a band of players, "that our bon hommes here might be finding out that hell does exist very soon — not another life in another body!" Guffaws and laughing.

Corba noticed a soldier lighting a torch from a campfire. Raymonde reached down and took her hand in his.

"Well, personally, I would like to enjoy the sunset with a nice wine so let's get on with it. Come on then, Lady, renounce your faith in order to spare the lives of your people." The laughing lord's eyes turned serious, looking directly at Corba with that icy glare that belonged to another time, another man. "Any change of heart and I could have them all mowed down in just a few moments, you know. I would make you watch before I burnt you so choose your words carefully, Lady."

Corba swallowed. Her soul railed against denouncing her faith, speaking against what she knew to be the truth, but she also knew that ultimately it didn't matter as every man and woman knew the truth as it lay inside them, all they had to do was stop and listen. Her words would not change the truth, but in this instance, they might buy more time for innocent men, women and children. Or at least spare them the ghastly ends they would undoubtedly find at the hands of Lord Guiscard. And may yet. Corba knew she couldn't trust him, but something told her she had struck a chord with him when she talked about giving them an easier time with less French bloodshed. Lord Guiscard, she realised, really just wanted an easy life. As long as he was kept entertained, that was.

With a deep breath, Corba released Raymonde's hand and stepped forward. Raising her hands to the sky she called in a voice she had no idea she owned.

"With Lord God as my witness, I renounce heretical Catharism, so abhorrent as it is to the one true faith of his Holiness. I beseech you all to look inside, into your hearts, to find the truth and I will see you all on the other side. In the name of Lord Jesus Christ, I bless you all, you, Raymonde, you, my fellow Cathars, you, soldiers, and even you, Lord Guiscard, with peace and love, just as He taught us. I am now ready to die. Lord Guiscard, I suggest you light the pyre or else you won't get to see that sunset with a glass of wine after all." With that, Corba smiled beatifically at Lord Guiscard and walked into the burgeoning flames, turning only to reach out a hand for Raymonde to take as he joined her.

"Flames again," he murmured to her as he wrapped his arms around her, the faggots at their bare feet smouldering and hot. "We have been here before, my love, haven't we?"

Chapter 9

"Aurora?" Jack's voice came to her over the centuries. "Aurora, you are dreaming again? Wake up."

And there she was, suddenly awake, the warm sheets beneath her back, the even warmer flesh of Jack's thigh beneath her hand. The smell of singed flesh ripe in her nostrils. Aurora shook it away and sat up, Jack next to her following suit. "You were trying to wrap your arms round me, but you were shaking and murmuring... I knew you weren't just after a cuddle... Or something else." Jack's voice was concerned despite the humour, his hand gentle on her cheek.

"Sorry... It was another life. I seem to be remembering them all so vividly just now."

"Another terrible end?"

"Yes... Fire... Again." Aurora leant into him.

"Have you ever had any peaceful ends?" Jack didn't mean to joke, but sometimes he really didn't know what to say. It didn't matter, though, as Aurora was distracted. She was remembering those cold eyes, the man in the café earlier and the cruel crusader who had sent her and Max to their deaths. Why was he in her life again now? And why was he following her? And as much as she adored the man who belonged to the chest her cheek was currently pressed against, she couldn't help wondering once more where Max was.

January wore on, perpetually draped in grey. Aurora felt as grey as the sky and strangely disconnected from the world around her. Walking the streets, she failed to find any of the beauty she could usually so easily find in the world, a stark branch against a bleached sky, a smiling wrinkled face, the soft purr of a cat. She went about her business as if taking part in a play she had rehearsed so often it had become second nature, too often so it had become automated, empty, meaningless. A dream she was in and yet not part of - a voyeur in her own existence. The only thing that seemed really real to her was the sense of disquiet, the churning anxiety in her solar plexus which forewarned of danger, portended doom. Even her scattered thoughts — Max, Jack, the cold eyes — never quite seemed to form into anything absolute, only fleeting glimpses of a truth she could never quite catch. Jack did his best to rouse her from her melancholia, but even he wasn't able to bridge the distance.

It was the first week in February when, after a silent dinner, Jack finally snapped.

"Aurora." His voice was desperate and sad rather than angry, but still brittle with frustration. "Aurora, please, tell me what I can do?"

Aurora regarded him from across the table, took in his large emotive eyes and his strong, manly face. Noted them as she would the detail of a painting in a gallery. She felt a faint sense of regret, sadness, even, but wasn't sure why.

"Jack." The name seemed to come to her from across a distance. "I'm sorry." What was she sorry for? "I don't know what's wrong with me... I can't put my finger on... Well, anything."

"Are you remembering?" Jack asked, anguished.

"Remembering?" Aurora was surprised. "No... Not remembering. The opposite. It's nothing. Like I have forgotten something really important and I can't remember what it is."

Jack looked at her, his face serious. "It was that dream. Do you remember? You've never been quite the same since."

"What dream?" Aurora asked with genuine confusion.

Jack slapped his hand on the table his temper fraying, his patience stretched thin. "Aurora! You were remembering, but you said it was a terrible end by fire."

"Fire?" Lord Guiscard — or was it, Lord Jonas' — cold eyes flashed through Aurora's mind, his sneering grin cruel as the fire took hold. "Yes. I remember fire and the man who sent me to the flames."

"What man?" Jack was pleased to see a flash of life back in Aurora's eyes, even as he felt a stab of fear, for what reason he couldn't quite say.

"The man with the icy eyes." Aurora looked up at Jack, seeing him again properly for the first time in weeks. "Oh, Jack, it's that same man. Remember? The one who has been following us."

Jack looked puzzled. "At the Christmas market?" he asked incredulously.

"Yes." Aurora was filled with energy now. "It was him, the same man. He has killed me twice before, that I can remember. He fills me with horror, Jack, it is like he has such a dark energy it drains all of mine, as if he is feeding on mine."

"But he hasn't been about for ages," Jack argued. "Since before Christmas."

Aurora felt her cheeks tinge. "Actually, I have seen him since Christmas. That day I had the dream I had confronted him in a café. Offered him help, actually, but he didn't say anything, he just looked at me with those eyes…and gestured that he would slit my throat.

"And you didn't tell me?" Jack sounded furious, his expression a mixture of horror and hurt.

Aurora shrugged apologetically. "I'm sorry, I am not used to talking about this kind of thing." Except with Max, she qualified to herself, and instantly felt a jolt of guilt at another secret she kept from Jack.

Jack's anger subsided leaving him looking weary. He rubbed his hands over his face before coming to put his arms around Aurora. "I can understand why," he said. "It is a lot to understand for those of us without the same insights as you." He kissed the top of her head. "Do you think he is a real threat, Aurora? Here and now?"

"Yes." It was so matter of fact. "But what exactly would I tell the police?"

Jack grunted a laugh. "But, sir, he killed me hundreds of years ago and he wants to do the same again."

"Ridiculous, isn't it?" Aurora enjoyed just being in Jack's arms, being there and feeling fully awake, for a moment. "The thing is, Jack, I need to work out why."

"What do you mean?"

"Everything has a reason. I need to work out why this man keeps coming up, why this pattern. It is the only way to truly stop him — it's what I tell all my clients, after all!"

"You mean like karma again?"

"Yes… It must be unfinished business of some sort… Or a karmic chord… Or a belief of mine."

"OK, well, while you work that out, how about I move in with you?"

Aurora laughed, honestly and truly for the first time in weeks. "Oh, the look on your face! All serious and anxious, yet as eager as a wee boy at the same time!" Aurora paused. "I would love that, Jack." Her answer surprised her more than it surprised Jack.

Jack brought a bag of his belongings over the next morning. Not enough to suggest he was selling his studio flat, but more than just a toothbrush. Aurora felt oddly reassured and pleased to see his toiletries next to hers in the bathroom.

It also took surprisingly little time for them to slip into an easy routine. Jack would be out most of the day working while Aurora saw clients and normally had at least started dinner by the time he got back. Their evenings were spent in quiet companionship, wine and music, books before the fire, movies and box sets, and of course, plenty of sex.

For a few weeks Aurora barely thought about her past lives and just lived in this one, enjoying some of those everyday moments, moments which sometimes in the past had depressed her for an overfamiliarity born out of hundreds, if not thousands, of years of memory. Jack too seemed as content as she had seen him, happy, it seemed, simply to sit next to her at night, happy to find her at home when he got in, happy to wake up knowing she was there.

Winter slipped into spring and with the lighter evenings, they both found themselves keen to be outside more, walking by the river or through London's parks, enjoying the enlivening scent of spring in the air and the joyous sight of daffodils bobbing gently in the light breeze.

They were warming their hands on take-out coffee while sitting on a park bench one day, relishing the spring sun on their faces even if it was yet to carry any real warmth in it, when Jack suggested they go on holiday.

"Holiday?" Aurora knew she sounded as if he had just suggested moving to Mars.

"Yes, Aurora, a holiday." Jack smiled at her. "You know, like people do. You must remember having one at some point in all your lives?"

Aurora sipped her coffee, wondering why the notion unsettled her so much. "Actually, I am not sure I do."

"Never?"

"Well, I can't remember every single thing at the drop of a hat, but I don't really remember going on holiday. Travelling, yes, though I always seem to live in or around the same area except for a few exceptions. I don't really remember travelling anywhere just for pure pleasure."

"Have you been on holiday in this life, then?"

"Well, sort of, I mean I've been to Glastonbury a lot for short breaks, and I have taken long weekends at the coast, but not a holiday like I think you mean. Not two weeks in the Caribbean drinking cocktails."

"Well, sounds like it is high time you gave it a try!"

"You know, I don't think, in all my lives, I have ever really been very far from London."

"Really?" Jack was surprised.

"I mean, I reckon I have roamed across most of the British Isles, and I know I lived as a Cathar in France, and I was in Paris for a while during the Revolution and maybe other places that will come back to me with the right trigger."

"Why do you think that is?"

Aurora shrugged. "You know, I have never really thought about it, but I do know there is a special energy in Britain, a certain magic, especially around Glastonbury and Stonehenge. Maybe I need to be close to that."

Jack thought about that. "I know what you mean. I think I've always been able to sense that as well. Why a Cathar though?"

Aurora shrugged. "There is a special energy there too. And there's something about the Cathar beliefs that resonates."

Jack paused, absorbing her words. "It doesn't need to be the Caribbean, though, you know if that doesn't feel right. We can go anywhere in the world. It doesn't even have to be in the summer."

Aurora smiled at him. "Did you have somewhere in mind?"

Jack returned the smile. "Well, I have always fancied going to Egypt, to see the pyramids."

An image flashed through Aurora's mind of her and Jack on camels, climbing pyramid steps and sitting on cushions beneath the shade of a Bedouin tent. It gave her a thrill and yet, mixed with her excitement, there was still that thread of memory. Shaking if off, she reached out for his hand. "Let's do it," she said, grinning broadly.

Geoffrey

Smoke filled the small chamber, making Geoffrey cough.

"Keep going, Geoffrey!" Master Bacon's voice called through the thick smog. "Hold your sleeve over you face!"

Geoffrey did as he was told and kept pumping the bellows, happy, as always, to do anything Master Bacon asked of him. Geoffrey was only eight years old, but he could remember all too painfully what life was like before Master Bacon rescued him.

Born into squalor, his family life had not been easy, but his parents' deaths three years ago had left him alone in this world. Young as he was, he begged for food at different hearths in return for completing menial tasks that were truly too much for his small frame. He did remember being met with some kindness at times, people taking pity on the scrawny child before circumstances meant they could do no more for him, but mainly he remembers cruelty and violence.

The drunken soldiers who promised they would feed him once he had eaten a plate of cow dung. How they laughed as he forced down mouthful after mouthful, tears streaming down his grimy face. The mean baker's wife who had made him work for hours in return for half a loaf, only to then claim he had stolen it. Despite his youth, he had been lucky to escape with just a beating. Then there were the older children who would kick him to the ground and steal his hard-won food, given half a chance, leaving Geoffrey to pull his rags closer round him and huddle, miserable and hungry, in the filth.

Only his memories of other times and places kept him going. He knew life didn't have to be like this. He knew life could change. He knew, instinctively, as well as from past experience in other bodies, that all the cruelty and violence came from fear and he could, at times, feel compassion for those who stole the bread from his mouth. And it was that knowing, that different perspective, that seemed to attract Roger Bacon to the boy.

He had been sitting on the step of the local wise woman's house with a basket of herbs to sell for her, in return for a hot supper and a bed for the night, when the friar, who, unbeknownst to Geoffrey at the time, was also considered a bit of a wizard, approached him.

"Child," he asked, his face kindly. "What have you here?"

"Herbs, master," came Geoffrey's schooled response. "Do you have an ailment, sire? The old lady in there could help."

"No, child. No ailment. Do you live with the wise woman?"

"She will give me a bed for the night for helping her out now and then, sir, but I don't really live anywhere."

"I see." The master looked at the child closely. "You have had a hard life, boy, haven't you?"

"Isn't hard to see that, sir," the child replied sagely.

"No, very true." The master chuckled tolerantly. "I can see more in your face, though, would you like me to tell you what else I see?"

"Go on then," Geoffrey replied, intrigued by the man. "As long as it don't cost me, 'cause I have nothing."

"Just a moment of your time, young master. I see wisdom beyond your years. You watch the world around you closely, but more than that, you understand. You understand what makes people do what they do, don't you?"

Geoffrey was unsure what to say. "You could say that."

"And you have memories, boy, don't you?" the master continued, unperturbed.

Geoffrey's eyes opened wide in astonishment. "How did you know that, sir?"

"I know lots of things, young man. I know that young boys like you need a home and good food. And I know young men with talents like yours need training and coaching. So, what do you say?"

"What do I say to what, sir?" Geoffrey asked, feeling a fission of excitement, knowing, as he did, with his uncanny insight, that this was an important moment for him.

"Coming to live with me. Becoming my apprentice if you will. You will be warm and fed and you will have a teacher. But most of all, son, I will become your friend and we all need one of them, don't we?"

Geoffrey nodded, wondering what it might be like to have a friend. "Yes, sir, I guess so. I need to finish helping the old woman first though."

Master Bacon smiled kindly. "I wouldn't have expected anything less, young man."

A day later, Geoffrey found himself the proud owner of a new set of clothes and even a pair of boots. He had his own bed piled high with blankets awaiting him and having enjoyed three meals in one day — plus a bath — for the first time he could remember in this lifetime, he could barely contain his excitement at the thought of getting into that cosy bed. Still, he sat by the fire, listening to Master Bacon that night with a look filled with gratitude and wonder. *This man really must be some kind of magician*, he had thought, unaware just how close to the truth he was.

In the next few weeks, Geoffrey discovered Master Bacon was remarkable in every way. He thought differently to anyone else Geoffrey had ever met and encouraged the child to do so too. He laughed loudly and often, giving thanks for the smallest of things in the same way. He carried out experiments that Geoffrey failed to understand but completely grasped the sense of excitement they generated in the master. Most of all, though, the master never failed to show the boy kindness.

Within days, Geoffrey was telling him all about his memories of what had been before, and to Geoffrey's astonishment, the man listened intently and asked questions as if Geoffrey was an equal. He was endlessly curious about the nature of Geoffrey's memories and in particular the moment of death in each life. The young boy struggled to find the words to describe it to the master, no matter how he longed to be able to do the sensation justice, as a way of repaying the man's kindness.

"It's like falling asleep and waking up all at the same time," he told him one night. "Waking up feeling like you are awake properly for the first time."

"And what do you see?" Master Bacon asked, looking at the child intently, his eyes alight with curiosity.

Geoffrey thought about this for a moment. "It's like light. White... But colours too. But it's not like seeing here at all."

"And do you feel scared?"

"Scared?" Geoffrey was genuinely surprised. "No, not scared. Happy." The boy thought about it some more. "Though it is not always nice to die... I don't like being stabbed or burnt."

"And you have been both?" Master Bacon was awed by the experiences this unassuming child must have had.

"Yes," was Geoffrey's straight-forward answer.

115

"And do you see a link between what happens to you in different lives? Like if you have been mean in one, someone will be mean to you in another."

"Yes… Though… It's difficult to explain. It's not like punishment, it is like you want to learn. You decide before you come back what you want to learn… Then you forget."

"Forget? But you remember?"

"Sort of… I mean, not clearly… It's like when something happens, I remember, but not before. Like when my ma and pa died. I knew we had decided that before. Still made me sad though." Grief streaked across his face.

"Of course, my boy, of course. Do you know why you had to experience that, though?

Geoffrey smiled brightly, his sadness vanishing. "Yes! So, I could meet you!"

And so it went, night after night, for a year. The only thing Geoffrey never mentioned to Master Bacon was Max. And then, one day, when Geoffrey was bellowing smoke as hard as he could and the Master's voice was getting equally hoarse from coughing and excitement, Max walked up the worn stone staircase to Master Bacon's study at the top of one of Oxford University's many towers.

"Doctor Mirabilis?" Max asked, standing tall and confident in the master's study for all the world as if he were the one receiving guests. His skin was dark, his voice heavily accented and his clothes sung of the exotic from every fold. His glistening purple cloak fell over shoulders cossetted in stiff gold. Even his sword, curved and cruel-looking, was encased in a bejewelled sheath.

Geoffrey held his breath. Max was a Saracen. "Max." His voice was so little of a whisper neither man heard.

"Greetings, young sir." Master Bacon didn't seem the least troubled by this invasion, or by Max's exotic appearance. "How may I be of service?"

"I hear you are a scholar of some standing, an alchemist too… A wizard, even?" Max's English was careful, considered, as if he found it difficult to twist his tongue round the harsh sounds.

Master Bacon laughed without rancour. "Some would say so. I think I am just observant. We could converse in French if you would prefer?"

The colourful young man smiled. "No. Thank you. I would like to be more comfortable with the English language."

Master Bacon smiled. "Well, perhaps you would like to take a seat and I will ask my apprentice here, Geoffrey, to fetch us something refreshing? Tea, perhaps?"

The man who was Max glanced at Geoffrey, was about to look away, thinking him of no great consequence, then looked again with a slight frown. Geoffrey waited, heart racing. Would he recognise something within him? But the Saracen youth shook his head and turned his attention back to Master Bacon. "Yes. Please. Tea would be perfect."

Geoffrey brewed the strange herbs Master Bacon loved to drink as tea, preferring it to beer or wine while he was working, his fingers clumsy with excitement.

His legs were shaking so badly he stumbled as he went to place the pot and mugs on the table between the two men, but kind as ever, Master Bacon simply steadied the boy and guided the tray to the table. The Saracen glared.

"Geoffrey has been with me a year. He is a quick learner, but like all young boys, he gets excited and you must forgive him." Master Bacon's gentle smile had a soothing effect as always and Max turned to Geoffrey.

"I am Anas al Razi," he said proudly, with the slightest incline of his head. "It is a pleasure to meet you, Geoffrey."

"It's a pleasure to meet you, sir," came Geoffrey's schooled response, all while his heart raced at being so close to the soul he had known since time began.

The master poured tea and asked his guest some genial questions about his travels and if this was his first time to Oxford, or indeed England. Anas answered cordially, but Geoffrey could tell, watching him intently as he was from his position standing behind the Master's seat, that he was desperate to turn the conversation to the reason he had come to find Master Bacon — or Doctor Mirabilis, as he had called him.

It seemed the master could sense his impatience as well, and after a few moments, he gave his guest a gentle, yet knowing, smile. "However, you have not travelled thousands of miles simply to tell me about the weather on the English Channel or your first impressions of our green and pleasant land, have you, young sir?"

Anas had the good grace to look slightly sheepish. "No, Doctor. Tales of your magic have spread far, but they also say you have wisdom and understand the nature of the universe, is that so?"

The master shook his head modestly. "I have been blessed with some insight, yes, but I don't think I would ever go so far as to say I fully understand the nature of God's creation."

Anas, his expression serious, ignored the modesty. "I hope you will be able to help me with dreams I have had since I was a child."

"Dreams?" Geoffrey could tell the master was interested.

"Yes, dreams. Except they are more than dreams. I don't know how exactly. I just know."

"Well, perhaps you could start by telling me about them?" The master topped up Max's tea and the young man slumped back in his seat as if taking him to this point had used all his energy. Geoffrey could tell that he was relieved too, relieved that the master was at least willing to listen.

"OK. I have dreamt like this all my life, as long as I remember. It is not like other dreams. These are like living. Like I belong in a different body, with different skin and sometimes..." Max's beautifully smooth caramel skin flushed a gentle pink. "I do such things as them..."

Anas, or Max, then went on to speak at length about the dreams, telling of scents and scenes from other times and places that had Geoffrey swaying on his feet as he too journeyed back through time and death, remembering, reliving, with Max.

By the time he finished, it was dark outside. "The worst, though, was the fire. Always the fire. I can remember the skin on my feet crisping as I stood on a pyre. I could smell my own flesh cooking. It would make me hungry if I could not feel the pain... I wake screaming because of the pain." Anas shrugged a little at his own black humour, looking to the Master with anguished eyes. "Can you help?"

Master Bacon leant forward to clasp the younger man's arm comfortingly. "First, I need to find the pisspot. While I am gone, perhaps you should speak to Geoffrey here." The look the master gave Geoffrey, told the boy clearly he was meant to confide in Anas, but as the door closed behind him, Geoffrey found himself suddenly shy.

Anas rose to his feet as the master left, his agitation causing him to pace the room, glaring balefully at Geoffrey.

"What do you have to say to me?" he finally asked, his voice filled with disdain and his eyes resting balefully on a nervous Geoffrey.

"I... Am... Ah... I... Eh..." Geoffrey stammered, the heat rising in his cheeks. "I mean... I..." Anas covered the room in two fluid strides to grab Geoffrey by the front of his tunic and pin him to the wall.

"Speak, serving boy. I can't imagine what a runt like you can have to say to me, but I believe in Doctor Mirabilis' reputation so I am bound to hear what you have to say. Speak!"

Anger overwhelmed nerves in Geoffrey, kicking his street instincts into play. With a deft foot, he caught Anas squarely on the shin and freed himself. Keeping the chair and table between them he glared back at the arrogant young man who was also Max.

"Don't you dare touch me! I might be a boy but I know more than you!" Geoffrey could feel tears in his eyes. "I know you. I have always known you. I know you better than you know yourself. Lifetime after lifetime, we know each other. I can tell you exactly what your dreams are about, because for me, they are not dreams, they are memories! I can tell you now that if you don't stop being such a... Such a... An arrogant yaldson... You will come back in the next life as a beggar... Or hopefully a fly for me to swat!"

Anas looked for all the world like he was going to murder Geoffrey when the door creaked and the master reappeared, taking in the situation in an instant. "So, you have started talking, I see," he said, his voice calm and gentle as always. "So, let me guess, where have you got to? Anas, you don't believe Geoffrey that he can remember his past lives? Or that your dreams might be your past lives?"

Anas glowered at the older man. Geoffrey spoke, suddenly afraid for the master. "Sir... It's not just that. I know who the young lord is, we have known each other before. I remember those lives he dreams about."

The master looked momentarily stunned, but then his natural curiosity took over and his eyes began to gleam. "Fascinating. Please, Anas, sit down, I vouch for this boy's word. He wouldn't say so if he didn't believe it to be true." A pale Anas somewhat reluctantly took his seat. The master gestured to Geoffrey to sit at the other side of the table in order for him to play mediator as he was sat between them. "So, Geoffrey. Please tell us what you know of Anas' dreams."

It was dark when Anas left. He hadn't said much more but he had listened intently to every word Geoffrey had said, asking the occasional question and sometimes staring into the distance, lost in his own thoughts. Although Geoffrey told him facts as he could remember them, he didn't tell Anas that they held a bond of love that existed beyond flesh and bone, life and death.

By the time he left, Geoffrey felt distinctly unsettled. The master, too, seemed concerned by his pale reticence and almost surly leave-taking. And as it turned out, they were right to feel uneasy, as the guards arrived before they were even out their beds in the morning.

"We are the sheriff's men," the leader announced to the crumpled old man as he stood before them, trying to pull on his robe. "We are here for the boy. Charges of unnatural goings-on."

They took Geoffrey away in chains and there was nothing the master could say to stop them. The old man grabbed the boy's arm as he was being dragged down the stairs. "I will get you out, Geoffrey. I am sorry, I feel this is my fault, but I will help you, do not fear."

Geoffrey believed him, but a lurching sensation in his stomach, as well as the curse of remembering so many other lives coming to brutal ends, made him fear that the master wouldn't be able to do anything.

Three days later, it seemed likely to be the case as Geoffrey huddled in the corner of the freezing, stinking dungeon, rancid straw beneath him and his arms held at an awkward angle by a chain through an ancient iron loop. The sound of the door bolts crunching into place rung in his head, anticipating what the next hearing of them, for better or for worse, might bring. When the sound came, Geoffrey felt bile, the only contents of his stomach, rise in his throat. The feeling of nausea was then aggravated by the unaccustomed brightness of the men's torches. Their strong hands grabbed his thin child's arms and huckled him and his chains out into the brightness of the courtyard above.

The master was there, exuding a quiet strength and peace, as always, yet Geoffrey could see he was pale and the thought of the master worrying made him quail. His knees would have given way beneath him if the two hulking men at either side of him hadn't already been more or less carrying his lightened frame. He gave the tiniest of nods as Geoffrey caught his eye, but the boy found himself unable to respond and instead looked away.

His eyes then found Max. Or rather, Anas, standing half hidden in the shadows of the towering castle walls yet still haughty in his glittering finery. With his uncanny insight Geoffrey knew instantly that Anas had somehow been the cause of his arrest. Yet even amidst his fear and lessened by physical weakness, Geoffrey could see beyond Anas' veneer as easily as if it were one of the veils worn by the king's dancers. The young Saracen was rocked by what Geoffrey had told him because he knew his words were true. He was scared and all he could think to do from his limited perspective as Anas was to take it out on Geoffrey. Somehow, he believed that by obliterating Geoffrey he would be free, but Geoffrey knew the truth had been spoken and could not be unspoken. Even if he died in the next moment on the greasy courtyard cobbles, Anas would always know that Geoffrey had spoken the truth.

And then Geoffrey's eyes alighted upon the inquisitor and his stomach scrunched again. He didn't know this man, but he had known so many like them through the years. In every life it seemed he encountered someone so terrified of life his only recourse was self-righteousness and the suffering of others. Always, it seemed to Geoffrey, it was done in the name of God. Or some God, anyway. Geoffrey wondered idly, how God felt about the innumerable injustices men carried out in His name. Maybe, if he remembered when he passed this time, he would see if he could ask Him… Or rather 'it', as he knew in a way that couldn't really be described as memory that God was not a man, or man was not made in the shape of God, God was everything and everything was God. God was all there was and lived in everything.

Lost in his thoughts, Geoffrey missed the inquisitor's words and received a deft blow to his cheekbone for it.

"Answer me, boy!" His silence had already drawn out the spite. "Your name?"

"Geoffrey, sir." He answered as respectfully as he could, unwilling to court another needless blow.

"Geoffrey, indeed. Do you know why you are here?" his voice boomed as he relished holding court.

"No, sir," Geoffrey replied, not quite in truth. "I've done nothing wrong." That, though, was the whole truth.

The inquisitor's eyes narrowed, his lips pursed as if Geoffrey carried a bitter taste. "We have received an anonymous letter telling of your unnatural abilities... you believe you have been reincarnated and can remember your lives. That doesn't sound in accordance with the teaching of Rome now does it boy?"

"No, sir." Geoffrey decided meekness might be the best option.

"It means heresy. And do you know what the punishment for heresy is, boy?"

Geoffrey shook his heads, unable to speak as he remembered the unbearable pain of fire consuming his flesh.

"Death. By burning." The inquisitor couldn't conceal his delight at the thought. "Purging. It is a favour to your soul, really, as we are transmuting your Earthly sins. Is that what you want to happen, Geoffrey?"

"Kindly sir, may I interject."

The inquisitor slowly turned his hateful gaze towards the master. "Ah, Doctor Mirabilis."

"Just a simple friar and scholar, my lord. One who carries the Lord God in his heart every day in the hopes of being a dutiful servant. And one who can vouch wholeheartedly for this boy here."

The inquisitor allowed a silence to take hold in the wake of the master's words, enjoying the suspense it created. Relishing the power, he had over the people before him.

"Really... Well, I wonder if maybe you should not be standing next to the boy in chains too, good friar, given the story as we have heard."

Geoffrey's eyes were darting from the face of one to the other, barely breathing as he waited for his fate to be decreed. He was willing the master to retort, to tackle bullyboy tactics with genial wisdom, as he so often did, but his lips moved mutely as he searched for the right words and found nothing.

It was in fact Anas who was next to speak. Geoffrey watched him with growing horror as he moved from the shadows to take centre stage.

"My lord inquisitor." Anas looked directly at Geoffrey, his expression inscrutable. "I am afraid I am the wrongdoer here. I sent the letter but I realise that my poor grasp of English… And my hastiness to see anything that goes against God punished has made me… What is the expression… Jump to conclusions?"

Geoffrey stole a glance at the Master who gave him the most infinitesimal shrug.

The inquisitor gave Anas a disparaging glance. "Who are you infidel?"

"My name is Lord Anas, I am a great friend of the Earl of Warwick." Anas meaningfully dropped the name of the most powerful nobleman in the land. "He will vouch for me and has indeed given me his ring in case I was of need of it." Anas opened his palm to revel a ring marked with the Earl's crest.

"The Earl of Warwick is a great man." The inquisitor was clearly weighing his options and was clearly unwilling to upset such a powerful figure, but his focus was still on Anas. "But tell me, infidel." The inquisitor's tone was desultory and yet there was a glimmer of something else in his eye. "Are you telling me you now believe you have been mistaken?"

The young Saracen smiled winningly at the inquisitor, obviously worldly enough to realise that the aged churchman's fire and brimstone didn't extend to dashing young men with skin like honey. "Yes, sir, I am truly most sorry, but perhaps we could discuss further over dinner? The Earl of Warwick is expecting me at Warwick Castle this evening and I am sure he would be delighted if I brought such a distinguished churchman as yourself?"

The lure of an evening in such influential circles combined with the promise in Anas' smile was too much for the inquisitor and he barely remembered to motion to the guards to let Geoffrey go as he rose from his seat and followed Anas from the courtyard with what could almost be described as a spring in his step.

The master rushed to the boy's side as he collapsed to the cobbles, already forgotten by the guards as they sauntered back to the guardroom, chains swinging nonchalantly from their hands, talking lazily about a game of dice.

"Geoffrey! Oh, Geoffrey, my boy, I am so sorry! Here, let me help you up and get you home." The master, Geoffrey thought as he was lifted into the man's arms with considerable ease, looked much older than he had a few days ago and though light with relief, he couldn't help but feel sad for it.

The master made him stay in bed for two days as he brought him bowls of thick broth, fresh bread liberally doused with honey or dripping and even beakers of ale. But Geoffrey was young, and despite it all, healthy, so, after two days, his young body was desperate to move. He was not long up, though, when he was overwhelmed by tiredness.

"See!" the master remonstrated with him, looking up for a moment from the manuscript open before him. "I told you to take it easy or you will tire yourself out, back to bed now!"

Geoffrey, who had got up like a lion not an hour before, obeyed like a lamb. Lying back down on his rugs with a sigh, he looked over to the master. "Will you read to me please, sir?"

The master looked up with an arched eyebrow. "From this manuscript?" He gestured towards the tome before him, knowing that Geoffrey knew fine well the medical textbook was not what the boy had in mind.

Geoffrey grinned back, content to play along. "No. Perhaps *Beowulf*? Or *The Battle of Maldon*? Or *Layamon's Brut*? Or…"

Geoffrey's happy contemplation of what his master might read to him was interrupted by a knock at the door followed by an anxious silence in the room.

The master moved sedately to the door, but Geoffrey knew he, too, would be worried. Instead of opening it, as he always would have previously, he called through the stout wood, "Who's there?'

"Doctor Mirabilis, it is me, Anas. Please let me in, I mean neither you nor Geoffrey any harm."

Geoffrey held his breath as the master hesitated, his eyes on the boy hunkering beneath his blanket. Eventually Geoffrey let out a long breath and nodded. The master opened the stout door.

"Anas." The master's voice was unreadable. "Come in."

The young man strode into the tower chamber, a flash of the exotic in his bright robes against the dark wood of the room's shelves and furniture, crammed as they were with all manner of books, scrolls and artefacts. Geoffrey could sense his pain even before he saw the tortured expression in his amber eyes.

"Geoffrey." His voice was pleading and weak, his fingers nervously knotting the hanging sleeves of his robe. "Geoffrey." He began again, his voice finding more strength this time round. "I am here to beg your forgiveness... And that of you, Doctor Mirabilis. Although what I did was unforgiveable... I allowed my own fear to take over. I know what you say is the truth... It just made me scared. I am sorry. I can't believe I nearly cost you your life." He shuffled in agitation, his eyes never leaving Geoffrey's face. "Can you forgive me?"

Geoffrey couldn't speak as an array of emotions washed through him. He could choose anger all too easily, but Geoffrey could so clearly see Max in the young man who stood before him in vibrant silks. His Max. His twin soul. Anger would achieve nothing. "Anas." The boy's voice sounded far wiser than his few years. "There's nothing to forgive. You took action to stop things going too far, and more importantly, you realise now that you were driven by your own fear."

Anas' face relaxed visibly. "Thank you, Geoffrey, thank you, you are a remarkable boy." He then turned to the master. "And you, sir? Can you forgive me too?"

The master's inscrutable face softened too. "It would be churlish of me not to be guided by our wise young friend here. Why don't we all have some refreshments?"

Months turned into years and Anas became a regular visitor in the tower study. He became like a brother to Geoffrey, teasing him mercilessly at times, and yet also listening intently when he spoke of the lives they had shared before. He also learned well from the master and discovered he excelled in complex mathematics in a way that baffled and bemused Geoffrey, who preferred to think in terms of images and allegories, stories and colours.

It was the autumn of Geoffrey's sixteenth year that Anas announced he was planning to visit Egypt and asked if Geoffrey and the Master would like to accompany him. The master, who now struggled to rise from his chair and who coughed intermittently the whole day long, smiled ruefully at Anas' bright-eyed enthusiasm. "Oh, Anas, my dear boy.

My bones are too old for such an adventure now, even while my heart still soars at the thought." Geoffrey felt his heart sink at the master's words. "But you must take Geoffrey, show him something of this world for him to remember in whatever life he leads next."

And so, it was with huge excitement tinged with sadness at parting with a frail Doctor Mirabilis, that Anas and Geoffrey set off, unaware that the old man knew the next time he saw Geoffrey would mean he was dying.

"The leaves are golden here, Geoffrey," Anas told him as they rode through the rolling hills toward a port and the ship that would carry them across the channel. "But in Egypt just now the sky will be blue as far as the eye can see and instead of green fields there will undulating sand for miles and miles."

"Will there be maids?" Geoffrey asked, undeniably a sixteen-year-old boy in this incarnation.

Anas laughed. "Yes, my young stallion, maids like you couldn't imagine! Just you wait until you see them dance... They have bells at their ankles and are draped in veils of the thinnest material possible... Thin enough to see everything but not quite." Geoffrey's eyes bulged as Anas continued. "But while I am sure we will have time for maids, it is the ancient mysteries we seek, my brother. We are going to explore the pyramids, you know about them, don't you?"

"Only from books," Geoffrey replied, still distracted by the images of maids Anas had conjured up for him.

"The reality will be very different, my brother, just you wait and see!"

The journey took many weeks, but Geoffrey didn't mind as there was always so much to see. In France he caught glimpse of his first tournament, where young knights took part in mock battles over many miles to hone their skills and earn their keep. The intent may not have been to kill, but Geoffrey saw plenty of blood and broken limbs. Unlike many boys his age, the sight didn't fill him with an urge to become a knight. Perhaps, he wondered, he had simply seen too much suffering in his lives as the sight only made him sad.

He did though revel in seeing the glistening white chateaus and tasting the strange cheeses the country had to offer. And Anas teased him mercilessly that he was becoming too fond of their famous wine.

"I am glad I follow Islam when I see you like that!" he teased one morning after Geoffrey had drunk himself to the point where he couldn't find his own bed roll.

The beauty of the Alps took his breath away and he wondered if he could spend the rest of his life just lying among the flower-dappled pastures, listening to the gentle chime of cattle bells as they grazed. But when they came to the Mediterranean Sea with its blue expanse and life-affirming warmth Geoffrey turned his thoughts to a life as a fisherman, spending his days peaceably mending nets and bumping over the gentle waves in a little boat, thinking of nothing much except his next meal and possibly a warm embrace when he got back to shore.

After a rough night on the large boat Anas had found to carry them across the sea, Geoffrey changed his mind. The sea carried them into a river and Geoffrey felt a frisson of new excitement. This was a different world again. Here thick reeds bordered the wide river and flat plains lay beyond, but it was the sky that enchanted Geoffrey. It was vast and far bluer than he could ever have thought possible. Geoffrey found it hard to take his eyes from the wispy white clouds drifting amiably across its endless expanse.

"Now, my young brother, we are in Egypt!" Anas announced grandly as he came to sit next to him on the deck. "Another day by river and we will get off and you will have your first experience of a camel."

"A what?" Geoffrey asked, running through memories of all his lives to see if he had experienced a camel before.

"A camel, you silly camel." Anas laughed as he nudged his young companion amiably. "You're telling me, with all your memories, you have never encountered a camel?"

"I don't think so, though I can't remember absolutely everything about every life. Besides, as I have told you, other than Atlantis, I don't think I have travelled far."

"Well... It is like a horse except it has a humped back and a similar disposition to Master Bacon when he has not had his morning tea."

"So, grumpy, then."

"Very, my young friend, but they are the best way to travel in the dessert and we have a long way to go yet."

"Where exactly are we going, Anas?"

Anas smiled at Geoffrey, his eyes dancing with warmth and love. "It will be better if I let you discover it all for yourself, Geoffrey, but believe me when I tell you, it will change your life."

Geoffrey accepted Anas' word. Despite what had happened in the past, he knew he couldn't help but trust the exotic young man who had been Max so long ago. And that night he dreamt of camels as well as dark skinned maids with intoxicating dark eyes.

The next day, Geoffrey came face to face with a real camel for the first time and saw Anas chuckling away to himself as he tried to mount the fractious beast. So as not to look silly in front of Anas, he found himself beseeching the animal mentally. *Please, camel, let me mount, I will be kind to you.*

To Geoffrey's astonishment, the animal stopped throwing his large head around, railing noisily against his reins as he was, and spun round to look Geoffrey directly in the eye.

Please, Geoffrey asked again inside his head, astonished by the wise look he saw in the camel's eyes and even more so when the animal lowered his neck to allow Geoffrey to climb on with greater ease. The young boy couldn't help but enjoy the look of bewilderment on Anas' face as the camel calmly stood with Geoffrey on his back.

A while later, once Geoffrey had got used to the strange undulating sway of the camel and had stopped being overwhelmed by the shifting sand dunes stretching out in every direction, he decided to try and communicate with the animal again.

I am called Geoffrey, he said, as he would to a person. *May I call you by your name?* he then asked politely, instinctively knowing that the camel's wisdom deserved respect.

The camel glanced back at the boy on his back yet again. This time with a look that could only be described as quizzical.

He then let out an almost celebratory grunt while, in his head, Geoffrey quite clearly heard the word, *Hikma.*

Thank you for carrying me so well, Hikma, Geoffrey answered. *I have never been on a camel before.*

I can tell, came the sardonic reply.

Do you mind if we talk as we travel? Geoffrey asked in his head, not quite believing he was really speaking to the animal.

If you like, Hikma said, though Geoffrey knew he was pleased.

That night, Geoffrey, Anas and their guide, Mehedi, camped beneath a flapping canopy, camels and people gathered tight around a fire as the temperature plummeted. Despite the cold, Geoffrey couldn't help wandering a little away from the fire so he could stare up at the heavens and the multitude of stars. The sight made him feel both insignificant and part of something much greater than he, or any other human, could ever conceive. When he returned, though, he couldn't help but ask Anas and Mehedi if the name 'Hikma' meant anything.

"It means wisdom," Anas answered as he peeled a fig with his knife. "Or, to be more precise, 'coming to know the essence of things as they really are'." Anas looked at him with interest. "Where did you hear it, young friend?"

Mehedi crouched on his haunches, striped robes wrapped tight round his legs. He watched the flames intently as he tended the fire, but Geoffrey could tell he was listening.

"My camel told me it is his name," Geoffrey said slightly defiantly, expecting to be mocked. Anas' handsome face broke into a wide smile, but it was far from mocking. He had a great respect for the young boy's unique perspective on life.

Mehedi, though, put his head back and laughed without shame and Geoffrey felt his cheeks redden. "No, no, my pale-skinned friend," Mehdi hurried to reassure him, "I do not laugh at you. It is a blessing for a camel to give you their name. I laugh at the perfection of it all. God does indeed work in mysterious ways." The Bedouin guide gave Geoffrey a toothy smile.

"How do you mean?" Geoffrey asked, mollified but still slightly hesitant.

"He gave you the name that you most need to hear., and my friend, I knew from the second I saw you that you are on a quest, a spiritual quest and that your travels in my country will indeed bring you to know the essence of things as they really are."

Geoffrey's head was full of many things that night as he fell asleep, snug beneath rugs and the light canopy, and there was no room for dark-eyed maidens in there.

They travelled many more days over the dunes. Geoffrey lost all sense of time in the endless sands, knowing only the searing, shimmering heat of day and the intense cold of night. And Hikma's conversation. The camel seemed to want to talk endlessly, and Geoffrey was happy to listen. The animal spoke of the history of the world and a time many eons ago when the deserts were covered in luscious grass, rivers and giant trees.

You remember too, though, Geoffrey, don't you? he asked one day as he was remembering the sparkling waters imbued with life-giving qualities that used to cover the Earth.

Geoffrey was taken by surprise. *Yes, I do,* he finally answered. *We called the place we lived Atlantis then.*

Yes, that's right. When everything was in balance and people understood the energies of the universe, how they flowed, the camel replied nostalgically. Hikma went quiet for a while after that and when he spoke again his voice was more serious than wistful. *Geoffrey, we camels carry a message for mankind, but we cannot impart it until humanity is ready to hold such wisdom again.* Geoffrey waited patiently for the camel to continue. *I want you to be the first human we give this knowledge to.*

The boy was stunned. *Me? Why?*

Because you remember. Because you understand more than most. And because you asked me my name, Hikma answered.

I would be honoured, Geoffrey answered.

Hikma plodded on in silence for a while more, before saying, *Water, Geoffrey, is the key to many things. Humanity abuses it, as it does so much else, but water needs to be cherished, blessed and respected. If treated properly, water can spread light across the world. Do you understand, Geoffrey?*

I think so. Geoffrey thought for a moment. *Water is life in many ways. We are made of water and water is life.*

Indeed, but water can become magical if we treat it properly. If you look with the eyes of your higher self, water is alive with energy and if blessed, that energy intensifies. Remember that, Geoffrey. This desert is what happens when water is neglected and abused. If you do one thing to help the world, let it be that you bless water.

I will, Hikma, for you, I will.

Saying goodbye to Hikma was one of the hardest things Geoffrey had ever had to do, but almost smiling, the camel put his forehead to that of the boy's. *All things have their time, my friend. I will always be in your heart and you in mine. Go forward with my blessing.*

So distracted by saying goodbye to the camel, it was only once Mehedi and his train had vanished into the distance that he realised they had arrived at their final destination.

Anas had been watching him closely, kindly waiting for him to compose himself. "Well now, Geoffrey, are you ready to delve into the mysteries of Thebes?"

"Thebes." Geoffrey tried the word in his mouth as he looked around properly for the first time. "I have heard of this place."

"Undoubtedly, it is a place of ancient magic and mystery, you should feel right at home!"

And Geoffrey did. He would remember that first walk with Anas for the rest of his life. Through the brightly festooned markets where wares, noisy sellers and shoppers all — laughingly, seemingly — jostled for a spot, a place at the fruit stall, a space to feel the quality of the silk merchant's fabrics or a seat beneath an awning on an upturned barrel for a glass of cooling tea. He stopped dead in his tracks at the sight of his first dancing snake, a cobra, Anas told him, deadly poisonous as well as prolific.

"Watch your feet constantly," he told Geoffrey, only half teasingly.

But Anas did not stop in the markets, or down the narrow, but much cooler, side streets where veiled children ran around or carried water jugs, women tended herb gardens on roof terraces and an old man sat on stone steps, watching the world go by with dreamy contentment.

He kept walking and Geoffrey kept following until he finally asked, "Where are we going, Anas? Do we not need to find lodgings?"

"We have lodgings, Geoffrey. But they are not to be found in the city. It is not long now."

It was nearly dark when Anas stopped. Exhausted, Geoffrey had long since stopped drinking in his surroundings, aware of only the way his weary feet were scuffling through the sand. Still, he couldn't contain the gasp he gave when he looked up. Living with the master in Oxford, he was used to impressive scholarly buildings, and their long journey through Europe had exposed him to grand castles, sprawling manor houses and ruined grandeur of all sorts, but nothing had prepared him for the sight that befell him on the outskirts of Thebes. Bathed in the magical milky white luminosity of the full moon, an army of giant stone warriors stretched into the distance on either side of a massive stone portal doorway sitting, indomitable, at the top of a dozen wide steps. These warriors, though, had strange bestial heads, almost like a fox, Geoffrey thought, or possibly a wolf.

Anas enjoyed seeing his young friend taken aback at the grandeur. "They have been here thousands of years," he told him. "I felt like you the first time I saw them. Like I was dreaming, is that not so?"

"Yes," Geoffrey spluttered. "Although I am not sure if I dreamt of these animal soldiers it wouldn't be a nightmare!"

Anas laughed. "They are not to be feared! At least not if you come to this place pure of heart. They guard the ancient secrets of Thebes, ancient wisdom which you can only access if you prove yourself worthy. Are you worthy, Geoffrey?"

Geoffrey looked at Anas with a growing sense of trepidation. "Is that why I am here, Anas? To be tested?"

Anas smiled. "I don't know, Geoffrey. We will just have to wait and see." As enigmatic as his smile was, Geoffrey was reassured by the warmth and love there. He knew, as he had learnt through life after life, that he must trust. "These are our lodgings, Geoffrey, shall we knock?" Anas asked, his face bright with excitement.

"I suppose so," replied Geoffrey, his stomach dancing with butterflies.

Inside was even more extraordinary, and if anything, a little more intimidating than outside. The Legions of Anubis, as Geoffrey quickly discovered was how the stone guardians were named, stood to deft attention in rows upon rows on either side of high-vaulted corridors lit with a thousand lamps and torches. A white-robed, shaven-headed priest led the way round corner after corner, each corridor the same as the last, until, eventually, they reached a courtyard. Geoffrey breathed in the still warm but fresh air gratefully.

Without a word, he gestured for them to sit on cushions by a fountain. A tray carrying a cloth-covered ewer, beakers and a bowl of figs had apparently been awaiting their arrival.

Happy to be seated, Geoffrey looked around him, taking in wide, shaded but open corridors on all four sides of the courtyard, decorated with beautifully intricate fretwork. The courtyard itself was abundant with blooms of every colour and every shade. The fountain, at least four times the height of Geoffrey, was aglow with seemingly magical golden lamps. High above, though, Geoffrey could still see the stars and it was on them he gazed as he lay back on his cushions, grounding himself with the awe-inspiring sight of the night sky. It was something so comfortingly familiar to him, as he had looked up at it through lifetime after lifetime, and yet something that never failed to thrill.

"Why did you want to come here, Anas?" he asked the older man as he too made himself comfortable eating a fig.

Anas looked around him. "As ever, Geoffrey, I seek knowledge and this is a place of ancient wisdom. I hope to be allowed an insight into some of it."

"Why did you bring me?"

Anas smiled at the half-man, half-boy, his eyes filled with affection, and Geoffrey realised for the first time, respect. "Geoffrey, you have far more wisdom than you realise and far more knowledge than most of the other people in the world put together. As soon as I thought I would like to go, I knew I had to bring you. Call it divine prompting. Call it God. Call it whatever you like, but I know you are meant to be here. Perhaps the whole reason for my existence, and the long journey we have been on since I first met you, was to bring you here, to this moment. Perhaps it is only part of my soul's purpose, but if that was all I am destined to do then it has been an honour." Anas dipped his head in a respectful bow, leaving Geoffrey feeling like he might just cry tears of joy and yet he couldn't quite explain why. Sometimes he forgot that Anas was Max. Perhaps that made him sad.

Geoffrey didn't know how long they had been sleeping when another white-robed priest woke them. He noticed groggily that the stars were a little less visible in the darkness above, suggesting the sun had started to rise. The priest bowed and spoke in a language Geoffrey couldn't understand.

"He is apologizing for our wait," Anas whispered to him as they fell in behind the man. "And says we are to be bathed."

"Bathed?" Geoffrey's horror forced Anas to catch a snort of derision.

"Come now, Geoffrey, I know it is not the practice in England but it really won't do you any harm."

"By men or women?" Geoffrey demanded.

"Which would you prefer?" Anas asked mischievously.

Geoffrey soon discovered that he was to be bathed by more of the white-robed priests and couldn't decide if he was relieved or not. But he couldn't argue that once he had got passed the embarrassment of being disrobed and having every inch of his body scrubbed, the experience was actually quite wonderful. The bathhouse, shimmering in a wondrous golden light, was built from the purest white marble and smelt of a heady mix of oils. Geoffrey, used to such smells in the master's study, could pick out rosemary, lavender and lemon, but the others were strange, though no less beautiful, to his nose.

He lay back in the wide bathing pool, ignoring Anas over at the far edge, and wondered at the pleasure of letting his body float in the warm water, his skin glistening with a combination of cleanliness, scented oil and the golden hue of the place. And then he started to remember. Remembered other worlds when he had bathed, sometimes as a woman, sometimes not. In one memory, possibly his earliest memory, he seemed to remember a large bathing pool filled with crystals. He remembered how it felt to absorb their pulsing energy when you lay in that crystal clear water, how you rose from the bath feeling alive and alert in a way he couldn't remember feeling since.

Lost in such thoughts, it took Geoffrey a moment to realise he was being watched. His eyes opened reluctantly to see another priest standing at the edge of the pool, staring down at him, smiling. Geoffrey could tell instantly that this man was held in respect. He wore the same white of the others, but he exuded a peaceful confidence which spoke to a subtle power and a certainty about self.

"Welcome, Geoffrey," he said, smiling broadly. "Sadly, we have no such crystals here. Perhaps you would prefer if I called you Cas?"

Geoffrey was staggered. "No, no thank you, Geoffrey is fine." Then after a moment, he said, "You speak English?"

Is that what we are speaking, Geoffrey? The voice Geoffrey was hearing, and he realised, belatedly, his own responses, were all in his mind. But before he could do anything other than stare in surprise, two other priests were ushering him from the bath and into a clean robe. It was obvious he was meant to follow the high priest, as he could only be, who was already walking away. He was hurrying down a golden-lit corridor after him, when he realised he had never even given Anas a backward glance.

The high priest had sat Geoffrey down opposite him in his chamber, both on low-cushioned seats with curved backs made entirely out of gold. Servants brought food and wine, which Geoffrey tucked into hungrily, before leaving them to talk in peace.

"I am told you remember Atlantis," the high priest said by way of opening gambit, his bright green eyes watching Geoffrey keenly.

"Yes. I remember a time I believe is what we call Atlantis." Geoffrey, normally wary about revealing too much of his unique memories, especially to strangers, couldn't help but trust this man. "Did Anas tell you?"

The man smiled. "In some ways, but I have other ways of knowing things too." He sipped his wine. "Will you tell me what you can remember of that time?" he asked Geoffrey, his voice wistful and filled with reverence.

"I can try… Sometimes I don't remember very much but then something will remind me."

"Like the bath?"

"Yes. You might need to ask me questions."

The high priest considered this for a moment or two. "What if there was another way?"

"How?" Geoffrey asked.

"If you allowed me, I could place my hands on your head and read your memories. I understand it is a very intimate act, but I hope you sense you can trust me."

Now it was Geoffrey's turn to pause, and for some reason, before answering, he asked, "Where's Anas?"

The high priest smiled sadly. "I am afraid he has left the temple. He knew this was not the time for him to be here."

Geoffrey felt a swell of panic. "But Anas is Max... He was in Atlantis too... I need him with me." He knew he sounded like a petulant child, but he couldn't help it.

"I am sorry, Geoffrey, it was Anas' choice. He, too, is wise and he listened to his own inner voice. He knew that it was important for you to be here without him. We will look after you, Geoffrey, have no fear."

Looking into those soft green eyes filled with love, Geoffrey didn't doubt him for a second and gestured to show he was willing to let him read his memories.

Sometime later the next morning, Geoffrey woke in a large bed in which he was naked except for a light cotton sheet. Thin white curtains billowed at a tall window as sunlight streamed in, bathing Geoffrey in a warmth that reminded him of days in his early childhood when he would nestle against the back of the baker's oven to keep the freezing cold at bay in winter. He was glad he was alone. He needed to understand what had happened during the night. The high priest sifting through his memories of Atlantis in a way that brought them back to Geoffrey as if he was living them all over again. And yet, just when he could remember every second with Max, and their life together in what seemed like a magical world, he had lost Anas. Perhaps forever, or rather, for the rest of this life, Geoffrey simply didn't know. It seemed he was meant to be here and he felt that in his bones in the same way that he knew not to be scared as he would come to no harm in the temple.

But, while Geoffrey was intrigued by the temple and keen to remind himself of wisdom he knew he had known before, he couldn't help but feel as if he had somehow lost his freedom. As if greater powers had stepped in and taken control of his life. He knew the best response was to 'let go and let God', as the master was always so fond of saying, to follow where he was being led and trust it was for his highest good. But in this life, Geoffrey was still just a young man bursting with life and curiosity and he was desperate to go his own way, for a while, at least.

It wasn't long, though, before he knew it simply wasn't an option for him just now. Servants brought him food and the part of Geoffrey who was still the little boy begging for scraps couldn't quite believe that he was being served so. Then, once he had been dressed, the high priest came to see him.

Sitting on one of the low chairs embossed with gold, he watched Geoffrey as he paced around the room getting used to the sway of the white robes around his legs. After a moment, he spoke. "Geoffrey. I will not beat around the bush. I have come here this morning to ask you if you would like to ask to be initiated into our priesthood."

The high priest spoke on, telling Geoffrey it was not an easy path, but one that was full of wonders and one, he had known long before he had read his memories, Geoffrey was born to, but Geoffrey did not hear because he knew with a diamond-like clarity that his answer was yes.

Five years later, Geoffrey was alone in the desert, sitting crossed legged on a sand dune watching the stars dance in their inky home. He didn't know how long he had been there, but it was one of his favourite things to do. He felt as if he travelled out amongst them, followed their light beams through time and space, universes and dimensions, returning to his body feeling oddly invigorated and filled with wonder. It was during these astral journeys that he remembered more about his lives than he had done ever before and even began to wonder if there might have been other incarnations beyond the fringe of their known universe.

He felt he learned more in these night-time sessions than he had in the temple, where even their most secret knowledge was a little like a child re-reading a favourite story to Geoffrey. He knew it for the truth, but he knew it was only part of the story and that the missing pieces were even more wondrous. Not that he hadn't enjoyed his time at the temple. He had. He was respected and treated as an equal to all. He enjoyed a good life, even when initiations, ceremony and ritual called for abstinence, fasting and privations of the harshest sort.

One of the hardest for Geoffrey was when he spent many days locked naked in the pitch-black labyrinth of tombs and tunnels below the temple with nothing but his instincts to lead him to safety. His eyes had never grown accustomed to the complete absence of light and when it seemed to crowd in on him, suffocate him, even, he was surprised to find it was the dungeon he had been condemned to by Anas back in Oxford that he remembered. And yet, in time, his instincts could tell when an animal approached in the blackness. The cockroaches and snakes, the beetles and lizards. He grew capable of sensing an opening, a turn in the corridors, by the slightest change in the air or the merest trace of scent, the dust of old bones no longer there or the long-burnt incense of a burial service many thousands of years before. Or was it the atmosphere he sensed? Was it the remnant of old memories that he was really tapping into? He had emerged truly feeling as if he had survived the hardest of initiations, feeling reborn as he was meant to do, after just seven days, only to discover nobody had ever come out alive before.

Life in the temple could also be sweet. The priests understood the power of sex and Geoffrey was happy to take part in rituals where he made love to the priestesses of Isis. A joining of equals, the bringing together of the divine masculine and feminine in an ancient and sacred act, much like the one he was meant to participate in so many years ago on top of a British tor before Sienna stepped in with her knife. Indeed, Geoffrey relished many aspects of life at the temple, but now he knew change was coming. He didn't know what form it would take but he knew it was fast approaching, just like the servant running across the dunes towards him.

"Adom! Adom!" he called, using the name he had been given. It meant 'one who received help from the Gods'. "Sire, you have a visitor. It is urgent, you must come quick."

"Max." Geoffrey knew in a heartbeat and had risen to his feet even before the next, racing back down towards the temple with his priestly dignity left to the wind.

Anas was standing in the central courtyard, his fist clenched around a goblet. He had aged well beyond his years, with deep lines and a dusting of grey at his temples to testify, as well as a greyness to his pallor, but his sparkling eyes remained the same.

"Geoffrey." His smile was warm despite the news he obviously had to break. "You must come, the master is dying."

They made good time, first by boat to the south coast of France and then on horseback, barely pausing to sleep and eat, it seemed, as they almost flew through the enticing lavender-filled meadows. They arrived in Oxford just short of a month after they left and Geoffrey never even paused to remove his riding gloves before he was by the master's bed.

The old man's face crinkled at the sight of him. "My dear boy, you are a sight for sore eyes." His voice was weak, rasping. "I have been holding on to see you, I knew you would make it." He reached a papery hand to touch Geoffrey's sun-kissed cheek, raising his head a fraction as he did so. "You look like a lord from a far-off land." He smiled, then coughed a little. "I know, though, you are a priest now, though, if truth be told, Geoffrey, you always were." He let his head fall back into the pillow and closed his eyes. "Tell me, Geoffrey my son, tell me all you can of your adventures. I think that's just what I need to hear to carry me away to meet my maker."

And Geoffrey did. He sat crouched by the bed, the old man's hand in his, still enclosed in the dust of the journey, and told the master, the man who had saved him, all about the wonders and miracles of the Egyptian temple, watching as all tension eased from his tired face. Finally, the last breath fluttered, with his soul, Geoffrey couldn't help thinking, from his lips. A kiss to the cold forehead was all he could muster as tears took hold. Geoffrey, more than anyone, knew it wasn't the end, but the master had perhaps been the closest he had had to a true parent in all the lives he had lived so far, with the exception of the first.

Grief overwhelmed Geoffrey for a week or more, but as the master began to visit him in his dreams, once more looking hale, hearty and full of mischief, Geoffrey felt more at peace.

One morning, he sat looking around the master's study, wondering what he was to do with all the old professor's worldly possessions when he noticed Anas properly for the first time since he had torn him away from Egypt with his sad tidings.

"Anas?" he asked. "Are you well?"

The older man looked up, ready, it seemed, to shrug off Geoffrey's concern but when their eyes met, something gave in Anas, his shoulders slumped and he ran weary hands over his pale face. "I am sick, Geoffrey."

Geoffrey took a second to let the news sink in before a rush of emotion swept through him. How had he been so remiss? How had he missed it? How had he let Anas struggle on supporting him in his grief while all the while he was sick himself.

"Oh, Anas! What ails you?" Geoffrey rushed to his friend's side, looking intently into his gentle, sparkling eyes. Eyes which were, for a moment, Max's rather than Anas'.

He smiled weakly. "Something I will not recover from, Geoffrey."

"What do you mean?" Geoffrey felt panic rise inside him. "No, Anas, that can't be true, you are still a young enough man, there must be something we can do. I learnt things in the temple and we could visit Old Marjory, she has herbs for everything…" Anas held up his hand, his other reaching around his ribs in a gesture Geoffrey belatedly realised had become second nature to his friend.

"Geoffrey, please, I know you mean well but it is no good. I have been to see everyone I can think of and I have accepted that my time is limited."

For a long moment, Geoffrey never moved or uttered a word, a million emotions caught in his throat. Finally, he reached forward and laid his hand over Anas'. "Sorry, I was thinking more of myself than you, Anas. I know better than anyone that death is not the end, but I always hate losing you."

Anas smiled again, still weak. "I would ask a favour of you, Geoffrey."

"Anything." Geoffrey's eyes were damp.

"I don't think I have more than a few weeks left, months at best, I would like to spend them here, in the master's rooms, with you, if possible?"

"Of course," Geoffrey answered. "I will arrange it all."

Geoffrey was as good as his word. He arranged with the university for them to keep the master's rooms for as long as was needed. As autumn settled in around them, they both settled into a hermetical routine. Using funds left to him by the master — enough to keep him for the rest of his life — he paid for Mistress Alban, the master's housekeeper, to come in once a day to clean for them and to leave them food for the day.

She normally arrived not long after dawn, carrying a large tray covered with a white cloth hiding eggs, bread, cheese, apples and some kind of soup and stew in a clay pot. She would put a kettle over the fire to heat for tea while Geoffrey got up and dressed, then set to sweeping and clearing while he made tea and took a steaming beaker to Anas as he lay in bed. The world seemed to shrink to just the two of them. Outside, the smoky autumn days drew a mist around the master's tower, keeping them safe and cosy inside.

While Anas was still well enough, they would spend some of the day making an inventory of all the master's belongings, wondering what should become of each book, map or strange artifact, both men thinking hard about what the master would have wanted, where he felt they would do the most good. In the evenings, they would lounge beside the fire, watching the flames and talking. Much of the talk was of their pasts, shared and otherwise, and Anas was keen to hear as much about Geoffrey's time in Egypt as he could, but as the nights grew longer, and darker, it seemed, and with Anas' health failing, many of their conversations turned to death.

"Can you remember the actual moment of death, Geoffrey?" he asked one night as the wind and rain pummelled the wooden shutters. Geoffrey let his mind wander into his many lifetimes before answering.

"I remember the moment of death in each life very clearly. It differs depending on how you die. When it is sudden and violent, it is true that a thousand thoughts seem to flash through your mind in that instance. Sweet memories, loves, losses, regrets, long forgotten images. When you are old, though, or sick, it is more of a gradual process. You can sense it coming and the process of sorting through your memories of this life happens more gently over days or weeks, even."

Anas sighed and shifted slightly in his chair, his sickness making it uncomfortable for him to sit in one position too long. Geoffrey heard the wheeze in his chest as he did so but knew not to offer help. He settled again and regained his breath. "I am at that stage now," he said, with as much acceptance as sadness in his voice, but before Geoffrey could say anything he continued. "What I really want to know is what do you remember of what happens next? After your soul has fled your body."

Geoffrey smiled. "I do have memories, but they are much harder to describe. It is more of a feeling than anything else. A lightness, an incredible expansion. It is like laughing at a delightful, joyous realization. There are so many... Beings... There, waiting to welcome you... Then, after that, my memories become much more indistinct." Anas noted the beatific expression on Geoffrey's face. "I can tell you this, Anas, I have never once feared death. I have regretted it coming so soon at times, and sometimes feared the method, but never feared death itself as I know there is nothing to fear."

Anas nodded in acknowledgement but spent the remainder of the evening lost in the flames of his own thoughts and memories.

As autumn gave way to winter, Anas's body gave way too and he was soon too poorly to get out of bed. Geoffrey was content to care for him with the love that filled his heart, reading to him now at night rather than trying to engage his exhausted friend in conversation. Finally, as midwinter approached, Anas was no longer able to speak and refused what little food and water he had been taking and Geoffrey knew it wouldn't be long. He sat for three full nights next to his friend's bed, holding his hand, reading to him or sometimes just passing comment, knowing with his priest-honed instinct that he could still hear him. His breathing was growing harder when he opened his eyes for one last time.

"Geoffrey." His voice was no more than a whisper, Geoffrey crouched beside his bed, clutching his hand, the exact position in which he had said goodbye to the master not so many months before. "My life is flashing by just as you said… I know I don't have long…" He breathed deeply, garnering whatever strength he could for what he wanted to say. "I only have two regrets… Having you sent to prison… And never telling you that I loved you, Geoffrey. I hope when we meet again, I can remember you as Geoffrey the way you remember me in all my guises. Hataa naltaqi mujadadaan, my friend. Until we meet again."

Death was not the end, Geoffrey knew. He also knew Anas was free from pain and happy beyond any Earthly possibility now, but he still sobbed the rest of the night.

It took him many more months of hiding out in the master's old tower, mourning the two most important people in this life, until he felt ready to emerge once more. It was springtime and as he wandered out into the world brimming with life, he felt as if he had once again been reborn, or possibly as if he had escaped after many months in a dark dungeon. For many more weeks, he simply walked the country around Oxford, enjoying the sight of newly budding leaves, hedgerows bustling with life and the smell of a new beginning in the air.

Then, one day, it dawned on him that he must go and a week later he left with all that he could carry on a horse, not to return to the master's tower for another forty years, when, this time, he was there to face his own death. Something he did so with a relish that those who met him at that time could never understand. He told the porter at the gate that he had come home to die with a cheery smile. He found a replacement for Mistress Alban and told her with unbridled gaiety that he would pay her handsomely given he wouldn't need her services long as he was happily dying. And so it was, he once more settled back into the tower after forty years of travelling the country, learning and experiencing, trusting the universe to provide and always gaining a reputation as a wise man and even healer, to die. He donated and gave away his belongings and distributed his wealth with joyous delight and lived with no more than a fire and a comfortable bed for company. He needed no more and so it was he spent his final days happily lost in memories until one bright, sunny evening, he took one last deep breath in and with one word gave his last out, a sound that sounded for all the world like a sigh of contentment. Max.

Chapter 10

Jack looked down at Aurora as she slept, noting the strange, dreamy smile of contentment and knew she was reliving another time, another life. He could tell when it happened now and had heard that name more than once, yet Aurora never mentioned it to him. Still, Jack was more worried about the man she told him she kept seeing, someone else from another time, but unlike the mysterious Max, this man posed a very real threat.

Unable to sleep, he manoeuvred himself from beneath Aurora's outflung arm to get himself a glass of water. Without thinking, he wandered into the living room of Aurora's flat, or, rather, their flat, he corrected himself. Or at least their home for the moment. Moonlight cut across the floor, reflecting brightly on the highly polished wood, like a long pale finger beckoning Jack to follow. And follow he did until he found himself looking down onto the street below, taking in the cars parked as brightly lit in the moonlight as if it were day. The figure standing, leaning against the wall, across the road waited just long enough for Jack to catch sight of him before vanishing into the trees and bushes at his back. With an innate knowing that he later wryly attributed to spending too much time with Aurora, he knew that was the man that Aurora had seen. He also knew he had somehow been waiting for Jack to see him. An urge overwhelmed him to run down into the street and chase after the shadowy figure, but he knew it was pointless as the mysterious man would be long gone by the time he arrived in the moonlight.

He spent the rest of the night sitting in the armchair, brooding and by the time Aurora came yawningly through looking for him, he had decided that he would find the man and confront him no matter what it took. A little bit of the warrior Sloan was still in there after all. He also decided not to tell Aurora about his midnight encounter — she would only worry.

"So, two weeks in Egypt, are we agreed?" Jack was on his laptop a finger hovering over the enter button.

Aurora, snuggled beneath a blanket next to him, cup of tea in hands, smiled. "Go for it!"

"Done!" Jack's returning grin was ecstatic. "In three weeks', time, we fly to Karnak."

"Can't wait! Did I tell you I had a dream when I remembered that I had visited Egypt before? I lived in Oxford but I spent a few years there training as a priest."

Jack smiled. "Why does none of that surprise me?" He thought that that was probably the dream she had the night he saw the man in the street a few days ago. He had kept his eyes open ever since but hadn't seen hide nor hair of him. "By the way," he asked, trying to sound casual, "have you seen that man again? The one you confronted in the café?"

"No." Aurora didn't sound like she thought it was odd for him to ask. "I have been thinking, though, it might be a good idea for me to undergo some kind of regression like I do with my clients and see if I can work out why he is here."

"Who would do that for you?" Jack asked, his face concerned.

"Actually, I was thinking Felicity could do it, she has some training. But I think I would like you to be there too." Aurora watched him closely.

"Me? I know nothing about that kind of thing!"

"Oh, I think you have a bit of a natural instinct for that kind of thing, actually, but I think I would just feel safer knowing you were there." Aurora heard herself sounding like a scared little girl.

Jack sat in silence, wondering why he felt uneasy about the whole notion, but finally he agreed. "OK, then, let's do it. I think we should find out all we can. Before we go to Egypt or when we come back?"

Aurora mulled for a moment. "Before we go, then maybe we will have some answers and be able to relax more."

"OK, arrange it with Felicity." Jack pulled her close for a cuddle but Aurora sensed his unease.

A week later, the three of them were gathered in the front room of Aurora's flat. Jack had met Felicity briefly a few times before and liked her, but tonight her cheerfulness irked him. Unreasonable as he knew it was, it was just his own worry clouding his normally tolerant nature.

"So," Felicity enthused, teacup swaying dangerously about in her dancing hands, "this is exciting! The tables are turned! We are to find out a bit about Aurora's past lives! I can't believe you have never been tempted before, Aurora, given what you do for a living." Aurora had warned Jack she had told Felicity very little. She had rarely told anyone more than a very little these last few hundred years, that was until she met Jack. "You never know, maybe you too have been lovers before, eh?"

"Actually, Felicity, I am interested in finding out more about someone I dreamt about."

"Ooh! Even more interesting. Who is this then?" Her excited eyes flashed from Aurora to a morose Jack and back again.

Aurora swallowed. "A man with icy blue eyes. I have dreamt of him a few times and I think he might have done something horrible."

"A historical baddie. OK then, let's track him down!" The sheen had been taken off her enthusiasm, though, as she finally sensed there might be more going on here than she had realized.

All three of them were silent as preparations were made. Aurora lit candles while Felicity blew incense into life. Jack simply sat in the armchair, leaning forward pensively, hands clasped and forearms resting on the top of his thighs.

"OK, then. I think we are ready," Aurora announced, her voice trembling slightly with trepidation. "Strange to be in the hot seat, so to speak," she added, smiling weakly as she made herself comfortable in the reclining chair where her clients normally sat.

"Blanket?" Felicity asked, her demeanour much more serious now. "I know the fire is lit but you can get really cold when you go under."

"Thank you," Aurora answered with a weak smile. "Let's do it."

A few moments later, Aurora was breathing heavily and the temperature in the room seemed to have dropped. Jack never took his eyes from her face.

"OK, Aurora." Felicity's voice carried a cultivated calm. "Keep breathing as you travel backwards in time. Back to the moment of your birth and into the darkness beyond. That warm comforting darkness. Can you feel it, Aurora? What does it feel like?"

"It is warm, dark, but also light... I am part of the light but also me..."

"That's good, Aurora, just relax and enjoy that feeling." Felicity paused for a moment. "I want you to find another time now, another incarnation. The time when you knew the man with the cold, pale eyes."

Aurora shifted uncomfortably beneath the blanket, a brow creasing her forehead. Jack instinctively started to rise from his chair, but Felicity raised a hand to stop him.

"Aurora... tell me where you are." Her head was rocking gently side to side now, her lips making indiscernible sounds. "Aurora? Can you tell us what you can see?"

"It's dark... Very dark... I can hear footsteps... He is coming..."

Isabella

Isabella held her breath. Maybe, just maybe, the footsteps would keep going, echoing along the corridor and find mischief elsewhere. She couldn't remember hiding from him here before, he might not think of looking for her here, not in a linen trunk. Not in the wooden depths beneath the folds of heavy tablecloths used only on special occasions. Would he? The echoing, angry steps had stopped to be replaced by a heavy silence. Isabella swallowed her breath and fear, silent tears on her cheeks. Why did this life have to be like this? With him, of all people.

She had felt herself quite blessed when she had been born this time into a prosperous family, not nobility but wealthy and content in their rambling red brick farmhouse with a large hall and acres of orchards and woodlands. An only child, Isabella's childhood had been happy, nonetheless. Summer days spent running barefoot between the apple-laden trees, her beloved dogs at her heels, autumn collecting those same apples and taking them to cook in the kitchen where she would sit sipping last year's warmed cider while watching as the cheerful old woman transformed those apples into pies and sauces, cakes and tinctures. Winter by the fire in the great hall listening to her father read from one of his many books. In spring she would ride out over her father's lands, marvelling at the world coming back to life again after the cold, stillness of winter. It was a home filled with love and laughter, with an open door and visitors aplenty. Her memories of past lives haunted her less and even while she felt curious about when she would meet Max in this life, she never felt concern about his absence.

So, when her mother told her Sir Richard Lacy was to be their guest for dinner she only smiled pleasantly. At fourteen, she was excited as she had heard all about Sir Richard's good looks and skills as both a horse- and swordsman from her friends in the neighbourhood. It was only when she interrupted the chat of Sir Richard and her father to be introduced, dressed in her most becoming violet gown, that she realised she already knew Sir Richard. She felt as if she had been dipped in an ice bath as she curtsied and offered him her hand, as manners dictated she must. Her inability to look into those cold, pale eyes was taken for maidenly modesty and when she did manage to hold his malicious gaze, the glitter of greed and power she saw there made her shiver to her bones.

From that moment, she knew this life was to change forever. Her parents thought she was shy and nervous at the thought of becoming a bride, but she was simply numb with horror as her parents set out their intentions then planned for the nuptials without requiring any real input from Isabella. As they sat side by side at their bridal feast, Isabella could sense the potency rise in the man who was now her husband. He was filled with lust and hunger, desire and machismo. But there was something else too, Isabella knew, because she had seen it before as he murdered her children before her. The hate, the misogyny, the power.

And she was right. The violence overspilled before they had even consummated the marriage. The moment they were alone, he had her pinned to the wall with a hand round her throat. Her attempts to fight back were met with cruel yet delighted laughter. Her mettle only aroused his passion and desire to hurt. And so began their marriage. Isabella prayed for the spells when her husband would be called away to fight or travel on the king's duty, as only then could she breathe, sleep, rest. Those were blissful days of tending her kitchen gardens and learning to make tinctures and medicines from Sir Richard's housekeeper. She was a kindly and wise woman in her fifties who did everything she could to protect and educate Isabella, even though they both knew that when the rider came to announce the lord's return, there was precious little to be done except rub salve on the bruises and pretend, in Sir Richard's presence, that there was nothing amiss, or they would all suffer.

As Isabella hid in the trunk, she knew she wouldn't be saved by a servant happening along the corridor or a maid cleaning the floorboards. The moment they knew the lord had returned, they would all ensure they were as far away from him as possible, leaving their unfortunate mistress to her fate. Not out of unkindness, but out of the need to ensure their own survival.

Isabella felt like she was about to burst when she heard the creak of hinges. Instinct told her he was in a particularly foul mood, confirmed just moments later when his hand grabbed her by the hair at the back of her head. She was viciously pulled from the trunk and dropped on the floor, unable to right herself before the backhand knocked her the length of the corridor.

It was only when she could focus once more that she realized he held his riding crop. The blows came thick and fast, the pain overwhelming as the whip cut through the cloth of her gown and tore her flesh. Isabella tried to protect herself, holding a chair between her and her husband, only to find it shattered by an angry kick. Backing away as best she could, she gasped in relief to have made it to the door, only to find it locked. It was then the red mist descended. Isabella roared like a lion as she found her feet, ignoring the whip coming down upon her shoulders and head. In one deft move, she ran at her husband, catching his torso as he exposed his body with an arm held high to inflict another blow. With another guttural snarl and with a show of strength that came from she knew not where, she pushed him backwards out of the window. As she looked down on the awkwardly lying body below, she hoped he was dead.

He wasn't. But he was broken beyond all repair. He could no longer walk or look after his own basic needs. Nor could he talk beyond moans and grunts. Sometimes he would look and point at Isabella, turning puce with the effort of trying to form his grunts into accusatory words, but Isabella simply looked coolly back, and the servants blandly ignored him. They all guessed what must have happened — it didn't take much when they saw their young mistress cut to ribbons — but without any discussion, they all simply decided that their lord had fallen and was now a poor cripple.

Isabella found herself leading the life of a caring wife tending for her terribly injured husband. Spooning pottage into his mouth. Wiping the drool from his chin. Always wondering if she would ever feel guilt or sympathy. She had been numb since the day she had set eyes on him in her childhood home. And then, one cold winter's day about three years after the day 'of the terrible accident', as it was called, a servant told her she had a visitor.

"Aurora, sweetie, Aurora, are you OK?"

"Yes." Her hand sought Jack's face. "Yes, I am OK." Aurora sat up gingerly, aware of two sets of eyes watching her closely. "It's OK, both of you, I really am OK."

"Are you sure?" Felicity was clearly concerned. "That was quite… Intense."

"It was, I know, but it is the past and it helps me understand."

"He hurt you." Jack's taut jaw betrayed the intensity of his emotion.

Aurora reached out to take his hand. "Yes, he did, but that was hundreds of years ago. I didn't even remember anything about it before just now."

"He was vicious." Jack's voice wavered. "Brutal. He could still be capable of the same now, Aurora. He's dangerous."

"Jack's right, Aurs," Felicity added.

"I know, it is true. But it might be he is acting out without really understanding why he is doing what he is doing. He probably doesn't remember; just knows he is angry and that for some reason his anger is directed at me."

What she didn't say was that she didn't need to stay regressed to remember what else happened in that incarnation. The hypnosis had been enough to open the floodgates and she could now recall what happened later as if she was remembering a night out a few weeks ago.

The visitor that day was Max. Or rather, in that lifetime, it was Richard's brother, Ralf. He had been in the Holy Land for the last few years and Isabella had never met him, otherwise she would have known, as she did, the second he walked into the bedchamber where she was feeding her husband as if in a daze, who he was. Or had been.

He had been filled with horror at the sight of his brother, but he quickly let Isabella understand that he knew what his brother was like. He had heard the story of how he had beat her and had suffered at his hands himself in their childhood.

150

In time, they became close and somehow Richard understood what was happening. When the two of them were together, he would try in vain to raise himself from his pillows, to speak, to call them out as his face turned a dangerous shade of red and the spittle gathered in the corners of his mouth, only to collapse in impotent frustration back into his pillows with an anguished moan. It was as they lay together in the early hours of the morning that they came up with a plan. Discussed it in hushed whispers, even though the household slept around them.

It took many weeks, and for Isabella, much anguish, despite it all, but she knew it was the only way. At times, she would remember other lives, especially Atlantis, and know that what they planned would be looked on as a fall from the love and light by which they lived, and she knew the balance would be redressed in other lives to come, but none of that mattered. In her state of numbness, she could only think of the peace that would come of being rid of Richard and being able to live the rest of her life quietly with Max, or, rather, Ralf.

In the end, it was all too easy. They concocted a poison and between them fed it to Richard in small doses over months, so his body gradually gave way and his demise seemed nothing other than inevitable. A result of injuries sustained in the fall. And when he passed, Isabella did sigh with relief, and for many years she did live peaceably and happily with Max — Ralf — but as she grew older, she was filled with a sense of dread. She would wake in the night having dreamt of Richard stalking her through lifetime after lifetime, making her watch once more as he killed her children, sneer at her as she dared to imagine he wanted more than his leg over, and in some time, in a strange time and place, making her suffer more than she had ever suffered before. Aurora knew without a shadow of a doubt that the man lurking in the shadows was Richard — Lord Jonas — and she knew his distorted sense of justice meant danger for her and Jack.

She was quiet and withdrawn after Felicity left. Jack watched her with worried eyes, but with a keen instinct for what she needed, he let her have her space.

It was only when they were lying in bed that night, a shaft of moonlight breaking through the curtains the only light, that she told him the rest of the story. Almost inevitably, for reasons she still couldn't quite understand, she still left out Max.

"I killed him," she announced to the dark, certain Jack wasn't asleep.

"Sorry?" His voice was clear if bemused. "Who?"

"I killed Richard. In that life, after... I now remember what happened after we stopped the regression. I killed him."

Jack took a moment to digest that news. "I can't say I blame you. Can you not remember killing people before? Given what you have told me, I must have killed many as Sloan."

"Yes, I have, but this was premeditated. In the time I knew you as Sloan you only killed in battle. Did what you had to do under extreme circumstances. I slowly poisoned Richard quite deliberately over months as I was supposedly nursing him."

Jack tightened his arms around her, burying his lips in the hair on top of her head. "Aurora... I can't judge you for that. He beat you. He was brutal. You would have been traumatized."

Aurora sighed. "Perhaps, but you would have thought, me of all people, would have known better. Him being here now, a possible threat to both of us, is because I killed him then."

Jack held her tightly. "And if that's the way it works, why am I not being slain on a daily basis by all the people I killed as Sloan?"

Aurora couldn't help smile a little at his tone. "It's not usually quite as literal as that, and besides, perhaps you have been bumped off repeatedly in all the lives you have led between then and now."

"OK, so maybe your killing of Richard was karma balancing for when he had wronged you before?"

The thought lifted the weight on Aurora's heart a little. "That could be true," she admitted. And then, twisting herself round so she was face to face with Jack, she said, "You know I am tired of thinking about the past. Let's think about now... And then make plans for our holiday!" And with that, she kissed him with the same delicious passion she remembered from all those years ago, all the while unaware that outside in the dark, their window was being watched.

Chapter 11

Aurora had her entire wardrobe laid out on her bed. The sight gave her a thrill. It wasn't so much the thought of going on holiday, but the normality of it all. She was undoubtedly looking forward to being on holiday with Jack for two full weeks. Two weeks of sun, fun and laughter in the here and now. Two weeks of not remembering or wondering about the shadow from the past that lurked behind every lamp post. Jack — an experienced traveller — had packed his one modest rucksack and was currently making breakfast as he tolerantly waited for her last-minute addition of a second suitcase. Folding a few more dresses into the second case, she zipped it closed with a satisfied flourish and walked through to find the cup of the coffee she could smell brewing.

Jack looked up from the cooker and smiled the smile that still made her stomach flip even after all these months. Serious eyes crinkling round the edges, his mouth wide and inviting amidst just enough stubble to be sexy, in Aurora's opinion.

"Is that you, then?" he asked, still smiling.

"Yes! Remember, this is my first proper holiday."

"How can I forget?" He nudged scrambled eggs on top of sourdough toast. "Grab yourself a fork, the taxi will be here in twenty mins."

About seven hours later, the plane was coming into land. Aurora had been watching out the window in wonder as the plane flew low over Karnak, happily contemplating the next two weeks. A short taxi ride through the intense heat and they were unloading their luggage into the welcome air-conditioned reception of a five-star hotel.

"You never told me it was so nice!" Aurora cried in delight as she took in the white marble flooring and the sumptuous fountain in the middle of the foyer.

Jack grinned in response. "I wanted it to be a surprise!"

"It is, it's amazing."

"Well, what would you like to do first? Swim? Eat? Drink? Take a trip to the spa? Or just collapse in a couple of sun loungers and sleep away what's left of the day?"

Aurora laughed. "Oh, can we do that please? I can't remember the last time I was so lazy!"

"Long overdue, then, in my opinion!"

The next few days were spent indulging their laziness. They lay next to the sea, read books by the pool, sipped cocktails on their balcony and sometimes, when the heat was simply a bit too hot, even just lay naked on top of their bed. Their idleness was punctuated only by the occasional swim, a trip to the bar and lovemaking.

Finally, four days in, Aurora started reading a guidebook and decided some exploring was in order. "How do you feel about a trip out of the hotel tomorrow?"

"Must we?" Jack asked from his prone position, but Aurora knew he was ready.

"Yes. We are only a few miles from Karnak, we have to go and see it."

"OK, then, you win, but the day after we go back to doing nothing but having sex and sunbathing."

"Deal."

The next morning, they rose with the sun and Aurora felt her spirits soar in the hazy redness of the early morning. Already warm, there was a light breeze which carried a sense of anticipation for the day ahead.

"It's a special place, is it not?" Jack asked as he came to stand beside her on their balcony.

"It really is. I know I have visited Egypt before, but I actually feel like I am seeing it all anew, for the first time, almost."

"I am glad." Jack smiled down at her. "You are making history, rather than remembering it, today!"

Aurora felt a quiver of excitement. She knew today was going to be special.

The hotel provided a light breakfast of fruit, pastries and coffee on the terrace while their jeep arrived at the entrance. In less than an hour, they were parking near the temple complex. Aurora could barely contain her excitement as she clasped Jack's hand, following behind their guide

154

as he led them to the top of a mound. By now, the sun was reclaiming his power from the night and the heat was already dancing along the surface of the sand. Aurora was glad of the light scarf wrapped round her head and neck and couldn't help but feel a flurry of excitement at the sight of Jack in his own Lawrence of Arabia-style keffiyeh. But all thoughts were swept from her mind when they reached the summit of the small mound and saw the view of the ancient temple complex laid out before them blushing red in the early sun. She actually gasped.

"It's extraordinary." Jack's voice was filled with awe as he let his eyes sweep over the vast array of ruins.

"It's powerful," Aurora responded. "Can you feel the energy?"

Jack couldn't quite suppress a slightly sardonic twitch of an eyebrow, but after a moment, he nodded earnestly. "Yes… Yes, I do feel it. It's ancient, but it's like the air thrums." A few seconds later he grabbed her hand again. "Come on, let's go and explore!"

Cas

Cas was up early and enjoying watching the world come to life as she followed the foot-worn path through the emerald meadow where many and myriad wildflowers were just beginning to open their delicate petals to the morning sun. Her hound, Luna, loped by her side as she had done every day since she was a baby. Pausing only to tune into the joyous songs of the birds, absorbing the messages they carried from the universe and responding with an outpouring of love and gratitude from her heart. But it was only for a moment or two as she was on a mission to get to the temple for what was an important day. She had just turned thirteen years old and it was time she learnt more about her soul's purpose as an adult in Atlantis. As the shimmering pillars of the temple glinted in the morning sun, she felt a frisson of excitement and quickened her step, her distraction making it easy for Max to sneak up behind her and take his friend by surprise.

He laughed heartily as she squealed in fright, although he knew she wasn't really scared and her wide grin told him she was happy to see him as always. His dog, Solas, was already tumbling happily with Luna.

"Where are you going so early, Cassie?"

"The temple," she replied with just a little pride in her voice. "I have been called to find out about my soul's purpose."

Max's eyebrows raised in surprise but he was filled with happiness for his friend. "That's great, I haven't been called yet."

"You will be soon," Cas replied kindly.

They walked on amiably for a while, Max handing Cas a bright shiny red apple from the satchel he wore slung over his chest. "What do you hope to hear?" he asked her after a while.

Cas took another bite of her apple as she considered her answer. "I am trying not to have any expectations. I trust that everything is as it should be and that everything will work out perfectly."

"Yes, but... Is there not something you would really like to have in your future?"

Cas smiled. "Love and happiness!" she answered blithely. "However, they may come." She nudged him playfully. "What would you like to be part of your soul path?"

Cas was surprised to see him blush a little, then, without giving her an answer, he threw his apple core to the earth, throwing up a quick prayer of gratitude and called out his challenge, knowing well that Cas could never resist. "Race you to the temple!"

When they arrived, red faced and panting, the priestess was standing at the top of the steps waiting for them, smiling tolerantly. "It is a fine morning for a race," she said by way of greeting. "Max, why don't you go to the kitchen for some bread and honey. Cas, catch your breath as you follow me?"

A while later, Cas, much more composed and having regained a sense of calm, sat cross legged at the heart of the temple surrounded by lit candles and crystals of all shapes and sizes. Being this the temple of love, though, they were all delicately pink in colour. Except the crystal standing majestically before her, which was a glorious purple. Cas was already lost in its pulsating eminence, letting herself acclimatize to its energy before the real work would begin. The priestess, followed by six others, came to stand in a semi-circle behind her. Together they raised their arms to the heavens, visible through the roof high above.

"Powers that be, almighty source of love, light and all that is, we call upon you to be with us here today in this moment. We call upon this child's guardians and guides to surround her and through this crystal, this great gift of Lady Gaia, to reveal her soul path."

Together the priestesses raised their voices in a sonorous chant, a sound that Cas felt in her body in the same way as she felt the pulsing emanations from the crystal. In time they merged within her to carry her on a journey to tap into the knowledge of her soul. With her eyes closed, she sensed herself surrounded by swirling, translucent colours merging together to create the shapes of many beings of light. Cas felt as if she could lose herself in their light forever, all thoughts of her life in Atlantis forgotten. Eventually, one being stepped forward and smiled benignly at her then spoke. "I have lots to tell you."

A while later, Cas sat with the high priestess in her garden, surrounded by lush green leaves and delicately coloured flowers. Luna sat pressed close to her knees. She drank gratefully from a glass of pure crystal-clear water bubbling up from the ancient spring beside them. The priestess waited with eternal patience for the girl to speak, knowing that she needed a little time before she would be ready. It was only when her glass was empty that she spoke.

"They told me this incarnation would not last long." Cas's voice trembled a little as much as she tried to sound neutral and grown up.

The priestess smiled gently. "We have known for a while that we are approaching the end of this chapter, Cas. It is nothing to fear. You have just seen what lies beyond the veil and it is nothing but loving."

"I know, it is lovely, but I quite like being here, now, as Cas and..."

Again, the priestess smiled knowingly. "And with Max."

Cas looked at her with surprise, she hadn't been sure that's what she was going to say herself but the moment she heard the words from the priestess she knew them to be true.

"Yes, and Max." Cas frowned.

"It's not really all you were told, though, was it?"

"No... They said my soul purpose could be deemed a blessing or a curse and would follow me through incarnation after incarnation."

The priestess looked thoughtful. "We all bear karma, from lifetime to lifetime and as the vibration of the planet drops, the energetic fields will become denser, people will become more disconnected. They will forget so much and accrue more karma as they live to survive and gain without connection to all that is. Perhaps that's what they were referring to?"

"No, my guides were quite clear. They said I will have memories of all my lives, although I won't always be able to see the threads that move through them, only hints and suggestions. They said I will remember more clearly than anyone else and that I would need to learn to live with that, and one day, I will need to use all my memories for something important. They said it will be important many years in the future."

The priestess leant forward and laid her hand on Cas' arm. "That's a lot for young shoulders to understand."

Cas shrugged a little. "I understand that I will remember — a bit like we sometimes do anyway — but I am not sure what that means for me."

The priestess placed her hands on Cas' head. "I don't think you are meant to just now, Cas. My advice to you is to be in the moment as much as you can for what time we have left here. Love Max well and store up as much information and wisdom as you can for the future."

"That sounds wise." Cas grinned up at the beatific woman she had known and loved all her life. "Like you are a priestess or something!" Youthful exuberance replaced the disquiet of only moments before. "I think I will go and find Max and race him back to the village." Luna was off before Cas could raise herself from her seat.

"Aurora… Aurora… Where are you?" Aurora came to at the sound of Jack's voice to find herself leaning against the shaded side of one the giant stone monoliths. He was crouching down in front of her, his hands on her shoulders and his eyes filled with concern.

"I'm here… I'm back," Aurora said weakly, her tongue thick and her lips dry. Wordlessly, Jack passed her a water bottle. Aurora drank deeply then looked around. "What happened?"

"You said you felt a little funny and wanted to sit down for a while in the shade. You told me to go off and explore, but I was worried so came back after about fifteen minutes and you were in a sort of trance. Were you remembering?"

"Yes. But it was different this time. I know it is important but I am not sure how. Can we go back to the hotel and I can tell you all about it there?"

An hour or so later, showered and in clean clothes, Aurora and Jack sat on their balcony looking out over the sea, each picking at grapes and sipping cool tea. Aurora had told Jack everything that had happened, only, though, making passing reference to Max and never by name. Why, she was still not sure.

"You are telling me you remembered being in Atlantis?" Despite it all, Jack couldn't quite hide his incredulity. "I mean, everywhere else you have told me about has been a real, historical place."

"Actually, I have always known about Atlantis, remembered it, I have just never dreamed about it like this. I sometimes do have dreams at night where I remember what it was like... Everything seemed brighter, cleaner, fresher somehow... And I remember people from then really clearly... But I have never experienced anything like that. I feel like it was a message from the universe, to somehow explain everything that's been happening."

"Like the man who has been following you?"

"Yes that... And you."

"Me?" Jack seemed genuinely surprised.

"Yes... The way we met, my memories of you from before... It is all part of it. As I have told you before, I have loved people before and had relationships, but this is different, especially compared to my experiences of the last half dozen incarnations or so."

"Is it like everything that has ever happened to you is coming to some kind of head?"

"Yes," Aurora agreed. "Yes, that's exactly what it is like. But also like I have to pass some kind of test — a really important test — but at the moment I can't help but feel like I am missing something." Like Max, she thought silently. And yet, as she looked into Jack's eyes across the table, she found herself hoping perhaps for the first time in thousands of years that Max simply wouldn't appear this time round.

Aurora and Jack spent the rest of the holiday lazing in the sun, Aurora, on occasion, a little preoccupied as she tried to fathom what was happening to her. ... The memories coming back thick and fast and her increasingly strong feelings for Jack. The anonymous man who had been following her played on her mind too — was he dangerous? He had been in the past, she knew that well, but she also knew from her work in this life that he may be confused, hurt and desperate to heal now. Jack was kind and patient with her, allowing her time to think but also pulling her out of her reverie often enough that, by the time they boarded the plane home, they did so with the reluctance of anyone who has had a lovely holiday.

But a few days after landing, they had settled back into their, by now, comfortable routine of work and leisure, still happy to spend as much time together as possible.

Aurora was glad to find herself content just to live day-to-day once more and rather than brood on past lives memories, Max and her mystery man situation. That was until she went for a drink with Felicity.

It was a bright, sunny evening, warm and enchanting and they were sitting at a table outside the kind of pub that had been there for centuries looking over the Thames. Aurora felt a fleeting jolt of remembrance as she remembered that she had been to the pub about two hundred years before. The sounds, sights and smells of the raucous riverside tavern overwhelmed her for a second and then subsided as quickly as they came. By the time Felicity arrived, rushed and flustered, as usual, she was a picture of happy calm.

"Well, hello there!" Felicity gushed as she bent to kiss Aurora's cheek. "You certainly grabbed a top spot."

Aurora smiled. "I also took the liberty of ordering us a bottle of their finest chilled Sauvi."

"Excellent." Felicity grinned at her as Aurora dutifully poured her friend a glass. "Cheers," she said, tapping glasses. "So, you look well." Felicity's eyes danced with mischief.

"I am well, thank you. We had a lovely holiday and I'm still feeling the benefits of all that sun, sea, rest…"

"And sex. Yes, you don't need to finish that sentence — I know a happily satisfied woman when I see one."

"Are you jealous, Flick?"

"No! Yes… Well, not really, Daniel and I do just fine, thank you."

"I'm glad to hear it, how long is that now?"

"A few months, I mean we…"

Aurora had stopped listening. Leaning against the river wall, wearing jeans and a tight grey t-shirt, with legs crossed at the ankle, hands resting on the stone at either side of his hips, was Lord Jonas. Or whatever he was called in this life. His cold, icy eyes staring straight at Aurora.

Their eyes met, and try as she might, Aurora couldn't look away. Somewhere, her mind was aware that Felicity had stopped talking.

"Aur, what's wrong? Aur?" Felicity followed her glance to where Lord Jonas still sat, a smile now curling on his lip. "Is that him?" Her voice was a stage whisper, prompting the man who had been Lord Jonas to smile nastily before moving cat-like towards them.

"Yes, it is him." He spoke to Felicity, but with his eyes on Aurora. "Who am I then, Aurora?".

Fear tightened in her throat as images flashed unbidden through her mind of the man standing before her killing her and Max's children, then, later, in another life, laughing as she burnt. Words would not come.

He smiled again. "Not like you to be so reticent, Aurora, is it? Cat got your tongue?" Then, bending down, his lips came close to her ear, his voice sibilant. She could feel the moisture on his breath as he whispered, "I remember." Straightening up, he then turned and walked away without a backwards glance.

Jack was furious when she told him. "He did what?" His eyes blazed and suddenly it was as if Sloan the warrior stood before her, not Jack.

"He told me he remembered." Aurora was still shaken. "He must mean that he remembers those lives too. I can't think what else it could be."

Jack paced the floor of the flat. "But how did he know how to find you? Did he follow you?"

Aurora threw up her hands. "I don't know, Jack, I really don't. I didn't get any sense of being followed, but… It was a busy night. The sun was shining — everyone was out!"

"I know, I know!" Jack came over and put his hands on either side of her head. "Sorry, I don't mean to make it sound like I thought this was your fault, I'm just worried and I don't know what to do. I mean, I can't imagine we can go to the police." His face told her he knew what her answer would be before she said it.

"And tell them a man who has been nasty to me hundreds of years ago is stalking me through London again?"

161

Jack grimaced. "Maybe we don't need to tell them that part? Just that you are being followed?"

"Maybe. He was different this time, Jack."

"How d'you mean?"

"He was more like Lord Jonas than he was before... He was more confident, more cruel-looking... Before I always thought he was scared or at least shy. Now, though, it was as if Lord Jonas was there right before me."

"So, what do you want to do?"

Aurora shrugged and then melted into his arms, saying nothing for a blissful moment. "I really don't know."

Jack kissed her hair. "I don't think you should go out alone for the time being."

Aurora jerked back. "Oh, Jack, that's impossible."

"Well, have you got any other suggestions?"

They were both silent, but the next day, Jack came home with a dog. The large, imposing grey and brown mongrel fell in love with Aurora at first glance.

"He is a rescue," Jack told her as Aurora let the dog place his large head in her lap so she could scratch behind his ears. "I had heard about him last week when he had been rescued from a scrapyard where he was being used as a guard dog. The people didn't treat him very well, but like most dogs, show them a bit of love and they are putty in your hands. That said, he is trained and he would guard you with his life."

Aurora bent down to kiss the big dog's head. "What's his name?"

"They didn't give him one."

"What?" Aurora was aghast. "How could they not give him a name?"

Jack smiled sadly. "We can pick a good one for him."

Aurora looked into the dog's striking blue eyes and for a moment she thought of Lord Jonas, but dazzling as they were, the dog's eyes were filled with love and trust. The absolute opposite of Lord Jonas.

"I've missed having a dog," Aurora said, suddenly quite sad. "I haven't really thought about it until now but I have had lots of dogs. I had a dog when I knew you as Sloan, do you remember?"

Jack shook his head regretfully. "No."

"Maybe we should name him Sloan?" She smiled up at Jack. "You were courageous, valiant and loving as Sloan and that's what we need of this beautiful big ball of fur now. What do you think?"

"It's perfect." Jack smiled. "I'm glad you like him; I was worried you might freak out and tell us both to go!"

"Hardly! How could I? I love him and I love that he is a rescue."

"Good. I will certainly feel better about going out to work now I know you have Sloan here at your side."

Jack sat down on the sofa next to Aurora. A few minutes later, Sloan jumped up between them, wriggling his bottom to make room before settling down as if he had never known a different life.

Rosalind

Picking up her skirts, Rosalind ran as fast as she could through the London street, leaping nimbly out of the way of the crooked limbs of beggars lying on the filthy, hay-covered stones and ducking quickly away when privies were emptied above her head. People, dogs, cats and even rats got caught up in her mad chase, only slowing when a horse and cart got in her way. Needing to press on, she risked life and limb by diving beneath the cart's wheels, bare dirt-smeared legs flashing in the bright daylight and starting to run through the streets once more. She had to get to William as quickly as she could. She had a very important message to pass on. One that simply couldn't wait for carts or decorum. Finally, she arrived at the theatre doors, breathing hard and heavy, clutching at the jutting ribs on her side.

"William! William!" she called into the empty stalls, knowing he would be lurking somewhere. He loved to sit in the stalls and imagine his next play coming to life on the stage, sometimes scratching notes on the paper he carried with him and other times just losing himself watching the players in his own mind.

"Will! It is I! Rosalind!" Holding her skirts high above her knees, she ducked in and out of the benches, her eyes searching for her friend, the man who had always tried to help her. He even listened to what others called her mad ramblings, about other times and places. Rosalind knew they were her memories and she didn't care if people believed her, but it was nice that Will did. He tried to feed her and clothe her too, but Rosalind was too free a spirit to be held in one place too long. Even by the promise of three, square meals and a warm bed. Not that Will ever tried anything with her, he was too kind and caring to take advantage of a young girl. He really did just like to talk to her and wanted to help her stay warm and fed.

"Rosy! Rosy! I am here!" Will appeared from beneath the stage, shirt undone clutching sheaves of paper. Rosy could tell right away he was tired and looked every one of his forty-nine years. "Good God, girl, where have you been? You look like you haven't eaten for weeks."

Rosalind couldn't answer. "Will! Will! I have to tell you something!"

"What? What is it, child?"

"I have found Max!"

"Max, you say? You have found him?" Will knew who Max was and never for a moment considered brushing aside the girl's momentous news.

"Yes! Yes! He is a lad, one of the Baker Boy gang — can you believe it?"

"No and yes, Rosy. Come, let's go and get ourselves some food and you can tell me all about it."

Rosy let Will place a fatherly arm around her shoulders and lead her gently out of the theatre and towards his rooms.

They were fine apartments going by the beautiful dark rose polished wood on the floors and walls and the furniture spoke of a man of means, but when writing, Will lived in chaos. Clothes were strewn all over the floors, used crockery and wine glasses were piled high everywhere you looked, but more than anything, there were papers. Papers scrunched in balls on the floor, paper scattered across the bed, paper piled high and tied with ribbons.

Somehow, though, the man navigated his way through it all with ease, gesturing Rosalind to take a chair that he had cleared of debris and producing clean cups from a dresser and even a wooden board carrying fresh bread and cheese.

"Here, Rosy, you must eat." He handed her a slab of each. "Before you tell me a word about Max, I insist you eat all of that while I fetch ale. Then, my child, we can talk."

Rosalind dutifully ate, relishing the taste even while she tried to rush down the mouthfuls in her excitement to speak.

Will set a frothing tankard next to her to wash it down with and then, only once she had swallowed the last mouthful, did he let her talk.

"Well, now, tell me everything, child." He smiled fondly at her.

Rosalind took a deep breath. "It was last night. I have been helping out a pharmacist north of the river for a few weeks. I enjoy the work, learning about the herbs and things. He would let me sleep in his outhouse and he gave me some food each day."

"Not very much, by the looks of things."

"No, he wasn't a very nice man and liked keeping me hungry. He said it makes me keener to help."

"Rosy! You should have come to me!"

Rosalind ignored the plea. "Anyway, last night there was a huge fuss. I heard banging and raised voices so I crept to the back door to see what was happening. There were three men, one injured, and they were looking for the pharmacist's help, looking for something for his pain. One of the men who had carried him in was Max. I know it."

Will smiled. "I am pleased for you, my child, I know how much finding him meant to you. Did he recognize you?"

"No." Rosy shook her head sadly. "He doesn't usually anyway."

There was a comfortable silence as they both got lost in their own thoughts.

"Rosy," Will said finally, "you said he was a member of the Baker Boy gang; how do you know?"

"Why, they were wearing those red kerchiefs tied round their arms. Do you not know that's how you know someone's gang, Will?" Rosalind loved to tease the old playwright.

He smiled tolerantly. "No, my child, I am not as *au fait* with the ways of the street as you are. Do you know how the lad came to be injured?"

Rosalind looked away a little discomfited. "They had been fighting."

"And?" Will asked, looking directly at the young woman.

"He had been run through by a sword."

"And the other man?" Will asked pointedly.

"I am not sure…" Rosalind looked away.

"Rosy?"

"I think he might have died."

Will closed his eyes, uneasiness shifting in his stomach. "Rosy. I know you don't want to hear this, but I think you should stay clear of Max... Or whatever he is called now."

"Mathew."

Will didn't ask how she knew. "Mathew, then, but the fact remains, if he is in a gang then he will lead a troubled life. My child, you could end up dead."

Rosy shrugged a little. "I need to speak to him."

"Do you?" Will asked gently.

Rosalind thought for a long moment. "Yes. I can't explain it, but I do. Maybe after that I can forget him. For now."

"And how will you find him?"

"He said he would come back to the shop tomorrow for more medicine."

Will leaned back in his chair. "Well, child, please stay here tonight and have a proper meal. Will you promise me that?"

"Yes." Rosalind gave him a smile.

"Good. And perhaps a bath?"

Rosalind threw a crust of bread at him, but an hour later she was soaking in a tub next to the fire as a slightly bemused playwright poked ineffectually at her dress as it lay soaking in a bucket.

Then, wrapped in a blanket, and back in her chair she devoured a large bowl of beef stew with slice after slice of thick bread. She gasped like a child when Will then presented her with a sugar cake decorated with pink icing. Finally, she curled up in a makeshift bed in the corner of the room while Will sat musing at the fire well into the night.

By the time he woke up in the morning, Rosalind was long gone, taking half a loaf of bread and another sugar cake with her.

Rosalind jumped every time the door of the pharmacist's shop opened, the little bell jangling as it dangled on its string. It was a busy day and by the time the pharmacist returned from lunch, her nerves were shredded. Then, late in the afternoon, he finally arrived, nervously looking back over his shoulder into the alley beyond. Rosalind was lucky, the pharmacist had drunk too much punch with his lunchtime haunch of venison and had retired to his bed for the afternoon.

"Can I help you?" Rosalind's voice shook just a little, her eyes drinking in every detail of a face so familiar and yet completely strange. Mathew glanced at her, but his eyes were more concerned with roaming the shop and the people passing outside.

"I told the pharmacist I would come back for medicine for my friend." His voice was flat but strong.

Rosalind smiled a little, hoping it was conspiratorial. "Yes, I remember."

He looked sharply at her. "What do you remember?" Suddenly he was all business.

"I was here the other night when you came... For help. How is your friend?"

Mathew swallowed tightly. "He is living. Just. He needs more medicine." He looked directly at Rosalind, her Max and yet not.

"Yes... I have it here. Just give me a moment."

Rosalind retreated in the back room, taking her time to find the package left by the pharmacist, wondering what she could do or say to prolong the exchange, when the bell on the door clanged once more. In a heartbeat, Mathew was there beside her, hiding behind the curtain that divided the back room from the front counter.

"What—"

His hand clamped over her mouth; his lips close to her ear. "Be quiet." A knife teased the underside of her chin. He cocked his head and listened to whoever was outside, no doubt pacing impatiently wondering where everyone was. "Call out — say you will be a moment."

Rosalind nodded almost imperceptibly. "Just a moment." Her voice sounded raspy.

"Now go and serve him. He must not know I am here. If you give me away, I will slit your throat, understand?"

Rosalind nodded once more, again barely perceptibly.

With butterflies in her stomach, Rosalind smiled as best she could and served the man quickly, the green kerchief round his arm explaining why Mathew did not want to be seen by him.

When the door slammed behind him, the man that was Max emerged silently from behind the curtain, the knife dancing easily in his palm and a satisfied smile on his face.

"Very good." He smiled at Rosalind. "What's your name?"

"Rosalind. Or Rosy."

"Pretty name for a pretty girl." His smile was rakish and Rosalind couldn't help smiling back. In one fluid movement he flicked his cap from his head, bowed ostentatiously to Rosalind and headed for the door. As he held it open, the ting of the bell still vibrating through the air, he turned back to her. "There's something about you, Rosalind." He smiled, his eyes flashing speculatively. "I would like to see you again."

"I'm here every day," she replied, eyes sparkling.

It was a few more days before she saw him again. He slipped in just before the doors were shut for the night, on silent feet, raising his finger to his lips to tell Rosalind to be quiet.

Somehow, he hid himself in the folds of the heavy door curtain, just feet away from the oblivious apothecary as he readied the shop to close.

"Get the broom," he barked at an astonished Rosalind. "Don't stand gawping, girl, I have an appointment to keep."

She rushed to the back of the shop obligingly and set about sweeping the floor, her whole being pulsating with the awareness of Mathew — or Max — hiding so close by. As she swept near the curtains, she could feel his breath on her neck. Her body turned to liquid.

It was only once the apothecary stomped out the back door into the evening summer sun that she felt herself let go of the breath she didn't realise she had been holding and turned to the figure lurking in the folds of the dark material. He emerged laughing, delighted at his own daring.

"The old man had no idea I was there!" He grinned at Rosalind, suddenly looking boyish rather than dangerous, as his hand reached out to grab Rosalind by the waist. Her skin beneath her dress burned but she deftly spun away.

"Sir, be careful where you place your hands. I am a lady." The look in her eyes was anything but ladylike.

"Indeed." He stepped so close to her their noses were almost touching, his hands, though, stayed on his hips. "Well, would this lady join me for dinner?"

"Well, since you asked so nicely."

Together they walked along the Thames in the sunshine, their arms grazing as they talked lightly, laughing often. It was warm, the sun was high in the sky and the world looked bright and full of opportunities.

Mathew bought them pies and flagons of ale from the stands that lined the waterways and spread his short cloak on the grass beneath a tree for Rosalind to sit on. Once they had had their fill, they lay close together, talking idly.

"Where are your family?" Rosalind asked him, deliciously aware of his hand casually roaming over her bodice.

Mathew sighed a little. "They are all dead."

"I'm sorry. Mine too. Plague. What happened to yours?

"My father was killed in the king's service. When our landlord heard, he threw us out of our home. We were homeless and my mother tried to keep us safe and fed but it was too much and she just died. After that, it was me and my two sisters. I was only eleven. They were five and seven and I tried to look after them but…" His voice cracked. "But… One night they were taken by these men. I think they were dockers. I found their bodies the next morning. I buried them and came to London. I joined the gang not long afterwards."

"Oh, Mathew, that's terrible." She grasped his hand.

"They are my family now." He rolled over so he could look her in her eyes. "I know we do things that might seem wrong to a lot of people, but we look after each other and our own. It is us against the world." His words were brave, but Rosalind could see the hurt and anguish in his eyes.

She pulled his head to her breast so she could stroke his hair, wondering at a world where people suffered so much that they couldn't really be blamed for doing all they could just to survive. So, Mathew and his cronies might steal — or worse — who could blame them? What choices did they have? As she lay there, though, with Max in her arms, a small voice inside her whispered, *There's always a choice.*

Mathew started popping into the apothecary every day. Each time he brought something for Rosalind. To begin with, it was a flower or a cake, but then it was a new silk wrap or even a silver locket. In time though, her joy at his attention began to turn to uneasiness.

"Mathew," she told him one evening as they walked arm in arm, "you don't need to bring me gifts every time. I am happy just to see you."

"You deserve trinkets. Why not?" He smiled down at her. "You need to enjoy what comes your way, sweeting."

"I enjoy when you come my way!" She smiled back. "But where do you get them from?"

"Let's just say *they* come my way." His voice was gentle but firm. "Now let's say no more about it. Come, I'm thirsty, let's get some ale."

One evening, they were sitting close together on some barrels, hands entwined, watching a street performer when there was a commotion from the gathered crowd. Rosalind felt every sinew on Mathew's body come to life, his eyes flashing everywhere. Two men spilled from the crowd in an angry embrace, barrelling into the performer as he juggled, knocking him to his knees.

Mathew was up on his feet in a moment, spotting the flashes of red and green amid the chaos. Rosalind saw him slip his knife into the palm of his hand. What happened next, she could never properly recount. People pressed around her, obliterating her view of Mathew and the other men. There was shouting and then screaming. The crowd jostled first one way and then the other, and then, as Rosalind held up her arms trying to push her way through the press of bodies, there was a horrified gasp and the way parted before her. Red liquid pooled at her feet. Before she had a chance to take in anymore, Mathew grabbed her arm and catapulted them both into the alleyways of London's docklands.

They ran and ran, knocking over people and stalls as they went. Eventually, Mathew pulled her into an open doorway. They stumbled in exhaustion into the musty darkness beyond. As she lay in his arms catching her breath, Rosalind suddenly realized Mathew was laughing.

Pulling herself to her feet she rounded on him. "You are laughing!"

He smiled up at her, his arms draped casually over his knees. "Oh, come on, that was fun!" He stood up, still breathing heavily. "Don't tell me your heart isn't beating fast, Rosy?"

"Of course, it is, but I am not laughing! It was not fun!" She was angry.

"Wasn't it? I loved it!" His eyes were bright, filled with excitement.

"Mathew, someone died back there, don't you care?"

170

He shrugged. "People die every day. At least it was one of them, not one of us."

"Oh, Mathew, how can you think like that? They are still people. It doesn't matter what colour of gang you are in, we are all people."

"Doesn't matter?" Now he was angry too. "Doesn't matter? It's all that matters. It is us against the world and the only way to survive is to strike first, hurt first, kill first. We have to stay on top at all costs."

Rosalind backed away from him, her vision blurred with tears. Once out in the sunshine, she turned and ran. She felt like she was running for her life.

Unsurprisingly, her feet once more took her to the Globe Theatre. She ran sobbing into Will's arms as he stood watching the players rehearse one of his plays.

"Break, everyone!" he called as he ushered Rosalind into the stalls, patting her back as a father would a daughter. "Come, child, what has happened?"

Rosalind told him all, everything that had happened since she had last been there.

Will was silent once she had finished. After a while he said, "Two men died."

"What?" She looked at him in horror.

"The street performer and a member of the Fleet boys."

Rosalind was white. "The street performer? Fleet boys? Do they wear green colours?"

"I believe so. They were both stabbed."

Rosalind crumbled. "I can't believe that's Max."

Will put his hand on her head. "You must stay with me, child. Do not return to the apothecary. Stay here, I will look after you."

She nodded mutely, there was nothing else to do.

Rosalind took to bed for two days. Will brought her food which she nibbled at and ale which she drank thirstily in moments. On the third morning, he threw open the shutters early, letting in all the noises and smells of a busy London morning as well as the bright sunshine.

"Morning, Rosy," Will called brightly. "You need to get up today, child. You have moped long enough; it is too glorious a day to stay hidden away. Besides, there is a performance tonight and I need your help. We are to have a cannon as part of the play tonight!"

Rosalind sullenly got up, had the bath Will insisted she have and even put on the new gown he had bought for her.

"There, child, that's better." He smiled when he saw her. "The colour is perfect for you, a dusky rose like your cheeks."

"Thank you, Will." She was grateful despite her misery.

"Now, have some food and we will get to making preparations for tonight."

The performance was in full swing and Rosalind stood in the wings, enraptured. She was always astonished by the plays Will created and always got lost in the words, the way they flowed, their cadence, the emotion they invoked.

She was so engrossed she never heard Mathew approach; never knew he was there until his hand went over her mouth.

"Shh!" he whispered in her ear. "It is just me. Are you not pleased to see me?"

He smiled down at her as if nothing had ever happened. Then, with no words coming from Rosalind's mouth, he bent to kiss her.

"NO!" It was a whisper but there was enough force in it to stop the young man in his tracks.

"Oh, come on, Rosy! Don't tell me you are still upset?"

"Mathew!" Rosalind held her hands to her forehead, too close to him for comfort due to the lack of the space in the wings. "Upset? Upset? Yes, I am upset. Two men died. Two men died because of the man I love!"

Mathew looked at her in delighted bemusement. "You love me?" His eyes danced mischievously. "Look, it is worth it then, isn't it? I have found out you love me!"

Rosalind was apoplectic. "Worth it? Are you aware of what you are saying, Mathew? Worth it?"

"Hey! Come here, it is OK, Rosy." He tried to put his arms round her waist, to pull her closer to him.

"No! Stop! Go away, Mathew, I don't want to see you!" She pushed hard, so hard he fell back into the metal hooks and ropes fixed to the wall. The pain and humiliation instantly transformed into anger.

When he looked up at Rosalind, his eyes were filled with hate. "Nobody touches me like that, Rosalind. I will make you suffer for that."

His face contorted with rage, he lunged towards her, staggering forward as Rosalind's fleet-footing carrying her away into the space beneath the stage. In amongst the wooden jousts holding up the stage, it was difficult to move, and in the gloom, it was hard to see where she was going. She didn't need light to know that Mathew was close behind her, she could sense his anger. It was like being chased by a malicious volcano.

She fell over a joust. He grabbed her ankle. She kicked out, catching his cheekbone, and freed herself. He lunged closer and brought her down over a protruding beam, winding her. Somehow, she fought her way free once more and emerged out the other side of the stage to the backstage area where props were left in readiness of the players. There were blunt swords, crowns, goblets and even a lit torch stuck in a bucket of sand in readiness for the cannon that Will had been so excited about. It was as good as being in a cupboard as the only exit was onto the stage.

On stage, the players were lost in their performance. The audience held rapt. Mathew pulled himself from the dustiness beneath and sneered at Rosalind. He knew she had nowhere to go. It took him just one step to corner her. He used his body to press her into the corner as he grabbed her hands. Stuffing a rag in her mouth he grabbed a cord from the nearby prop table and tied her hands to a hook above her head. Tears cut through the dust and grime on her face.

"Still upset, Rosalind?" His voice was quiet, his face just inches from hers as he followed her tears with his finger. "Good. This time you have good reason to be because now you are going to die." She struggled at her bindings, railed against the rag stuck in her throat. Uttered guttural sounds that only made him smile even more widely. "We had something good, Rosalind, but you ruined it. Now I need to get rid of the taste it has left." Turning around, he grabbed the torch from the sand bucket. "Fire is good for getting rid of rubbish, don't you think, Rosy? It is quite transformative, really, isn't it?" His eyes looked crazed. "Any last words? Anything to say? Sorry, perhaps? Ah, no, you can't speak, can you? Ah well, probably for the best. Goodbye, Rosalind."

He brought the torch close to her body, looking like he was about to set fire to her dress and paused. Breathing heavily, desperately, she hoped he had changed his mind, come to his senses.

"No, too easy," he almost said to himself. "You need time to realise the mistakes you have made. Repent, even. If you believe in God, that is. Do you believe in God, Rosalind?"

Her answer was no more than a muted scream against the filthy cloth in her mouth. The movement though dislodged the rag allowing her to speak.

"Max! Please stop!"

"Max?" Mathew paused, his eyes softening as if trying to remember something and couldn't quite.

"Who's Max?" He looked at Rosalind for a long moment, his face anguished and confused but with a gentleness it had lacked before.

"You are Max, Mathew, you are strong and kind, you don't want to do this."

Mathew floundered, struggling with the bubbling emotions and the sense of something unremembered, something whole and wonderful, triggered on hearing the word 'Max'.

"Mathew please." Rosalind pushed her advantage. "This isn't you, not really. Things don't have to be this way." Rosalind knew she had said the wrong thing as Mathew's face instantly closed as if a shutter had been drawn down.

"Don't I Rosalind?" His eyes burned with pain once more. "What choice do I have? All I have ever known is death and loss, but now I am taking control."

He turned, calm and in charge, looking around him for what he needed. Within moments he found the gunpowder to be used in the canon, and with a pleased smile at Rosalind, he set about drawing a line of powder from the bottom of her dress to the stage. Then, with one of those fluid graceful gestures he was so good at, he dumped the torch and was gone.

If anyone ever knew he had been there it was just as a vague awareness of a dark figure fleeting across the back of the stage, an actor in the wrong place, no doubt.

Rosalind watched the powder catch and flicker, licking up the powder as it caught her skirt, her screams lost amongst the raucous noise of the audience. Her body heaved with sobs and fear, and as she felt the first of the torturous heat on her legs beneath her skirts, all she could think was, *Not fire again.*

Aurora was careful not to wake Jack as she slipped out of bed, the smell of smoke still acrid in her nose and throat.

She made herself tea and settled into her armchair, wrapped in her cashmere throw, to ponder. Sloan looked up curiously from his place on the rug but quickly decided to return to sleep. Aurora had always been aware that death by fire had been a recurring theme in her lives — how could she not — but the fact seemed to be being drawn to her attention by the universe in the most brutal of ways in the last year or so.

She had always dreamed of Atlantis and the end shared by her and Max there, but now she was dreaming — or remembering, in some cases — all those lives that came to particularly brutal ends and fire was definitely more frequent than any other means. The dreams — or remembering's — were also happening in chronological order so it was hard to shake off the sense of some kind of endgame approaching.

The dream she had just had was 1613. She knew because she knew that was when the Globe had burnt down. She had remembered before she had known Shakespeare and visiting the rebuilt Globe as a tourist a few years ago had brought back a draft of memories of being there as the original players rehearsed and performed the great plays, but she hadn't then remembered being part of the end.

So, she still had four hundred years of memories to catch up on and then what? Would Max appear then? She also knew, with the wisdom of someone who could remember their many lives in the same way most people remembered childhood Christmases, that she needed to unravel the layers of karma she and Max had created together. In the past, she always assumed the bonds of love between her and Max overrode any karma created, but her memories now were showing her that there was a lot of complex shared history between them to unravel. He had killed her in 1613 again; was that an act of redress or had he accrued more karma? And what about Lord Jonas, as she couldn't help but think of the man currently stalking her as what part did he play? Or did he? Perhaps he had nothing to do with Max and he was simply, with the intense anger of his previous personalities, looking for revenge of his own for the life in which she had murdered him.

And what about Jack? Her wonderful brave warrior soul? Even if Max, in whatever form, did appear, was she willing to sacrifice Jack for him? She simply didn't know. Part of her wanted to try and forget about it all and simply carry on with their day-to-day lives like ordinary people, but another part of her was determined to try to bring it all to a head. Could she speed the process up, she wondered? Could she go into a deep regression to delve into her next meaningful life rather than wait for it to find her? Her instincts told her that was probably not a good idea and while, for the moment, she decided just to see how things played out, she stored it away as a possible course of action if needed in the weeks to come

Jack made her jump as he leant down behind her and kissed the top of her head.

"Sorry, I missed you." His voice was heavy with sleep and desire as his mouth sought out the back of her neck, making her gasp with pleasure. "Come to bed." She did, and for the rest of the night, Jack was the only man who filled her thoughts — and her body.

Chapter 12

It was a few weeks later before Aurora saw any further sign of Lord Jonas, nor had she any more dreams or remembering's beyond the usual flash of recognition when she met someone new or visited somewhere different.

It was a bright late August day and having closed the door behind her last client of the day — interestingly, a woman who she had known briefly about six hundred years ago as a young lord — she knew she couldn't stay inside any longer. Jack had asked her to think carefully about going out alone, but the call of the birds and the sunshine was too strong. Anyway, she would have Sloan with her to protect her.

So together they headed out into the London streets, Aurora taking simple pleasure from the buzz of happy activity she felt all around her. After taking no heed of which direction they were headed, they finally ended up at St James' Park, where Aurora decided to buy ice creams for herself and the dog.

They were sitting happily together on the dry grass enjoying the cones, Aurora leaning amicably against Sloan's broad back, when a shadow fell over them, followed almost instantly by a low growl from Sloan's throat.

"So, you have yourself a guard dog, do you? Or should I say another one. What's the other one called? Jack, is it?" Lord Jonas sneered at her.

Aurora was not going to be drawn into unnecessary chit-chat. "You said, last time, that you remember," she said in a neutral voice, a steadying hand on the back of Sloan's neck, helping to steady her own nerves. "What did you mean?"

"I think you know what I mean. I know you remember, too. I know you recognized me from before."

"Who do you think you are then?" Aurora asked, sounding nothing more than casually interested even as his cold eyes flashed towards her.

"I remember lying in bed unable to move or speak. It was your fault I was there and then you killed me so you could go off with my brother. I cursed you then. I couldn't speak but I cursed you with all my being."

He sat down beside her. He would have been elegant and attractive if he didn't radiate hate. Instead, he moved with twitches and jerks as if he couldn't quite keep the anger inside. Aurora resisted the urge to move away, his body was only an inch away from hers. She could feel Sloan's hackles rise as he shifted to watch the man sitting next to her.

"I have always been angry, even when I was the tiniest of boys. I always knew I was angry at someone for something, but I didn't know what or who. Until I saw you, that is. At first, I didn't understand why I felt the way I did at the sight of a strange woman, but then I started dreaming. So, Aurora, you owe me. The question is, how are you going to repay me?" He turned his head so he could look at her, his face deadly serious.

Aurora felt her throat tighten with fear, her heart race in her chest. Sloan responded by getting to his feet and growling. "I think it is time I left before my dog here decides you are dinner." Aurora got to her feet then looked down at the man who was Lord Jonas.

"Sir, you have a short memory as I think you will find that death was payment for your cruelty in that life and others. You are owed nothing." She turned to walk away when he called after her.

"My name is John, by the way. I thought you should know when the times comes for the balance to be paid."

Aurora walked on without looking back, but when she got back to the flat, she was violently sick. By the time Jack came home, she had made a decision, one borne from both instinct and a need to put some distance between herself and the man she now knew as John.

"I am going to Glastonbury," she said from her place in her armchair, cushion hugged to her chest, Sloan at her feet.

"OK," Jack replied, obviously unsure what to make of her announcement. "For a weekend?"

"No." Aurora knew she wasn't being fair on him, but by this point, she didn't know how else to be. "Maybe a month or two."

Jack was silent, watching her intently. "Is there something we need to talk about, Aurora?"

"No… Yes…" Her voice trailed away as the first tears rolled down her cheeks. "Sorry, I am being ridiculous."

"What's happened, Aurs?" Jack knelt beside her, his strong arms round her.

"He found me again today."

"Lord Jonas?" There was steel in Jack's voice.

"Or John, as I have discovered he is called this time round."

Jack's jaw tensed. He was angry and felt helpless. "Aurora, I had said it was best if you didn't go out on your own."

"I wasn't alone, I had Sloan with me, but honestly, Jack, do you really think I can never leave the flat unless you are here? That's madness."

"I know… I know… But I want you to be safe." Jack stood up, rubbing his face in his hands. When he stopped, he poured them both a brandy. Handing one to Aurora, he sat down wearily on the couch. They both took a drink. "So, is that why you want to go to Glastonbury? To get away from him?"

"Yes. I feel safe in Glastonbury, Jack… It's a special place… Full of ancient magic."

"I don't doubt it, but this guy seems to be able to find you wherever you are, will being there make a difference?"

"Maybe. I don't really know but my instincts are telling me to go."

"What did he say to you today?"

"He wants to punish me," Aurora said flatly. Jack leant forward on his knees, glass in hand, eyes downcast. "Jack." Her voice was filled with emotion, reading his weariness as having had too much of her strange life, lives. "This isn't your problem."

His head came up quickly, his face angry. "Not my problem? Aurora, how can it not be my problem?" He stood up and started pacing. "As long as it involves you, Aurora, it is my problem. Don't you see? I love you. I want to sort this out for you, but I can't. I hate that I can't and I hate that I can't find this guy and punch his lights out. I hate I can't do any of the normal things a person would do in this situation, like go to the police. But most of all, I hate seeing you sitting there looking like that. That's what I can't stand, Aurora, and that's why it is my problem."

Aurora let her tears fall. "I know that… But what I mean is, if it is all too much — and I mean all of it, my memories, dreams, remembering you from one thousand five hundred years ago — then I wouldn't blame you for wanting out."

Jack stopped pacing and came to kneel before her. Tipping her chin with his finger, he looked down at her with eyes brimming with anger, frustration, hurt and love. "Do you want me to go, Aurora?"

"No." Her voice was a whisper.

Jack leant his forehead on hers. "I don't want to go either. I can't help feeling like Sloan would have known what to do." He slumped to the floor next to her, one arm across her knees and took a large drink of brandy.

"He might have done, Jack, but he wasn't perfect, you know. And he is in you, anyway, I see it every day."

Leaning into each other, they sipped their brandies and contemplated what came next.

"Let's go to Glastonbury together," Jack said eventually, turning to look at her. "We can work it out… I can work from there for a while… So can you, I imagine."

Aurora held his face in her hands, her heart swelling with such love and gratitude she couldn't speak for a moment or two. "Are you serious, Jack?"

He smiled tiredly. "Yes, I am. But we need to take this seriously. We need to go soon but we also need to make a plan. And we need to make sure he doesn't follow us. Deal?"

"Deal." Aurora wrapped her arms around him. "I love you, Jack."

Three days later, they were ready to go. A story about heading to Brighton for a few weeks had been bandied about. Jack closed his studio and told his contacts to email. Aurora found them a little cottage to rent for a few months not far from the Tor. Then, with due seriousness, they left a trail for John to follow, first taking a taxi to the train station and buying tickets to Brighton. They even boarded the train, except, rather than going all the way to the seaside town, they got off at Gatwick Airport and collected Jack's Range Rover from where he had left it the day before in the overnight parking. Then, finally, with a sense of freedom, they set off for Glastonbury, their entire lives now contained in two suitcases, one handbag and Jack's kit bag. And Sloan, of course, happy to be on an adventure with the people he loved.

For the first time in months, Aurora began to feel a lightness of being, and more than anything, she loved how it was reflected in Jack's smile. She even felt calm when Jack suggested they pop into see her parents for a coffee en route. For the first time in this life, she was able to see beyond the shadows of their previous life together and see the worry, love and confusion in her parents' eyes. It wasn't an easy visit as such, but Aurora left feeling like she had laid groundwork for the future and as if she had made an important step in this life. They seemed to be delighted by Jack too.

On arriving at the cottage, they felt at home right away. By the time they got there, taking a protracted route that involved even more coffee breaks as an added precaution, it was dusk and the silhouette of the Tor was only just still visible against the deep lilac sky. With the earliest possible suggestion of autumn there was also a discernible chill in the air. Jack — so like the warrior, Sloan, in more ways than he knew — instinctively went to the fireplace and within minutes had a fire going. Aurora, meanwhile, found two mismatched glasses from the little kitchen and brought them back through to the cosy living room — complete with low-beamed ceiling, an inglenook and a bay window made up of small stained-glass diamonds — with the bottle of red they had picked up on the way.

As she snuggled next to Jack on the throw-laden sofa, she breathed out a contented sigh.

Jack kissed her forehead. "Happy?"

Aurora snuggled closer. "I feel like I have come home."

"Me too," replied Jack.

They both slept soundly that night and the next day Aurora set about showing Jack round. They climbed the Tor, enjoying the freshness of the early autumn air, sat in quite reflection together next to the ancient Chalice Well and poked about in the many alternative and New Age shops on the high street.

"I like it here," Jack announced over organic coffee and raw chocolate and beetroot brownies.

"I'm glad." Aurora smiled at him, her mouth full.

"I like the way you look here," he added, his eyes bristling with suggestion.

"Oh yeah?" Aurora replied, eyes matching his for sparkle.

"Yeah." Jack gave her that lopsided smile that made her insides turn to liquid silver. "Relaxed. Happy. Lively."

"I am not surprised, I have always loved living here — I have done, many times — there is a really special energy."

"I take it you were happy here?"

"Happy? Not always. I was murdered here at least once. But when I was here, I always felt like I was exactly where I was meant to be."

"Murdered?"

"Yes. On top of the Tor."

"Of course." Jack smiled. "And do you get no sense of Lord Jonas or John here?" He was serious now.

"I don't know, Jack. Though I think I would sense him."

"I hope so. I will need to go away in a few weeks for a couple of days for work.

"I know. Sloan and I will be fine, I am sure."

They next few days were spent settling in and walking Sloan round the sacred landscape surrounding Glastonbury. When they weren't eating cake and coffee in the town centre, they were lounging happily in the cottage, reading books or making love. Jack would deal with his business on his laptop while she started to put up posters in shops offering her services.

For Aurora, though, it felt like a wonderful holiday from life. She knew she would miss Jack when he went away, but there was always any number of interesting talks, classes, gigs, and meditation sessions going on in Glastonbury so she knew she would be OK.

So, it was with a light heart after many dream free weeks, she kissed Jack goodbye on the doorstep of the cottage and returned to the warmth of the living room to drink her morning coffee. Jack had made it in the cafetière so it was strong and aromatic. None the less, moments after finishing her cup, she was sound asleep on the couch in front of the fire.

Prudence

Prudence stood on the upper floor, staring out of the window overlooking the high street. All looked normal from behind the casements. People milled about, going about their daily business — travellers arrived and left the inn, housewives ducked in and out of shops and market traders called and bantered at the market cross in a bid to sell their wares. Children ran wildly weaving in and around people, animals and market stalls, causing the good folk of Glastonbury to call out in anger, but that was completely normal as well. As was the group of old soldiers sitting singing in the sun as they enjoyed a tankard or two of ale. Even the sight of a wild-haired old man in worn and torn robes carrying a staff as if he was about to part the Red Sea was nothing that unusual.

But she could sense trouble. She could always sense when something was amiss or when something was about to happen. Glastonbury was the kind of place though where that kind of thing was accepted. In other places, she would have been killed as a witch — she knew because she could remember those lives in which that had happened to her. But in Glastonbury, everyone quietly knew and understood that there were people that could see or sense more than others, that an old wise woman was worth ten court physicians and that there was an energy that pulsed beneath their feet in the earth itself, regardless of what the *Bible* said. There were even whispers of gatherings on top of the Tor on certain nights where unspeakable things occurred, but in Glastonbury nobody really bothered. Prudence knew all about the kinds of things that happened on top the Tor from other lives, but even in Glastonbury, she thought it was, well, prudent, not to mention them. She had been well-named.

This morning, though, she wished she had a greater ability to see what was to come because she couldn't stand the twisting and nauseating sense of impending doom about which, without discovering the cause, she could do nothing about. Instead, she kept looking out of the window, senses on high alert, hoping to find some clue to the cause.

It could, of course, be partly due to the civil war. Largely protected from it in Glastonbury, they knew what was happening elsewhere and it was edging ever closer to their magical little town. Only last night, her husband, Thomas had been talking about skirmishes nearby, but he hadn't seemed unduly concerned. Prudence, though, could sense something coming and in this magical town, she knew she wouldn't be alone.

Wrapping herself in her thick cloak, she headed out onto the streets. She wasn't shopping, just sensing the atmosphere. Everything seemed normal down the high street and even in the old, ruined abbey grounds she couldn't sense anything other than the feeling of general unease she had had all morning.

In her search for greater insight, she climbed the Tor, remembering with every footstep all those other times she had climbed the sacred hill in previous lives as both priestess and seeker. She paused at the Chalice Well to allow answers to come to her as she sipped at the holy water, but nothing came. It was only as she walked along the ancient processional way to the thousand-year-old oak tree that she found what she was looking for.

"You can sense it too, then," the old woman sitting at the foot of the tree asked as she approached.

"Morgan." Prudence was delighted to see the old wise woman. "Yes, I can feel it too, but I don't know what to do. I wish I knew what was coming."

"Violence and death are coming, my child," Morgan said plainly, without grief or sadness. "There's duality in the world and it is setting people against each other."

"What can we do though?" Prudence asked.

Morgan smiled serenely. "Nothing. Or everything, depending how you look at it. Send blessings out into the world and let the will be done." She gestured nonchalantly at the sky. Prudence didn't respond. "Maybe that will be enough to protect yours and yours, my dear, but if your time has come then your time has come and there's nothing all God's angels can do about it."

"And has my time come, Morgan?" Prudence spun round to face the lady, her dark eyes bright beneath her bonnet and cloak pulled tight over her shoulders.

She smiled knowingly. "Do you think it is your time, Prudence?"

"Maybe." Prudence looked out over the sacred landscape spread before her. "Not that I am scared of death. I'd rather be dead than to wonder what is about to befall and know it is bad."

The two women stood in contemplative silence for a while.

"If you want my take, my dear," Morgan finally said, "your fate is not sealed as yet, and no offence, there is something much more important at stake today and it is too important — for everyone, both here and around the world, — for us to try and stop it from happening. Or, rather, Prudence, that you try and stop it from happening."

Her heart was no less easy as she wandered back to the house, but it leapt at the sight of Thomas dismounting from his horse in the street before sending it away in a flurry and vanishing through the thick oak doors with a harried step and a plume of dust from the road. Prudence hurried in after him.

"Husband," she called out as she entered the receiving room, bobbing the slightest of curtsies. He was alone. "Forgive me. I am surprised to see you." He looked agitated. Prudence went to pour him a goblet of wine as he withdrew his gloves and cloak.

"Thank you, my wife." His voice was taut with anxiety and he drank thirstily before looking down at her. "I don't have much time, I need to muster the town."

Prudence took a deep breath. "Are troops approaching? Which side?"

"Both, Prudence, my darling. Both. We are to be caught between the two and that's just about the worst possible situation we can find ourselves in." He finished his wine. "Prudence." He cupped her chin so she was looking up into his gentle and caring face. "Once I leave, you must get the servants inside — and anyone else you think needs a place — and you must do it quickly. Have the doors barred before the turn of the next hour, do you understand?"

"Yes, my lord, but what about you?"

"I will come and let you know it is safe as soon as I can." He squashed his lips to her forehead in a clumsy but loving kiss and was gone.

Prudence only took a moment to gather her thoughts before she was also back out in the street, ushering people inside the house. As she had promised her husband, by the time the church tolled the hour, the doors were barred. She had even ordered barrels and furniture to be piled against the inside doors in case soldiers tried to break their way in. Now the household, plus a few stragglers — about thirty souls in total — were gathered in the upstairs rooms awaiting her orders.

"Now, everyone, well done on securing the house. Boys, it is your job to stand watch. Stay in the windows overlooking the back courtyard and let me know if soldiers breach the outside gates. We can see clearly from here if anyone tries to breach the door." Prudence took a deep breath. "I think we should bring some supplies up to these rooms so we can barricade ourselves upstairs, if that's necessary."

"John and I will block the staircase, ma'am," the groom offered.

"Good idea, Ralph. Then all we can do is sit and wait to see what happens."

And wait they did, for hour after hour, making them all glad Prudence had ordered supplies brought up. For her part, she sipped slowly on a goblet of red wine and stood watching the street, unable to shake off the sense that something momentous was about to happen. She watched a lone rider blaze a trail through the debris left behind by people retreating indoors. A group of earnest townsmen, deep in conversation as they hurried to where Prudence imagined the elders, and Thomas, gathered to plan and seek talks with the leaders of both armies. Several cats slunk from the shadows, only to retreat on sensing the atmosphere. Dogs, too, didn't linger to scratch amongst the rubbish and even the pigeons seemed to have silently retreated to the rooftops. It was almost dark by the time she saw any sign of soldiers. Just one or two to begin with, but then it seemed as if they streamed out of every alleyway and side street.

Extinguishing the lamp nearest to her and stepping carefully behind the shutter so they could not see her, she watched intently. Ralph appeared at her shoulder. "So, they are here at last, are they?"

"Yes, it seems so, and in some numbers, but can you tell what side they are on, Ralph?"

"By the looks of the red they are wearing, they are Cromwell's men."

Prudence looked on as the men moved through her town, impressed by their discipline as they made their way to wherever they had been ordered to go without interfering with their surroundings at all. "However," she went on to ask, "where are the others?'

"I think that's them coming now." Ralph nodded down the street as a quick flash of light followed by a loud bang drew the attention of a few hundred faces in the street below them.

Within moments a full-blown fight had started. Men's bodies, locked in combat, slammed against the thick oak outer doors that lead straight onto the street.

Prudence gasped, but Ralph placed a steading hand on her arm. "It's OK, ma'am, they would need several shire horses to kick through those doors."

But by then, Prudence was no longer listening, because somehow, in the melee below, she had spotted a face. Max was there and he was fighting as one of Cromwell's soldiers. "Shut the door behind me, Ralph."

She was heading out of the house before anyone could stop her, pulling away the piled furniture from behind one of the doors just enough so that she could ease it open and slide out. She knew Ralph might hesitate, but she was pleased when she heard the bolt slide back in place and the barrels and furniture being pushed back behind the door.

Incredibly, none of the men fighting just inches from her seemed to even notice her as she stood with her back pressed to the hard oak. She could not, though, see Max anymore. The smell of smoke and unwashed male bodies filled her nostrils, the clang and clatter of metal-on-metal rang in her ears, and before her eyes, limbs thrust and flailed by the flickering light of a burning building further up the street. But Prudence ignored it all as she scanned the scene before her for a glimpse of Max, or the tall blonde soldier that he was in this life.

With her back to the wall, she began to make her way up the street, her eyes never leaving the fracas before her. About fifty steps from her front door, the fighting eased and there was only a handful of men in the street, none of which were Max. In the relative quiet, though, Prudence could see the men take note of the lone woman creeping along the edge of the street and quickly ducked down an alleyway and up a back staircase to find a vantage point on a low roof.

From where she stood leaning over a low wall, she could see the fighting a little way down the street to her right. The men she had left in

187

the street below were heading up to the left, swords hanging in their hands, ready to flash and kill once again at a moment's notice. They were Cromwell's men, she thought, and Prudence, wondering where they were going, decided to follow them in the hopes of finding Max.

The thought of seeing him in person overrode all sense of her own danger. Ducking through the parallel backstreets, she kept up with the soldiers, her ears tuned to the soft fall of their feet on cobbles and the gentle clang of their equipment as they walked. They spoke not a word.

It wasn't long, before Prudence realised they were heading out of the town towards Wearyall Hill, home of the holy thorn planted there by Joseph of Arimathea. She never stopped to wonder why, she simply kept going, stumbling in the dark, trying to keep sight of the shadowy shapes of the soldiers ahead of her, in the hopes of seeing Max.

If she been thinking straight, she may have realised before it was too late that she had been heard. Instead, the first she knew she was in trouble was when the hand closed over her mouth and a strong arm wrapped round her body, holding her arms tight to her torso. Instinctively, she struggled and tried to kick backwards at her assailant, but she knew it was pointless. Whoever had a hold of her was simply too strong.

"Easy, girl. Calm down." He sounded like he was soothing a horse, but with some skill he held her with one hand and bound her hands with the other.

A second soldier arrived carrying a torch, sword held before him. The light of the flame lit up the face of the solider who had captured her and in the space of a heartbeat she knew it was Max. She gasped. He was watching her intently, his face handsome, if worn. His eyes intense but gentle, care-worn but wise. An experienced soldier and a man to be respected.

"Not a good night to be out and about, lady." He stood before her, at least a head taller and twice as broad. "Especially not on your own." Prudence felt her stomach tighten. What was he implying? As if reading her mind, he instantly sought to reassure her. "Don't worry, my lady, as long as you are in my care no harm will come to you." He gave her the tiniest of bows. "However, we do need to understand what you are doing out here on your own. Here is not the place, though, let's get to camp."

188

Men appeared all around her and one took her by the elbow to guide her along the dark path. It seemed like an eternity of stumbling along with the man's fingers pressed into her flesh before she saw the first flickers of the camp lights. It wasn't a large camp, rather just an overnight stop for the leaders and a few dozen men. There was one large tent flanked by half a dozen smaller ones, while foot soldiers were making themselves comfortable round small fires.

Max — or, rather, Captain Fleming, as she had heard him called — gave orders to his men in a quiet, confident voice and then nodded for the man holding onto Prudence to take her into the largest tent. He even held the flap open for her himself. Prudence found herself staring into his thoughtful brown eyes as she ducked underneath it, desperate to see some flicker of recognition or connection. His returning look was merely quizzical. The tent was lit by a single lantern and was empty except for a low bed on which sat a lean, older man in shirt and jacket, both loosened as if he were about to prepare for bed.

"Captain." He spoke with the tone of a man in command. "How goes it?"

"Skirmishes in the streets, sire, but we are achieving our objectives."

"Good, glad to hear it. What have we here?" He nodded in Prudence's direction. "She is no wench."

"No, sire, I think not. I found her between here and the town. It appeared she was following us."

"Indeed?" The older man looked at Prudence curiously, his bushy grey eyebrows raising in interest. "A spy, do you think?"

Prudence opened her mouth to object, but Max raised a hand to silent her. "I can't imagine so, sir, but I thought it best to wait to question her until we were back at camp."

The older man stared at Prudence, his lips sternly set. "Well then, lady, let's start with you name."

"Sir." Prudence bobbed a curtsey as best she could with her arms bound. "My name is Prudence Shardrake and I am the wife of Master Thomas Shardrake, one of the alderman of the town."

"So, a gentle lady, though that was already evident from your clothes. Can you explain how you came to be out on your own, in the dark, in the midst of such unrest as we have on our hands tonight?"

Prudence took a deep breath. The truth wasn't an option, but she knew her life depended on the story she told. "Sir. I know I am in terrible trouble. My husband bade me to stay locked indoors, but my pet dog got out and I came out to find him, sir. I followed him out into the fields but I lost sight of him."

The general stared hard. "Your dog, madam?"

"Yes, sir, he is very dear to me."

"Did you not have a servant to send, lady?"

"Yes, sir, I should have, but they were all otherwise engaged trying to protect our home and as I was the one who saw him run away, I didn't want to waste time. I never expected to be out this far or late, I thought I would find him in the next street and be able to call him home."

"And his name?" Max, or, rather, Captain Fleming, asked, his lips twitching ever so slightly with amusement.

"I'm sorry?" Prudence stammered.

"The dog's name, my lady."

"Oh, my apologies. It's a she actually. Erm… She is called… Max."

"Max?" The General looked both disbelieving and also exhausted all at once. With a rub of a weary hand over his face, he motioned for Captain Fleming to take her away with the other. "Keep her bound overnight. We will work out what to do with her at daybreak."

Prudence thought she was to be left outside tied to a post like a horse, but as it turned out, Captain Fleming was too much of a gentleman to allow that to happen. He brought her to his own tent and even let her have his bed, albeit with her bound hands secured to the bedpost. Tied as she was, Prudence could only lie on her side, looking into the tent.

She tried to keep her eyes closed in order to gather her thoughts, and if she were honest with herself, to give Captain Fleming — Max — a little bit of privacy as he readied himself to sleep on the ground. The compulsion to look at the man she had known as Max was too much, though, and she found herself watching him from the cot. She took in the strength of his shoulder as he shrugged off his leather body armour and then let his quilted red jacket fall to the floor, leaving him standing in just his stained white shirt and breeches. She watched as he rubbed the strain from the back of his neck and rolled his shoulders with a deep sigh to release the cares of the day. There were many, she imagined.

"It would be best if you slept, milady." He spoke without even glancing in her direction.

Prudence paused only briefly before answering. "Difficult to sleep, Captain, when I am not sure what fate befalls me in the morning."

Now he looked at her, a smile dancing on his lips. "No harm will come to you, lass." He smiled at her, his eyes sparkling from a nest of creases. "Not unless you are a spy, that is."

"No!" Prudence tried to sit up but found herself having to lie back down again. "Of course not. I really am just in the wrong place at the wrong time."

He gave her another smile, drily lopsided this time. "Ah yes, the dog." Prudence held her tongue. "You may be just in the wrong place at the wrong time, but something doesn't add up and my dear general will be determined to get to the bottom of it in the morning, so either you get some sleep or you spend time doing some hard thinking."

He turned away from her to splash his face with water from a bowl. He was towelling himself dry when she spoke again. "There was no dog."

"You surprise me." He was drying his hands, his tone utterly unsurprised.

"It was you." Now he was surprised.

"I'm sorry?"

"I was following you. I had seen you from my window and came out to find you." Prudence spoke plainly and the simple resonance of her words struck the captain as he sat next to her on the cot.

"Now why would you do that?" he asked, genuinely interested.

"I thought I recognised you." Again, Prudence felt there was nothing she could do except speak the truth.

"From where?" His eyebrows creased in concerned interest.

"A long time ago." Prudence held his eyes, her heart beating fast.

"When? Where?"

"Another lifetime." Prudence's voice was a whisper.

"Are you talking about reincarnation?" Captain Fleming's voice was strained. He was, after all, in this life, a roundhead and a staunch Protestant. Belief in reincarnation would amount to witchcraft.

"Maybe. Do you not believe in more than one life?" Prudence asked with plaintive openness, all the while knowing she was dancing with death.

"No, my lady, I do not, and I suggest that by morning you don't either." And with that he rose from the cot, grabbed a blanket and curled himself into a ball on the ground beside her. His back toward her.

Prudence hardly slept at all and smelt morning in the air before she saw the first blush of light through the thin material of the tent. The captain hardly moved all night, but instinct told her he hadn't slept much either. With the first trill of the birds, he was on his feet. Washing and dressing without a word. In moments he had vanished from the tent.

She was just getting to the point where she thought she would need to relieve herself where she lay when a young soldier came and untied her. He even turned his back as she used the chamber pot and then, with reasonable gentleness, escorted her from the tent by pulling her along by her bindings as if she were a donkey.

Prudence found her mind strangely calm as she walked through the bustling camp, ignoring the inquisitive glances from soldiers as they doused fires, checked gunpowder and polished their muskets. She was taken beyond the tents to the hill beyond where a group of half a dozen men stood, deep in conversation. Prudence could see that one of them was Captain Fleming and bile rose in the back of her throat. How she would like a flagon of small ale or a cup of nettle tea.

"Ah! The good lady of the town," the general announced as they approached. "It seems your presence here is most fortuitous. We have a duty to perform today on behalf of Lord Cromwell himself and it is good we have a local to witness our little moment of history."

Prudence looked from the general to Captain Fleming in confusion. "I'm sorry, I don't understand."

"No need for you to understand, my lady. Just stand and watch and then we will ensure you are returned to your husband forthwith. As long as you can answer a few more questions to my satisfaction, that is." The General turned away, undoubtedly assuming that his word, now spoken, was enough to end the matter. "So, my lords, we are here this morning to witness the execution of the will of our Lord General Cromwell. It is believed by the ignorant folk of these parts that this tree was planted by

Joseph of Arimathea and is considered to carry healing properties as a 'holy thorn'. Of course, this is nothing more than mere superstition and we are to free the people of these parts of their enslavement to such nonsenses on this misty morning by cutting down the supposedly 'holy' tree."

Prudence, sleep deprived, cold and hungry as she was, never thought before speaking. "No! You cannot!" All eyes turned to her, but it was those of Max, or, rather, Captain Fleming, that she sought. "This is a sacred tree, please don't cut it down; it would be sacrilege. Heresy, even." His eyes were hard but not without some compassion, but it was the general who spoke.

"Quiet! We have no need of your opinion, woman, and certainly not one voiced in support of such superstitions!"

"It is not a superstition! This tree is so important to the people of these parts. Why cut it down? Don't you sense its power?" Prudence's eyes were a little wild by now. "Oh, is that it? Maybe it is because you sense its power that you want to cut it down? Is that it?" She was silenced by a hand across her face.

She was horrified to find the hand belonged to Max, or, rather, Captain Fleming. The men eyed her with distaste and the general's look was filled with venom as he said, "Captain Fleming, proceed with the axe."

With a last slightly pitying look at Prudence, Captain Fleming turned, his hands loosening an axe from his belt, to look at the tree that sprung from the staff of Joseph of Arimathea returning to Glastonbury after the Crucifixion of Christ, returning, many believed, to the same sacred place of ancient wisdom that he had brought a young Jesus to learn. But with nothing more than a barely audible sigh, Captain Fleming lifted his axe and brought it down with a sickening thud into the holy wood. Prudence couldn't stand it and without a thought for herself, lunged at the tree ahead of the second blow. It lodged between her shoulders rather than in the wood. But it was all to no avail as, once the axe had been removed from her flesh and her body drawn to the side, Captain Fleming — Max — continued his assault on the holy thorn until it lay decimated on its side next to Prudence.

Chapter 13

It was pitch black when Aurora awoke on the couch, confused and disorientated. She had been asleep all day and judging by the depth of darkness outside the cottage window, it was late. Wind and rain were rattling the same windows in their old casements. It was also cold, the fire having burned down to ash.

Sitting up, Aurora shivered. Rubbing her eyes, she tried to wake up properly. Sloan looked at her balefully from the rug, having not been out since Jack had brought him back from their early morning walk. Bending down, she massaged behind his ears and kissed the top of his big head by way of apology. How could she have been asleep for so long? She had slept the night before and had just finished a strong coffee. The dream — or memory — had been so vivid though, it was as if she had lived it all again in real time. Was she somehow slipping back into the past rather than just remembering? Was being in Glastonbury somehow effecting how she remembered?

Standing up, she pulled a throw round her shoulders and knelt next to the fire to coax it back to life. Once the flames were once more licking at the black bricks of the chimney, she stood, intent on pulling the curtains shut on the night and heading to the kitchen to make tea, but something in the garden made her stop in her tracks. A figure, she was sure, standing stock still, despite the elements, about thirty feet from the window at the edge of the hedges and trees that formed the garden's boundary. The figure, she was sure, had to be John. Or Lord Jonas.

Taking a deep breath, she tried to act as if she hadn't seen him, closing the curtains briskly but without panic. As quickly as she could, she made her way to the front door and drew the bolts across, realizing with a shiver that it had been unlocked the entire time she had been asleep. As she stood leaning against the back of the door, her heart racing, Sloan whimpered by her side. The poor dog hadn't been out all day. Trusting her instinct, she now unlocked the door and opened it wide to let Sloan out into the garden.

"On you go, pup, have a good sniff around." The dog instantly shot out, barking ferociously at the hedges where Aurora had seen the figure, just as Aurora had hoped he would. She was sure she heard the tell-tale breaking of twigs and branches as whoever they were — Lord Jonas or otherwise — scarpered.

Aurora made herself stand in the doorway, throw tightly wrapped around her shoulders for a full half an hour to allow Sloan some time to do his business and sniff about. The dog came back in of his own volition and Aurora instantly headed to the kitchen to check the back door and put out Sloan's dinner. She also decided to pour herself a glass of wine rather than a cup of tea. Carrying it through to the living room, she also picked up her phone. There were sixteen missed calls from Jack. He answered at the first ring.

"Are you OK? Where have you been? I've been so worried since you didn't answer." She could hear the fear and relief in his voice.

"I'm OK. I'm so sorry, I've been asleep. Despite your potent coffee this morning, I fell sound asleep on the couch not long after you left. I've not long woken up."

"Did you dream?"

"Yes. It was really vivid."

"What happened?"

"I was here, living in Glastonbury, nearly four hundred years ago. I was there when Cromwell's troops cut down the holy thorn. I tried to stop them and they killed me."

Jack was quiet. "Maybe Glastonbury wasn't such a good idea," he said finally. "Is it making things more intense?"

"Yes, maybe, but I think I need to be here, Jack. I can't explain why." She decided not to mention the figure in the garden. Instead, she asked Jack about his day, told him how much she missed him and how much she was looking forward to seeing him in a few days.

When she hung up, Sloan reappeared, licking his chops appreciatively. Without invitation, he leapt onto the couch next to Aurora and she couldn't have been more pleased to have him there.

Unsurprisingly, Aurora didn't sleep much that night and as the rain and wind calmed down, the burgeoning sun promised a glorious autumn day. She decided to take Sloan out for a long walk — partly to make up for the day before and partly to help clear her head.

Her spirits soared the moment she was outside; the light just breaking in the otherworldly way that Aurora always felt was unique to that part of the world. She felt like she could so easily slip through the veils of light laying across the land into another realm. There was also what Aurora though was a perfect wind, just brisk and cold enough to be refreshing and invigorating. Sloan galloped around joyously too, his tongue lolling happily out of the side of his mouth.

Aurora was unsurprised when she found her feet taking her naturally to the top of the Tor, following in her own footsteps from many lifetimes over. Standing on the summit looking out over the sacred landscape bathed in golden light, she could sense the ley lines beneath her feet, the energy pulsating out round the planet from this incredibly powerful place.

Taking deep breaths, she felt strong and powerful herself. She had a sense of connection and that, on some level, she held all the wisdom she needed and understood exactly why she could remember all her lives — and deaths — why she was so in love with Jack in this life — yes, she was ready to admit she was in love — why Lord Jonas was stalking her in the here and now, and of course, why there was no sign of Max. It was with a great sense of peace that she and Sloan made their way back down the Tor, past the Chalice Well and to one of the many cafes on the high street just in time for opening.

Aurora would admit to herself that she was putting off going back to the cottage for as long as possible. Not because she didn't want to be there, but because she feared seeing Lord Jonas in the garden once more. As she wandered around the town's streets with Sloan in tow, she found herself taking double takes at men as they passed and wondering where John was now. Could he really have followed her to Glastonbury? They had thought they had been so careful.

Eventually, though, weariness drew her back to the cosy little cottage where she could quite happily have lived with Jack forever. Did she really just have that thought? She stopped herself dead in the street. There had been no pause to think of Max at all. No pull through the thousands of years and hundreds of incarnations. No wrench in the gut. No sense that there was no meaning to life without that one person that had always filled it someway, somehow.

After a moment, she began to walk on slowly. Perhaps loving Jack in this lifetime was bringing something to a natural close. Perhaps her obsession with Max through lifetime after lifetime had been unhealthy, born from her unusual ability to remember, and it was time to let it go and live differently. Would Max leave her alone to live that life though? He hadn't shown up so far. A smile slowly crept over her face. All she had to do now was free herself of Lord Jonas, and for once, Aurora might be offered a chance to live free of her memories.

She let herself into the cottage with a lightness in her step, the hint of smokiness in the air making her want to light the fire and pour a glass of red wine. Just one more night and Jack would be home.

Rose

Rose leant over the dock wall so she could get a better view, unable to quite believe what she was seeing. Ships jostled for position along the Bristol Channel, but it was the one closest to her that held her attention, swaying and lurching as it was beneath the tumult of activity on board. Sailors in their dirty white trews and worn striped tops leapt ably and barefoot from deck to dock and back again under the watchful gaze of commanding officers in frock coats and tricorn hats. Bales of unknown materials were winched and unloaded while barrels of provisions were rolled down board ramps to find a place in the substantial holds.

None of this is what caught Rose's attention, though; she had seen it all so many times before. What captured her every sense, were the chained men standing proud, defiant and yet beaten on deck, their ankles and necks shackled by heavy chains rubbing at their dark skin. Here were the slaves that Rose had heard so much talk about in this life and as she stood looking, seeing nothing but worn out and miserable men, her heart bubbled over with compassion. She remembered meeting people with such dark skin in other times and places in those memories she instinctively knew not to share, but in those other places everyone had been happy equals. Here, though, they were being treated as inferiors.

Treated in the same way as oxen or donkeys, not that Rose believed people should treat animals so either.

"You taking an interest in our slaves, missy?" The voice was friendly and Rose turned to see a sailor standing next to her, his limbs strong and tanned. His face weather-beaten but gentle. He was only a few years older than Rose. She also knew in less than a moment it was Max. The knowledge made her stammer her answer.

"Yes, sir. I have never seen men so."

"They are strong brutes, that's for sure. Makes them worth their weight, I believe."

Rose was watching his face keenly, fascinated as always by the strange combination of familiarity and newness, but the man's words — Max's words — jolted her. "You misunderstand me, sir. I don't mean their shape, I mean I have never seen men so treated, like animals."

The sailor looked at her, eyebrows raised. "Your compassion does you proud, miss." He looked over to the men, barely even moving as they stood weighed by their chains. "I don't suppose I've ever thought of it like that. I certainly wouldn't like to be treated the way they be." He gave her a lopsided smile. "I suddenly feel lucky to be the sailor I am."

Rose's heart swelled with a mess of feelings. He was here. The man her heart and soul craved for through endless years and incarnations was standing before her and part of her longed to do nothing but take him in her arms and tell him how overjoyed she was to have found him again. Yet her heart and mind were distracted by the plight of the men standing, looking so proud and yet forlorn, on the deck of the ship.

"Miss, are you quite alright? Maybe the sun is too warm for you out here? Or maybe it is the smell? Too potent for a lady's nose?" He was genuinely concerned.

"No, thank you, I am quite fine." She smiled at him, wondering suddenly if he was about to vanish from this lifetime as quickly as he had arrived. "How long are you in dock for, sailor?"

He grinned now. "A few weeks, by God's, while we get repairs."

Rose smiled too, her heart fluttering as her mind whirled with possibilities. "And those men?"

"Some are to be sold, I believe, but most will be held until we are ready to sail again."

Rose nodded her acknowledgement of his words. "Sailor, may I know your name?"

"Certainly, miss, it is Able Seaman Jones. Harry Jones."

Rose offered her hand to kiss. "A pleasure to meet you, Able Seaman Jones. My name is Lady Rose Wardlow. I wonder if you would do me the honour of being my dinner guest tonight?"

The sailor's eyes widened in surprise, his cheeks clearly reddening beneath his tan. "Lady." He bowed slightly. "I am sorry, but I am just a sailor."

"Able Seaman," Rose interrupted him, "I am well aware of who you are." More so than he realised, she mused. "And it is you that I am inviting."

With a wave of her hand, her manservant, George, emerged from where he had been discreetly standing and stood by her side, well used to his mistress' unusual habits. "George, please make sure this man knows where to come for dinner and make sure he has everything he may need to attend." Rose didn't want to shame him by overtly referencing his lack of proper attire, but she also wanted to ensure he had no reason to feel he couldn't take up the invitation. She knew George would handle it perfectly. "Until this evening," she said with a small smile to Max — Harry — and without further ado, turned on her heel and walked briskly to where her carriage awaited, unaware of the ship's captain watching intently from the poop deck.

Rose was in a complete fluster as she readied for dinner that evening. Her entire wardrobe was scattered around her dressing room and her bemused dressers were desperately trying to work out what dress she wanted to wear as she veered from a delicate and suggestive pale blue satin gown that revealed her shoulder and décolletage — for Max — to a dark green taffeta with a high neck and full sleeves — a dress suitable to discuss the business of slaves.

In the end, she settled for a pale gold dress with a wide skirt and lace trims which hinted alluringly at the flesh beneath while remaining modest. The colour, she knew, suited her pale complexion. Her hair was piled high on her head, decorated with pearls, with some wispy tendrils round her face.

She paced the rug in the receiving roomas she awaited her guest and felt almost weak with relief when the footman came to tell her he had arrived. Rose stood by the fire, hands clasped before her and smiled in anticipation of seeing the man she had loved throughout time. Except the first man through the door was not Max. The one who came sheepishly in his wake, though, was.

"My lady, may I introduce Captain Oliver Bradshaw and Able Seaman Jones." The footman bowed before retreating and closing the doors.

Standing in front of Max was another figure from Rose's pasts. An unwelcome one, the one she would always think of as Lord Jonas. Her mind reeled but lifetimes of experience helped her to show none of her surprise. "Captain Bradshaw, welcome to Oakridge House." Rose gave her gloved hand for the captain to kiss, managing to ignore the instinctive desire to draw away from his touch, her skin crawling even beneath the soft silk of her glove. Then, turning to Max, she gave a genuine smile full of warmth, noticing it went a long way to quell the uneasiness in his eyes. "And Able Seaman Jones, it is a true pleasure to see you again. Please do sit."

The three of them took their seats round the fire as a servant poured drinks. Captain Bradshaw leaning back in his chair, legs wide with one boot resting nonchalantly on his knee, for all the world as if he were relaxing at home. Able Seaman Jones, sitting on the edge of his chair in his new breeches and jacket — undoubtedly provided for him by George — as if he would rather be anywhere else in the world. And Rose, smiling warmly as if she were hosting a bridge party for her lady friends, trying to quell the waterfall of emotions she was feeling inside. Her joy at finding Max, her unconditional love for that soul, the shock of finding Lord Jonas here in her living room, her terror of him born from several lifetimes of pain and a strong compulsion to help those poor souls she had seen chained on the dock. With a sip of wine, she composed herself and focused her attention on Lord Jonas.

"Captain Bradshaw, you are very welcome to my home, but I don't seem to remember issuing an invitation?" She sensed Max — Able Seaman Jones — baulk and saw him take a long drink of his wine as he stared intently at the rug.

"No, indeed, Lady Wardlow, and please do accept my humblest apologies." He was like a cat that had got the cream, Rose thought as she watched him lean forward in an insincere little bow, his lips twitching smugly. "I decided it was my duty to attend as I couldn't help feeling there had been some mistake when I heard that Able Seaman Jones here had been invited to sup with a lady. Alone as well, it seems. You are not married, Lady Wardlow, am I right?"

"Widowed, Captain Bradshaw, five years now. And since then, I have run my husband's estates — hugely successfully, I might add — run my own households and keep rules and company as I see fit."

"Quite an extraordinary list of achievements for one so young and a female at that." Captain Bradshaw eyes glinted as he eyed Rose.

"I don't believe us females are capable of any less than any man, Captain Bradshaw." Her own eyes glinted back. "More, quite often, in my experience." Lord Jonas — for in that moment it was indeed Lord Jonas looking back at her — grinned malignantly at her. Rose chose to ignore him and turned to Able Seaman. "Able Seaman, how do you fare this evening?"

"Very well, my lady," he replied a little hesitantly. "I am grateful to be invited to your home."

"It is my pleasure, Able Seaman. I enjoyed our chat on the quayside this afternoon and I had hoped to hear some more about your time at sea and experience of the slaves."

The sailor smiled warmly, if a bit shyly, at her. "I will happily answer any questions you have, my lady."

The captain guffawed. "Just as well I came after all, Lady Wardlow, I doubt this ruffian has anything to say that you would like to hear."

"We shall see about that, Captain Bradshaw. Now let's go through for dinner."

Dinner would have been strained if Rose had let it be, but she had plenty of experience of keeping a steady flow of conversation which, in the main, she directed at Max while ignoring the captain's increasingly sneering and nasty jibes.

"So, Able Seaman, tell me how you come across the men - or cargo, as Captain Bradshaw likes to call them." Her tone was undeniably barbed.

"My lady, we capture them from their lands." The man who was Max looked pained at the confession and Rose laid her hand over his in sympathy. The captain snorted into his wine glass.

"No need to feel sympathy, my lady. They are savages. They are running around in the jungles and deserts, scrabbling around in the dirt for food. We are doing them a favour."

Rose stared at the self-satisfied officer with a hard glint in her eye, unable to keep the sarcasm from her voice. "Oh, it certainly looked that way on the dockside earlier today."

"Forgive me, Lady Wardlow, you are but a female and I can't complain when you are by nature a little soppy. Believe me, we must not let compassion overrule our heads or these savages would kill us in our beds and quite probably eat our still warm flesh." The captain said those final words with relish.

"Perhaps, Captain, but this mere female can't help but wondering if they would have been any danger to us at all if they had been left in their homelands with their families."

He let out an amused strangled sound. "My lady, there go your female sensibilities again. We are superior to them in every way. It is our right and place in the world to have dominion over them, surely you can see that?"

Rose lifted an eyebrow archly. "My good captain, I certainly agree that if you and one of those men were to stand side by side, I would certainly be drawn to look less favourably on one, even consider one inferior, as you say."

The captain considered her across the dinner table where the remnants of their meal lay. "Perhaps you wouldn't feel so much from the heart, Lady Wardlow, if you were to meet these brutes up close." There was an undeniable threat and one, Rose knew, he was enjoying.

She shivered and drew on all her self-control to not let it be seen. Looking up, though, she realized Able Seaman Jones — Max — was looking at her knowingly from where he sat, nervously toying with the stem of his glass.

"Maybe, Captain Bradshaw, you could indulge a silly lady and give her the fright she deserves?"

202

He smiled, maliciously. "I certainly think a little dose of reality wouldn't do her any harm. Why don't I take you to meet our savages?"

"I would be delighted to make their acquaintance." Rose smiled innocently back at the man who seemed to shadow her steps through time. "Shall I arrange for my carriage to collect you in the morning?"

There was that smile again. "Actually, I was thinking more of now, Lady Wardlow, why not? A dark night to meet some dark-skinned brutes. What say you, Able Seaman?"

"Nothing, Captain. Though I would be happier if the lady wasn't to venture out at night."

"Come now, Able Seaman, what harm can she come to with you and I there to protect her?"

The captain would have his way and half an hour later they were rattling over cobbles in the darkness on their way to the warehouse where the men were being kept. Rose was glad Max sat next to her while the captain lounged across, backing the direction of travel, smiling with vicious delight.

It was Max who helped her from the carriage and who muttered in her ear when the captain was distracted, talking to the guards, that she was just to stay close to him. "I will do all I can to take care of you, my lady, I'm not right sure what the captain is up to."

"He certainly has an air of a man up to something, Able Seaman, I am glad you are here." She squeezed her hand lightly on his forearm just before the captain turned back and offered her his arm.

"My lady, please do follow me. I would hold on tight to my arm if I were you and I would also advise you to raise your skirts with the other. These men soil themselves where they stand, as beastly as they are."

"Do they have much choice?" Rose countered, determined not to let him rattle her despite her instinctive desire to pull as far away from his as she could.

"They could show self-constraint, like a gentleman." He sounded ridiculous and she couldn't believe he didn't know it.

"I have seen many gentlemen behave worse than beasts," Rose countered once again.

"That's their prerogative, my lady. Able Seaman, do you have the keys? Well then, open the gate."

Max fumbled with the keys by the light of the one torch lodged in a sconce. Eventually, the iron gate swung open with a theatrical creak. Max grabbed the torch and lit the way for the captain and Rose, the orange light dancing across flesh and chains as he moved to light more torches attached to the far wall.

When the light finally settled, Rose almost stepped back beneath the baleful, curious and plainly anguished eyes that stared back at her, wondering what this woman before them in her fine dress meant now for their future. She smiled hesitantly, instantly aware of seeming exactly how she didn't want to appear — like a kindly superior white woman looking at specimens in a zoo.

With a defiant step she moved forward, shaking off the captain's arm and held her hand out to the nearest man.

"Hello, sir, my name is Rose."

He stared at her as if she had landed from the moon, but she held his eyes and continued to smile. Bringing her hand back to lay it on her chest, she simply said, "Rose." She then held her hand back out to the man.

Slowly he raised his own hand, shackled and blistered as it was, and took hers, nodding ever so slightly. Rose repeated the same process with all twenty plus men in the room. "I don't know if you understand any English," she said finally. "But I don't agree with what has happened to you. I believe you deserve to be at home with your families, on your own lands. I will do everything I can to help you."

The captain uttered his now trademark guffaw.

Rose rounded on him. "Captain. I want to buy freedom for these men. I don't care how much it costs but they are to be brought directly to my home."

"My lady, you can't surely…"

"I can, Captain Bradshaw, and if it is not through you, it will be through those in far higher places. I have more than enough money so you may as well claim the credit of a ridiculously successful sale or, I imagine, simply skim off a healthy wedge for yourself. You are that kind of man."

The captain stood glaring, red splotches on his neck telling of his displeasure. And yet, as a man greedy for wealth and never keen to upset those who could smooth his path as he climbed the slippery social ladder, he knew he would do as she asked. He motioned to the guards while Rose spoke quietly to George.

"Take them home, George, feed them, bathe them and clothe them and let them rest. Let them know if you possibly can that they are going home."

George nodded and smiled. "Yes, my lady." He would never be a man to have any truck with slavery. Then, as the men were being freed and ushered from the room, with George and Max doing their best to reassure them without a common tongue, one stepped to Rose and grabbed her hand. "I know. Thank you."

Rose pressed his hand in return. "I'm glad, please tell the others. We will make arrangements for you to go home as soon as possible."

The man nodded then shot a glance at the captain. "Be careful missus, that man has darkness in him."

"I know. I will. What's your name, sir?"

"Ade, missus."

"Well, Ade, please make my home your own. Perhaps we will be able to talk properly before you go home. I would like that."

"Me too, missus." Ade left with a flash of a beautiful smile and Rose was left in the dank warehouse room with nobody except the captain.

"Well, Lady Wardlow, you certainly have the capacity to surprise me."

"Good, Captain, expecting the expected leads to slow wits." Rose began to walk towards the door, desperate to get out from the dark, clammy place, fetid with human waste. She was even more desperate to get away from Lord Jonas.

"So eager to get away, my lady?" He pulled her back by her elbow so her back was now against the wall. "Why don't you stay for a moment... Perhaps pay off a little of your debt?" His eyes glistened with lust, power and anger. A dangerous combination.

Rose pushed at his chest, but he was immobile and he simply pressed her back against the wall.

"Now, now, my lady, behave. If you don't, I might find myself needing to use some of these now redundant shackles." He let his fingers trail down her cheek, his sour breath damp on her skin. "You might look quite pretty with an iron round your neck." He grinned, that grin she knew from so many lives. Almost charming, filled as it was with life. If it weren't so malicious.

"Let me go, Captain. I will make you pay for this." She couldn't move.

He sneered. "My lady, I don't think you are in any position to bargain, much less threaten. Now let me see if I can lift this skirt. Beautiful material."

Rose began to thrash where he had her pinned as his other hand expertly struggled beneath her skirts to find a way in. She was screaming, but he didn't care and it was that which was almost his undoing as he never heard Able Seaman Jones as he brought a large jack iron down on the back of his head.

"Come, my lady, quick." Max grabbed her by her hand and pulled her after him. They only stopped when they were by her carriage.

"Is he dead?" She was breathless.

"No, I know how to hit a man without killing him."

"Thank God." Rose swept her hand over her forehead, struggling to remain in control of her emotions. "For your sake, I mean, Able Seaman. I don't want you getting into any trouble for helping me like that. I am sorry you got embroiled."

"Well, ma'am." Able Seaman looked almost rakish as he smiled at her with a lightness she had never seen. "I think the boat free of trouble has long sailed. I never liked the man and I didn't like being part of taking and keeping those men. Time for a different life for me."

"What will you do?" Rose resisted the urge to stroke his face, suddenly aware of all the love she had ever felt for him bubbling over in that one moment in time.

"I'm not sure. I need to gather my things and then get away as quickly as possible."

Rose nodded. "Do what you need to do as quickly as you can then come to me; I will help you." With that, Rose smiled once more at his sweet face, and with his help, climbed to her carriage.

"Thank you, my Lady. You are one of a kind." And despite the horror and shock of the last hour or so, Rose couldn't help but smile.

The next morning, Rose slept late, despite her awareness of the many extra bodies in her home.

She had come home to find the bemused men sat around the kitchen eating plates of hot pottage over slices of meat and bread. George had been organizing a system of bathing, and one by one, the men were being washed and having their wounds cleaned before being offered clothes. Rose knew they were being billeted in the upper rooms, hardly luxurious but hopefully having a bed each and a hot meal was an improvement for the time being. With a smile, and quick hello, Rose had retreated to her room with the tumult of emotions tumbling inside her.

It had taken her a long time to sleep, to shake images of Captain Bradshaw — or Lord Jonas — from her mind and trying not to let her love for Max overwhelm all her thoughts. It would have been almost impossible that she and Able Seaman Jones could live as husband and wife, even if he had any interest in such, under normal circumstances, but the circumstances they now found themselves in made it utterly impossible. Was he a deserter? A runaway? Or could he just simply walk away? And what about Captain Bradshaw? Would he be so ashamed of his own actions last night he would not seek retribution? Instinct told Rose there was no chance of that and her niggling feeling of foreboding was borne out when a message came — Able Seaman Jones had been arrested.

Rose was up and dressed in moments, her mind reeling. George was waiting for her on the other side of her bedroom door.

"As far as I can ascertain, my lady, he was picked up on his way here."

"On what charge, George?" She looked at him in horror as she strode though the halls of her home, causing staff and guests to look on in wonderment. "Oh no! Please don't tell me. Is Captain Bradshaw dead?"

"No, my lady, though that might actually have been preferable."

"How so, George?" Rose was now rushing down the front steps to the waiting carriage.

"It is Captain Bradshaw who has brought the charges against the able seaman. They are holding a hearing this morning."

"Damn that man! I must go to the court at once and tell them what really happened."

Her carriage rattled away leaving George standing on the top step, watching her go with a desperately uneasy feeling in his stomach.

Rose paid no attention to the men who tried to stop her entering, ably ducking beneath the arms of the sentries to push open the heavy doors of the room which was to be Able Seaman Jones' — nay Max's— courtroom.

"Gentlemen," she called in ringing tone, "let this young man go at once!" She carried the weight of authority and conviction, all three men behind the desk looked up, their interest overriding their irritation, while Able Seaman Jones looked around, startled but relieved. Only Captain Bradshaw looked unsurprised and less than pleased.

"Lady Wardlow," he intoned darkly by way of introduction to what were obviously his three superior officers sitting behind the desk, hair scrapped back in low ponytails above their starched collars.

Rose took them in at a glance. They were all, momentarily anyway, allowing her interruption in part out of curiosity and in part out of deference to her sex, looks and title. Their patience wouldn't last long, she could see, and she knew instinctively that the tall, lean man in the middle was the one she needed to focus her energy on — his eyes were sharp, but kind and he had the taut musculature of someone who had done their time and knew hard work. She could bet he was an incredible fighter. He would not, though, tolerate anything other than facts and plain speaking.

"Sirs, I beg that you forgive the intrusion." She looked plaintively at the man in the middle and saw the tiniest movement of his eye in response. She wasn't sure what it meant but she pressed on. "I had to come here as soon as I heard about Able Seaman Jones as I had to make sure you were in full ownership of the facts."

"We know he attacked his senior officer, Lady Wardlow, I am not sure what else there is to know?" asked the pudgier of the men on the left.

"I am sure Captain Bradshaw has given you his version, undoubtedly omitting to mention his assault upon my person, which this young seaman was saving me from."

There was gasping and muffled whispering from the bench. Captain Bradshaw had turned puce and glared at her balefully.

"Lady Wardlow," the capable one said, "you do understand what you say?"

"Of course, sire. I simply speak the truth."

"We are to understand that, after dining with you, alone, Captain Bradshaw and Able Seaman Jones took you to meet the slaves — which you then bought and released — after which, Captain Bradshaw molested you?"

"Yes, sir, that's about it." Rose could sense his disdain.

"Where was this meant to have happened, Lady Wardlow?" the pudgy one asked this time.

"In the cellars where the slaves had been kept. He threatened to chain me and do unspeakable things to me. I couldn't move and would have been at his mercy if Able Seaman Jones hadn't come along."

The three officers looked at each other, slightly flustered by such straight-talking from a lady. Papers were shuffled, knuckles were wrapped on tables and Captain Bradshaw, wiser than Rose in these matters, obviously, turned the full power of his reptilian smile on her.

Finally, the pudgy one called for order — although they were the only ones making any noise — and then cleared his throat. "Able Seaman, please rise."

Rose watched the young man get to his feet in his shackles and admired his bravery. He stood tall and straight and without any sign of nervousness.

"We here find you guilty of attacking a senior officer and as such, you are to be sentenced to death. You will be hung from the gibbet at sundown unless there is an appeal for clemency from your accuser." The pudgy man looked like he knew there would be none and then turned his attention to Rose. "No doubt you will find this harsh, but we have laws for a reason. I thank you for your interruption nonetheless, goodbye, Lady Wardlow." He nodded at the guards to escort her from the room.

"But no! Wait!" Rose refused to move. "You say you have laws, well what about Captain Bradshaw? Should he not be punished?"

Everyone exchanged weary looks.

"It is your word against his Lady Wardlow. Good day to you."

Rose found herself sat back in her carriage with her eyes overspilling with tears. In the last day, her life had been turned upside down - ever since she laid eyes on Max again. And yet she couldn't just leave him to his fate. She had to at least go and see him, see if he had any last requests.

It was another arm though that caught her as she half-stumbled from the carriage in eagerness to see Max. "Captain Bradshaw. Forgive me but I would rather not see you just now if you don't mind. I have business to attend to." Rose made to move past him on the busy wharf front.

"Ah, but my dear Rose, we too have business to take care of."

Rose spun to look at him, his arm still gripped around her arm, oblivious to the fisherman and peddlers pushing past them in their noisy, odorous gaggle. "What do you mean, Captain? Speak plainly."

He had no intention of speaking plainly. He sneered instead. "You really don't want to see the young seaman swing today, do you?"

"Of course not, nor does he deserve to."

"You have quite a soft spot for him, in fact, my lady, do you not?"

"He is a fine young man with a bright future ahead of him, if he was allowed to have it."

"Perhaps he could."

Rose looked at him sharply again. What was he suggesting? "Once again, Captain, I beg you to speak plainly." She was at the end of her tether.

"Well, what if there was a way you could save the young seaman?"

"They said they only way was for you to beg clemency and why would you do that?"

"I might. If there was a reward in it for me."

Rose felt the colour draining from her face. "What do you mean?"

"Why, my lady, I am asking you for your hand in marriage, of course." He smiled down at her, looking for all the world like a charming lover to the outside world, while to Rose he looked like the devil incarnate. And yet she knew the devil had her trapped, she had no choice but to say yes.

Able Seaman Jones was let off with a whipping. Rose was made to watch, standing with her arm in that of her betrothed. The young man begged Rose to reconsider, but she was resolute and as he sailed away on the next ship to America, she began her life as Mrs Bradshaw.

Her husband, meanwhile, happily fashioned himself as a lord and made the most of her wealth. The greatest source of joy for the rest for her short life was to know that Max was starting a new life far away from Captain Bradshaw and around thirty slaves would hopefully be back in their homeland and with their families. Rose herself died only two years after becoming Mrs Bradshaw following a short illness. Doctors could never identify what was the matter with her, it was simply as if she decided just to stop living and so she did.

It was the taste in her mouth that brought Aurora out of her dream. Stretching out, creaking limbs, she wondered when the last time was that she had brushed her teeth. Or, perhaps, she wondered, she was tasting the last flavours of Lady Rose Bradshaw a woman who had simply allowed her system to shut down after having found herself inextricably attached to Lord Jonas. John. The man who kept reappearing in her own lives and never in a good way.

Aurora lay for a moment, eyes still closed. In all the lives she remembered, it was he who wronged her, yet it was him who, in the here and now, believed he owed her revenge. They both participated in the dance of karma, they knew, and she knew she must have drawn these experiences to her through agreements for growth or, given the world was an outer reflection of the inner, as a manifestation of her own thoughts and beliefs. Or as a balance for her own actions. She would write, she thought to herself, or perhaps draw a mind map to try and work out the energy cords connecting them through lifetime after lifetime. Perhaps if she could do some work to release those repeating patterns and stagnant energies then John would simply leave her alone. Miraculously discover a passion for giant butterflies and emigrate to the Congo. Or even suddenly see the world as a place of love and set up an animal sanctuary. The universe was a miraculous place, after all, she thought as she stretched once more and eventually opened her eyes.

John was standing with one hand on the mantelpiece, looking down into the remnants of the fire. For a disconcerting moment, Aurora thought she was looking at a staging for *Wuthering Heights* and before her was the brooding Heathcliff. He certainly gave off a darkly intense energy, as she imagined Heathcliff would. Aurora felt panic rise in her throat.

"Where's Sloan?" Her fear made her speak out in haste, when perhaps she may have taken a moment more to collect her thoughts and form a plan.

"Ah, so Sleeping Beauty wakens. I thought I was going to have to kiss you."

And there it was, the same reptilian smile Aurora remembered seeing as Rose on Captain Bradshaw. For a moment, time and lives slipped and slid together as John and Captain Bradshaw became one and the comfortable mauve sofa in the cottage morphed into a chintzy pink chaise longue.

"Don't come near me." Aurora sat up and glared at her intruder. "Where is Sloan?"

"So concerned about the dog." The smile again. "Don't worry, he is in the kitchen sleeping. He will be out for eight hours at least."

"I suppose I should be grateful you didn't kill him." Aurora's tone was steely.

"I am not sure what you think I am, Aurora?" John looked at her with faux hurt and surprise.

"You told me you were going to have revenge on me. Although, let me tell you, John, I remember a lot of my lives and every time you show up you cause me pain and suffering, so I would think karma would be on my side."

"So, you remember, do you?" John stepped closer to her, his eyes filled with an eagerness. He reached out a hand and allowed one finger to idly, almost imperceptibly, caress her jaw. "You will have to tell me all about them, although I think you will find that, on reflection, you were always at fault. My memories might not be as clear as yours, but I do remember you clearly. Always so strong-willed, proud and filled with a knowing… You always seemed to know what was happening… What I was thinking. Your downfall, Aurora, is all your own."

"Jack will be home soon."

That smile again. "No, Aurora, he won't. He left you a voicemail. He won't be home until the morning, just in time to take care of Sloan, in case you were still worrying about the dog. Not you, though, because you, Aurora, are coming with me."

"And how exactly are you going to make me do that, John? I am a fit and able woman and you aren't exactly Mr Universe there."

Aurora was on her feet edging backwards towards the door, John watching her casually. Too casually, she realised, just a moment before she noticed him look behind her and clearly catch the eye of someone there. There was someone else in the cottage. A split second later, her world went black.

Gerard

Gerard's feet were freezing, but at least he didn't feel the rats nibbling. He had no energy to shrug them off anymore. The pain in his stomach was harder to ignore — and he knew if he didn't get food soon, he would die — but even that thought wasn't quite enough to make his weakened, starved limbs move. If he died, he thought idly, he would be dead before he was fourteen years old. He knew he would have to move at some point, but right at that moment, even lying dying in a sewage-filled gutter in the few rags that he had left was preferable to doing anything else at all.

Lady du Bonnieres — Lord Jonas, he knew — had thrown him out into the street for no reason other than that the very sight of him drew out her spite. She must remember him in some way, he thought, from those other lifetimes.

Anger coursed through his own veins at the thought and gave him enough energy to get to his feet. Food. He must find food. Gerard had been stumbling around for the best part of the evening — time was nebulous — without any luck when someone appeared at his shoulder.

"Young master, can I help you?" Gerard turned toward the voice, his weakened senses swimming uncomprehendingly. "You look cold and hungry."

Gerard narrowed his eyes to see a young woman, older than him, but young, and while she was dressed plainly, she was wrapped up warmly beneath a good quality wool shawl and a thick fur-lined cap. It was the face though that had Gerard's full attention. It was a face he knew and loved well, even though he had never before seen it with such smooth sallow skin and amber eyes. "Max," was the only word he could manage.

"I am sorry, I fear you are delirious, master. My name is Claudette, come with me and I will get you warm and fed."

Gerard knew the dangers of going with people in Paris, especially the way things were. Children were kidnapped and put to work, or worse. With the aristocracy being dragged to the guillotines by the dozen, the poor's attempts to redress the balance of equality had simply ended in chaos. Now no one had enough food and no one ever felt safe, but this young woman had Max's soul and Gerard was unable to do anything other than allow her to gently hold his arm and follow.

She led him down the quieter side streets, expertly ducking away from trouble and unwanted attention until they came to a better cared for road. Opening a heavy iron gate, and then locking it behind them, they went down a tidy alley and up a well-maintained flight of stairs, to an appartement. Gerard could see a warm welcoming light and couldn't help but wonder who was at home.

Claudette opened the door. "I am home, Papa. I have brought a young master. He is starving."

An elderly man shuffled from a room in slippers, an ornate shawl over his shoulders. "Well done, well done, Claudette. One less on the streets tonight. Come in, young man, do you have a name?" Gerard moved his lips, but they were so blue and weakened with hunger no words emerged. "No, indeed, names are not important. Come in, let's get you sat by the fire and then get you some food."

A while later, Gerard wasn't sure if he hadn't died. His rags removed, he had been given warm, almost new clothes and his frozen feet were unthawing in a tepid foot bath. He was sitting next to the fire with a thick blanket around his shoulders and a tray on his lap with as much bread, cheese, ham and soup as he could eat. It was more comfort than he had known in a long time and even while he relished being able to feel his toes and having a stomach no longer cannibalising itself, he couldn't help but wonder.

Living on the streets tends to make a person wary, even someone with Gerard's unusual ability to remember so many other times and places. People in this time and place, he knew, rarely showed altruism. There was always an exchange, a desired one or otherwise. And Gerard knew that even though he and the girl that was Max shared a history — and love — stretching back to the beginning of time, that didn't mean she could be trusted in this lifetime. Hadn't Max killed him before several times over?

Having eaten plenty for the moment, he laid down his spoon and regarded the old man sitting seemingly benevolently across from him. His eyes were kind and encouraging.

"On you go, young master, eat as much as you like."

"Why?"

The old man chuckled. "Why? Because you need to eat, young man. You were close to death when my daughter brought you here."

"Where am I?" Gerard knew he sounded truculent and ungrateful. Or was it just suspicious?

"My home." The old man gestured around him. "It's not much but we are lucky, I know. We have a warm, dry, comfortable appartement and plenty of food." The old man and youngster stared at each other a moment. "You are wondering why I have so much when so many have so little, aren't you?

"Yes," Gerard said shortly. "And why you care enough to give it to me."

"Ah, I see. Yes, yes, I have seen it before. You youngsters on the street believe nobody capable of some simple kindness." The old man looked into the fire, shaking his head sadly. He spoke quietly, almost to himself. "It is very sad that so few believe in kindness anymore. So, so sad. What will become of people if there is no kindness, indeed?"

"You want me to believe you are just being kind?" Gerard asked, his doubt wavering.

"Yes, young master, I do. But perhaps I am not being completely altruistic as I don't like seeing people suffer so would rather try and alleviate it where I can. I get a lot of joy from seeing people come back to life, so to speak, with a little warmth, food and kindness."

"So how do you have enough to share?"

The old man looked at him closely. "I have friends in the country. They make sure I am well enough provided for that I can offer some charity."

Gerard looked into the fire, suddenly feeling very sleepy. "But what about tomorrow? I have a full belly tonight but tomorrow I will starve."

He never heard the old man tutting sadly as he pulled the blanket over his shoulders.

When he woke, Claudette was busy in the kitchen, humming softly to herself as she chopped vegetables. He watched her surreptitiously for a moment from behind half closed eyelids, taking in the healthy flush in her cheeks and the lustre of her hair.

She must have sensed him. "Morning, sleepy bones," she said without looking up. "The jakes is down the hall. Once you come back you can have some breakfast — even though the time for that is long past." She threw a smile at him and he didn't know what else to do but obey, unfolding his body, creaky as it was from a night curled in the chair like a cat

On his return, there was a plate of scrambled eggs, a bread roll and hot coffee awaiting him. Gerard fell upon them as if last night's feast had never happened. Claudette smiled tolerantly.

"I'll just finish this and be gone," he murmured half-heartedly through a mouthful of bread.

"Gone? Why?" Claudette asked, genuinely surprised.

Gerard looked nonplussed. "I thank you and your pa for helping me, but I know I need to keep moving on. It's just the way of it."

"You don't need to go anywhere, Gerard. Not unless you want to, that is. Do you?"

Gerard thought about his life, the cold, the hunger, the fear and almost in an instant decided there was absolutely nowhere for him to be and no reason for him to go. Least of all because here, standing before him, was Max.

"No. I don't."

"Good." Claudette smiled, seemingly genuinely pleased. "Once you have eaten, you can help me peel some potatoes."

Many years passed and Gerard learnt all there was to know about love and kindness from Claudette and her papa, Luc. Luc had once been a successful watchmaker, but his business had dwindled as wealthy people fled the city and aristocrats lost touch with their heads. He always lived humbly and managed to keep his home well stocked and supplied. And then there were the friends in the country who Gerard discovered were actually all those dozens of people who Luc and Claudette had helped. Young couples they had taken in when they had nowhere to go before sending them on to a new life. Families with lots of children they had kept fed when the only alternative would have been the workhouse or starvation, now set up on farms many miles away and even an old aristocrat they had saved from the guillotine.

216

"He is just a man and a good one at that," Luc had told an aghast Gerard. "I don't believe any man has the right to decide who should live and who should die. We are all equal in the eyes of the Lord."

Gerard, though, had no desire to move on and neither Luc nor Claudette showed any signs of wanting to encourage him to do so. He earned his keep by doing heavy chores and the more manual labour, but to Gerard, it never felt like work, just as though he was part of their little team. That's certainly how Claudette and Luc made him feel, and in time, he too helped take care of other unfortunates as opportunity arose. Nobody else stayed as Gerard did, though, and in time he almost forgot that he had never lived there.

He never forgot, though, that Claudette was Max. Gerard never said anything to Claudette about his memories, but he was certain she had a sense of their shared history as there was undeniably a special bond between them. A bond which they saw sanctified before a priest in the year that Gerard turned twenty years of age, with Luc looking on delightedly, alternately clapping and wiping tears away. The little family was almost blissfully happy, so much so that Gerard forgot all about Lord Jonas, or Lady du Bonnieres, as she was in this life.

They had been married around eighteen months when their world came crashing down around them. It was a few days before Christmas and the weather was bitterly cold. So cold, Gerard was reminded of the winter Claudette had rescued him from certain death. Icicles formed on the ends of noses, breath puffed from mouths like smoke from chimneys, and despite their efforts, bodies littered the streets. Their comfortable but modest appartement had been bursting at the seams with those who would otherwise have frozen to death. Dozens had been sent to new lives in the country, thanks to Luc's extensive network, but still, every evening, he helped weakened, embittered souls up the same steps he had once stumbled on so many years before.

At nearly eight months pregnant, Claudette no longer ventured out onto the streets with him, but instead worked tirelessly to ensure a large pot of soup or stew was always boiling over the fire.

Gerard was just heading out once more, after having settled a young girl, probably no more than twelve, into the same armchair he had been cossetted in on the night Claudette saved his life. The night sky was dark and glimmering with stars. It was likely to be the coldest night yet, he thought to himself as he pulled his thick cloak around him, and felt a burst of gratitude for the thick, lined gloves Claudette had made him. He caught himself smiling broadly, unable to contain his happiness yet again.

Despite the horrors they sometimes saw around them, this life had been good to them, he often thought. They had warm clothes, good food and a solid roof over their heads. They also loved each other wholly and completely. But perhaps more importantly than anything else, they derived a huge sense of satisfaction and contentment from being able to help people. It gave them both a huge thrill to see people thrive who had come into their lives as wraiths. The fact that Claudette was also Max simply added another layer of wonder to Gerard's happiness. He was truly blessed, he thought. And then three men barred his path.

"Can I help you, sirs?" he asked, his voice not giving any hint of fear.

The three lumbering figures said nothing but moved closer to Gerard, closing in on him in a three-way pincer movement. He felt panic rise in his throat as his brain raced through escape routes, but darkness descended before he had a chance to make any move.

When he awoke, he was tied to a chair with a hood over his head. A metallic taste in his mouth told him he had been bleeding, he thought possibly from his brow and his lip. The thumping pain in the back of his head told him he was probably bleeding from there too. He pulled at his bindings but all that achieved was intensified pain from where the rope bit into his wrists. Instead, he forced himself to sit still and took three deep breaths of the musty grainy air inside the old grain sack over his head. Panic rose in his throat but with each breath it subsided to be replaced with sadness.

Images of Claudette rose in his mind. He saw her bent double in grief, clutching her extended stomach. He saw her screaming in pain as she gave birth to their daughter early. He saw her cradling the lusty little girl, that she would name Geraldine, in her arms, knowing that he would never see her in reality. Tears were streaming down his face when the hood was torn from his head.

Blinking in the brightness, he struggled to refocus in the yellow glow from the one lantern, but it was only moments before he recognised the figure before him in the dark, cold, stagnant room. A room filled with the scent of death and sawdust. Lady du Bonnieres. Or Lord Jonas in another form, bristling with anticipation at the cruelty she was expecting — hoping, even — to inflict.

The old woman grinned viciously at him, so wide she carelessly showed the gaps at the back of her mouth where she had lost teeth. Gaps that, when in polite society, she was so careful never to show.

Gerard decided not to wait for her to start. "So, it is you who is going to kill me," he stated bluntly. If he was going to die, why let her have it all her own way?

Her eyes sharpened beneath her powdered wig, bejewelled with pearls, the weight of which forced her to move as if she were carrying a heavy water pot on her head. And yet she still managed to pace restlessly, her deep olive silk skirts rustling. "What makes you think I am going to kill you?" she asked, deciding to play the game rather than follow his blunt lead.

"I know it. I would like to know why, though. Will you tell me?" He saw her lips purse and her jaw tightened. With a flash of insight, he realized she didn't really know. "You don't know, do you?" His voice was goading, delighted, even. "You don't understand why you don't like me so, do you?"

Her hand cracked across his face like a whip. "Stupidity. You were always stupid. I can't stand to be around stupid people and you incensed me with your gawping and foolishness. You didn't even have the sense to show me due respect, to fear me as everyone else does." She was spitting as she spoke, constantly pacing and flailing her arms in agitation.

"That doesn't make sense, though, does it?" Gerard was emboldened. Sad as he was, he never feared death, knowing, as he did, what was waiting. "You can't really explain, can you?"

"I CAN! See, you are doing it now, driving me mad with your idiocy."

"That may have explained why you threw me out on the street without good cause all those years ago, but not why you have tracked me down after all these years, had me kidnapped and now plan to kill me. That's not rational, my lady." Now Gerard was smiling.

"Rational? How dare you challenge my rationale?" Her eyes were wide with rage.

"I can challenge it because I know. I remember. I know you hate me because of what has passed in previous lifetimes, but in truth, it is me who should hate you. I have always suffered at your hands whereas you have never been able to take responsibility. You see your own guilt when you see me, your own inadequacies and *that's* why you want to kill me."

Gerard knew the blow was coming, even before he felt the blade strike his neck and for one sweet moment, he felt exultant and free. Then, before he slipped out of his body and towards the light, his last thought was once more of Claudette and baby Geraldine, and this time he saw them lying in a pool of their own blood and he knew without a shadow of a doubt that Lady du Bonnieres would be responsible.

Chapter 14

It was a cold, misty morning. Autumn had truly arrived in Avalon and if he had not been worried, it was exactly the kind of morning Jack would have relished. The trees, leaves growing into their goldenness, bristled with just a hint of frost and the swirling mist carried that evocative scent of earth and smoke which, for Jack, encapsulated the season.

Instead, he walked quickly from the layby where he had parked his Range Rover to the cottage, focusing more on why Aurora hadn't answered her phone than the seasonal delights that surrounded him. As he approached the front door, though, his steps slowed, now fearful of what might be beyond the worn blue painted wood. He slid the key into the lock and turned, the sound too loud in his ears. The door glided open smoothly to reveal an empty hallway except for Aurora's boots slumped next to the bottom step and her thick outdoor coat hanging on its hook next to Sloan's lead. They clearly weren't out on an early morning walk.

"Aurora?" he called into the emptiness, the echo of his own voice intensifying the panic building in his chest. "Sloan? Sloan, boy, come here." He added a shrill whistle for good measure and waited once more, standing a foot in the doorway almost crouched as if expecting a blow at any moment. If only he had realised his stance unconsciously echoed that of the warrior he had been so many years before. He listened. Was that a rustling from the kitchen? He wasn't sure, but taking a deep breath, he slowly made his way through, glancing into the living room as he passed, knowing it would be empty. He paused once more outside the kitchen door. It was closed. Bile rose in Jack's throat with the growing sense of wrongness. It was never closed to allow Sloan to come and go as he pleased. "Aurora?" he called again. "Sloan?"

The rustling once more, and perhaps a whimper? With a burst, Jack pushed open the door to see Sloan's large fluffy body spread out on the slate tiles, breathing hard. He never lifted his head but a faint rumbling in the back of his throat let Jack know he knew he was there.

"Sloan, buddy, it's OK, I am here." Jack knelt beside the big dog and lifted his head into his lap, stroking his ears back from his face. "What happened, mate? Where's Aurora?"

The dog looked up at him with pained eyes. Jack could have sworn he felt guilt and anguish. He also noticed the spittle gathered round the animal's muzzle and knew he had to get him to a vet.

An hour or so later, Jack was once more pushing open the cottage front door, carrying a still dopey Sloan and placing him on his giant cushion by the fire. A few minutes later, he had a blaze roaring in the hearth, wanting to take the chill off the room and keep Sloan warm. The vet had said he had been drugged and to keep him warm and hydrated. He then made a pot of coffee then returned to the living room with his phone in his hand once more. He had tried to call Aurora another six times since he had found Sloan, but he had never expected an answer.

He knew now that someone must have drugged Sloan with the purpose of getting to Aurora. He knew, too, with a simple knowing, that that person was John — Lord Jonas. What he didn't know was what he had done to Aurora if she were still alive and what he should do now. Under normal circumstances, he wouldn't have hesitated to go to the police, but he knew his story of past lives, karma and ancient grudges travelling down through the centuries simply wouldn't be believed. Or would simply make him prime suspect.

He took a long drink and stared into the flames, trying to ignore his churning stomach. He needed to think clearly, to try and work out what John was likely to do. *What would Sloan do?* he asked himself, meaning his warrior former self, not the dog, but the question just made him chortle disconsolately. He couldn't feel less like the ancient warrior right now.

He wondered if John had a car as, if so, they could be hundreds of miles away by now and anywhere from France to Glasgow. And yet something told him they were not far away. There was something about Glastonbury that drew them all here, something that made this place special for Aurora and therefore connected to both him and Lord Jonas too. But where? It was a place steeped in myth, magic and legend. There were any number of places in the surrounding countryside that might provide a perfect hiding place or place to… Jack stopped his train of thoughts there. He couldn't let himself think about what else John might be planning to do with Aurora. He simply had to find them.

Sloan's head, dopey as it still was, lifted from his pillow and a sharp knock at the door followed shortly afterwards, echoing heavily through the cottage. Jack got up warily, motioning to Sloan to lie back down when the loyal dog tried to raise himself to go too. Cautiously he approached the door and peered out through the small arched window, half expecting to see John staring balefully back. Instead, there was an eccentric-looking lady in her mid-fifties wrapped in a deep purple cloak and wearing flowers in her hair, smiling expectantly up at the window as if she knew he would peer out before opening the door.

He did so and looked out questioningly. "Can I help you?" His voice, he was ashamed to say, was less than friendly.

"Jack, isn't it? Pleased to meet you. My name is Morgana Star, I came as soon as I heard. May I come in?"

Jack stepped back to let the vision in purple into the hall, almost without knowing he was doing so, and then followed her a little lamely through to the kitchen where she flicked on the kettle and started to make tea from the contents of the basket she had been carrying over her arm.

"Now, coffee is not the thing for times like these. We need something to open the senses. Something like…" She rifled through small packets of aromatic herbs. "This!" She smiled up at Jack in triumph. "Mugwort!" She was back in the basket again. "And maybe some rose," she added, coming out her basket once more, "for flavour."

"What do you mean 'times like these'?" Jack asked, trying not to be distracted by the basket of herbs.

"Why, your Aurora has been taken, hasn't she? I heard it being called out across the land with the first rays of the morning sun. Such a wonderful light your Aurora has, not that I have had the privilege of meeting her as yet, but I sensed her the minute she arrived in Avalon… As for the other fellow, the one who has her, his energy is very dark… Murky. His soul will need lots of cleaning after this is all said and done."

Jack held up his hand. "Please, Morgana, can you start from the beginning?"

The woman turned to look knowingly at Jack, her eyes sparkling amongst wrinkles that spoke of a lifetime of smiles. She took a moment to read his face, and satisfied by what she saw there, she nodded decisively. "Very well, but first I insist we make tea."

"Do we have time for tea, Morgana?" Jack's nerves were frayed and he was worried that every second that passed somehow placed Aurora in even greater danger. If she weren't dead already.

"Jack, Aurora is alive and unharmed. Don't ask me how I know, I just do. We have time for tea and to go about this properly. No time to waste, but time for tea so pass me those cups."

A little while later they were sat on either side of the fire with Sloan lying, still dopey, between them. His nose twitching at the delicate aromas of rose and mugwort tea. Jack tried not to scrunch up his nose distastefully and forced himself to take a sip. It tasted better than he expected. Morgana finished her sip with a loud appreciative, "Ah!" Only then did she once more look over at Jack.

"As I said, I have been aware of Aurora from the moment she arrived in Glastonbury, just as I have been aware of her every time she has visited in the past. There is something here that keeps drawing her back, not that that is anything unusual, Glastonbury is a place of special energy and many people feel it calling to them."

Jack nodded, urging her to keep going. "Some of them come to my attention — there are many people with strong energetic fields — but I don't think I have ever encountered anyone with an aura as strong as Aurora's. Living, at any rate. Merlin has an incredible energy and he lights up the whole of Avalon when he pays a visit, but then he is no longer in a body."

Jack chose to ignore that, though given everything he had learned since meeting Aurora, who was he to argue? Maybe one day he would have a pint with Merlin. "So, you can sense her?" he asked.

"Yes... Though it is more than that... I pick up on what she is feeling." Morgana looked closely at him once more. "It is as if she is one person but also another, many others; would that make sense to you?" She watched him closely. Jack felt his tongue thicken in his mouth as he wondered how much to say.

"Yes," he finally admitted. "Aurora has a unique ability, you see." Morgana looked on expectantly, clearly waiting for further explanation.

Jack swallowed once more. "She can remember all her lives." It was now his turn to watch Morgana. "All the way back to Atlantis."

"Ah! Now that is interesting. I have known people to remember bits and pieces, but generally they have to go searching for them through regression and meditation, but you say she just remembers them?" Her eyes were keen.

"Yes. She says it is in the same way as you or I remember a holiday or childhood Christmases."

"How extraordinary. That must get confusing, no wonder her energy is so huge and many coloured. It is like she is many people at once."

"And not," Jack said, with sudden clarity. "I think Aurora is, in this lifetime, the closest she has ever been to her core being. Since Atlantis, anyway. I think that's why things seem to be coming to a head now."

Morgana looked at him. "You and she have been together before, is that right?"

"Yes, we were lovers about one thousand five hundred years ago."

"Mm… Yes, I can sense the bonds between you, very strong and beautiful, if you don't mind me saying… But they are not the only ones. I see others, including the dark cords which seem to be surrounding you, her and even this cottage right at the moment. Do you know anything about them, Jack?"

"I think so," he replied taking another drink of tea. "There's been a man following her on and off for about a year and it turns out he is the reincarnation of a man who keeps cropping up in Aurora's lives and doing her harm… Although he seems to be the one with a chip on his shoulder and revenge on his mind. I believe the first time Aurora encountered him was about one thousand years ago. He seduced her and then abandoned her before, many years later, reappearing only to make her watch as he murdered her family. The other incarnations have been equally brutal and Aurora always on the wrong end. Although there was one life in which Aurora poisoned him, but then he had been an incredibly abusive husband."

"Interesting, and do you think that's why he wants revenge?"

"In part. He just seems to be fixated on her, as if he somehow believes her to be the root of all his problems."

"He is a very out of kilter soul, certainly, I can sense that from the dark energy cords he is sending out. Now, what about the other energies I see around her? There is one very strong energy although it isn't close just now, who might that be?"

Jack pursed his lips and thought hard. "I have no idea, I am afraid. Aurora must have met hundreds of people through her lifetimes."

"Very true. Well, I think it is time to do what I came here to do. Drink up and I think we will turn off the lights and shut the curtains."

As the room fell into dimness, Jack added a few logs to the fire and urged it back to life with a poker, making it sizzle in protest. Morgana rustled back from pulling over the curtains and sat back in her seat with her back very straight, her hands smoothing and settling her skirts around her. She took a deep breath in, then out, then closed her eyes. Jack watched in bemusement while, outside, the first stirrings of an autumn storm stirred.

For a few minutes, Jack watched Morgana's closed face while listening to the encroaching wind finding its way down the chimney to infuriate the flames of the fire. Rain now also battered against the window. Aside, though, from the occasional crease across her brow, Morgana made no noise or movement for a good few minutes. Finally, she cleared her throat.

"Aurora? Is that you?" Her voice sounded reedy, as if coming from far away. "My name is Morgana, I am a friend. I am with Jack and we are trying to find you." Morgana now swayed in her seat, her back upright and her hands pressing into the top of her thighs as if to keep herself anchored. "Aurora, can you hear me?" Her swaying was more pronounced. "Don't try to speak, my dear, just send me pictures... Anything at all that might help us find you."

Jack sat forward in his seat, desperate to know what Morgana could see but unwilling to disturb her in case she lost her... connection, for want of a better word... with Aurora.

"I can see trees, is that right, Aurora?" Morgana was concentrating hard. "But you are inside... Somewhere dark... And somewhere that smells... A distinct smell... Makes you sneeze... Oh, I see horses. OK, that's good. Can you give me anything else, Aurora?" Morgana jumped in her seat and opened her eyes with a start. She looked drawn.

"What happened, Morgana?"

The woman reached for her empty tea cup and tried joylessly to take a drink. "He came back. I don't think he knew I was connected to Aurora but his dark energy was enough to cut us off." She sighed and rubbed her face. "I am sorry, that is very tiring, do you think I could have a coffee?"

With coffee made an impatient Jack quizzed Morgana mercilessly as she sat now slumped back in her chair, coffee cup in hands and feet stretched out towards the warmth of the fire.

"Was she unhurt?" Jack demanded for the umpteenth time as he paced the room.

"As far as I could tell, Jack. She certainly never sent me any pain signals or images of injuries."

"But she was bound?"

"Yes... Her wrists, certainly, and she was gagged."

"In a room?"

"Of sorts... I couldn't' see it clearly as it was dark and it was full of stuff. I am afraid, though, I couldn't clearly see what any of the stuff was. There was a sense of a storeroom... Or somewhere where someone hoards."

"Do you think it is nearby?"

"She has not left Avalon," Morgana said with complete certainty.

"But somewhere with trees."

"Yes, I think Aurora must have caught sight of trees as they arrived."

"And a smell of horses. She is allergic... She would sneeze... And have itchy eyes and throat. It would make being bound and gagged even more miserable for her." Jacks voice was filled with despair.

Morgana finished her coffee and sat up. "Jack, there's nothing more you can do tonight. The storm is quite literally raging and I have no sense he means immediate harm to Aurora. He has a plan, that much I can sense, but I am not sure what it is at all." She looked at him. "My advice to you is to try and get some sleep. I will meet with some of my fellow priestesses and we will see what more we can try to find out by whatever means we have available. I will come back here in the morning." She stood up and retrieved her cloak then turned to face Jack once more. "I don't know how much this means to you, Jack, but you have the support of the entire community of Avalon. Aurora is one of us and we intend to keep her safe."

With that, Morgana left. Jack wasn't sure if once outside, she jumped on her broomstick, but he had no energy to wonder for long or even smile at his own levity. Instead, he collapsed onto the couch, and to his own surprise, was asleep within minutes.

Claude

Claude couldn't help watching her. His eyes were drawn to her in a way over which he had no control. She knew it too and while she sometimes nodded and gave him a small smile when she caught him, Claude knew she wasn't interested. It pained him greatly. Ever since he had come to stay at his family home while nursing an injury picked up at Waterloo, he had been entranced.

That first morning home he had hobbled on his crutch out into the garden, keen to be outside in the summer sunshine amongst the scents of the famous rose garden. It was here he first set eyes on her. She had been kneeling on a cushion, gently pruning a rose bush, smelling each bloom with a look of complete joy before placing them in her basket. Her fair hair was scooped in a low bun beneath a straw sun hat. Over her coffee-coloured gown with lace cuffs, she wore a pale green apron embroidered with exquisite flowers and foliage. Aware she was being watched, she looked up at him and smiled and Claude felt his heart twist and turn unexpectedly.

"Hello, you must be Master Claude." She stood up and presented her hand to him, looking at him strangely, searchingly, as if recognizing something in his features, before letting her face slip into a gentle smile. "My name is Lottie, I am Lady Alexandria's tutor."

He reached for her hand with his own, wishing he was not leaning on a crutch. "It is a pleasure to meet you, Lottie, though I am no longer a master these days, but a colonel." He winced at his own pomposity. "But, please, you must simply call me Claude."

"Thank you, Claude. I was sorry to hear about your injury, I hope you are recovering well?"

"I am, thank you. I was lucky the bullet went clean through. I will only need this for a few more weeks." He gestured disdainfully at the crutch.

"I'm glad." She smiled earnestly but was obviously not inclined to linger and instead bent to retrieve her basket. "Now, if you will excuse me, Lady Alexandria and I will be painting this morning and these beautiful blooms are to be our study." With that, she swept away, full of poise and calm, leaving Colonel Claude Fletcher standing, staring after her like an uncouth schoolboy.

From that moment on, Claude devised every opportunity to be in Lottie's presence, much to the sometimes annoyance and other times delight of his sister, the fourteen-year-old Lady Alexandria. The young lady adored her big brother, but like all siblings, could get annoyed if his presence stopped her from getting her own way.

"Why were you following us about again today, Claude?" she remonstrated with him over dinner one night. "I would have thought a colonel in the British Army would have better things to do than hang around two ladies trying to catch butterflies."

"Alexandria, mind your tone, as I keep telling you, you are a lady."

"Lady Smlady! Lottie and I were going to go swimming in our under garments if he hadn't been around."

"Alexandria!" It was their father this time. "Perhaps your tutor needs to adopt stronger discipline measures rather than encourage you to frolic in that manner."

Alexandria stuck her tongue out in response, careful to make sure her father never caught her, however.

"I am recuperating, sister, and the exercise is good for me," Claude responded, trying not to look flustered.

"Pah! Nonsense, brother, you like Lottie. It is as clear as day to anyone with eyes."

"You don't know what you are talking about, Alexandria."

His sister was laughing delightedly now, crowing in delight at his discomfort and oblivious at the curious and disapproving glances between her parents. "I do! I can see how you flush whenever she is close and you never stop looking at her! You are like a dog gazing longingly at a bone it has been told it can't have!"

"Enough, Alexandria!" Her father's voice cut through her youthful delight. "Go to your room. I will be up to see you presently."

Alexandria flushed and went pale, but her father's tone was enough to see her slip demurely from her seat and leave the room to await her punishment.

Once their daughter had left, their parents looked curiously at Claude. "Well, son, is there any truth in this?" his mother asked.

He could feel himself blushing but sought to maintain some dignity. "I think she is a very alluring young lady with many talents and charms, certainly," he managed, trying to sound as dispassionate as possible.

His mother saw right through it though. "Oh, Claude! You fancy yourself in love with her, do you not?"

"She is a governess, Claude!" his father chimed in, looking at his son with horror at the thought that their family line could potentially be diluted by someone of the lower classes. "You do know you cannot possibly have a relationship with her, never mind marry her, do you not?"

Incensed by his parents and with his judgement clouded by his feelings, Claude decided to take matters into his own hands. Once the household was asleep, Claude, dressed for the road, crept on silent feet with only the slightest of twinges in his injured leg, to Lottie's room. He knocked gently and waited, his breathing shallow. When he heard nothing, he knocked again. No answer. With a sense of panic, as if the world was closing in on him, he brazenly reached for the door handle. In the gloom, he could see her shape beneath a patchwork blanket, her shoulders rising heavily in deep sleep. He took a step closer.

"Lottie." His voice was a stage whisper, but still not enough to wake her. He took a step closer and reached out a hand to her shoulder. Lottie sprang awake, sitting up, spinning round and pulling her blankets protectively to her chest all in one movement. Her scream was only just stifled by Claude's hand over her face.

"Hush, Lottie, it is me, Claude, you know I would never harm you." He knew he sounded strange, not quite himself.

"Claude." Lottie relaxed a little when she realized who was there. "What are you doing here?" She noticed how his eyes looked a little glazed.

"Lottie, you must know that I love you... And I know you don't love me... Not like that, I mean..."

She tried to stop him. "Claude, this really isn't proper, you can't be here saying these things to me."

He took her hands and held them to his chest, sitting close to her on the bed. "I know, but I have no time for proper, Lottie, as I fear this might be the only chance I get. Come away with me tonight... I will be a good husband and I think in time you will come to love me, we could have children together..."

"Claude! Please don't say these things... I don't want to leave here. I like being here."

"Why? Why would you want to be a governess to my wild sister all your life? I am offering you the life of a colonel's wife..."

"Claude, I love your sister as if she were my sister... She is important to me... Important in a way I can't explain... You must forget this has ever happened..."

"You love Alexandria? What do you mean? You would rather stay with her then be with me? I don't understand..."

Claude could feel a sense of rage building inside himself, a rage he couldn't really understand, born out of hurt, rejection and disbelief and a deeper, older feeling he sensed but had no grasp on. He felt it building inside him and could see in Lottie's face that she could see it too. It was a matter of who could move quickest, and thanks to his still injured leg, in this instance it was Lottie. She dived for the door and ran for the stairs in nothing but her nightgown and cap. Claude caught up with her quickly, though, and grabbed a hold of her before she had made it down the top two or three stairs. She screamed, scared enough now she didn't care if she woke the whole household.

"Claude, stop it! Please leave me alone!" She fought with all her strength to get her arms free and managed enough to claw at his face with her fingernails, but just as she thought she was going to be able to shrug him off and run, he lashed out, caught her legs and sent her tumbling down the stairs to her death.

When the family and staff found Claude, he was sitting weeping like a heartbroken child at the top of the steps, Lottie's broken body a crumpled heap below.

Jack woke with a jolt. The fire was burnt to ashes in the grate and a wind was howling as if tormented by grief. It felt like the roof of the cottage was about to be ripped asunder. Sloan was curled into a tight ball on the fireside rug, his eyes, though, were open and wary.

Jack swung his feet to the floor and paused for a moment to rub hands over his face, agitating the two-day stubble, and then through his already tangled and tousled hair, giving himself a moment or two to shake off the strange dream and come to terms once more with the facts of his life. He was sitting in a cottage in Glastonbury, Aurora was missing — likely kidnapped by a vengeful character who has stalked her through time, although he only knew that thanks to his gut feeling and a middle-aged witch, or priestess, or something, who appeared out of nowhere — and he couldn't go to the police because the story was just so farfetched. Or could he? Why couldn't he? He didn't have to say anything about past lives, he could just say Aurora had gone missing and that she had been bothered by a stalker, couldn't he? Why hadn't he thought about that before now?

He rubbed his face again and shivered. The room was freezing. He glanced at his watch. It was three a.m.; he couldn't go to the police just now, but he would go first thing in the morning and say he had waited to come to them in case she had just taken herself off for time on her own. Jack knew he would look suspicious, but he couldn't see another way right now and he certainly didn't have any other way of finding Aurora, other than hunting down every property that housed horses in Somerset, as seen in Morgana's vision. Or maybe he could? What was less mad? Jack didn't know any more, but giving himself another shake, he decided that at that particular moment he needed to do something practical.

With a spurt of energy, he knelt by the fire, giving Sloan a reassuring pet, and resurrected the fire. A few minutes later, he had also had a quick shower and shave and redressed in jeans and a warm woollen jumper — the soft navy one Aurora had bought him last Christmas. The feel of it made his heart and stomach turn over as fear and panic rose once more.

"Aurora," he whispered to the cottage, "I will find you, I promise." Taking a deep breath, he remembered what Morgana had said — she was safe for the time being. His job was to think clearly and formulate a plan. For that he needed coffee.

He placed a tray with a full cafetière of strong coffee and a plate piled high with homemade biscuits and cakes (bought from the market) before him on the footstool. Pouring himself a mug, he sat back with two oaty biscuits. Sloan leapt onto the couch beside him and happily settled down to wait for his share, while Jack settled back in the couch to stare into the flames. He didn't have any psychic ability that he knew of, but perhaps if he let his mind quieten and his gaze soften on the flames, something would come. He didn't know where that knowledge came from, but he thought it sounded like the kind of advice that might work, so, after munching one biscuit and giving the other to Sloan, he drank a large mouthful of coffee and then took two big breaths and allowed his gaze to get lost in the flames.

He wasn't sure how long he sat like that when a voice clearly rang out in his head — *remember your dream*. He sat up, a puzzled look on his face as if waiting to hear the voice again. He did and the surprise of it made him gasp out loud. The dream? Now wide awake, he let his brain call back the details of the dream — or was it a remembering? — of a young man called Claude, perhaps about two hundred years ago, who was obsessed with a young governess called Lottie. He let the images flash through his mind until he stopped on one of Lottie smiling and laughing with complete delight as she played in the garden with Claude's younger sister. It was Aurora's smile, the same laugh. Lottie was Aurora, but in that life, she didn't have eyes for Jack, or Claude, as he was then — at all — in fact, all her attention was on Alexandria

Jack sat up on the edge of the couch, his body taut and alert as if ready to start a race. What did it mean? Why did he dream that dream now? Was that the kind of dream Aurora had when she remembered her past lives? With a sudden sigh, he fell back into the couch and closed his eyes again. It was all too much for his very ordinary brain. He had accepted he was once a warrior called Sloan — he sometimes felt as if the memories of that life danced tantalisingly close at the edges of his mind — but all the different strands and threads of connections through different lives, personalities and experiences were just too much for him to get to grips with. He wondered how Aurora coped.

"Oh, Aurora! I so wish you were here," he said to the cottage and Sloan.

To his astonishment, moments later, the door went. It was not quite five a.m. When he opened the door to a flurry of leaves and rain, he saw Morgana and three others, holding their cloaks tightly around them.

"We need to speak," Morgana said without preamble as she pushed past Jack into the hall, shaking her cloak out as she went.

Bemused and without arguing, he stood back to hold the door open for the three others who all, in a way reminiscent of Sloan the dog, shook their cloaks out in the hallway too. Jack surreptitiously wiped the fine spray from his face.

"Please come through, ladies," he said wearily, leadingly them into the living room with his mind numb to any wonderings as to what they could possibly have in mind. "Shall I make tea? Coffee?"

"No time just now, Jack. We are on a tight deadline and have to act fast if we are going to get Aurora back, and it has to be said, rid Glastonbury of the dark energy that man has brought. We need your help and we need to work quickly."

"OK," said Jack, flatly, no longer surprised by anything and too tired to feel any hope. "Just tell me what you need me to do."

Alma

"Mr Dickens, it is a monster of your own creation, you must accept responsibility," Alma said as she sipped her coffee.

Her cloak was steaming, along with those of all the coffee shop's other patrons who had taken shelter from the thick snow falling from a darkening sky in the cosy room with its large fireplace. A veritable blaze roared in the hearth, surrounded by small tables packed tight with patrons gathered like pigs around a trough. Innumerate candles added to the warm golden glow, while holly boughs, bedecking almost every available space, ensured nobody could forget Christmas was only days away.

Mr Dickens, a crease on his brow, leant back as far as he could in his seat without compromising the large woman at the table behind him. "I suppose you are right, mistress, and it is not that I am not grateful for the success or the revitalization of Christmas spirit it's just…"

"Yes?" Alma eyed her friend mischievously over her coffee cup as she took another revitalizing sip of the thick brew.

Mr Dickens glowered but it soon melted into a self-effacing smile as he saw his friend's eye twinkling. "It's just I wish it didn't feel so forced... Most of them are only pretending to have Christmas in their hearts... For the sake of appearances... Fashion, even... To be seen... I wish it came more naturally."

"I grant there may be some for whom that's the truth, but I believe there are many who have simply been reminded of the true meaning of Christmas and all the magic that comes with it, thanks to you and your book, so please don't look so disheartened. Tell me, what are your plans this year?"

Mr Dickens brightened. "Children, of course, my dear Alma! Dozens of them, it feels like, all running riot round the Christmas tree, fuelled by sugar plums and ginger ale!" He grinned at his friend. "And you, my dear? Can I not prevail on you to join us?"

It was Alma's turn to look glum now. "It is very kind of you, Charles, but I must stay with my plans to go away for the festivities."

"Why, though, Alma, will you not tell me what is worrying you?"

"It is nothing, I promise you. I leave this evening and will be back the first week in January so, if you permit me, I will call upon you then."

"Of course." Mr Dickens watched his friend closely and couldn't quite suppress the feeling that he would never see her again.

The carriage ride gave Alma time to think. She was travelling west, out of London, to join friends at their country home in Somerset, in the countryside near Glastonbury. In any other circumstances, she would have been delighted to be spending Christmas with people she loved in such a glorious setting, but Alma couldn't help but feel like she was fleeing for her life. Many times, during her journey, she leaned out of the carriage window to look back down the road she had just travelled, always relieved to find it empty. Yet the niggling worry would build once more, compelling her to again look out, just minutes later.

She only felt safe when she arrived at her friends' grand Elizabethan manor house where she was ushered into a room with a warm fire. She had a glass of wine pressed into her palm before she even had the chance to remove her gloves. Caught between exhaustion and relief, it took her a moment to register the other guest, but when her host, and oldest friend, Emily, noticed their eyes meeting, she jumped to introduce them.

"Ah, Alma, how rude of me, please let me introduce Mr Nathan Avery, an old friend of my Rubin's."

Mr Nathan bowed over Alma's proffered hand, his eyes speaking of a deep recognition he couldn't place or name.

Alma could, though; here was Sloan, once again. She would know him anywhere. As she drew off her gloves and returned his smile, she wondered, as she had done so many thousands of times during her lifetimes, how neatly the universe always set things up. She knew she may well be in need of a warrior before the festivities were over.

"Madam, what brings you all the way to Somerset for Christmas?" Nathan looked searchingly and not without appreciation at Alma, as dishevelled as she was from her journey.

But before she could answer, Emily jumped in. "She is in hiding, Nathan, can you believe it!" Emily's voice was light, but Alma could tell she was concerned.

Nathan looked back at Alma, his face also showing concern. "How so?"

Alma took a deep breath. "I am being threatened, Mr Avery."

"Nathan, please," he replied automatically. "Threatened by whom, may I ask?" His interest seemed genuine.

Alma and Emily exchanged glances, mentally summing up how much to say. "There is a man, a very highly respected man, a lord, even, who will not take no for an answer." Alma looked into the fire, rather than dare to look into Nathan's eye, worried she might see Sloan there and reveal too much. How could she tell the man before her, embodiment as he was, of a man she once loved, that she was being stalked by a man who had dogged her through many lifetimes with a passion-filled hatred that was beyond reason and rationale?

Emily understood because her wonderful friend was Max and she had admitted to Alma that, in this lifetime, she had some memories.

Nathan remained calm but even more concerned. "Are you at liberty to tell me this man's name?" he asked.

"It is probably best I don't, Mr Avery... I mean Nathan. I would rather like to try and pretend he doesn't exist and enjoy Christmas, if you don't mind obliging?"

"Certainly, madam." Nathan smiled at her, his brown eyes crinkling in a way that made Alma's stomach lurch.

"Alma, please," she replied with a warm smile.

Christmas Eve dawned bright, crisp and even and Alma felt her spirits rise. With the house decked in miles of evergreen boughs, deep red bows and even glittering snowflake decorations that danced and glinted where they hung in the frost-covered windows, Alma found it hard not to get caught up in the excitement. And with Nathan there, with a ready smile, a quick hand and an endless supply of dry wit, she even found herself laughing with joyous abandon in a way she felt she hadn't done in a very long time.

After a leisurely and late breakfast, they wrapped up with muffs and mufflers to go skating on the frozen lake. The sky was already darkening as they traipsed home, red-cheeked and merry, for a warming hot cider. They then headed back out to chop down the large pine tree already earmarked to be the centrepiece to the festive celebrations, much to the excitement of Emily and Rubin's troop of children, all under the age of ten. A sumptuous feast was then enjoyed by all before everyone joined in decorating the tree and singing carols.

By the end of the evening, Alma felt a delicious peace descend on her. In her desire to enjoy the sensation for longer, she decided to wrap herself in her cloak and slip into the garden to look up at the stars, bright and many against the blackness of their eternal backdrop. The crunch of feet in the crispy snow gave away the man who approached her and her heart only skipped a beat for a moment as she turned round, knowing it was Nathan but fearing for a second that it might be Lord Jonas.

She smiled to see him in his overcoat, cigar in one hand, a brandy in the other. "It is a beautiful night," he stated by way of hello. "Nothing quite like standing beneath the stars and seeing them in all their glory to put your life into perspective."

"Truly spoken. They remind me of what must lie in between, beyond the world as we know it."

Nathan gave her a quizzical look. "Between?"

Alma shrugged off her comment. "Sorry, the combination of Christmas, wine, snow and stars is making me sentimental."

"You sounded profound to me." Nathan turned towards her, dropping his cigar to sizzle in the snow as he did so. Attraction shone from his eyes with an intensity that made Alma shiver, while memories of Sloan, naked and tattooed, flashed through her mind. She moved forward to meet his lips before he had even started dipping his head and there they stood, beneath a universal canopy, lost in a kiss.

Everyone gathered the next morning in the drawing room for a casual breakfast while presents were exchanged. Alma couldn't help but exchange more than the odd glance with Nathan, while Emily watched with an inscrutable expression.

After church, where Nathan and Alma sat next to each other, pressing as close as they dared, it was home for games before dinner. Alma squealed in pretend protest when Nathan caught her beneath the mistletoe.

The meal was another sumptuous board laden with treats, including a huge goose, a ham, pheasant and myriad of honey-glazed and roasted potatoes and vegetables.

Afterwards, everyone collapsed before the fire, sipping wine and lazily chatting, oblivious to the dark figure lurking beyond the heavy velvet curtains, closed behind the sparkling tree. To those ensconced in the glow of a warm fire, a thousand candles and easy, comfortable company, it seemed as if all the world was at peace and ease. The man who lurked beyond the boundary of light and love in the shadows was, though, intent on destroying it all.

As if obeying a power beyond her ken, Alma stood up and announced she would take a turn of the garden. A few moments later, after he had heard the door close behind her, Nathan rose and announced to the room that he felt it was his gentlemanly duty to follow Alma and make sure she didn't slip on the ice.

Emily, lying lazily against Rubin, glanced up at her husband knowingly. "It seems you were right, my dear."

Rubin smiled down at her, his kind eyes twinkling. "It does seem like our Nathan is taken with Alma."

"Now we have a quiet moment, though, I might as well see if we too can play lovers." He produced a sprig of mistletoe and dangled it suggestively above his wife's head. "I managed to save this from the lovebirds." Emily smiled up at the man she adored just as a horrifying scream rent the air.

Outside, they found Nathan wrestling a man to the ground. Beside them, on the ground, lay Alma in a pool of dark, sticky liquid, stark against the snow even by starlight.

As Emily fell to her knees next to her soulmate of eons and howled at the heavens, Rubin dived to help Nathan hold the man responsible, but he was quicker and more feral. In just moments he had managed to shrug both men off and flee into the darkness.

Chapter 15

Aurora came to with a jolt and instantly shivered, unsure if it was the temperature in the barn making her cold or the memory of her blood seeping out onto the snow that night about one hundred and fifty years ago.

Struggling within the confines of her restraints, she sat up and leant her head back against the wood of the post behind her. It was cold in the barn and by the depth of darkness she could gauge between the slats of wood, she could tell it was still early and yet her senses told her the first stirrings of dawn were not far away. Her lips were dry around the gag, her head thumped and the coldness made her bones ache. She was also ravenous, but all she could think about was that Sloan — or Jack — had been in her memory.

She had thought they had only shared one lifetime before, but now she had remembered their fleeting romance that Christmas all those years ago while Max had incarnated as her best friend. And yet, once again, Lord Jonas had been the means of her demise. It must all mean something. Was Lord Jonas' centuries-old vendetta robbing her of her appointed death, she wondered?

She knew, in a way many people didn't understand, that the way of your birth and death was decided before you incarnated. It was the bit in the middle that was free will unless someone somehow managed to disrupt that divine plan. Was this happening again here and now? Or maybe her greater awareness this time as she pieced together the many memories she was reliving with greater clarity than ever before, would help break the cycle. Maybe this time she could be ready for Lord Jonas when he came. With that thought, she once more slipped into an uneasy sleep.

Marjory

Running on silent feet, Marjory slipped out of the house into the deserted street. The dark was inky but still she kept to what would have been the shadows, her back pressed against the cold stone of the houses where people quietly went about their evenings trying to stay safe behind their shutters. Perhaps they were pretending that the war was not still raging three years after Hitler invaded France, that thousands upon thousands had not been murdered and that every day their own survival hung by the thinnest of threads.

And perhaps Marjory's life was even more vulnerable than most as she was here as a spy. She had volunteered as soon as war had broken out. Having watched the rise of nationalism and the dualization of Europe, with nations, cities, neighbours and even families broken down into 'us and them' and the gang mentality that always leads to division, hate and ultimately death, Marjory had been preparing. She had become fluent in French, German and a host of other languages. She had taught herself customs and mannerisms and absorbed as many other subtle pieces of information as she possibly could. The kind of thing she knew could mean the difference between life and death as an undercover operative. Perhaps her unique perspective on life, her knowledge of the eternal, also made her perfectly suited as it made her less afraid of death. The war office had had their doubts to begin with, but she soon proved her worth.

She had now been in deep cover in her current persona — Sabine Chirac — for just over a year. An inordinately long time for a spy, but she knew she was reaching some kind of crossroads which would either mean fleeing 'back to Blighty' or her death.

Pausing at the corner of her street, she used all her senses to gauge what was happening in the world around her. She could smell cigarette smoke but knew it was coming from a nearby house, as was the stench of cooked cabbage. Probably all they had had for dinner. Her eyes had adjusted to the darkness but with no moon or stars, she could only see dim outlines. Nothing, thankfully, to arouse her suspicion and she knew the slight rustlings she heard were no more than foxes sniffing round the rubbish bins.

After a moment, she moved on, careful as always on silent feet. She had to make it to the airfield to collect the air drop at exactly the right time and she had no idea if their coded messages had reached friend or foe. Her fellow agent — a young man from Yorkshire — had been shot a few days before and his body showed clearly how they had tortured him. How much he had given away was anyone's guess. But this drop was too important to cancel. She knew that the plane, fast approaching through the darkest of nights, could save many lives and even change the war. With her senses on high alert, she picked up her pace through the streets until she reached the fields beyond.

Half an hour later, she was crouched in bushes next to the inconsequential field that would shortly act as a runway. With a finely tuned ear, she picked up the drone of the engines. Holding her position, she waited for it to draw nearer, experience having taught her exactly what point she needed to dash out and set the flares to guide the pilot. The muffled sound descended before the small aircraft emerged, flying with no lights, and came to rest between the quickly extinguished flares. Always wary, Marjory hung back in the bushes after dousing the lights, unsure if the plane was a trap or if the SS were also waiting in the bushes, guns primed.

A man carrying a large equipment bag jumped from the plane, the pilot preparing to take off before the door had even closed, and Marjory had no choice but to run forward and greet the new operative. She was nearly face to face with him before she realized it was Max.

A while later they were sitting by the light of a single candle on either side of a rickety kitchen table in a safe house, deep in the woods. Marjory was trying hard to focus on the job in hand when in reality all she wanted to do was drink in the face of the being who had been with her since the beginning of time. He was handsome in this lifetime — called Henri, though obviously not his real name in this life — perhaps about forty years old with wise, clear eyes that Marjory knew would inspire people to follow him. She guessed he was of high rank, someone who could lead the operation they were planning. There was a map spread out before them.

"The Führer is due to arrive here on Saturday. That gives us three days to plan. I need to meet the local resistance tomorrow; can you arrange that?" Marjory nodded, feeling gauche. "Are they reliable?" Henri's eyes searched her face.

"Yes. They are all good people." Marjory thought she sounded pathetic, but Henri just continued to gaze at her steadily and continued.

"Good. This is a once in a lifetime opportunity, we will never get it again, do you understand?"

"Yes, I do. It is what I have been waiting, hoping and planning for, sir."

"No need for the sir. Tell me about the local SS — who is the most concerning?"

Marjory took a deep breath and marshalled her thoughts. "In the main, they are the mildest of SS, only really willing to take action if something happens right under their noses. That all changed a few weeks ago when SS-Oberst-Gruppenführer Krause arrived. He is cruel. Vicious. And seems to be watching everyone constantly."

"He will have been sent to clean up ahead of the Führer's visit. What's he been doing?"

"Mainly making examples of locals. He shot an old farmer in the market square for not answering him, even though his wife tried to explain he was deaf. And he shot a girl who worked in the local café because she turned down his advances. He also ordered several low-level criminals to be hanged in public and their bodies left for the crows. People are keeping to their homes even more now, terrified of answering doors." Marjory paused and looked down at the document-strewn table between them.

"There's more, isn't there? Are you on his radar?"

"No. At least I don't think so. I have been here so long now, and the German troops have changed fairly often, so I think I have managed to avoid any suspicion. My story is so easy and plausible."

"But?"

"Yes, there's a 'but'. Another operative was captured last week. His body was found a few days ago. He had been brutalised."

"What did he know?" Henri's eyes sharpened but not without empathy.

Marjory swallowed. "He didn't know about the plan, but he knew about me."

Henri mulled this over for a moment. "Not ideal but can't be helped." He looked at her seriously, his face shaped and shadowed by the flickering candlelight. "You must get home and do nothing unusual for the next few days."

"Bit late for that, or have you missed that we are in a broken-down hut in the depths of the woods, long after midnight?"

He offered her a wry smile but continued. "Still, don't attempt to contact me or do anything except your job and chores. I will contact you when I need you, do you understand?"

"Yes, sir." Marjory couldn't help sound sullen.

"Henri," was his only response as he lost himself in the maps and papers in front of him.

Marjory slipped out into the shroud of darkness and back to the place she had really begun to think of as home.

Keeping up the pretence of humdrum normality was torturous. She smiled and called 'bonjour', stood in line for the meagre bread rations, washed clothes and passed hours working in the small library which had, amazingly, been kept open despite the war ravaging the world around them. People always need stories, Marjory used to think to herself as she smiled and nodded to the locals who came in to browse the shelves and select their evening's escapism. They also came for news, though, she knew. They had newspapers and magazines from beyond their small town, out of date but still news. And sometimes people posted flyers carrying messages. 'Just letting you all know Pierre is getting better' always meant something more to someone. Marjory knew it was one way they used to pass messages back and forth between operatives and resistance members.

Then, when the shifts she normally enjoyed were over, she would head back to the house she shared with her 'uncle' Alfred, a man she had grown to love as her own. Together they would dig up a few frugal vegetables from their small garden, milk the goat and rustle up a meal to be washed down with a glass or two of local wine and a game of backgammon.

Every second seemed interminable to Marjory after Henri arrived. Wise as always, Alfred knew something had happened. He didn't ask to begin with, but just watched her with worried eyes. Finally, two days after Henri landed, he looked up from the backgammon board and said simply, "C'est fini n'est pas?"

"Oui," was all she said by way of a reply, but she did reach across the table and hold the old man's hand hard.

By the time a message arrived from Henri, she was sick with tension and no longer knew whether to feel nervous, scared, excited, happy or sad. The red cloth was tied to the clothesline when she went out to check if their hens had laid eggs in the first haze of daybreak. She knew it meant he would find a way to speak to her today, it was a warning for her to be watchful and ready. More like on tenterhooks. For hours. Finally, he came into the library, late in the afternoon, unshaven and rough-looking. Dressed like a field worker.

"Bonjour." She nodded politely, giving no sign of recognition despite there being nobody else in the library at that point.

"Bonjour," he responded in a gruff voice. "I am looking for a book. Called *Midnight in the Woods* by Jacques Blanc, do you know it?"

"I do, sir, but I am afraid we do not have it in stock at the moment, je suis desole."

Henri grunted, turned and left. He knew Marjory had got the message. Just as Marjory knew that night, as she quietly closed the door behind her, leaving Alfred dozing in the chair, that she would never be back. She knew, too, she was probably signing Alfred's death warrant and the thought tore at her heart in a way that made her want to collapse to her knees and sob.

By the time she arrived at the hut in the woods, the leaders of the resistance were already there, listening keenly to Henri as he laid out the plan. They went through it time and time again through the course of the night. By the time the first flush of sun started to dissolve the mist, they were all in place, armed and determined that, by the end of the day, the Führer would no longer be living, even if it meant the deaths of them all.

And it would all have gone perfectly if, just as the Führer's car and outriders headed towards the part of the road where they lay in positions on either side of a small bridge, explosives in position, guns in their hands, a tractor hadn't come the other way, pulling a trailer full of children, none older than about six. They all looked at each other, eyes filled with horror then looked at Henri to make the call, but he too was trapped by a terrible decision and made the call too late.

It was all over in a few minutes. Henri lay dead, as was one of the resistance leaders. The other and Marjory knelt, side by side, in the road, their hands on the heads and guns pressed into the backs of their heads. The children watched in silent horror from the back of the trailer, forced off the road with the tractor by the momentary chaos that had erupted before them.

From the Führer's car stepped a pair of jackboots. With deliberately slow steps, they moved round the bodies to stand before Marjory. A leather glove grasped her chin and there, staring down at her with the coldest of smiles, was Lord Jonas. In one fluid movement he dropped her chin, shot the Frenchman by her side and walked away. "Bring her to me."

Hours later, broken, beaten and tortured to beyond endurance, Marjory lay naked on a cold, wet, cellar floor, and with a broken shard of glass, cut her own jugular. As her blood seeped out to mix with the rancid water, a blessed numbness taking over her limbs, she realized that in all her incarnations this was only the second time she had ever taken her own life.

Aurora awoke, cramped and frozen, on the hay-strewn floor. She knew before she had opened her eyes that John — Lord Jonas — stood looking down at her. Breathing deeply, she took a moment, but he had been watching her closely.

"I know you are awake." His voice was light, keen, alive. "You were dreaming. Again."

He watched nonchalantly as she struggled with her hands, bound as they were behind her back, to sit up, to give herself a little bit of a fighting chance at least. Her hair, wild and flecked with straw, fell annoyingly in her eyes. John calmly leant forward from where he stood leaning against some farm machinery and gently smoothed it back, taking his time and assuming intimacy by arranging other strands behind her ears. He pulled the gag from her mouth.

"Better?" He smiled at her, as a man would a wife, for all the world as if this was normal, as if they were chatting over breakfast, and yet there was a glitch in his voice. A tell-tale tautness that spoke of the cruelty and danger behind the faux affection. "So, what were you dreaming of? Can't have been pleasant."

Aurora glared at him, uncertain of how much to say. John laughed. "What's so funny?" she asked around a thick tongue and parched lips.

Reaching behind, he found a flask and poured a hot drink. With utmost gentleness once again, he held it to her lips and allowed her to take a sip. She let out an involuntary gasp. Coffee. Hot, sweet and the first food or drink she had had in more than twenty-four hours. John's smile broadened.

"You asked what's funny. Why this, of course, and the similarity to the dream you just had. I remember, too, you know. I had you at my mercy then, too, didn't I? I remember what I did to you and how long you lasted." He looked down at her fondly, with love, even, and then gazed into the middle distance, his expression dreamy. "I hurt you so badly and yet you still managed to surprise me by taking your own life." He gave his head a little shake as if, all these years later, he still couldn't quite believe it. "Not this time, though. No, indeed."

He bent down again and gave her another sip then hunkered down before her, a hand cradling her cheek. "This is the end, Aurora. This time I stop it all. By the time I have finished with you, this time, there will be no coming back. You will not die this time, you see, you will cease to exist. As you anyway."

He ran his fingers over her face, following the arch of her eyebrow, the curve of her cheek, the line of her jaw. "You want to know why? Well, it is simple. It is so I am finally free of you… Or free from your power by placing you under my power. You… Aurora… Make me do things, make me behave badly… And yet, it is like you are always punishing me too. I can't escape."

Aurora swallowed, her skin shrinking from his touch. "Nobody makes you do anything, John. You always have a choice."

"No." He stood up and turned away in anger. "I didn't choose to be slowly poisoned by you and my brother."

"You chose to beat me, your young wife, daily though."

"You deserved it."

"So did you!" Aurora retorted, her own anger rising to be met with his hand crashing down on her cheek.

247

"Enough!" he roared. "Tonight, by the dark of the new moon, it will be over and you will cease to exist as a person with free will... You will be mine completely and utterly." Aurora couldn't help the tears. "You may as well remember the final life we shared before this, Aurora, as you will never again have another opportunity."

He turned to walk out of the stable, but Aurora called after him. "He will come, you know. He will come. Even if it is after my death, he will come."

"Who, Aurora? Who will come? Sloan or Max?" Aurora flinched more at the words than she had at his blow. John now grinned down at her with the vicious grin of Lord Jonas. "Did you think I didn't know?" This time he did walk away, laughing, and Aurora couldn't think of a thing to say.

Daisy

They called it the Summer of Love and Daisy knew why. It many ways, it reminded her of the heyday of Atlantis, where unconditional love was a continual state, where everyone lived with empathy and compassion, and judgement and intolerance were unthinkable. She could see traces of it in the hippie movement, the talk of the Age of Aquarius, and she enjoyed being part of it.

She loved what seemed like endless summer days in the parks of London, sometimes lazily listening to music or ponderously contemplating the nature of the universe and sometimes losing herself completely in dance or lovemaking. It was like a spell had been cast and for a while they were all living out of time, and her lover — Max, known as Paul in this lifetime — was so reminiscent of her youthful soulmate in Atlantis that, for a while, she was happy just to lose herself in being with him, ensconced in the haze of love and community spirit.

Of course, Daisy saw the cracks appearing before many others. She understood that while 'free love' was OK in theory, while people still acted out of ego rather than from their higher selves, such careless giving of the body created the push and pull of co-dependency, regardless of the physical liberation. Few knew what it meant to be truly centred, to love themselves first and foremost and therefore, by giving their bodies so freely, they were still vulnerable to doubt, self-loathing, fear and guilt. The drug-use created more fracturing in people's energy fields, leaving them even more susceptible to emotional problems. Then, of course, there were those who sought to capitalize on the vulnerable. This was how she met Lord Jonas in this lifetime.

Unlike many others, she only had one lover — Max — and she didn't do drugs. Through her unusual perspective, she had more awareness than most and could also see how many so-called gurus acted out of ego and drew followers and devotees as a way to satisfy their own needs, rather than as truly enlightened beings. And this was exactly what Lord Jonas — or Apollo, as he called himself in this incarnation — was doing when Daisy first encountered him.

She and Paul were at a festival, idly wandering barefoot and with painted faces around fields filled with musicians, dancers, yogis and gurus, holding sessions of every type of meditation or chanting imaginable. A droning sound coming from a teepee caught their attention, and ducking under the door flap, there sat Apollo in a haze of smoke and incense, eyes shut, a crystal stuck to his forehead, hands raised in submission to the heavens as he led those gathered in a chant. Daisy knew in an instant it was Lord Jonas and instinctively began to back out of the teepee. Paul, sensitive to her feelings as ever, reached out to grasp her hand as he followed her out, his handsome young face filled with concern. They were almost back out into the early autumn sunshine when they heard a voice.

"Travellers, don't go." His voice was silky, as if every word was a performance just for the listener. So hypnotic that Daisy and Paul found themselves pausing and unwillingly turning around to face the smoky inners of the tent.

Apollo had come to his feet, white robes flowing around him. "You were brought here for a reason, please sit, just for a moment, and take some tea with us." His dazzling blue eyes landed on Daisy, and like a mouse caught by the stare of a snake, she found it impossible to do anything other than obey his will.

They sat near the fire and accepted cups of herbal tea while Apollo watched them intently with the assumed smile of a wise old benefactor, before beginning to once more address those gathered eagerly around the fire pit. Daisy felt a strange feeling in the pit of her stomach and knew something terrible was going to happen.

Daisy tried several times in the next hour or so to leave the teepee, but Paul was entranced. Apollo smiled his encouragement every time he asked a question.

"But, Apollo, are we not led to believe that we have the answers inside? All we need to do is listen to our hearts?" he asked.

Apollo nodded his apparent astonishment at Paul's insight, his eyes sparkling with a wickedness that could have been mistaken for passion. "Why, yes, Paul," he answered, as you would to nursery children. "However, in this busy day and age it can be difficult to hear what that wise inner voice is saying. That's why the universe has seen, in its incredible wisdom, to send me. My soul mission is to act as translator for people like you, Paul, whose hearts are pure and are following a path of enlightenment but just need a gentle guiding hand, like a father showing you how to shave for the first time." His smile was all innocence, but Daisy caught the flash of a smirk of delighted disbelief behind the façade. Apollo lifted his gaze to catch hers and caught her derision. He couldn't quite contain the instinctive lip curl and Daisy saw that too.

Standing, she pulled at Paul's arm. "Come on, Pauly, he's a fraud, let's get out of here." Apollo watched her, eyes fiercely dancing like a wolf readying for the kill.

"C'mon, Daisy." Paul sounded like a petulant child. "Let's just stay, this is cool. This man knows what's what."

"No, he doesn't, Paul, open your eyes, for God's sake. Your little finger is more enlightened than he is, you should just try stopping and listening for once."

"I am listening, sweetheart, and I like what I hear. Sit down and really tune in, man, you will hear too."

"I meant to your own heart, Paul, not HIM."

Apollo smiled, his grin board and devilish, but everyone else in the tent still seemed to see the guru they wanted him to be.

Paul pulled her back down beside him and tried to put his arms around her soothingly. "Daisy, babe, chill. Please, just a few minutes longer, I am really getting this, I want you to, too."

Daisy sat back down, her mind racing. She didn't want to stay in the tent a minute longer with Apollo — Lord Jonas — but she didn't want to leave Paul — Max — either. She was filled with a horrible sense of dread and an even stronger sense, born from lifetimes of experience, that she couldn't stop what was coming, no matter how hard she tried.

When Paul passed her the joint rolled by Apollo himself, she shook her head angrily, refusing to even look as he drew in a deep drag and exhaled with a sound of pleasure. Apollo smiled and nodded, happily in cahoots and yet Daisy knew it was her he really watched. She doubted he really toked either. A suspicion that came to fruition when everyone else around them flopped to the floor, muscles turned to jelly, minds turned to mush, and Apollo picked his way through the flaying arms and bursts of giggles to find a seat beside her. Her muscles tensed involuntarily. She wanted to say something sharp and cutting but in fact she found she had nothing to say to him. With eerie uncanniness, his words echoed her own thoughts. "What, nothing to say?" he asked with feigned gentleness.

She looked him in the eye. "Is there any point?" she asked.

He guffawed softly. "Probably not. I have urges I can't control and you bring them out more strongly than I have ever felt before." Daisy ignored him, her mouth dry. "Would you like to know what they are?

Daisy found her voice of generations. "I have a fair idea. Aren't they always the same? Are you not bored yet of causing pain and suffering? Especially to those who challenge you, am I right? You love to make them submit as how dare they challenge you! Don't you ever think, oh wise one, of taking personal mastery? Don't you know that we are the masters of our own emotions, we create our own reality by our thoughts and our choices so if you believe you are being slighted it is of your own making. If you feel like you are not given the recognition you deserve it is because you don't give yourself the recognition you deserve. You need to cause pain to others to escape your own pain within; you could do something about it but you don't want to, do you?"

Apollo held her eyes with an intense and yet earnest stare. "Touché, Daisy, but could the same not be said about you? Why do you keep creating these violent ends? Are you not in some way responsible? Could you not change your repeating fate too?"

With that, Apollo stood, white robes swirling, and ducked out of the teepee, leaving Daisy shaking with both indignance and the dawning of a truth.

Her many lives were of her own making, just as his were his. It was like having a bucket of ice-cold water poured over her head as patterns swirled and formed before her eyes. She saw clearly for the first time how the energy she was giving out had been mirrored back to her perfectly each and every lifetime, including the deep self-loathing she felt, born from a deep sense of responsibility for what happened to Atlantis — and to Max. And yet there was only one question rippling up from deep within. More important than how she had created these patterns was what she was going to do to change her future? With a sudden urgency, she stood up and stormed out of the teepee to find Apollo, leaving Paul staring after her with unfocused eyes.

She found him, eventually, sitting on a rock at the edge of the festival site, looking for all the world like he had been waiting for her, his robes billowing a little in the gentle wind.

"Well?" he said with an annoyingly self-satisfied little smile.

"You are right. I need to break the chain for myself. For me to be free." There was that smile again.

"What do you propose? A meditation? Call on higher beings?" The smile was outrightly sarcastic now. "Visualise a cleansing flame burning away the cords that bind us? Come now, Daisy, it will take more than that." He leapt nimbly from the rock and grabbed her by the hand. "Come, let me show you."

Daisy tried to break free of his grasp but it was useless — his grip was too strong and her increasingly strident protestations were lost in the growing hubbub of a burgeoning festival as dusk set in.

He pulled her between tents, camper vans and bodies lying languidly — sated, stoned, immaculate — between guy ropes and fires, tie-dye cloths and wafts of joss sticks. Far away from the teepee, at the heart of the party, he pulled open the back door of a van and pushed her onto the damp carpet lining and musky bedding in the back. His body, hard beneath the flowing gossamer robes, was on top of her before she could protest, one hand expertly clamped over her mouth while he grabbed her wrists with the other.

"Don't struggle now, Daisy, remember you created this... You wanted this... You must have on some level or else you wouldn't be here now, writhing beneath me."

Daisy's lips bruised beneath his sweaty palm as she tried to argue, tried to fight, tried to deny she wanted this.

"You will never break the chain because deep down you want me... You want me to put you out of your misery." His eyes were bright now, hard as agate. His body clearly hungry, but she knew instinctively that was not what he had planned. He smiled a smile filled with venom. "How you would love for me to satisfy you first... Like I did all those years ago when I was Lord Jonas and you were the serving girl... Oh what you would give to be back there again, but you are out of luck, Daisy." His body had her pinned to the fusty bedding. "Tonight, you die and your death will give me power, power you couldn't ever imagine, more than any of your other deaths has given me." He smiled down at her again, almost gently, as his hand slid from her mouth to her throat. "Any last words, woman of a thousand lifetimes?" Daisy opened her mouth to scream but her voice was lost to the tightening hands round her throat, the swelling pain in her chest and the blessed blackness when it came.

Aurora came to, spluttering, tears streaming down her face. "I need to kill him," she cried desperately to the emptiness around her. Then, as she regained her composure, she said, more quietly this time, with resignation, sadness and resolution, "I need to kill him this time." Leaning her head back to the wood behind her, she begins to sob, because for once, she simply couldn't see another solution.

Chapter 16

Jack wasn't sure if he was awake or dreaming. Or in a nightmare. He stood on top of Glastonbury Tor, surrounded by a group of witches. He couldn't think of anything else to call them, and if truth be told, he knew they likely wouldn't mind being called witches. Together, they had spent the day in preparation for this moment. Jack couldn't claim to really understand what it was all about, but it had involved lots of incense, meditation and pungent teas.

Now the sun was just beginning to set as they swayed in their circle, eyes closed, murmuring enigmatically and occasionally urging Jack to think of Aurora. He closed his eyes too and focused on his memories — Aurora standing, feeling the rays of the sun on her in Egypt, Aurora looking on fondly as his family indulged in their Christmas traditions, Aurora looking down at him in bed, her hair falling over a naked shoulder.

"That's it!" called Morgana. "I can sense her! The ley lines are showing me where to go — follow me!" With cloaks billowing in the dusky half-light, the group fell in behind Morgana with Jack taking up the rear. He longed to sprint forward and quiz Morgana about where she was leading them, but she had warned him staunchly not to interrupt. He would hate to break whatever energetic connection she had with Aurora, if she did indeed have one, a little cynical inner voice reminded him. The part of him that believed reminded the little cynic that there was always hope, and besides, what other choice did he have?

The odd little group scurried — there was no other word for it — in Morgana's wake, trusting her footing as darkness descended. The steep sides of the Tor gave way to fields, then the springy branches of stripped trees whipping at their faces. Jack could smell the earthiness of the land beneath them, hear the crunch of leaves and twigs under foot but he could see next to nothing. He wished he could somehow tap into the part of him that was Sloan. This would have been a normal day for the warrior, he imagined. He might also need Sloan's strength and grit when — if — they found Aurora.

Together, they stumbled on for what seemed like an age until finally Morgana held up her hand and gave a short sharp 'shh'. Beyond the branches, Jack thought he could see some building on the other side of an area of open land about the size of a tennis court. A tingling at the back of his neck told him more than his physical senses ever could, though. "She's here," he whispered, his voice barely audible.

"Indeed," Morgana answered in equally hushed tones. "What we need now is a plan."

Jack glanced in her direction in the deathly darkness. "Have much experience in planning rescues, Morgana?" he asked huskily.

"No," she responded flatly. "But I imagine we should start with a recon, don't you think? Fallow, you have the softest step, how do you feel about having a creep about and seeing what you can see?"

The mousy thirty-something nodded succinctly and immediately floated off silently across the open ground to the buildings, her dark cloak proving the perfect disguise.

The moments ticked by in silence, eventually becoming minutes. Jack had long since lost sight of the gentle movement of Fallow's cloak that gave a clue to her whereabouts, but he still strained in the darkness to catch a glimpse, hoping upon hope that by some miracle she may even return with Aurora.

After around ten minutes had passed, he grasped Morgana's arm more roughly than he intended. "I am going to look for them both," he spoke through gritted teeth, days of tiredness and frustration now threatening to shatter what little grip he had left on his self-control.

"Patience," Morgana answered gently but definitively. "Fallow is returning. I can see her."

Jack once more stared desperately across the velvet depths but could see nothing more than the merest hint of walls. He was just about to burst out of the thicket to go and look for himself when a wraith-like figure emerged from the dark on silent feet.

"I have found her," Fallow's soft voice intoned with excitement as soon as she was back in the safety of the thicket. "She is in one of the outbuildings. On the floor, asleep." Jack cradled his head in his hands, gulping air in sheer relief as Fallow continued. "I worked my way right around the building to see if I could find a way in, but everything was locked. The doors even had chains and padlocks as well."

"Well done, Fallow, at least we know where she is." Morgana patted the younger woman's arm.

"Any sign of HIM?" Jack's voice was tight with strain and Fallow simply shook her head. "Good. I am going to get her." And with that, Jack burst from the thicket without any thought to who heard him.

The women watched his broad back vanish into the shadows in silence.

"What do we do now?" one of them asked.

Morgana gave a little sigh. "We wait until we are needed," she replied eventually. "I have a feeling this is something he needs to do on his own."

A dozen strides from the thicket and Jack's resolve wavered. Why he hadn't even asked Fallow which of the outbuildings held Aurora, he didn't know. He could at least have paused long enough to grab something as a makeshift weapon, but here he was, alone in the dark with empty hands, feeling his way around a damp stone wall just as Fallow had already done just minutes before. Through the dark he realized he could hear the gentle snorting of contented horses and decided to follow the sound. He was in search of a stable, after all.

Railing against every instinct, he forced himself to take his time. Step by step, letting his feet fall as quietly as possible, he didn't want to alert Lord Jonas if he was close and he didn't need the horses and whatever other animals nearby to set off a chorus of alarm. He suddenly wished he had brought Sloan, though if the dog thought Aurora was somewhere close, there would be no stopping him. He understood. Every muscle on his body felt tightly wound and desperate just to surge forward and find the woman he loved, but instead, he crept along, his eyes boring into the inky night and his ears primed for the tiniest sound.

The whinnies and snorts grew closer. Jack turned around a corner and saw a dim light coming from beneath a half-opened stable door. He knew instinctively that that's where the horses were, but not Aurora. He moved on, keeping to the wall furthest away from the open stable door as he moved around behind the first stable, understanding now why it had taken Fallow so long to explore what was a much more complex array of farm buildings than they had first thought.

Around the next corner, Jack found himself on a lane, the lighter broken stone of the surface allowing him to see it arc about twenty feet around a slight bend and into some thick trees. Jack followed a hunch and followed it and there, at its end, was a much smaller stable building, lying dark and desolate at the heart of a small grove of trees.

"Aurora," he whispered, hoping that somehow, she could hear him, sense his closeness. He was next to the stable's walls in a few strides, searching for a way in or at least a window — there must be a window or how else did Fallow see her? He cursed himself again for not taking the time to question the witch more closely.

And then he found it near the back corner — one small window giving him a view into the dank interior where, somehow, there was just enough light coming from somewhere to let him see Aurora, hands bound behind her back to an upright timber, collapsed in on herself, head lolling. Sleeping, he told himself. Jack's heart leapt at the sight of her and then panic swelled from his stomach up to suffocate him. He had to get in. He had to get in now. Running back, he pulled frantically at the door, as futile a gesture as he knew it would be. He ran back to the window, Aurora hadn't moved. This time he ran around the other way to find yet another door, smaller this time but still locked and reinforced with a chain and padlock, but once again he pulled and strained, trying to pull it open. Nothing.

He ran back to the small window again. Aurora still hadn't moved. In frustration he banged on the window with his fists. Nothing except unnecessary noise. No movement from either the window or the love of his life, where she lay crumpled, held up only by her bound hands round the pillar. He felt tears threaten, panic and impotence on the verge of drowning him. Looking wildly around, his eyes fell on a large branch from a tree. Without thinking any further, he picked it up and with all his force, crashed the piece of wood through the window, shouting Aurora's name as loud as he could as he did so.

Back in the thicket, the gathered women heard the crash of glass and the anguished calling of a name, like an animal in the most terrible pain.

"So it begins," Morgana said matter-of-factly. "Be ready to move, ladies." She nodded towards a figure as it moved around the buildings in the same direction as Jack.

Oblivious, Jack dragged himself bodily through the serrated ring of what was once the window, ignoring where the broken glass, wood and metal gouged and scratched at his flesh, lacerating his clothes like a knife through butter. All he cared about was getting to Aurora, so close now he could smell her, his senses enhanced by fear and adrenalin. Blood coursed through his veins, thundered in his ears and soaked into the shredded cloth of what had once been his shirt and jumper, but none of that mattered as he was now in the stable and on his feet, hurtling like an injured gorilla towards where the woman of his heart lay like a rag doll.

"Aurora! Aurora! It's me, Jack, wake up!" He righted her body, pushed hair from her filthy face and slapped her face in an attempt to rouse consciousness, gently at first and then with greater force. Giving up, he reached behind her to loosen the rope that tied her hands, all the while speaking loudly to her as he would to a child, horse or dog. "Come on, Aurora, you must wake up! Before he comes back!"

"Too late." The voice came out of the darkness behind him, calm, confident and carrying an undeniable trace of smugness, as if he was announcing himself as the winner in a raffle at an amiable evening to raise funds for charity. "I am back. Lovely to see you, Jack."

Propping Aurora up against the wooden beam, he slowly turned round to face Lord Jonas, his eyes casting around for anything within arm's reach he could use as a weapon. But before he could even catch more than a glimpse of the dark figure, something hard and cold walloped the side of his head and blackness descended. When he awoke, Aurora was gone.

"Nooooo!" he screamed to the heavens in agony and frustration and would have happily allowed himself to crumple in defeat if Morgana hadn't appeared at his side.

"It's OK, Jack, we are on their tail, they are heading to the Tor. He had an accomplice, but we took care of them. Now, can you stand? Can you manage?" Jack swallowed the bile that rose in his throat as he stood, his head thundered and the cuts around his torso twinged unremorsefully.

"Just about. If you lead, I will follow." Silently he called upon the spirit of Sloan to give him strength.

He stumbled and stuttered his way over the uneven ground of the field until they reached a track, and then continued to stumble and stutter his way along the gravel, never taking his eyes from the back of whichever cloaked woman bobbed silently before him. After what seemed like a lifetime, the track started to rise steeply up towards the now starlit sky. Jack suppressed a groan. And then another.

"Keep going," murmured a dark shape beside him. "We are not far away. They are round the other side; they won't see us approach."

He could offer no more than the barest of nods in response as his feet continued to trip and falter. A hand took an elbow and then another one the second. Somehow he felt almost as if he was weightless, gliding almost up the sacred hill, his body momentarily freed from pain, from the weight that had pressed down upon him from the moment Aurora had disappeared. He was sorry when he once more felt the solid Earth beneath him.

"They are over there," a voice whispered in the deep silence of the night. Jack looked, his eyes now accustomed to the darkness, and what he saw filled him with a far greater horror than anything he had witnessed in the stable below. Aurora stood before Lord Jonas, swaying slightly, as he lifted her hand and placed a ring on the fourth finger of her left hand. Jack would have called out in horror if Morgana's hand hadn't clasped his arm.

"Wait," the woman hissed in his ear. "Something is to come. Something has to happen. We need to get closer so we can hear."

Crawling along the cold earth, the grass of the tor rough beneath their hands, they edged closer to where Lord Jonas now stood with his arms wrapped around an inert Aurora.

"You are mine now," they heard him say, his voice jubilant as it carried on the wind. "It is for eternity, this time, Aurora, there will be no escaping me this time, no betraying me, no leaving me."

Aurora seemed numb with confusion. "What do you mean? What is the ring for...? I never betrayed you... It was you who betrayed me..." She slumped in his arms, her strength giving out.

259

Lord Jonas cradled her, almost gently, almost as if he really did love her. "Ah, Aurora, don't you understand yet? Don't you understand? You are mine. You have always been mine to do with as I please. It is impossible for me to betray you." Aurora's head swayed back.

"But... But... I am not yours... I am nobody's... We are all one, but each our own..."

"No, Aurora, I need you..."

"You need to control me... That's not love!" Aurora struggled in his grasp, rousing herself from her shock.

Close enough now to see the frown on her face, her struggle to marshal her thoughts evident on her face, Jack couldn't hold back anymore. "STOP!" he called out, his voice his own and yet, on top of that windswept Tor, it sounded almost as if it was the universe itself speaking.

"Jack!" Aurora's voice was weak but filled with relief. Lord Jonas' face, however, was thunderous.

"Well now, what do we have here? The boyfriend again? Delivered into my lap perhaps? Maybe this is even more perfect than my plan." Lord Jonas let go of Aurora, not noticing that she collapsed to her knees. "And what else? Some witches, eh?" He laughed nastily. "Of course, what better place to employ the help of a few witches than Glastonbury! Full of kooks who think they have power when the fact is they know nothing of power." He sneered at the women as they gathered round Jack. "And as for you, boyfriend, how could you think Aurora could ever really love you, you have no awareness of anything."

"I know I love her."

"Pah!" Lord Jonas scoffed. "You know nothing. Do you think she loves you?"

"Yes." Jack's answer came quick, clear and confidently.

"Really?" he goaded.

"Yes. You don't think she could love you, do you?" Jack shot back. "A man who has terrorised, abused and used her over lifetimes? You don't know what love is. You think control is love. You... You..."

"Try to find love through dominance and manipulation." Aurora struggled to her feet, weak after hours of captivity and little food and water. "You have never understood, Lord Jonas, have you, that to love and be loved, you need to love yourself first. You have never liked what you see when you look in the mirror so you project and try to find a way of making yourself feel better by acting the way you do… But you have it all wrong. Controlling me, owning me, dominating me, will never make you better."

Quick as a flash, Lord Jonas backhanded her across the face with one hand and pulled a gun from inside his jacket with the other. "Enough! I am not here for New Age pontificating! I don't want to hear about how I will be a better person if I love my inner child. I don't want to be a better person. I am me and I am powerful, and yes, I want to control you, dominate you, see you submit to me because you never truly have and I can't abide that."

There was spittle at the corner of his mouth as he dragged Aurora to her feet once more and pulled her into a rough one-armed neck hold. The gun he held steadily aimed at Jack. "I might have taken great delight in drawing this all out and seeing your face when I suggested you ask your beloved who Max is…" Jack glanced from Aurora to Lord Jonas and back again, his face a picture of confusion. "Ha, ha, I can see you have no idea! Jacky-boy doesn't have a clue what he is up against! Well, what does it matter, after tonight none of it will matter. And you have to admit it is funny, isn't it? Funny how your failed rescue attempt, has played right beautifully into my hands. Tonight, Aurora will become my eternal bride and your death, Jack, will seal our souls." And with that, he vanished into the darkness beyond the cusp of the hill behind him, dragging Aurora in his wake.

"He means to sacrifice you!" Morgana called over the wind as Jack rushed forward to follow. "Maybe us all!"

"There's only one of him though!" Another voice came through the air, but Jack ignored them, interested only in following Aurora. He could see they did not go directly down but were on the spiral ceremonial path that had circled the Tor for time immemorial. Jack ploughed on, stumbling downward as he tried to keep them in sight. After a moment or two, they had vanished and it took Jack a few seconds to realise they were once more climbing to the summit before he lost sight of them again.

"They are back on top," he called to the cloaked figures following him. Scrambling back up the steep hillside, they became aware of a faint orange glow from the hilltop and Jack felt fear run a cold finger down his back. It did, though, add strength to his failing limbs and moments later, he, too, was standing by the light of a quickening fire, blinkingly searching for Aurora. Then he saw her, once more bound, as she stood in the middle of St Michael's Tower next to the burgeoning flames.

"It will make a beautiful site, will it not?" Lord Jonas stepped behind him and placed the nozzle of the gun to the nape of his neck. It will go up like a candle… A huge candle seen for miles around… You, me and Aurora taken in fire to live again in another life… Except this time — thanks to your blood — Aurora will be mine from the moment she is born. To do with as I like."

"You will pay for this." Jack's throat was tight.

"What? Karma, you mean?" He made a disparaging noise in his throat. "I have been dodging karma for eons, it doesn't worry me."

Now if was Jack's turn to guffaw. "You think you have been avoiding karma?" He turned to stare down the barrel of the gun. "You've never known the love Aurora and I have… You are so miserable you need to make other people miserable… I would say your whole life is one huge karmic kick in the ass." The butt of the gun hit him on his cheek.

When he came to yet again, groggy and wracked with pain, he was on the ground near where Aurora lay bound and perilously close to the steadily growing fire in the middle of the tower, being cradled by Morgana.

"Jack!" Aurora was sobbing. "I am so sorry. This is all my fault."

Through the fog of the blow, Jack tried to speak, to tell Aurora it was not, it was the fault of Lord Jonas, but a piercing pain through his head had him falling back into Morgana's lap with a groan.

"No, dear," Morgana spoke calmly, "it is all his own responsibility. That's the whole problem. He isn't taking responsibility for the energy he gives out into the world and the lives he creates for himself. He would rather be a victim and a bully, but then the two things are one and the same. But we must not hate him, we must feel compassion."

"Now that's what I like to hear." Lord Jonas reappeared in the tall archway to the open tower on top of the Tor, gun raised at the group huddled on the ground. "If you feel such compassion towards poor little me, witch-woman, you will be happy to perform the wedding ceremony.

262

Your followers here will come in handy too. No such thing as coincidence, eh? Looks like the Goddess is on my side tonight bringing you all here like this and landing you all in my lap!" He threw a piece of rope at Morgana. "First things first, you can tie his hands — tightly, now, I will be checking."

Lord Jonas watched her work, then, standing before them, his eyes blazing with a strange power, he pulled Aurora to her feet to stand beside him, ripping off the ring he had placed earlier on her finger, and told them his plan. "So, this is how it is going to be. Aurora and I are to be wed. But to help bind us together forever, a blood sacrifice will go down a treat — that's where you come in, Jacky-boy. Don't worry, I am not going to cut your heart out or anything, a simple slit throat will suffice. I will enjoy that bit. Witch-woman, you will then marry us as we stand in a pool of Jacky boy's blood... Then... Just as we kiss... You and your other witchy women will kill us." He said the words lightly, with relish. "Just light the tinder I will place around us from the fire I have already started so we — all three of us — go up in a glorious flame of transmutation!" He smiled madly now. "Our bodies will melt away and our souls will rise, eternally bound to each other, and when we next come through the veil of amnesia, Aurora will be mine, all mine... No Sloan, no Max, just me!"

Aurora whimpered where she stood, her arms aching in their binds. Through tears, she sought Jack's eyes and saw her own terror, pain and sadness reflected there. She couldn't let this happen to him, but what could she do?

"You are forgetting one thing, Lord Jonas." Morgana's voice was as calm as ever. "How will you make us light the fire for you? It is a crucial moment, is it not? Has to happen at an exact time?"

Lord Jonas turned his most horrible of grins on her. "Because if you don't, I will shoot all of you witchy women right where you stand and light the fire myself... The energy of your deaths will carry us over nicely, I am sure. Don't you see? By asking you to light the fire, I am showing my compassionate side, I am giving you all the chance of life, isn't that nice of me?"

He laughed devilishly. "Now... The time is right... Let's get on with this." Lord Jonas untied Aurora's hands, his gun still held tightly in hand. "No funny business now, or it's bullets all round, do you hear?"

"Sounds like a blessing," Aurora spat at him, but before Lord Jonas could respond, it was Morgana who spoke.

"Now, child, remember, don't feed the hate. Love is the only way. Unconditional love." Aurora caught the older woman's eyes for a moment, a calm grey pool in the sea of raging emotions all around them and she felt herself calm in response. Perhaps there was hope after all.

"Witch-women," Lord Jonas barked, "there is a pile of straw and kindling over there, surround the three of us. Soak it with the paraffin. You will also find a torch already in the fire to use as a light. I have a knife here, I will hand it to you when the moment is right to slit Jacky-boy's throat, probably best if you do it as I will have my hands full." He leered horribly at Aurora "Though I am not giving you a knife earlier than needs be. Don't think I am that daft, do you?" He winked nastily at Morgana.

Aurora breathed deeply as the women silently went about their business, using the precious moments to gather her thoughts and her energy. She needed to be calm and centred. Closing her eyes and determinedly ignoring the proximity of Lord Jonas, she breathed deeply three times, focusing on feeling peace in in her heart. She had to be able to act from a place of love.

"Hurry up, women!" Lord Jonas was bristling with excitement. "That will do! Now, Priestess... let's start the ceremony!"

Morgana stood before the pyre, her fellow priestesses behind her, her eyes on Aurora, still calm, and yet Aurora could see she was taking as much time as she possibly could.

Taking a deep breath, she began, "We are gathered here tonight in the eyes of the Goddess to witness the union of Lord Jonas and Aurora Flowers. I call upon the Goddess to be with us tonight and imbue all our actions with love and purity."

"Careful, woman," Lord Jonas interrupted. "Stop trying to interfere, just get on with it."

Morgana swallowed and started to speak again. "May the Goddess bless this union and allow the words spoken as vows of love to be binding for as long as love exists." She held Aurora's eyes meaningfully. "Lord Jonas, please speak your vows."

The man, still holding his gun, held Aurora's cheeks between his hands to ensure she was looking directly into his eyes. "I, Lord Jonas, pledge that my soul now has complete dominion over the soul of Aurora Flowers forever more, through all time and space." His eyes glittered dangerously and Aurora supressed an ice-cold shiver that ran down her spine. Her mouth was dry, but Morgana nudged her gently.

"And your response, Aurora?" Once more laden with meaning.

"Yes." Lord Jonas bristled again, obviously relishing the thought of her rebuttal, her fight, the scream of her soul against his dominion.

Aurora took a deep breath. "Lord Jonas, I accept you as my husband." Jack groaned in horror. "For now, and forever more. I accept you with unconditional love and forgiveness. I know that your actions come from a place of pain and hurt and I offer you nothing but love in return."

Lord Jonas looked confused. "What... I don't need your love, Aurora, I want your submission. Submit!" His gun was now raised at her head. "Submit!" Jack groaned again as he struggled to rise to his feet.

"No." Aurora was now as calm as Morgana's eyes. "I offer you love, Lord Jonas. I look at you and see a hurt, lost and lonely little boy who needs love and that's what I offer you."

He forced her to her knees, she could feel the paraffin soak into her trousers. His gun pointed right between her eyes. "I said submit!"

"I put up no resistance, Lord Jonas, if my death is to be now, then so be it, but I want you to know that I have no fear or hate of you any longer. I have only love."

She closed her eyes and awaited the bullet. She could sense the man's panic. But instead of shooting her, he pulled her roughly to her feet and pointed the gun at Morgana. "Declare us married, now!" Almost in the same movement, he thrust a knife into her hands. "Then slit his throat!" Aurora gasped, she couldn't help it and she saw Lord Jonas' eyes flicker with pleasure. "Still love, Aurora?"

"Yes. I don't want you to kill Jack, but I forgive you and I still love you, that lost angry boy." She breathed into her heart and felt the words to be true.

The gun was now levered at the priestesses behind Morgana. "Finish the job, woman, or the priestess dies," Lord Jonas growled angrily.

With a tremble in her voice, she intoned, "I now declare you man and wife. You may now kiss the bride."

Lord Jonas turned his panicked eyes to Aurora who, now feeling an eternal peace descend upon her, returned his anguish with a beautiful heartfelt smile. "I offer all of myself in love, Lord Jonas. Kiss me."

He hesitated. She could see the pain, confusion, anger, frustration and loss all flash across his eyes. Love was something he didn't know what to do with.

"Kiss me," she repeated. Calm and filled with a power beyond her own ken, Aurora encouraged him gently, but rather than give in to the kiss that he had thought would give him power and dominion, he turned away, raising his gun.

It went off with an ear-splitting bang and Aurora saw one of the priestesses fall to the ground. It went off a second time and ricocheted off the ground. The man that had been Lord Jonas, dropped to his knees, head bowed with the gun still in his hands. Aurora could see he was crying, his shoulders juddering as he sobbed lifetimes' worth of grief, hurt, resentment, frustration and ultimately a lack of love.

Aurora bent to him and held him. "Let it out, Jonas, let it all out. It doesn't need to be this way."

"Slit his throat!" he spluttered at Morgana, though his face crumpled and contorted with hundreds and thousands of years of pain. He raised the gun once more at Morgana. "Kill him!"

"No," Morgana said simply and stood looking down at him, peace radiating from her every pore.

Aurora held him more tightly. "Look at me, John. You don't need to do any of this. You don't need to kill any more. You have a choice, take responsibility and create a different future. You can be happy; you don't need to control people for that." She could feel the waves of rage and anger sweep through him. "You can let go of all of this, leave it in the past and move on. It is possible, John, I promise you."

"Promise? You?" He swung around, his attention now firmly on Aurora. "What do your promises mean? You promised me once to be an honest and dutiful wife and you poisoned me. How dare you!"

"You forget that you beat me day in day out in that life. Actions have consequences. We reap what we sow. But you can change the future now, right now, all you have to do is let go of the anger and find peace."

He was on his feet now, gun raised at Aurora's head. "I don't want peace!" he screamed. "I want you. I want to see you submit… Now!" His eyes were frenzied, Aurora could feel her calm beginning to waver, her eyes watching his fingers tense on the trigger.

"No, Jonas." She held her voice steady. "I will not submit, I only offer you love."

"Submit!" His finger flexed.

"No!" The muscles bulged, the trigger moved a millimetre.

"I said SUBMIT!" Spittle landed on Aurora's face. His finger increased pressure on the trigger; it would take little more.

"No." Aurora had tears streaming down her cheeks now too. She never saw the finger squeeze further as she now closed her eyes, and thinking of Jack, she waited for the dull thud, the pain and then the darkness. That familiar darkness, that death that was really an awakening, a slip back into the reality of the universe as the door closed on another act on her soul's eternal journey. But it never came. Instead, she felt a gust of air on her face followed by a thud and a groan.

Her eyes opened and Jack was already on his feet before her. His arms wrapping around her and squeezing her close, holding her so fast and tight she thought her ribs might break.

"Oh, Jack, please, you are going to break me." For the first time in what seemed like weeks, months, even, Aurora felt herself laughing. "What happened?" Looking past Jack, she looked at Lord Jonas where he lay on the ground. "Is he dead?" She felt a wash of sadness at the thought.

"No, just stunned. I caught him on the lower back of his head with the hilt of his own knife. Morgana slipped it to me when he wasn't looking. After she had somehow freed me with it without either of you knowing."

Morgana stood up from where she had been kneeling next to the priestess who had been shot.

"Your friend?" Aurora asked anxiously.

"She will be fine." Star smiled. "Us priestesses have quite a few skills. Like you, Aurora. Maybe when this dust all settles you will become one of us."

Strangely, there was no question in that statement and Aurora felt the subtle energies of the universal threads moving, just a little, and settling down into position like an old dog in a new bed.

"What now?" Jack asked. "The sun will be up in a few hours."

"Well," Morgana said, as calm as ever, "I suggest we clean this place up and carry our man here down to your cottage where I am hoping we can find some hot tea and maybe a biscuit."

"Oh, and Sloan!" Aurora's voice was worried.

"Yes." Morgana smiled. "Of course, Sloan. We also need to get your warrior here cleaned up and taken care of." She said nodding towards Jack, drawing Aurora's attention for the first time towards the tatters of Jack's bloodstained clothes.

"Oh, Jack." She leant into him, careful not to hurt him. "Let's get you home."

Somehow, by all helping each other, the bedraggled and crooked group managed their way down the Tor's steep sides to the cottage. It took quite a long time, but despite the exhaustion, pain and cold, it was a journey enfolded in peace.

Once inside, Morgana took control, ordering the uninjured sister priestesses — Agnes and Fallow — to light a fire and boil the kettle while she set to looking at wounds. Aurora, knowing she wasn't seriously hurt, slipped away and stood for long moments beneath a hot shower before returning, feeling a million times more human in leggings and an oversized navy sweatshirt. She came to sit next to Jack on the sofa who was leaning back, his head lolling with tiredness, as Morgana tended the lacerations around his stomach. Aurora could see she had an array of balms, washes and ointments laid on a table at her side.

"Never leave home without them, eh?" Aurora asked with a smile.

"I had a feeling I would need them." Morgana smiled back. Just then, Agnes appeared with a groaning tray. Aurora could have wept at the sight of a full cafetière and a plate loaded with hot buttered toast.

"Oh, thank you," she said as Agnes paused before her to allow her to grab a slice of toast, her voice heavy with the sincerest gratitude she had ever felt. "Jack, can you manage some toast?" she asked, her brow creasing with concern as she looked at the man she loved. His answer was barely a murmur, but he did manage to shake his head to convey his feelings.

"Don't worry," Morgana reassured her, he just needs a good night's sleep and plenty of rest. "Much like you. I would also like to treat all your bruises and cuts."

"Thank you, but I think maybe you need to tend to... Sorry, I don't know her name."

"She likes to go by the name Sparrow." Morgana smiled over at the woman curled up in Aurora's armchair like a field mouse. "But her wound is tended, it was not much more than a scrape, really, and she is doing the best thing she can for herself right now — sleeping, and I am sure, focusing some healing energy to her wound."

Agnes handed round cups of coffee, the tantalising smell rousing Jack enough for him to be able to raise his head. "Ah... Just what I need."

"Sleep is what you need, young man."

"This won't stop me sleeping," Jack muttered through a long draught of the hot drink. "Ah. Shame it didn't have brandy in it."

"You don't need it, trust me, I will give you something much better shortly." Morgana winked at him.

Jack roused himself a little as something crossed his mind. "You said he had an accomplice..."

"That's right!" Aurora suddenly remembered. "There was someone with him. Here in the cottage —that's how they got me."

"It was a 'she', actually. Tied up and hidden for the moment, safe until daylight when we can let them go, I think."

"And what about him?" Fallow asked, her voice filled with a slightly irate compassion. Lord Jonas sat sprawled across the opposite armchair to the one Sparrow was currently curled up in, having never moved a muscle since they had unceremoniously dumped him there on their arrival. How they had managed to carry the unconscious man down from the Tor, given their own decrepit physical state, was beyond Aurora, but what could they have done? Despite everything, they couldn't just leave him. Aurora thought they may well have had some help, from the fairies, the spirits of the Tor or the Goddess, herself. She wasn't sure but she had a strong feeling someone had helped.

"What are we going to do with him?" Jack asked, alerted by the strong caffeine hit.

"I'm really not sure," Aurora answered as she leant gently into Jack's side, his arm snaking naturally around her shoulders. "Let's see what happens when he wakes up. And when we speak to his accomplice." And at the thought, Aurora felt nothing but peace.

Two months later.

Jack couldn't stop grinning. And judging by the way people smiled back at him — wide smiles that broke into a small, delighted laugh — he must have looked a bit of a grinning fool, but nobody seemed to mind, least of all him. And why shouldn't he? This was his wedding day, after all.

After everything they had gone through together, getting married as soon as possible just felt so right for Jack and Aurora. Amazing, really, given all she had told him about Max and how she had never, before now, felt complete without him in her life. How each lifetime became a search for the soulmate, who had been the young man she had married all those thousands of years before. Whether he be man, woman or child, she never felt quite right until he appeared, distracting her even, it appeared, from the sinister and repeated appearances of the soul of Lord Jonas. Until now, that was, until she had fallen completely and utterly for Jack in a way she hadn't done for anyone in a long, long time. Now she said she barely thought of Max, she knew his soul was where it needed to be and she was where she needed to be. There would always be a connection, one that existed beyond time and space, but here and now, Aurora loved Jack. And Jack loved Aurora.

There had been lots of conversations in the two weeks following the night on the Tor. They had needed to rest, to process, to put it all to bed, which was something they never had any problem doing. And afterwards they felt shiny, clean and ready for a fresh start. As if history had been written clean and they were alive here and now to dream a whole new world into creation. As the saying went, the world was their oyster.

They weren't alone in feeling like that, either. Lord Jonas — John — had undergone something of an epiphany too. Whatever forces were at work on the hill that night had shifted something deep down and he was finally ready to delve into his own actions, take responsibility and accept the love Aurora had offered him for what it was — an unconditional demonstration, a pure act which had led to his own transformation. It was a very humble, sheepish, even, John who finally left them after three days of rest and some genuine heart-to-hearts. There was work to be done but he had left them with heartfelt hugs and promises to stay in touch from a monastic retreat in Italy and let them know of his progress. His accomplice — a susceptible young woman — was now under Morgana's care and thriving.

His departure had left Jack and Aurora free to contemplate their own future which turned out to be a path which had led Jack to standing before the gorgeous Goddess alter in Glastonbury's Goddess Temple, a large portrait of the Goddess in Her winter garb, smiling knowingly down on him and attended on by smaller statues and candles. Jack took a deep breath of white sage smoke and turned round to look at the door once more. He wasn't waiting for Aurora, he was waiting for the priestess who was going to perform the hand-fastening ceremony. She had been away for the last three months on retreat in Mount Shasta so neither Jack or Aurora had met her, but they had all communicated often by email and the arrangement felt just right. She had flown in this morning, and with only a few minutes before Aurora was meant to arrive, she had yet to put in an appearance.

Morgana smiled at him. "Stop panicking, she will be here at exactly the right minute."

Which, of course, she was. The tall and stately older woman, with salt and pepper hair drawn up in a loose bun and wearing a loose, deep purple, velvet robe as if she was born to it, swept in moments later. Smiling beatifically at the gathered guests, she nodded to Jack in acknowledgement.

"May the Goddess bless you," she said by way of greeting, her voice deep and sonorous, filled with gravitas and humour. A woman who knew herself, this world and all others innately, Jack thought. Then he was just glad she was there.

"Thank you." Jack smiled back just as the sound of harp music started, indicating Aurora's arrival. She walked the short distance to the alter on her own, with just Felicity at her back. Her parents stood bemused yet proud in the front row, having spent more time in the last couple of months with their daughter than they had done in the previous two decades. Aurora had chosen a deep blue dress of the softest wool with long sleeves and cinched in at the waist with a silver circlet belt. Her hair was bundled loosely on her head and she was crowned by another silver circlet. Her eyes, dazzling with heightened blue thanks to the colour of her dress, never left Jack's as the naughtiest of smiles played round her lips. By the time she stood next to him, it had formed a grin to match his own and he couldn't help but lean in to kiss her in greeting.

"Children of the Goddess…" The high priestess raised her arms to start the proceedings and Aurora managed to turn her eyes from Jack to face forward and hear the words that would bind her to Jack, but instead, it was another name that came crashing from her lips.

"Max!" Aurora stared at the high priestess in stunned disbelief and Jack felt his blood run cold as he realised just what had happened.

Unfazed, the high priestess simply nodded in acknowledgement. "Beloved, I am delighted to see you again. And ecstatic to marry you, here and now, to Jack."

Aurora laughed, a laugh lighter and freer than any Jack had ever heard her laugh before. "I am so glad it is you, Max, I really wouldn't want anyone else marrying us."

"Hecate, actually, this time." The woman smiled and Aurora looked back at Jack with such love he knew he didn't have anything to worry about.